PRAISE FOR KENNEDY RYAN

"Ryan is a powerhouse of a writer." —*USA Today*

"Kennedy Ryan is one of the finest romance writers of our age."
—*Entertainment Weekly*

"Few authors can write romance like Kennedy Ryan."
—Jennifer L. Armentrout, #1 *New York Times* bestselling author

"Every time I think Kennedy Ryan can't possibly raise the bar any further, she proves me wrong in the most delightful way possible."
—Katee Robert, *New York Times* bestselling author

"Every time Kennedy Ryan sits down to write a book, she is hunting big game from page one."
—Sarah MacLean, *New York Times* bestselling author

"Kennedy Ryan writes the stories we all need to read."
—Lexi Ryan, *New York Times* bestselling author

"Opening a Kennedy Ryan book isn't simply reading a fantastic book. It's an experience. Kennedy Ryan slays us with her words and leaves us wrecked in the best of ways."
—Naima Simone, *USA Today* bestselling author

"Kennedy Ryan is the queen of emotionally poignant love stories. No one writes about social issues with such subtlety and depth while also providing a uniquely gorgeous romance."
—Giana Darling, *USA Today* bestselling author

"Three things I can count on when I read a book from Kennedy Ryan—breathtaking prose, being schooled in a compelling story line, and falling head over heels for deeply rooted characters. She never disappoints."　　　　　—Kate Stewart, *USA Today* bestselling author

"Kennedy Ryan always delivers a story with emotion, power, and off-the-charts sexual tension."
　　　　　—Robin Covington, *USA Today* bestselling author

"Kennedy Ryan breaks me apart and puts me back together every time with her gorgeous prose and deeply human characters who tear their hearts out for one another."
　　　　　—Andie J. Christopher, *USA Today* bestselling author

"Kennedy Ryan writes with surgical precision that slices right through your heart."　　　　　—Sonali Dev, *USA Today* bestselling author

"Kennedy writes these gripping, touching, romantic, transportive books every single time."
　　　　　—Denise Williams, author of *How to Fail at Flirting*

BEFORE I LET GO

KENNEDY RYAN

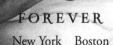

FOREVER

New York   Boston

Forever
Hachette Book Group
1290 Avenue of the Americas, New York, NY 10104
read-forever.com
twitter.com/readforeverpub

First Edition: November 2022

Forever is an imprint of Grand Central Publishing. The Forever name and logo are trademarks of Hachette Book Group, Inc.

The publisher is not responsible for websites (or their content) that are not owned by the publisher.

Print book interior design by Abby Reilly.

Library of Congress Cataloging-in-Publication Data

Names: Ryan, Kennedy, author.
Title: Before I let go : a Skyland novel / Kennedy Ryan.
Description: First Edition. | New York : Forever, 2022. | Series: Skyland novel | Summary: "Their love was supposed to last forever. But after two devastating tragedies, Yasmen and Josiah Wade realized love alone couldn't solve everything…or keep their marriage together. It's taken a year since their split for Yasmen to finally start feeling like herself again. To finally be able to breathe again. But the more she sees Josiah-whether it's parenting their two children or working together at the restaurant they co-own-the more Yasmen realizes she may not be ready to completely let go of everything they had together. Like magnets, Yasmen and Josiah are always drawn back to each other, and one almost kiss soon leads to more. It's hot. It's illicit. It's all good…until old wounds start resurfacing. This time, will they have what it takes to make forever last? Or is it already too late?"—Provided by publisher.
Identifiers: LCCN 2022026036 | ISBN 9781538706794 (trade paperback) | ISBN 9781538706817 (ebook)
Subjects: LCGFT: Novels.
Classification: LCC PS3618.Y33544 B44 2022 | DDC 813/.6—dc23/eng/20220627
LC record available at https://lccn.loc.gov/2022026036

ISBNs: 978-1-5387-0679-4 (trade paperback), 978-1-5387-0681-7 (ebook)

Printed in the United States of America

LSC-C

Printing 1, 2022

To the strong girls,
To the hustlers,
To the superwomen,
Tend your hearts with ruthless care...and rest.

AUTHOR'S NOTE

Before I Let Go is a story of joy, healing, and recovery. Consequently, it is also a story, at least in part, about loss. When we meet Yasmen and Josiah, they are emerging from the most difficult season of their lives and embarking on a time of joy.

With that said, there is some reflection on past difficulties, including: a stillbirth, loss of loved one (past/off-page), discussion of complicated grief, depression, and passive suicidal ideation (no attempt). Please know these topics were approached with the utmost care, and in consultation with those for whom this was a lived experience and with several counselors/therapists. They were kind enough to beta read for me, so I hope I achieved my goal when writing, which is to edify and do no harm.

THE BEGINNING

JOSIAH

"In the middle of the journey of our life
I found myself within a dark woods where the straight way
    was lost."

—Dante Alighieri, *Inferno*

Do people remember the exact moment they fall in love?
I do. Yasmen brought me homemade chicken noodle soup when I was so sick it hurt to blink. Tasted like day-old dishwater. Not sure how you mess up chicken noodle soup, but my girl managed it. She watched me expectantly with those long-lashed doe eyes. God, I'll never forget her expression when I spat that soup out, but it was so bad and I was too sick to even play it off.

For a second, Yasmen looked distressed, but then, despite feeling like someone dragged me over hot coals and needles, I laughed. Then she laughed and I wondered if this—finding someone you can laugh with when everything hurts—was the stuff happily ever afters were made of. Not the sugarcoated kisses and hot-air balloon rides and romantic walks under a full moon. My whole body throbbed with whatever plague infected me, but that day Yasmen made me happy. In the midst of a raging flu, she made me laugh.

And I knew.

I tipped over from wildly attracted and more-than-slightly

pussy-whipped into the real thing. Into love. That moment is soldered into my memory. It's one I'll never forget.

And here, just months later, so is this one.

"What do you think?" Yasmen looks up from something she's working on at the card table in the middle of the living/dining/kitchen zone of my dilapidated one-bedroom apartment, complete with impoverished student decor.

"Think about what?" I ask, sitting down in the raggedy chair across from her.

"Grits."

"Baby, please don't make grits again. I'm still recovering from the last time you tried."

She glares at me without heat, the corners of her mouth fighting a grin. "Boy, not cook grits. Have you even been listening? I said what if you name your *restaurant* Grits?"

In an unprecedented move, I took a girl home for Christmas. She and my aunt Byrd hit it off right away, and by New Year's Eve, the two of them were scheming about a restaurant I could open using my MBA and Aunt Byrd's family recipes.

"Oh, yeah. Sure. Grits." I scoot my chair closer and push back the fall of braids cascading over Yasmen's shoulder. "Sounds good."

"Sounds good?" She lays the back of her hand across my forehead. "Are you sick again? The Josiah Wade I know picks apart every suggestion and always has a *yes, but* on the ready."

She's not wrong. My father was a military man, a stern taskmaster who never settled for anything a day in his life. He planned each move like a military campaign. Control, discipline, and reason propelled him up through the ranks. That's what he instilled in me even in the short time I had with him before he passed away, but all of that goes out the window in this moment when I realize that I not only love Yasmen, but I want to love her for the rest of my life.

"Marry me."

The words slip out soft and certain. And I *am* certain. An actuary running a dozen risk assessments couldn't be as certain as I am right now. Yasmen and I belong together.

She drops her pen and her mouth falls open.

"Wha-what?" Jerky breaths stutter over her lips and her eyes go wide.

"Marry me."

Improbably—because this, *all of this* is as out of character for me as a goat tap-dancing—I sink to one knee in front of her, heart skydiving in my chest. Full-on romantic movie proposal posture. I reach up to cup her face, the beveled bones and delicate curves fitting perfectly against my palms.

"I love you, Yasmen."

She nods, her expression dazed. "I know. I—I love you, too, but I thought we'd wait until you finished grad school."

"I'm almost done. One semester left. Your lease is up next month. Perfect time to move in with me." I sweep my arm around the sparsely furnished, shabby apartment. "Don't you want to join me in this lap of luxury?"

She snickers, a wide smile breaking out on her beautiful face. The first time I saw her, my friends laughed because I stopped in the middle of whatever bullshit I was saying and stared. That's not me. No matter how fine, no girl ever dropkicked me at first sight the way Yasmen did. I want to see her smooth brown skin, these sweet, full lips, the thick fan of lashes, on my children.

"You're crazy," she whispers.

"I'm sure of you." I trace the silky dark arch of her eyebrow. "Are you sure of me?"

And I see it. I see the calm, the certainty, the *love* suffocate her doubts, smother the hesitations. She leaves the rickety chair, goes down on her knees to face me on mine, and scatters fleeting kisses across my face. They ghost over my lips and eyes like butterflies that float out of reach before I can grab them. I want to capture her face again, make her be still so I can kiss her back, but my hands hang at my sides, numb from the magnitude of what's happening. Finally, she takes my hands in hers and looks directly at me. Tears pool in her eyes and slip over her cheeks.

"Yes, Josiah Wade," she breathes. "I'll marry you."

My body comes back to life and I pull her into me by the curve of her hips, press my palms into the warm suppleness of her back. She's all tight heat and temptation. In the absence of a ring, I seal our pledge with a slick tangle of tongues and tears.

The kiss is hot and sweet and ravenous. This, *this* must be how forever tastes.

I'm sure of it.

CHAPTER ONE

YASMEN

You rarely see good things in the rearview mirror.

A lesson I should have learned by now, but I flick a glance to the back seat anyway, watching my daughter break the rules. Her brother in the passenger seat beside me is just as bad.

"Guys, you know it's not screen time." I split my attention between the interstate and the two of them. "Put your phones away, please."

"Mom, seriously?" My daughter Deja's sigh is heavy with a thirteen-year-old's exasperation. "I just finished school *and* dance lessons. Gimme a break."

"Sorry, Mom," Kassim says, lowering his phone to his lap.

Deja expels another breath, like she's not sure who irritates her more, me for making the rules or her brother for following them.

"Brownnose," she mutters, gaze still fixed to her screen.

"Deja," I say. "That phone is mine if you don't put it away."

Her eyes, dark and gold-flecked, clash with mine in the mirror before she sets the phone aside. It's like staring back at myself. We're so much alike. Skin as smooth and brown as polished walnut. Her hair, like mine, prone to coil and curl, always contracting at the slightest bit of moisture in the air. Same stubborn chin hinting at a will to match.

"She's just like you," my mother used to say when as a toddler Deja barreled into mishaps despite my warnings to take care. When she'd pull herself up to run off again with fresh scrapes and bruises. "Serves you right. Now you'll see what I had to put up with raising you."

I always thought it would be a blessing, mother and daughter, two peas in the proverbial pod. And for a long time, it was...until thirteen. God, I hate this age. I can't seem to get anything right with her anymore.

"So how was your day?"

I ask because I want to make good use of all this time we have in the car commuting. They've only been back in school for two weeks, and I should start this year as I mean to go on.

"Jamal brought his lizard to school," Kassim says, his amused eyes meeting mine in a brief sidelong glance. "And it crawled out of his backpack in class."

"Oh, my God." I laugh. "Did he catch it?"

"Yeah, but it took like twenty minutes. He's fast. The lizard, I mean." Kassim twists a button on the crisp white shirt of his school uniform. "Some of the girls started screaming. Mrs. Halstead stood on her chair, like it was a snake or something."

"I might have freaked out too," I admit.

"This one was harmless. It wasn't like a Gila monster or a Mexican beaded lizard," Kassim says. "Those are two of the poisonous types found in North America."

I catch Deja staring at the back of her brother's head like he sprang from Dr. Who's TARDIS. With Kassim's constant stream of factoids and fascination with...well, everything...it probably sometimes seems like he did.

"Never a dull moment with Jamal," I say with a chuckle. "What about you, Deja?"

"Huh?" she asks, her voice disinterested, distracted.

When I check the mirror again, I only see her profile. She's studying I-85 through her window. The six o'clock traffic is basically a parking lot, a fleet of Atlantan commuters inching forward and negotiating tight spaces in a game of vehicular Tetris.

"I was asking how your day went," I try again.

"It was all right," Deja says, eyes fixed on the traffic beyond her window. "Dad's at the restaurant?"

So much for connecting.

"Uh, yeah." I tap the brakes when a Prius cuts in front of me. "You guys can eat dinner there and your dad'll take you home once you're done."

"Why?" Kassim asks.

"Why what?" I wait for the Prius to decide what he wants to do.

"I mean where will *you* be?" Kassim presses.

"It's Soledad's birthday," I tell him, carefully switching lanes. "We're taking her out to dinner. Make sure you get your homework done. I don't want you to fall behind."

"God, Mom," Deja sighs. "We're barely back from summer and you're already up our asses."

I ping a sharp glance from Kassim in the front seat to Deja in the back.

"Day, don't cuss."

She mumbles something under her breath.

"What was that?" I flash a look at her in the mirror as I pull off the exit. "You got something to say?"

"I said it." Defiant, resentful eyes snap to meet mine.

"I didn't *hear* it."

"Is that my problem?"

"Yeah, it is. If you're big and bad enough to say it, say it loud enough for me to hear it."

"Mom, geez." She pinches the bridge of her nose. "Why are you so…ugh."

I have a thousand replies to that, but all of them would only worsen the tension between us. If I had spoken to *my* mama that way, she would have pulled over to the shoulder and popped me in the mouth. God knows I love my mother, but I don't want that. I draw a calming breath and try to remember all the ways I promised myself I would do things differently with my kids, landing somewhere between gentle parenting…and my mama.

I stop at a red light, turning to glance over my shoulder, meeting

Deja's hard stare. It always feels like she's fortifying a wall between us, piling up the bricks before I can touch her on the other side. I miss the girl who loved our pillow fights, s'mores over the backyard firepit, and Saturday morning mommy-daughter manis. Is it all part of growing up, or are we just growing apart? Or both?

"Your dad and I expect you to set a better example for your brother," I tell her.

"Well, Daddy's not around as much anymore." She turns her head, shifts her eyes away from me, and stares back out the window. "Is he?"

Even though Josiah doesn't live with us, he's only two streets over and they see him every day. Still, my heart clenches with a guilt-tinged ache because as much as I'd like to believe it's only the big one-three that eroded things between Deja and me, I can't lie to myself. The trouble started with the divorce. Those eyes, before never far from sparkling with laughter, now seem too old for the rest of her face, and not just from seeing one more year pass, but from witnessing the dissolution of her parents' marriage over the last few.

"It's green, Mom," Kassim says.

Before anyone can honk, I accelerate with the cars around me, driving past the blue-and-white sign heralding that we're entering Skyland, one of Atlanta's most vibrant in-town neighborhoods. My shoulder muscles relax as we shift from the tension of the interstate to the more sedate pace and thinner traffic of Skyland's narrow roads. It pairs the charm and intimacy of a smaller community with proximity to the explosive energy and limitless options of a world-class city. We drive down Main Street, bordered by cobblestone walkways, boutiques, and cloth-draped tables spilling from the cafés onto the sidewalks. I exit the roundabout encircling the fountain in the center of Sky Square and keep driving until our restaurant, Grits, comes into view.

Downtown Skyland is a perfect blend of preservation and progress. The zoning gatekeepers have preserved many of the historic homes by repurposing them for business. Our soul fusion restaurant, Grits, is a shining example. The two-story Victorian with its wraparound porch stole my heart as soon as I laid eyes on it. The house had fallen into disrepair, but we had a loan from the bank, more ideas than we knew what to do with, and a stack of family recipes. Josiah had the business degree, but I brought the vision for an upscale, "down-home" restaurant that specialized in reinventing old Southern favorites. It took us awhile to get to "upscale." For a long time we were more "mom-and-pop," our entire operation squeezed into a small retail space on the south side of Atlanta. So much has changed, been lost, gained.

Besides the two humans in this car, Grits is what I'm proudest of. It's our baby too. Even when things fell apart between Josiah and me, we still had our three babies. Deja, Kassim, and this place, Grits. When we realized those were the only things holding us together, we knew it would be better to dissolve our marriage than to go on as what we had become.

Well, I knew.

When we arrive at Grits, I pull into a reserved parking space right up front and kill the engine. Kassim opens the door and is out and up the steps to Grits's entrance without another word. Deja gets out, too, and closes the door. Coltish, all skinny arms and giraffe legs in her plaid school uniform skirt and pink high-top Converse, she pauses to type, already glued to her phone again, before entering the restaurant.

I don't even have the patience to remind her about screen time. Let Josiah worry about it for the next couple of hours. I grab my suit bag from the trunk, start for the steps, and pull open the heavy front door emblazoned with our logo. As soon as I cross the threshold, a sense of accomplishment rises in me as thick and real as the smell of fried chicken and savory vegetables permeating the tastefully decorated dining room. It's a full house tonight, though lately every night is a full house. What a difference a year makes.

Across the dining room I spot Deja and Kassim standing with a man I don't recognize. He's of middle age and average height, and standing next to a petite woman dressed in a white chef's coat and slim-fitting pants. Vashti Burns's reputation and culinary expertise helped pull us back from the edge of ruin. Her dark brown skin is a gorgeous contrast to the auburn-colored natural hair she wears cropped close. Having less hair gives her high cheekbones room to show off. Her full lips spread, flashing straight, white teeth in a smile up at the tall man beside her.

Josiah.

My ex-husband is one of *those* guys. A man who captures your attention with the breadth of his shoulders and a purposeful stride, long legs devouring each step like he needs to get someplace but won't be rushed. I was a restaurant hostess when we first met. Josiah, waiting for a table with a group of friends, seduced my ears before I even laid eyes on him, that rich laugh of his unfurling like black silk ribbon and making heads turn. Turned *my* head. Not that he's had much to laugh about the last few years. Hell, none of us have, but he's laughing now, with our pretty new chef.

A group of laughing women spill through the front door, the perfume-scented clique of stilettos and body-con dresses crowding around the hostess podium. At Grits, your jeans are just as at home as your Sunday best. Or your *in da club* best in their case. Offering them a smile as the hostess checks them in, I walk toward Josiah and the kids. When I'm just a few feet away, Josiah glances up and his smile does that thing where it freezes at the sight of me and then melts completely into a neutral line. It stings a little, that the ease we used to share is gone. It's one of the things we never recovered from the most painful season of our lives. That ease came with love, with passion, with partnership. At least we're still partners, even if only in business and raising these kids.

"Hey," Josiah murmurs when I join their little group, his voice a low, deep, familiar rumble. "I didn't realize you were here. Thought you'd dropped them off."

"Uh, no." I pat the suit bag and angle a polite smile to Vashti and the stranger. "Just need to change before I go."

"Let me introduce you," he says. "Yasmen, this is William Granders, a food critic for the *Atlanta Journal-Constitution*. William, Yasmen Wade, my business partner."

A food critic. So that's why he's at Soigné, our best table.

"Nice to meet you, Mr. Granders," I say, extending a hand to him. He returns the handshake with a smile before taking a sip of his Bordeaux.

"Good to see you again, Yasmen," Vashti says, her voice well-modulated and pleasant.

"You too."

Even though Vashti's been here for about a year, we don't know each other that well. I was still on hiatus when Josiah hired her after a string of replacements failed following Aunt Byrd's passing. Vashti has the culinary training and that *something-something* Byrd used to say the most gifted cooks are born with. She's been a lifesaver, but something I can't put my finger on has kept the two of us from becoming friends. The customers and staff love her. My kids love her. Josiah...rests one big hand on her shoulder. The touch is innocuous. Platonic, but something about it...niggles.

"Hey, kids, let's grab a table so you can eat and get started on home-work," I say, offering Mr. Granders a smile. "Hope you enjoy your meal."

"How could I not?" He shoots Vashti an admiring look. "You've got yourself a rare gem here. Haven't had chicken and dumplings like this since...well, ever."

"We're very lucky," I agree with a smile.

"There's a booth at the back near the kitchen," Josiah says, dropping a quick kiss on Deja's hair. "I'll check on you guys in a bit. Decide what you want."

"Ribs," Kassim pipes up, licking his lips.

"Boy, you're gonna turn into a rib." Vashti laughs. "You get them every time. When you gonna try my chicken-fried steak?"

"Next time?" Kassim shrugs, his smile sheepish. If Deja's my mini-me, Kassim is Josiah's.

"Kids, let's go so Mr. Ganders can finish his meal," I say, looking back to the critic. "It was nice meeting you."

Once we reach the booth Josiah reserved, I grab two menus from the table and hand them to the kids.

"Figure out what you want," I say. "Your dad will come over to get your orders."

"I'm starving." Kassim opens the menu, eyes wide and scanning all the options.

"Eat. Home. Homework," I remind them, looking from one to the other. "In that order. Got it?"

"Got it," Deja says, her face obscured by the open menu.

"All right." I shift the suit bag over my shoulder. "I need to change."

I pick my way through the tables and smile at a few regular customers, but don't stop. The phone vibrates in my purse, and I know it's my friend Hendrix wondering where I am. I reach for my cell to reassure her I'm coming, but my steps falter midstride and I stand paralyzed in the empty corridor. To anyone else, it's just a stretch of hardwood flooring, the wide planks dark and polished, but my mind's eye superimposes an old stain spreading beneath my Nikes. And even though the floor has long since been scrubbed clean, I still see my sorrow embedded in the woodgrain. For months I couldn't walk through this place without my breath growing short and my head spinning. My pain was plastered in these walls. My ghosts and grief gathered around these tables. A knot of anxiety burgeons in my belly, and panic strangles me so tightly I can barely breathe, but I do what my therapist taught me.

Deep breath in, slow breath out.

Deep breath in, slow breath out.

At first I can only manage tiny sips of air and my head spins, but each breath deepens, lengthens, deploys life-giving calm to my tingling extremities. Repeating that cycle a few times slows my heartbeat and loosens the band manacling my throat. I've exorcized a lot of my demons. Not all, but enough to at least walk into Grits without running right back out. I'm ready to reclaim the space that loss and shit luck tried to take from me.

When I open my eyes, it's just a floor, polished to a high shine. There was a time I would have fallen over that cliff, breath-deprived and panicked, and let my demons chase me from this place I love so much. A tiny smile crooks the corner of my mouth and I take one step and then another.

So this is what getting better feels like.

Headed for the office, I pass the clamor of the kitchen. The clang of pots, the tantalizing scents, the raucous laughter and raised voices drift from the space that had always been Byrd's domain. I offer a quick wave to the crew as I stride toward the office.

"Private" is discreetly sketched into the gold plate on the office door. I walk in, closing the door behind me. Josiah is a man of order and discipline, and the office reflects that. When we shared this space, it was never this orderly. My side of our bedroom always looked like a natural disaster, while his side looked like…well, like *this*. Even though I'm getting back into the swing of things here at the restaurant, I haven't been using the office. And it shows.

The desk is clear, except for a few papers sorted into neat piles, edges lined up just so. Not a speck of dust would dare reside on any of the shiny surfaces. Josiah would be pulling his hair out if he saw our bedroom right now. I'm not one of those people who make the bed every morning. I mean, no one's in my room all day and I'm just climbing right back in at night. I like my bed waiting for me all rumpled like it was when I crawled out of it. Josiah? Sheets tucked tight like a can of sardines, corners sharp as a Swiss Army knife. He's one of those people who actually knows how to fold a fitted sheet into a tiny square.

Freak.

I walk into the en suite bathroom, shut the door, flop onto the closed seat of the toilet.

And sit.

Life comes at us fast. Responsibilities, kids, opportunities—it all rushes at us with projectile force. With all the things flying my way, I've learned to stop and check for dents and bruises. I've been the walking wounded before with disastrous results. Now I always pause just one damn minute to make sure I'm actually okay. Sometimes I gotta have a seat on a toilet, hoarding breaths, surviving between seconds. For mere moments, insulated by thin walls and a closed door.

After a few restoring seconds of silence, I stand to peel off the day along with my jeans and T-shirt. I search under the sink, praying I'll see the emergency deodorant I used to stash there.

"Yes!"

With a little sashay of my hips I apply the deodorant. My face is bare, so I pull out my "glam in minutes" kit and at least apply some coverage, color, and lashes. I washed my hair this morning, and the leave-in conditioner still tames my natural hair into a mostly curly, not-yet-frizzy, Afro-halo.

I may be winging it with my hair and makeup, but at least I know this dress is classy with a dash of freakum. Pink hibiscus flowers bloom across the emerald-green skirt and the bodice cups and molds my breasts like a lover. Not that I've had one of *those* since my divorce. I lift my arms, squinting into the bathroom mirror.

"Can you tell I didn't shave?" I ask the woman looking back at me. Eyes shining. Curls popping. That matte pink lippie is on point. Brows, fleek-ish. And yoga has done her body good. I'll never be the size I was before I had kids, and I'm fine with that. My health isn't a number on the scale or on a tag in my jeans. I feel good about my body because it gets me through this life. I want to be around as long as possible to see my kids grow up, so I take care of it. I can't remember when I last felt like this. I feel like...

"Myself." I give the woman in the mirror a grin. "I feel like myself." My purse vibrates.

"Dammit." I grab the phone and sure enough. "Hendrix, hey."

"Where are you?" My friend's husky voice holds an edge, but it always does. Her high-powered job and warp-speed life usually make her sound like she's poised to pounce on anyone she's talking to.

"Leaving Grits now. If I can ever get this dress zipped." I press the phone between my ear and my shoulder and stretch to reach my back. "You already at Sky-Hi?"

"Yeah. Walking in now."

"It's just up the street. Be there in less than ten."

"Okay. Bye."

I turn my focus back to the zipper, which stubbornly stays put at the middle of my back.

Screw it.

I'll ask the hostess to zip me up. I grab my stuff and leave the bathroom just as the outer office door opens and Josiah walks in. His glance skitters over me, starting with my curly hair and sliding to my bare toes.

"Sorry. I didn't realize you were in here." He strides over to the desk, opens a drawer, and retrieves a small stack of cards. "Granders wanted a business card."

"People still actually use those?"

The powerful shoulders shrug in the confines of his well-tailored suit.

"Apparently he does. I'll carve my name into a stone tablet if it means he'll write us a good review. We could use the visibility."

"Are things..."

I hesitate, unsure of where my question will lead. Josiah never pressured me when I couldn't drag myself out of the black hole, when just opening my eyes and breathing felt like a chore. He shielded me from how bad things had gotten financially at the restaurant. We thought we'd have time to train, to settle, to grow. Instead we lost Byrdie, our linchpin, in the middle of the biggest transition our little business had ever experienced. It wasn't until my fog started clearing that I realized how close we'd come to losing this place. To losing everything.

"Si, are we in trouble again? I can—"

"We're good." The hard, handsome cast of his features softens a little. "For real, business has never been better."

"If I need to do more around here, I can adjust some stuff."

"You're where we need you most." His reply is quiet but sure. His dark eyes, steady. "Knowing you've got the kids, their lessons, are serving on the PTA committees and keeping up with their grades, it's freeing me up to focus here and make sure we're all right. That we *stay* all right."

Both kids struggled some after the divorce. Deja especially became increasingly defiant and her grades have suffered. With Josiah handling so much at the restaurant after Byrd died, we agreed I would focus more on home and giving them as much stability as possible.

"Well, if things change, let me know," I say, forcing lightness into my voice, into the room. "Team Wade, right?"

That used to be our rallying cry when things got tough. Whatever needed doing, we did it together. A muscle in his jaw flexes, and he cuts his gaze away from mine to some point over my shoulder. Maybe to some point in the past, reliving the turmoil of the last few years like I do more often than I'd like to admit. His prolonged silence becomes smothering, and my breath shortens again.

"Anytime you want to be the one hauling Deja's ungrateful ass to dance lessons," I say wryly, hoping to dispel the heaviness that entered the room. "Lemme know. We can trade."

He shifts his glance back to me and the distant look in his eyes fades. "I'd rather work day and night. You can have that."

His full lips quirk at the corners, and I find myself smiling back. Josiah's face is interesting enough to make handsome look mundane, though the man is undeniably fine. The kind of fine that makes you lose your train of thought midsentence and bite your lip. Gorgeous dark skin gleams, pulled taut over the high sculpted bones of his face. To be so controlled, nearly austere, there is something boundless about his presence. Standing here with him, that energy, an amalgamation of ambition and audacity and swagger, swirls around us in the office. It's like being corked into a bottle with a typhoon.

His brows lift, querying. I'm staring.

"Oh." I turn my back to him, as much to recover my composure as to get my zipper up. "It's stuck. Can ya help?"

He doesn't answer, and his steps are so quiet I barely hear him cross the room, so the heat of his body warming my exposed skin startles me. The backs of his fingers brush over my spine as he pulls the zipper. It doesn't budge at first, so he has to tug. Even just that whisper of a touch reminds my skin how to goose-bump. I glance over my shoulder and up, my breath hitching when our eyes collide. The air around us practically crackles, charged with a familiar current I'd forgotten was even possible.

He clears his throat and slides the zipper to the top. "There you go."

I turn to face him and am unprepared for how close he stands. I'm barefoot and my view narrows to the broad chest and shoulders of the man in front of me. We're not alone like this often anymore, leading separate lives that only intersect at our kids and our business. Kassim and Deja are usually around, or staff, friends, coaches, teachers. It's rarely just us. We used to know each other better than anyone. Now I'm not even sure what he watches in the little free time he has away from this place, or really what he does at all.

"Have you seen *Ozark*?" I ask.

The thick line of his brows dips. "Nah. Should I?"

"It's one of the best shows I've seen in a really long time. The acting, directing. The writing is stellar."

I'm rambling. I want to shove a sock in my mouth to make it stop running.

"I'll have to, uh...check it out." He glances at the door. "I need to get back to Granders."

"Yeah." I reach into the bottom of my suit bag to grab my green heels, bending to slip them on. "I gotta go too."

He runs a thorough glance from my head to my shoes. "You look...nice."

"Nice?" I scoop up the suit bag, now stuffed with my clothes, and speed to the door, grinning over my shoulder. "Pfftt. I look amazing."

He shakes his head, allowing a small smile. "You look amazing. Have a good time."

"I'll try not to be out too late. And don't let the kids stay up all night, Si. They have school tomorrow."

"Like I'm the pushover parent."

We both know he is, so I just stare at him until his smile broadens to that startling brightness that will snatch your breath if you let it.

"Get outta here," he says. "I'll see you at the house."

The house.

Not home. Not the dream home we worked for and fantasized about for years. Now it's just the house where the kids and I live. Josiah's in the same neighborhood, but two streets over. I'm not sure why my thoughts keep revisiting the past tonight when my reflection, my mindset, *everything* has "future" written all over it.

"Shake it off," I tell myself, climbing into the car and pulling out of the Grits parking lot. "It's time to party."

CHAPTER TWO

YASMEN

It's Soledad's birthday," Hendrix mutters into her Moscow Mule. "You think she'd be eager for some grown-girl time, and yet she's late."

"She's on her way." I reread the text Soledad sent. "As of twenty minutes ago. She said Lupe's cheering practice went over, Inez is working on a science project, and Lottie had dance lessons."

I study Hendrix over the rim of my drink. She has a face as bold as her name, punctuated by sloping cheekbones and an audacious nose, nostrils flared to scent adventure and bullshit. Her dark, arched brows are as quick to pull into a frown as the wide bow of her mouth is to stretch into a smile. She gets shit done and is as driven to help people as she is to succeed. Helping people is, at least in part, how she defines success.

"How are your housewives?" I ask, sipping my French 75, the gin and the twang sloughing the edge off my frayed nerves.

"Girl, a whole-ass handful. The producer had the nerve to call and ask me to keep my clients in check. Bitch, *you* check 'em. My job was to get them there. Your job is to make sure they don't kill each other before the season ends."

"Seems like the more drama, the better the ratings, so what's her problem?"

"Yeah, there's drama and then there's..." Hendrix lifts her brows meaningfully. "*Their* shit. Fistfights, weaves yanked out, tires slashed."

"Sounds like high school."

"Or day care, and my degree is in PR, not babysitting. Though, for real, that feels like my job half the time."

She aims a smile over my shoulder. "Speaking of babies, here comes Mommy-in-Chief now."

I glance around and spot Soledad climbing the stairs to Sky-Hi's rooftop. She wears her usual slightly harried expression, but tonight it's paired with a butt-hugging red dress that screams *Work it, girl; it's your birthday*. Her dark eyes search the crowd until she finds us. A blinding smile lights up her pretty face. She's short and curvy, and springy sable curls bounce around her shoulders, reflecting the energy packed into her petite frame. She waves and crosses quickly over to our table.

"Sorry I'm late." She collapses into the empty seat, snatches the drink from my hand, and takes a long sip.

"For your own birthday celebration." Hendrix tsks. "Just glad you made it at all. Did you have to tie Edward to the refrigerator for him to stay home with the girls?"

Soledad's husband is notoriously absent from pretty much everything lately. Pink filters into the gold-brown of her cheeks. "He, um, had to work late unexpectedly and—"

"So who's with the kids?" I cut in.

"I called Mrs. Lassiter's daughter." Soledad fixes her gaze on the menu, avoiding the exasperation I'm sure is apparent in Hendrix's eyes and mine. "She's that ninth grader who lives around the corner. Lottie and Inez love her. Lupe's old enough to stay home and they'd be fine, but her cheering practice went late, so..." She shrugs philosophically.

"One night," Hendrix mutters. "He couldn't give you one night?"

I shoot Hendrix a quelling glance, silently urging her to lay off, but she's more likely to bite *your* tongue than she is to bite hers.

"Guys, come on." Soledad drops the menu and all pretense that it actually interests her. "Can't we just have a good time and not focus on Edward? He's in the middle of a huge project at the firm. It's a lot and he's doing the best he can."

I bet even she doesn't believe that, but I won't argue the point and spoil her birthday any more than her inconsiderate sperm donor already has.

"You're right!" I slam my empty glass on the table and signal for the server. "Let's get lit like we're not class mom in the morning!"

"One of us *isn't* class mom," Hendrix reminds, her laugh throaty and grateful. "And my apartment is literally around the corner. I'm walking, so I'll drink for us all."

Soledad and I *are* driving, albeit only around the corner, so we can't drink much, but getting lit *sounds* amazing. Our little trio is composed of disparate pieces that somehow work together. Hendrix, blissfully single and childless, is completely focused on her career and her ailing mother in Charlotte, splitting her time between the Queen City and Atlanta. Soledad doesn't work outside the home, but runs her household like a kingdom, leaving everyone awestruck by levels of organization and domesticity seemingly unachievable by mere mortals. She's a dash of Joanna Gaines, a sprinkle of Marie Kondo, and a big ol' scoop of Tabitha Brown, a dish served at a farm table on the finest china.

And then there's me.

Wrapped in all the trappings of a suburban housewife, except I'm no longer anybody's wife, and I run a thriving business with the man I always assumed I'd love forever.

"How are *your* kids, Yasmen?" Soledad asks, sipping the cosmopolitan the server set down after taking our orders. "Deja and Kassim okay tonight?"

"They're good. Grabbing dinner at Grits. Josiah's taking them to the house for homework once they're done."

"You two manage your . . ." Soledad closes one eye and twists her lips, apparently searching for the right word. "Your dynamic so well."

"*Dynamic?*" Hendrix casts me a look I've fondly dubbed sly-slutty. "Is that what you call it when your fine as hell ex-husband is there 24/7 for the screwing and you do nothing about it?"

There was a time when Hendrix's brashness would have left me sputtering and spewing my drink, but I'm used to her now. She spent all her shock value on me months ago.

"It's called co-parenting," I say. "And running a business together. If we want to do both of those well, it's best to keep things simple and platonic."

"You don't even want the occasional dip into that yummy honeypot?" Hendrix asks, a knowing smile gracing her full lips. "Josiah is—"

"Fine as hell." I smile at the approaching server carrying our food. "I'm aware. I was married to him."

"I bet Josiah put it down," Hendrix says. "You can look at him and tell he can fuck."

"All right. Enough." I try to play it off with a laugh, but talking about our former sex life is not what I want to do. "Don't creep on my ex."

"I mean no harm." Hendrix lifts both hands. "I come in peace and with the purest admiration for a man in his prime and a prime piece of man. I was just saying it seems like you probably got some good dick out of that marriage. Amirite?"

I did, but that was the last thing on my mind at the end. Our animosity and grief doused the passion we'd always taken for granted. Those last few months, we rarely even slept in the same room. My bed has been cold and empty for a very long time.

"I obviously don't know everything that went down with you two," Hendrix says. "But that's the kind of man I'd miss."

"Like you said," I tell her, staring into my drink. "You don't know everything that went down."

They never knew Josiah and me as a set, as the couple everyone envied. When I was going through my dark season, I lost touch with most friends I was closest to. Not their fault. I shut many of them out. I met Hendrix and Soledad through the yoga class my therapist recommended to help reduce anxiety and improve my mood at my lowest point. Soledad lives a couple of streets over, so I knew *of* her, but it wasn't until yoga that we really connected. The three of us hid on the back row watching everyone do their dog, cat, and cobra poses while we struggled to contort our out-of-shape bodies into the most basic positions. Maybe because I was so in need of reconnection, and they seemed to be, too, we grew close quickly. They don't look at me with that careful sympathy I see in the eyes of everyone who knew me before.

"I know you guys went through a lot all at once," Soledad says.

"Yeah, we, um...It was a lot." I take a fortifying gulp of my drink. "You know Josiah's aunt Byrd passed away soon after we opened in Skyland."

Pushing down the emotion that tries to break through the surface, I force myself to continue. "Business tanked. In that state, we couldn't hold our own in Skyland. Not with the quality of restaurants around here. Maybe we would have fared better if we'd stayed where we were. Stayed *who* we were."

But Josiah had always seen us turning the restaurant into an upscale destination spot. And it would have gone off without a hitch had life not hitched every which way but loose.

"You don't talk about it much, the divorce I mean," Soledad says. "Did you guys try therapy?"

"Josiah's allergic," I say wryly. "He doesn't do therapy. I wanted to, but..."

"At the church where I grew up," Hendrix says, "they always said you ain't got a problem God can't fix. What can a therapist do that God can't? That mindset kept a lot of folks from getting help."

"Josiah's reasons had nothing to do with faith," I say with a twist of my lips. "He just thinks it's a load of bullshit. Deja and Kassim talked some to a grief counselor at school, but aside from a rough patch or two, they bounced back okay. Couples therapy? Josiah didn't think it could help, and by the end, neither did I."

Things had gotten so bad, I felt like I was suffocating in that house, in that marriage, and I had to get out. It felt like the whole world was resting on my chest every morning, and it was all I could do to get out of bed.

And everything hurt.

That's the part of depression people don't consider, that at times it physically hurts. My therapist helped me understand that the back pain and the headaches I developed were most likely related to stress, and stress hormones like cortisol and noradrenaline contributed to my apathy and exhaustion. Which exacerbated my depression. It was an inescapable cycle that left me looking up at my life from the bottom of a well, the walls slippery, and seeing no way out.

And it all hurt, including being with the man I'd loved more than everything. After how we'd loved each other, the way we hurt each other was destroying us.

I've made a little bubble for my friends and me, one that protects my fragile joy and wards off the hurt of the past. I know I'll have to tell Hendrix and Soledad everything soon. If therapy has taught me anything, it's that you run from your pain in a circle. You end up exhausted, but never really gaining ground. I have to stop running, have to share with them all the ways life popped the seams on a world perfectly sewn together. For now I share a little at a time, and for tonight, I've shared enough.

I clear my throat and push out a laugh. "Is this a celebration or what? Let's eat before Sol ages another year."

The night turns out to be just what I needed, and I hope what Soledad deserves. She's the hardest-working woman I know and sees her life's mission as raising three beautiful humans to be confident women who make the world a better place. Some might judge that, say a woman as smart as Soledad could do so much more. I see the power in choosing your *own* more.

"So we doing this or nah?" Hendrix asks hopefully once we've settled the bill. "I got a roll of ones burning a hole in my Louis. Strip club?"

The answer is written in Soledad's eyes, sketched in the rueful tug of her lips. "Rain check? I actually *am* class mom in the morning, and I need to get home and check Inez's science project. I bet I'll have to help her because Edward..."

Edward is about as likely to help with that science project as Garth Brooks is to perform at the Apollo.

"Well, Edward had a long day," Soledad finishes with a smile as natural as my lashes. "And may have overlooked a few things."

"Hmmmmm," Hendrix grunts.

She really should patent that *hmmmm*. It's the most accomplished monosyllable I've ever met.

"Well, I have the care and feeding of my housewives tomorrow," Hendrix says and sighs. "The producers want me on-set to ensure no butt implants are harmed in the making of this next episode."

We share a cackle, and I relish the simple ease of authentic friendship where I didn't expect it and the evening breeze on my face. Georgia clings to summer as long as possible. August's bright green leaves still trim the trees lining Skyland's streets, but soon they'll be varicolored, the wind propelling them from the branches like a confetti cannon. In just a few weeks, they'll blanket the cobblestones under our feet.

I fish the keys from my purse and click the remote to unlock my car as we walk to the parking lot.

"Happy birthday, sweetheart," I say, reaching for Soledad.

Hendrix's arms enclose us both, and our little triumvirate huddles together, our perfumes and spirits mingling under the warm glow of the town's gas lamp streetlights.

"I love you guys," Soledad whispers, eyes bright. "There's nowhere I would have rather been than with you on my birthday. Thank you for making it special."

"I love you crazy broads too," Hendrix jokes, giving us an extra squeeze before releasing us. "Next year we are hitting up a strip club. This is *Atlanta*. How you gonna *not* go to a strip club?"

"I'm open." I grin.

"Yassss!" Hendrix high-fives me.

"Maybe next year," Soledad's mouth says, while the wide-eyed look she sends me says *neverrrrr*.

I climb into my car, chuckling as I picture staid Soledad and up-for-anything Hendrix in Magic City, tossing ones. I'd be in the middle enjoying the show onstage and off.

"Y'all still coming to Food Truck Friday tomorrow?" I ask through my rolled-down window.

"For sure," Hendrix says. "I'll be wrapped on set by then."

"Can't wait." Soledad opens her door and climbs up into a Suburban. She looks so small behind the wheel of that mammoth machine, but with three girls and their gaggle of friends, she can never have enough passenger space. "See you then."

The drive home is short, barely enough time to reflect on the day's events. A year ago, I could not have envisioned feeling this way. Feeling this *good*. A night out with new friends who feel like the sisters of my heart. Our business, not long ago on the brink of failure, restored, thriving, booming.

And then there's Josiah.

A shiver skims my spine, the memory of his fingers whispering across my bare skin when he zipped me up, coaxing to life parts of me long dormant and neglected. I'll probably always be attracted to him. Like I told Hendrix, he's fine as hell, but I can't let my body's natural response to a beautiful man with whom I have a complicated past, *and offspring*, fool me into thinking things should have turned out differently.

We were good together. Very good, in fact. Then shit happened. So much life-altering, earth-shattering shit, and not only were we not good together, but I couldn't imagine things ever being good again. It's time for us both to move on.

When Josiah and I dreamed of our restaurant over cartons of cheap Chinese, late at night while he was finishing his MBA, we didn't talk about living in an affluent neighborhood like Skyland, but as I drive past all the custom-built houses and three-car garages, I realize we got it. The garage door to the house we renovated together lifts. In the last gasping breaths of our marriage, it became unbearable to be in this house with him. How many nights did our arguments echo through the halls? But after the divorce, I couldn't bear to be here without him. It felt wrong and empty. To be fair, at that point, no place felt right. Not even in my own skin.

I rid the house of all our wedding pictures, but Josiah is indelibly stamped on every square inch, from the freestanding tub in our bathroom, to the large open kitchen, and the high-ceilinged family room. Every light fixture, paint color, down to the smallest detail, we carefully chose together. The only thing we never anticipated was losing each other in the process of gaining everything else. We executed every phase of our dreams right on schedule.

Graduation. Check!

Marriage. Check!

Start a business. Check!

Baby one. Check!

Baby two. Check!

Baby three…

I shake off the thoughts like shackles and pull into the garage. I made the right decision for us all when I asked for the divorce. I have to believe that. Anything is better than the volatile pressure cooker our lives became at the end.

Laughter reaches my ears when I walk into the kitchen and close the door behind me. I knew he would let them stay up late. I easily pick out the kids' giggles, mixed in with the low timbre of Josiah's chuckle, but I can't quite place the other melodic laugh. When I enter the family room I realize why.

I've never heard Vashti laugh like this before.

It lights up her face, an inner glow that spills into her eyes and over her cheeks. She wears a lovely dress the color of buttercups that discreetly outlines her slim, feminine shape. Her hand rests on Josiah's knee casually, at ease like she's touched him that way a hundred times.

Oh, my God. She probably has.

They've probably shared these simple intimate touches many times in secret, or at least without me knowing. I may not want Josiah for myself anymore, but I'm not blind enough to miss when someone else does.

And the simmering affection shining from Vashti's eyes tells me she wants my husband.

Ex-husband.

Plates litter the floor, along with cans of Diet Coke and LaCroix. A Monopoly board is splayed across the large glass table Josiah and I purchased from a furniture outlet in North Carolina. That somehow offends me most deeply.

On our table.

It feels like I interrupted them in a passionate embrace, twined together across the thick-paned glass in a pornographic pretzel, instead of playing a board game with the kids.

"Mom!" Kassim says, drawing everyone's attention to me standing in the doorway. "You're home."

I manage a nod, unsure of my lines in this farce.

"Vashti lost everything in Monopoly." Kassim points to the pretty young chef. He's oblivious to how this all looks and feels to me, but maybe Vashti isn't. She stands quickly and starts collecting dishes.

"Sorry about the mess," she says a little breathlessly. "I don't think we spilled any of the sauce from the ribs on anything."

If I *could* squeeze the voice through my constricted vocal cords, I still wouldn't trust it. Her words fall into an awkward silence I'm not sure how to break, or why it's there, for that matter.

"We got their food to go," Josiah picks up where she left off. "Vashti and I had been working all day, and were both ready to call it a night, so we just brought it home."

Once I finally find my voice, it's not to respond to him or Vashti, but to ignore them.

"Kids, it's way past your bedtime," I say, my tone bright and hopefully normal. "You have school in the morning. Did you get your homework done?"

"Yeah, it only took like twenty minutes," Kassim offers on his way to the staircase.

"Kassim," I address his retreating back. "Are you going to leave your trash here in the middle of the floor? You know that's unacceptable."

"FYI, Vashti," Deja speaks for the first time. "Just about everything is unacceptable in this house according to Mom."

I'm surprised by the sting of hurt. I know better than to let my daughter get to me. "Getting to me" is her new favorite pastime, but for her to strike in front of Vashti, who may be…something I didn't realize she was to Josiah…hits in a different way. Deeper.

"Fix that attitude, Day," Josiah responds before I have to, his voice somehow gentle *and* stern. "Your mom's right. You guys need to pick up after yourselves. She's not your maid, and I better not hear that you're treating her like one."

"Yes, sir," Deja replies demurely, gathering the dishes and heading toward the kitchen with Kassim.

"Thanks," I mutter, not feeling particularly grateful. "It's good seeing you again so soon, Vashti."

I'm trying to relocate the home training I lost when I found this woman in my house laughing with my kids, her hand all over my husband's knee.

Ex-husband.

"You have a beautiful home." Vashti flashes a smile at Josiah. "And I love hanging out with the kids."

"They love hanging out with you too." Josiah grabs his jacket from the back of the couch and slips it on. "But we should get going."

He proffers his car keys to Vashti. "Could you give us a sec, Vash? Wait in the car for just a minute? I'll be right out."

Surprise and what may be concern skid across her expression. A quick slide that she checks before it fully forms. Disciplined, this one. A great match for him in that at least.

"Of course." She takes the keys, and I don't miss the small squeeze she gives his fingers. "Night, Yasmen."

"See you tomorrow," I say, reining in my irritation, which is probably completely out of proportion to this situation, *but still real.*

Once she leaves the living room, walks to the foyer, and closes the front door behind her, Josiah looks at me, his expression guarded. I remember how this striking face looks happy, open. I haven't really seen him that way in a long time, but I do remember.

"Something you'd like to tell me?" I ask, perching on the arm of the couch, trying my damnedest to look harmless.

"Vashti and I—"

"What the hell is she doing in my house?"

Okay. That came out wrong.

Or maybe it came out exactly as I *felt* it, but I wouldn't have *said* it if my emotions weren't in freefall. He quirks a dark brow at me, his mouth tightening in the corners.

"Sorry." I clear my throat and smooth my dress. "You were saying?"

"You have no reason to be upset."

"Nothing makes a woman more upset than her husband telling her she has nothing to be upset about."

"Ex-husband," he corrects softly.

"Right." A stiff smile takes hold of my face. "Ex-husband, a *man* telling a woman she should stay calm. It's how we know shit's happening we should be upset about."

"Nothing's happening that shouldn't be." He gives me a look from under dark lashes that hides nothing and is unashamed. "Two consenting adults—"

"That phrase usually precedes fucking."

"And what if it does?" The release of his words is swift, sharp. A knife unsheathed like he was waiting for me to piss him off. "I'm single. She's single. You're acting like we corrupted the kids in some way. You're acting..."

Jealous.

He doesn't finish it. He doesn't have to. I'm not jealous. I'm just... *hell.* Thrown.

"I thought we agreed we'd discuss anyone we started dating being around the kids." I hesitate. "I mean, is that what this is? You and Vashti are, what... dating?"

He huffs an exasperated breath, like I'm bothering him with these basic questions and have no right to know.

Do I have a right to know?

I've been Josiah's friend, lover, business partner, the mother of his children, his wife. For the first time, I'm not sure where we stand. Where *I* stand with him. What I am to him.

"It's really new," he finally says. "We just clicked working so closely and started spending time together. And it's not like the kids aren't already around her all the time, so I didn't feel the need to introduce her to them. They may have guessed, but I haven't told them for sure."

"But you will?"

Why am I holding my breath?

"Probably. We've hung out a few times." He puts up a hand and shoots me a warning look. "And before you call me out on that, we said we'd give a heads-up for the sake of the kids. Not each other. I don't have to tell you when I start dating someone, and I don't want to know when…"

He does look away then. Drops his gaze to his expensive shoes.

"We've been divorced almost two years, Yas. We knew we'd move on. I honestly didn't think it would be a big deal."

Move on.

I'd just told myself it was good that we were moving on. And it is, but seeing him "moving on" in the house we built together, in the residue of the life we shared…I didn't know it would affect me this way.

"It's *not* a big deal." I stand to fluff the cushion Vashti's pert little ass was just seated on. "I guess I was caught off guard."

"Like I said, I haven't told the kids anything. Vashti's around at work a lot. It was casual. She was finishing up as we were leaving, and I invited her along. I didn't make a big deal of it, but I want to be honest with them."

He bites his bottom lip, and a sudden, ill-timed memory of those perfectly full lips on me assaults my senses. Kissing the curve of my neck. Sucking my breasts. Sliding over my stomach and down, down, down.

Crap. Crap. Crap.

"I want to be honest with you," he continues, completely oblivious to how my mind is flashback-fucking him. "Vashti's great and, though it may ultimately go nowhere, we want to see where this leads."

"What if it goes left? We could be out a chef. It took a long time to find her."

"Like I need you reminding me how long it took to find a good chef."

Funny how the words he *doesn't* say can sting more than the ones he does.

He doesn't have to say that when Byrd died I was in no shape to help, that he was the one at Grits from open to close. He wore all the hats—owner, manager, you name it—when I could barely hold up my head at all. Even now his eyes hold no accusation. Only memories that if we voice could shatter the tenuous peace we've managed to negotiate.

"Vashti and I did have that conversation," he says. "We agreed to keep work separate as much as we can. She loves her job and she's essential at Grits. Her cooking dug us out of the hole when Byrd passed."

"Just be careful, Si, and not only because of work." I gulp down hot emotion and force myself to keep speaking. "I don't want to see you get hurt."

His laugh, like so many things tonight, takes me by surprise. The sonic boom of it startles me, bounces off the walls and floods the room.

"What's so funny?" I venture after a few seconds of him laughing and shaking his head in seeming disbelief.

The humor in his eyes, if it was ever genuine, dissipates, leaving his gaze cool, flat. "The irony of you saying you don't want to see someone hurt me."

"I-I don't."

"No one in my whole life has ever hurt me like you did."

Shock shuts me up. I'm struck dumb, but the accusations he doesn't bother voicing, the grievances I didn't realize were so deeply held, screech in the silence. They blare from his eyes, fixed on me, not even a blink interrupting the unrelenting intensity of his stare.

"I'm the one who asked for the divorce, yeah," I say, suddenly unsure of something I should be certain of. "But we agreed."

"Is that how you remember it? Because I remember the worst possible thing happening to us both, to this whole family, and you shutting me out. I remember us losing..."

Don't say it. Don't you say his name. I can't hear his name right now. Not tonight.

"Never mind," he sighs, and it's my reprieve. He grips the back of his neck. "This shit is ancient history. I'm too tired for it."

I should press, demand that he finish the thought, but it, like so many other things we stopped saying when things got hard, remains buried under the rubble of our silence.

"I'm gonna go," he says and heads to the front door. "Early start tomorrow."

"Sure. Okay."

I trail him into the foyer. When he pulls open one of the wide French doors, in the sliver of space, in the breath of a moment, I see his Rover idling in the driveway. The interior light is on, Vashti's face clearly visible, her eyes alert and trained on my front porch. On Josiah. Her expression brightens with a smile, even as her glance drifts over his shoulder and briefly meets mine. In that tiny space, an understanding forms between us, and I know why we never clicked. She's not sure about me. About Josiah and me. It makes sense. Our lives tangle, vines running through our kids and our business. We have a history. A long, turbulent one. And even though we're no longer married, it's obvious we're still connected in so many ways. I can't blame her. I'd wonder too.

I could tell her she has nothing to worry about. The passion, the love, the fierce devotion that once existed between Josiah and me? I burned that to the ground long ago. Whatever remains is as cold and stiff as the look he slants over his shoulder at me before the door closes behind him.

CHAPTER THREE

YASMEN

"Everything looks great, Yas," Hendrix says, surveying Sky Square. Food trucks boasting restaurant logos and menus ring the area. Main Street has been blocked off and café tables and chairs dot the cobblestone road. Fairy lights wind through the trees, twinkling even though the sun hasn't set and there's still daylight. Vendors scurry, making last-minute preparations before the great citizens of Skyland descend in the next hour seeking good food and a good time.

"Thank you," I say, scanning the scene one last time. "I'm glad we got out here early to make sure everything's ready to go, though."

"Between the tostadas," Soledad says, licking sauce from the corner of her mouth, "the hot dogs, and the pulled pork, I think I've had a little of everything and Food Truck Friday hasn't even officially started."

"I know these businesses appreciate all the revenue and the traffic tonight will generate," Hendrix says, tossing what's left of a taco into a nearby trash can. "How's it feel to be Head Boss Babe again? Running thangs?"

I laugh and wave off her question, though I must admit that after barely leaving the house, being barely able to function for so long, it feels good to be doing something that benefits our community. When we first transitioned Grits from a mom-and-pop shop on the south side to our current location in the heart of Skyland, Josiah and I decided to get in good with the locals and endear ourselves to other business owners. I strategically assumed an active role with the Skyland

Association, an organization designed to increase community engagement, foster economic development, and strengthen ties between the private and the public sectors. I went from being the chairwoman, spearheading community activities on the regular, to being…well, not very involved at all, but Food Truck Friday signals to the board that I'm back and ready to go.

"I think we've checked all the vendors except Grits," I say, nodding toward our truck branded with the Grits logo. A few employees work the truck counter, attired in T-shirts and close-fitting caps, hair carefully hidden. There's no scrambling. No last-minute scurrying. Vashti has achieved the same order and calm for tonight's event that she elicits in the restaurant. I choose to be grateful. Her involvement means I'm more freed up to invest much-needed quality time with my kids without worrying Josiah has to handle everything at work on his own.

He has Vashti now.

"My people!" I say, dividing a greeting smile between the two employees behind the food truck counter. "How goes it?"

"It's all good," Cassie, Vashti's sous-chef, answers, but continues checking supplies. "We're ready for the stampede."

A gray-whiskered man emerges from behind the truck wiping his hands on a sauce-stained apron. "Now I know you better come get this hug, Yasmen."

I chuckle and step into Milwaukee Johnson's long arms. My dad died long ago, and this cook Byrd hired has improbably become the closet thing I've had to a father since. He smells like a dozen home-cooked meals, like all my comfort foods have been sewn into the lining of his clothes. My breath whooshes then releases into his shoulder, and I tuck my head under his chin, slinking my arms around his waist. He feels frailer, smaller than when we last hugged, like time is stealing not only years, but inches and pounds from his imposing frame. I pull back to peer up into his sharp features, leathered by time, but somehow still younger than his years.

"How ya been, Milky?"

His broad, bony shoulders lift and drop carelessly, but his eyes fill with sadness. "I still miss Byrd. They lie when they say it gets better. I think maybe I'm just getting stronger, so I feel it a little less."

By the time Byrd met Milky, she'd divorced three husbands and had just buried the fourth. She swore she'd never walk down another aisle, but Milky loved Byrd, and with what she had left, she loved him back. The food wasn't the only thing hot in that kitchen. They flirted and fondled, chased and caught each other, not even trying to hide that they'd found something special in their twilight years. Josiah and I used to laugh and say we hoped we had that much fire when we got to be their age.

"I know, Milky," I whisper, squeezing him a little tighter. "I miss her too."

He nods and pats my back before stepping away. "That Vashti is a godsend, though. She got that kitchen humming. Byrd woulda loved her food."

"Yup." My smile dries on my face like plaster. "She's great."

Wise, rheumy eyes study me and a gold tooth gleams at the corner bend of his smile. I force myself to hold his omniscient stare and resist the urge to squirm.

"How ya *really* doing?" he asks, gentling some of the usual gruffness in his scratchy voice.

"I'm getting there." I squeeze his hands, knuckles oversized from years of cracking them, smattered with fading grease burns. "Promise."

"Things won't the same without you. Glad you're back where you're s'posed to be." Milky grins and straightens his cap. "This event is something else. All the restaurants be empty tonight because the streets gon' be full. You did the damn thang, Yas."

"Thanks, Milk." I tap the aluminum counter jutting out from the truck. "You guys got it looking good over here too. Thanks for representing."

"You know if Vashti's running the ship," Cassie says from behind the counter, "it'll be tight."

"I'll choose to take that as a compliment," a low melodic voice drawls from behind us.

I turn to find Vashti standing there with a pair of silver tongs and a bottle of hot sauce.

"Oooh, hot sauce." Hendrix licks her lips. "If your fried chicken is as good as I remember, you can just run an IV from that bottle right here."

She slaps her forearm, and we all laugh. I smile in all the right places, but there is a definite tension between Vashti and me. Given the surreptitious glances she keeps sending my way, I suspect she feels it too.

"We do have a limited menu," Vashti says, entering the truck and disappearing beneath the counter. A second later she pops back up with a red-and-white-checkered food boat holding a crispy golden fried chicken breast. "But we got chicken."

"Oh, yes, hunty," Hendrix crows, reaching for the chicken with one hand and the hot sauce with the other. "I'm just gonna taste this right quick for you to make sure it's okay before the general public gets to it."

"Generous of you." Vashti laughs.

"Here comes the boss," Cassie says, shooting quick glances at both Vashti and me. "I mean, the other boss."

Josiah approaches with long, confident strides. Proud set to his head. Shoulders wide, body fluent with just a touch of swagger in his gait. He is flanked by Deja and Kassim, and trailed by one of the biggest dogs I've ever seen in my life.

Ottis Redding.

I'll never forget Aunt Byrd bringing this beautiful Great Dane with his shiny coat of unrelieved black to our house. A gift from her last husband, Herbert, the legendary R & B singer's canine namesake was just a pup when we first met.

"Herbert *would* give me the dog with the shortest life span," Byrd had half joked. "Since all he ever brought me was grief."

A wicked light in her dark eyes, she had added in an aside, "And sex. Whooo, chile, that man could lay some pipe."

My lips twitch even as my heart pinches. You had to smile when Byrd was around.

"Mom!" Kassim rushes ahead of Josiah and Deja and gives me a tight hug. I thought that by ten, he would have grown beyond this unabashed love for his mama. Boys usually do around now, but his affection for me is still open and uninhibited, even in front of his friends. Maybe he saw me sad for so long, he's afraid to withhold it from me.

"How was school?" I ask.

"Good." Kassim squints up at Grits's food truck menu. "Can I have ribs?"

"Oh, my God, with the ribs," Deja says, but smiles at her brother. The smile dims when she meets my eyes. "Hey, Mom."

"Deja, hey." I hate this tension with her, but I can't seem to fix it. "How was school?"

"Fine." She shrugs. "The usual waste of time, I guess."

I bite back the response that automatically rises to my lips.

"Good," I say, not wanting to ruin the night before it starts. "And, Kassim, if you want ribs, I guess you can have them."

"I thought you were gonna try something different tonight, Seem," Josiah says, joining our little group huddled around the Grits truck.

Kassim's expression turns pleading. "Can I change my mind? The ribs are the best thing."

"Well, I, for one, appreciate the compliment." Vashti laughs. "That's my grandmama's special sauce."

"Grandma knew what she was doing," Milky pipes in from behind the counter.

"Truck looks good," Josiah says, turning his attention to my friends. "Hey, Hendrix. Soledad, belated happy birthday."

They both practically simper under his attention. He does have that way of making you feel you and only you have somehow managed to coax out his reluctant charm.

"Everything okay back at the restaurant?" Josiah asks Vashti. Not me, but he already knows I've been focused on the event. I told him that myself, so it shouldn't sting that he consults with her instead of me, the actual co-owner.

Shouldn't, but does a little.

"Everything's great," Vashti answers, coming to stand beside Josiah. I wonder if I'm the only one who notices the way she looks at him, or if anyone else sees the longing her implacable exterior doesn't manage to hide.

"I'll still dash back over to the restaurant in a bit to double-check," Vashti adds. "Make sure the dinner crowd's going okay. Callile or I will be there all night."

"Can I go over with you, V, since the truck doesn't have the full menu?" Deja pleads with a warm smile, hands pressed together. "I want crab cakes."

When was the last time Deja smiled at me that way? Tried to spend any time with me? I know they're just walking to the restaurant together, but my jaw still aches with tension. Between finding out about Vashti dating my ex, playing games with my kids, and now winning my daughter over seemingly with barely any effort, I have to suppress my petty reflex.

"Of course." Vashti's smile broadens. "And we need to plan our Monopoly rematch."

"You're on!" Kassim nods, eyes lit up. His congeniality is only outpaced by his competitive spirit.

"We should teach them to play spades, Si," Vashti says, affection in her smile, in the hand she rests on his arm.

She exudes the same easy intimacy I noticed last night. By the way Soledad and Hendrix dart glances from them to me, they must notice it too.

Great. Interrogation forthcoming.

Hendrix's elbow to my side confirms it. When I look up, her eyebrows subtly lift, silently asking if I see this. I ignore her microexpression and decide I've endured enough of my ex-husband's budding relationship for now.

"I'd better walk around some," I say. "I should make sure the DJ is set up and ready to go."

"There's a DJ?" Soledad asks.

She may appear prim and proper and pinned up, but get a little sangria in her and put on some early two thous Backstreet Boys, and you got a party animal on your hands. I've borne witness.

"If he plays Tony! Toni! Toné!," Hendrix says, "I warn you right now, dignity is out the door and crunk will be activated. 'Feels Good' is my party anthem."

"Your anthem?" Josiah asks, humor bending the stern line of his mouth.

"Used to be 'Step in the Name of Love.'" Hendrix tsks and shakes her head. "But R. Kelly ruined that, pervert genius."

"And on that note," I interject before my son's quick mind starts digging for the specifics of the pied piper's sins. "I'm gonna go."

"We'll come with," Soledad says, pulling her phone from the slit pocket of her sundress. "I need to see if Edward's gotten here with the girls yet."

"I got my eye on the Blaxican food truck," Hendrix says. "I'mma surrender to the sexual tension that's been building between me and those collard green quesadillas ever since I got here."

"I wouldn't want to get in the way of that," I say wryly, turning to Kassim, cupping his face. "If you need me, text or call, okay?"

"All right, Mom."

"Don't wander off. Stay with me or your dad all night."

Kassim twists his lips like my maternal concern is finally getting to him. "I'm not a baby."

"She's right," Josiah says, his voice quiet but firm. "Don't make Otis have to come find you again."

Hearing his name, Otis perks up and barks loudly, nuzzling into Josiah's leg. A couple of years ago, Kassim got lost at the fair. After ten minutes I was ready to plaster his face on milk cartons and send out an Amber Alert, but cooler heads prevailed. Mainly Josiah and Otis. Maybe it was Kassim's scent, or something else, but Otis found him.

"I can count on you at least," I say, rubbing Otis's silky head.

"Collard quesadillas," Hendrix reminds me.

I respond with an eye roll while the others laugh. "Okay, let's get going."

We leave Kassim and Josiah at the Grits truck, while Deja walks off with Vashti, her animated chatter grating as they go.

"Um, was I the only one who didn't know your chef is smashing your ex?" Hendrix asks as soon as we're out of earshot.

"Shhh!" I hiss, glancing over my shoulder to make sure we *are* actually out of earshot.

"I saw it too," Soledad says, hesitation clear on her face. "I mean, I'm not going as far as to say they're already having sex, but there is obviously...something there, right?"

I pretend to be terribly preoccupied looking around to check each truck and make sure things are going smoothly. "Uh, yeah. I guess."

Hendrix takes my elbow and stops us in our tracks. "Is that woman fucking your husband?"

"Ex-husband." I shrug as if it doesn't matter to me either way, though deep down—hell, not even that deep—I know it does. "Josiah told me last night they're dating, but the kids don't know yet, so don't mention it."

"Are you okay with it?" Soledad frowns, before going on hastily. "I mean, obviously, you're over him and it doesn't matter to you if they're together."

She peeks from beneath a dark fringe of lashes. "Does it?"

"Not in the least," I agree.

"So what's the story?" Hendrix asks. "How long has this been going on?"

"He says it's pretty recent. They've been working together obviously and I guess they were…" I clear my throat. "Attracted to each other. She was at the house last night when I got home from—"

"Wayminit." Hendrix holds up a hand. "He had her up in your house?"

I give them both an entreating look. I have no desire to discuss Vashti and Josiah, and I don't trust myself not to betray a *not sure how I feel about this* vibe during this inquisition.

"Can we just drop it?" I beg.

"You sure you're okay?" Soledad asks, concern etched on her finely drawn features.

"Better than okay. I'm h-h-happy for him," I stutter…tellingly. "Happy for them both."

"Well, that was about as convincing as OJ teaching Sunday school," Hendrix mutters. "Look, even if you're over him, that first time either of you dates after the divorce is bound to feel awkward. I understand if you don't want *him* to know that, but we're your girls. It's safe with us."

Hendrix squeezes my hand. "*You're* safe with us."

Soledad nods, taking my other hand. "You can trust us."

I blow out a breath and lift my eyes to the sky, fixing my stare on the setting sun so I don't have to look at them when I make this confession.

"It feels…wrong seeing him with someone else," I admit. "But I have no right to feel this way."

"You mean jealous?" Soledad probes gently.

"I'm not jealous." I jerk my hands from their grasps. "I said it feels wrong, not that I'm jealous. We made the right decision when we divorced. We're better as friends. As partners and co-parents."

"Too bad you can't still fuck him, though, right?" Hendrix laments. "'Cause, ba-beeee, he looks *good*. And he got that smooth, Denzel kinda walk. That deep, chocolate voice. Your girl would be on that ex-with-benefits tip if I were you."

"Hen." Soledad slices her finger at her throat, the classic *cut it out*, widening her eyes pointedly.

"Oh, right." Hendrix pats my shoulder. "What I mean to say is, you're better off without him. You are both grown-ass adults handling this all very maturely."

"It's the first time either of us has dated," I say. "So it *is* a little awkward, but I'll get used to it."

"Well, we're here if you need us," Soledad says.

"While I really am enjoying this bitches bonding vibe," Hendrix interjects, "if that Blaxican truck runs out of collard quesadillas before I make it over there, that's hell *y'all* gon' pay."

Giggling, I walk with them to get this girl's quesadillas. I make my way around the Square over the next hour, pleased to see so much of the neighborhood out, eating, spending money. The vendors all seem satisfied, and the association members I run into congratulate me on a job well done. The night is going even better than I hoped and exactly as I planned. Kassim and Deja eventually make their way back to us when we are at the fountain.

"Got any pennies?" Kassim asks, looking longingly into the fountain.

It's not technically a wishing well, but Skyland residents have unofficially made it one, casting in so many pennies with their wishes that we've had to start removing the coins quarterly. The city donates any money removed from the fountain to a local shelter. It's not much, and we've even created a "fountain fund" for anyone who wants to add to what we give.

"I only have quarters," Hendrix says.

"Even better," Kassim beams. "I heard the bigger the coin, the better the wishes."

"I'm not sure it works that way," I say dryly. "But quarters will fatten the fountain fund, so go for it."

While Hendrix digs out some shiny change for Kassim, Soledad's oldest daughter, Lupe, joins us, explaining that her two sisters are still eating barbecue with Edward. She is, even at this young age, stunning. Soledad's mother is Black and Puerto Rican. Her father is white with rich auburn hair, and Lupe gets her deeply waved, bright copper from him. With Edward's green eyes and Soledad's smooth, tan skin, she's tall, already standing higher than Soledad's five feet four inches. Everywhere this girl goes, heads turn. Already. And she's only thirteen years old.

God bless Soledad.

"Hi, Mrs. Wade," Lupe says and smiles. "Hey, Ms. Barry."

She really is a great kid. Conscious of her grades, polite, and kind. I'm glad that since Soledad and I became friends, Lupe and Deja have gotten closer too.

"Hey, Deja," Lupe offers with an even brighter smile. "Missed you in English today."

Deja's eyes widen, snapping to my face and then back to her friend's. Lupe's smile dies with a quickness and she covers her mouth, obviously realizing too late she put her foot in it.

"Why weren't you in English class, Deja?" I demand, feeling my mother's hand on my hip and her stern frown possessing my face.

"I had something to do," she answers. I can tell she's trying to brazen it out, but she knows she's in trouble if she doesn't come up with a better excuse than that.

"Sorry, Day," Lupe says, chagrin all over her face.

"Mom, can we go now?" Kassim interrupts, borderline whining. "Me and Jamal are supposed to play *Madden*."

"And I need to record some videos," Deja says, glancing at her phone. "I can get one done tonight and the rest tomorrow."

"What kind of videos?" Hendrix asks.

"I'm a natural hair influencer," Deja says without missing a beat. "@KurlyGirly."

"I need to see the video before you upload," I remind her.

And to hear where you were during English class.

I don't say that part out loud, but the look we exchange lets her know she won't be doing one without the other.

"How could I forget?" Deja mutters, returning to her phone.

I know kids are way more web savvy than we were at that age, but

Josiah and I still have protections on our kids' devices and monitor their connections very carefully. We let Deja do this hair thing on the condition that her father or I have to see and approve everything she posts. We have all the passwords, and she already knows I will shut that thing down at the first sign of some grown man sending dick pics.

"I think we can start heading out," I tell them. "Things will be winding down in a few. Let me just alert one of the association members who offered to close since I handled the opening."

Before I can take one step, the DJ starts a song I'd recognize anywhere.

"Oh, no, they didn't!" Hendrix says, jumping up from her seat on the lip of the fountain. "Not my song."

Sure enough, the opening of "Feels Good" by Tony! Toni! Toné! blares across the Square.

"Come on, girl." Hendrix grabs Deja's hand. "Put that phone down and dance with me."

And amazingly…shockingly…beautifully…my petulant daughter dances. Not with the *I'm too cool for this* attitude I usually see these days, but with abandon. With joy. She and Hendrix throw their hands in the air, swivel their hips, drop it to the ground. Hendrix is completely unhindered by her vertiginous heels, matching Deja drop for drop. I'm not even sure Deja has heard this old R & B classic before, but she takes to it like it's BTS's latest hit. They're laughing so hard trying to outdance each other, they clutch their bellies. By the end of the first verse, Lupe and Soledad are up twirling around too. Watching those I love enjoy themselves, I'm transfixed, and for these glorious seconds, so happy. I've had some dark days the last few years. Days I wasn't sure how I'd make it.

But today.

Tonight.

Now, this is joy. I taste it in my laughter as Kassim grabs my hand and tries his best to twirl me around. I feel it in the spray of water on my face when we dance too close to the fountain. It leaps in my chest when I almost fall in, almost topple into a well full of wishes. I fix my eyes on the sky above, a blue-black quilt stitched with stars. With my arms stretched toward infinity, it feels for a moment like worship. Like a collection of sacred seconds consecrated to say thank you for friends and family and hope, that elusive emotion I didn't realize was such a rare commodity of the heart until I had none.

People talk about the stages of grief, but there is a stage of depression—at least for me—where you go from feeling pain so acutely you can't bear it, to feeling nothing at all. A blessed numbness after debilitating sadness. It's like laying a thin film of steel over your emotions. So thin it's diaphanous. You can see everything through it, but nothing actually touches you. I couldn't feel a thing, but I embraced it because at least I wasn't feeling pain. At that time, joy didn't stand a chance, but tonight I feel *everything*. And it is finally good.

Even after the song ends and Tony! Toni! Toné! has done it again, the laughter doesn't leave us. It bubbles up in me as surely as the water gurgles in the fountain. I glance over to the DJ, planning to give him a thumbs-up, and am surprised to see Josiah standing beside him, arms folded, a slight smile on his face when his eyes meet mine.

He was standing there when Hendrix said how much she loved this song. Did he...

I do the sign for "Thank you," touching my chin and dropping my hand. When the kids were young, before they could talk, we taught them a few basic signs. It's been years since I used it, but it was our shorthand in meetings, across crowded rooms. Josiah's smile glitches just the tiniest bit. No one would notice, but I do because even though we aren't married anymore, I've had years to learn the physiognomy of this man's features. After a pause so slight it's almost undetectable, he signs "You're welcome."

I'm still smiling when Vashti walks up beside him, tugging his sleeve. For just a second, he doesn't look away. My smile starts to fade, and Kassim tugs on *my* sleeve, reminding me about *Madden* and Jamal. Deja's back on her phone, her bottom lip slightly poked out.

It was nice while it lasted, and even though the song has ended and the droplets are already drying on my skin, I hold that moment of joy close. When I look back to the DJ booth, prepared to sign to Josiah that we're leaving, the spot where he and Vashti stood is empty.

He's already gone.

CHAPTER FOUR

∞

JOSIAH

I'm awakened by a warm tongue stroking across my skin like velvet.

I pry one eye open, dragging myself up from the pillows and thread count that dreams are made of to glare at the edge of the bed. Otis, of course, has pulled back the sheet with his teeth and is licking my foot like he does every morning.

"Dude, seriously?" I glance out the window, where the sky is still lavender tinged with pink, barely kissing dawn. "Can't we sleep in a few more minutes?"

The pitiful whimper at the foot of the bed becomes a whine. I know this drill. If that bladder gets any fuller, he will escalate to a full-on howl.

"Shit." I sit up, slide my feet into the leather slippers Deja and Kassim gave me last year for Christmas. I know Yasmen probably chose them because they bear the mark of the practical luxury she's good for, but they're still from my kids.

"Replacing the ones *you* mangled," I remind Otis, who doesn't look repentant in the least. I tap his head on my way out of the bedroom, and he follows me down the stairs and out the front door. Any hope I had of ever shaking this dog died long ago. He demonstrated his tenacity the first night I slept in this house.

The divorce wasn't quite final, but I needed a place to live. Instead of finding another tenant for Aunt Byrd's house, I moved in here. Of course, we all assumed Otis would stay with the kids. They walked him, fed him, played with him. I provided a roof over his head and the occasional acknowledgment of his existence.

I was considering the huge TV mounted on one of four blank walls, not even bothering to turn it on because who cares about Netflix when your life has been incinerated and everyone you love lives two streets over now…when my phone rang. It was jarring in that new *all by myself* quiet I hadn't experienced since before I married.

Yasmen's name and face flashed up on my screen. And for one wild moment, my heart banged in my chest. Had she changed her mind? Realized our divorce was a horrible mistake? As irrational as I knew that line of thinking was, I answered the phone with a pulse that refused to stop leaping.

"Yas, hey. Everything okay?"

You need me? You want me? Should I come home?

"I think Otis wants you."

It was the most disorienting thing she could have said to me at two o'clock in the morning.

I cleared my throat. "Sorry. What?"

"O-tis." Yasmen broke it down into small bites I could digest. "He won't stop howling. He's standing at your side of the bed resting his head on your actual pillow."

"What the hell? Why?"

"Gee, Si, let me find my human-to-Otis dictionary and ask him. I don't know why, but no one is sleeping tonight until you come home."

Not exactly the way I envisioned her invitation to come home.

"I'll be right there."

He couldn't want *me*. Because why? But sure enough, soon as I entered the kitchen through the garage, Otis stopped howling, stood on his hind legs, and licked my face.

"Dammit, Otis," I spat. "I have told you I am not that dude. Don't be licking my face."

He panted at my throat, huge paws pressing so hard into my chest I could barely stand under his substantial weight.

Yasmen leaned one shoulder against the kitchen doorjamb, lines of fatigue sketched around those pretty lips. A silk robe strained across her breasts, the tight belt emphasizing the fullness of her shape. My dick had swelled at the sight, and just as I was thanking God my T-shirt covered my erection, Otis nudged my shirt aside like some dick-detecting narc canine scenting cocaine.

"Otis," I snapped, pulling the shirt back into place. "Stop."

"I think at least tonight," Yasmen said, exhaustion patent in her voice, "maybe he sleeps at your place and we figure it out tomorrow."

"At my place?" What the hell was I supposed to do with a two-hundred-pound dog *by myself*? "Maybe we're misunderstanding what Otis wants. Maybe he—"

At that moment, Otis confirmed what I had always suspected. That he descended from some supernatural breed of wolf dog, because he calmly walked through the mudroom and out the door to wait quietly, *patiently*, at the passenger side of my truck.

"Is this some new trick you taught him?" I ground out. "Is this a prank the kids are pulling on us?"

"No, Otis wants to be with you. The kids will still see him all the time. It's not a big deal."

"Not a big deal, huh?" I retort, snapping back to the present at the butt crack of dawn, blinking blearily as Otis does his business in a patch of grass. "She's not the one following you around with *this*," I say accusingly, shaking the pooper-scooper Deja gave Otis for Christmas with its bedazzled handle. He looks at me in the way that seems to say, *Bruh, I'm the one stuck with you.*

And I would not put it past Aunt Byrd to have had a little talk with Otis and made him promise to take care of me when she was gone.

"She got us both. Told you to take care of me. Me to take care of you. She was a trickster."

Byrd was a lot of things. She was the strongest woman I ever met. She was indiscreet, conducting affairs and not giving a damn what any-one thought about it. She had shit taste in men, as proven by the four assholes she married. She was the first to laugh, the first to cry. She was selfless and generous and could cook her way into anyone's heart.

I don't think I'll ever get over losing her. Losing the woman who raised me. When both your parents are dead by the time you turn eight, you're absolutely certain that nothing is forever. No *one* is forever. My closest living relative was my whole world for a long time, and growing up I walked around waiting for the last shoe to drop. Waiting to lose her too.

And then one day I did.

"Damn, we're morbid this morning," I tell Otis as we enter the house through the front door.

He angles a long-suffering look at me that says *we*?

"Okay, *me*." I walk through to the kitchen. "You hungry?"

He assumes the position at the raised stainless steel dog feeder Kassim found. Once my son understood that Great Danes have some of the shortest life spans, he did what young geniuses do. Researched every single thing that might extend Otis's life, including a bowl raised off the floor so Otis won't have to gulp his food and water. According to Kassim, dogs as tall as Otis end up swallowing air with their food when they have to bend down to eat and it gets trapped in their digestive tract. Since bloat is the number one killer of Danes, Kassim is trying to outwit Otis's digestive system. Including putting him on a raw food diet.

"And guess what we've got for breakfast?" I pull out meat wrapped in white paper from the refrigerator, and Otis's ears perk, his tail beating a happy rhythm into the floor. "Yup. Vashti set aside chicken thighs for you."

Otis whines and lies down, sniffing the air like an exiled prince.

"Okay, every time I mention Vashti, you act all new." I give him a knowing look. "You think I don't see that? Give her a chance."

I pull a container of pureed vegetables from the refrigerator. He rests his head on his paws and stares at me unwaveringly, as if waiting to be convinced. I toss the pureed veggies into a bowl with the raw meat

Vashti sent home, crack an egg over it, and then top it with a little yogurt. At the sight of the bowl loaded with what Kassim assures me is a breakfast of champions, Otis perks up. Pulling his supplements from the cupboard, I add them to the goulash and set it in the standing dish holder. Otis rouses himself to dive in.

"I'mma leave you to it," I tell him over my shoulder. "I need to shower. We're taking the kids to the river."

A happy "woof" is his only response. I turn to point one finger at him. "I know you love the river. Don't say I never did anything for you."

I take the stairs and yell back, "But how could you ever say that when I do literally everything for you?"

I envision an air bubble over Otis's head that might read *Dude, get over yourself.*

"Yup," I say, of course *to myself* as I strip and turn on the shower. "You've lived alone too long."

The drive from Bryd's three-bedroom craftsman cottage to the dream house Yasmen and I designed together is less than two minutes, but may as well be separated by a millennium. I loved the chaos of young kids and their friends all over the place all the time. The partnership of managing their lives, of raising them under the same roof. Even though Deja and Kassim bounce between our houses, they spend most of their time at Yasmen's. Living alone without my kids was one of the biggest adjustments after the divorce. Both only children, Yasmen and I always planned to have at least four kids. By our first anniversary, Yasmen was pregnant with Deja. We waited a little while before Kassim. A few years later, we were excited to do it again. A pain so sharp I draw in a quick breath slices over my heart like a scalpel. I should be used to it by now, the pain, but it always catches me off guard, the freshness of it. After nearly three years, it still hasn't been dulled by time.

I consider that one more thing to never get over as I pull into Yasmen's driveway.

"Morning, Josiah!"

The greeting comes from the man standing on the front porch of the house next door, a modern blue-and-gray three-story contrasting with our more traditional white limestone. I get out of the truck and open the back door for Otis, who bounds up the steps of the house where we used to live. He settles in the corner by the swing, his favorite spot.

"Morning, Clint," I reply to the neighbor who moved in shortly after we did.

Clint's pale complexion and strawberry blond hair could make him look washed out, but his eyes are vivid blue and color climbs his cheeks. "Saw you last night at Food Truck Friday, but didn't get a chance to speak."

Before I can reply, Clint's husband, Brock, wheels a stroller through their front door and onto the porch, followed by their chocolate Lab, Hershey.

"Josiah," Brock says, his smile white against his dark skin. "Great event last night. Thank you guys for planning it."

"That was all Yas, but yeah, it was great." I nod to the stroller. "Is that Skyland's newest heartbreaker you got there?"

Both their faces light up and Brock turns the stroller to face me.

"That's right," Clint says. "Come meet our Lilian."

I climb their front steps and peer down into the stroller. Dark eyes set in a perfectly round face with smooth brown cheeks stare back at me. She has a patch of dark, curly hair, looks like she might have gas, and is just about the cutest thing I've ever seen. I stretch my finger out, and she grabs it, squealing and kicking.

"She likes you!" Clint says. "She never greets anyone like that. You charmed her."

I smile, but that sharp pain pinches in my chest again.

"Wanna hold her?" Brock asks, his voice eager.

I don't want to hold her. Not because Lilian isn't adorable. She absolutely is. I just avoid babies whenever possible. And of course, it's *not* always possible, but holding one...I'm about to refuse, but the happiness and anticipation sketched on both their faces has me stretching my arms out to take her. This was their third time trying to adopt. These guys often keep an eye on Kassim and Deja for us. They're over for dinner and have our family over all the time. They're good friends and I can't dim their light because I have shit I've never dealt with—*at this rate, probably won't ever deal with*—that makes it hard for me to hold a baby.

So I take her.

On instinct, I tuck the swaddling blanket around her tighter when it loosens. She fits perfectly into the crook of my arm, the same way Kassim and Deja did. The memory of when I last held a baby comes rushing up at me like the ground when you trip and fall. There's nothing warm or sweet about that memory, and I tense my jaw against the emotions it stirs in me, the ones I spent the last three years shoving away.

The front door to our house opens, and Yasmen walks out wearing her yoga pants and a fitted top that crops just above her waist, revealing a narrow strip of smooth skin that rich shade of Kelly Rowland brown. She stops short, her gold-flecked eyes dropping from my face to Lilian cradled in my arms. Something arcs between us in the small space separating the two porches, a tension that requires no explanation. I know it's because of the little girl cradled in my arms.

"Yasmen," Clint greets her. "Morning. We were just telling Josiah what a great job you did with Food Truck Friday. Everyone on the association is glad to have you back."

Brock is one of Atlanta's most prominent architects, but Clint owns Fancy, a pet grooming shop on Sky Square, and is an active member of the Skyland Association.

"Thank you." Her smile is stiff when she shifts the yoga mat slung over one shoulder by its strap.

"I guess the association's next big event is Screen on the Green?" Brock asks.

"Yup, next week," she says.

"Uh, here you go." I carefully hand the baby back to Brock. "She's gorgeous. Congratulations again."

"Thanks, man." Brock takes the baby and holds her against his shoulder, patting her little back. "We're taking her and Hershey for a walk down at the dog park. You and Otis wanna come with?"

"Maybe another time," I tell him. "I'm taking the kids to the Old Mill."

Hershey yelps and tugs at the leash, straining toward the steps.

"Looks like someone is eager to get out of here," Clint says. He carries the stroller down the steps, Brock trailing behind with Lilian in his arms. "Good seeing you, Josiah. I know you're around all the time, but we've been busy. Our anniversary is next week, and we want to make it in for some of Vashti's famous shrimp and grits."

"We still need to find a sitter," Brock reminds him.

"I can watch Lilian," Yasmen offers.

All the air is sucked out of the silence that follows her offer, and it's like we're standing in a vacuum, frozen.

"Yeah," Clint says, uncertainty dragging out the word. "If you want...if you're sure?"

Brock and Clint know how everything fell apart. They saw firsthand how it affected Yasmen.

"I can watch her," Yasmen says, splitting a level stare between the two men. "Really. I'll be fine."

Her last words, an acknowledgment that there was a time when she *wouldn't* have been fine watching a baby, seem to lift the net of anxiety that fell over the two porches.

"That's awesome, Yas. Thanks," Clint replies with a smile. "We better get on, but we'll talk deets."

"For sure." Yasmen meets my eyes for half a second before looking away.

I walk next door and up the steps to the front porch, where she stands. I want to ask if she's sure about babysitting, but her shoulders tense as if braced for a blow because she knows me well enough to assume that's the question I *would* ask.

Instead I stroll over to the swing and sit. Sometimes I wish I didn't know Yasmen so well. We both have these tells, secret passageways to our thoughts that took us years to find. No one knows her better than I do, and she knows me better than anyone else. So when she sinks her teeth into the pillowy flesh of her bottom lip, like she's doing now, it means she's working up to a subject she's reluctant to discuss.

"Kids ready?" I ask, giving her the chance to say what she needs to say. Otis puts his head in my lap, and I indulge him with a stroke at the sleek fur of his neck.

"Uh, yeah." Yasmen slides the yoga mat off her shoulder and leans against the porch rail. "But there's something I want to talk to you about first."

"What's up?"

"We need to get things under control with Deja. She skipped English yesterday."

"You sure?" I ask, frowning. "That doesn't sound like Day."

"She's been less and less concerned about her grades. It's the first month of school and I'm already worried. She was an honor student before."

"She's been through a lot, Yas. We all have."

"I don't need you telling me what we've been through. What Deja's been through."

I stiffen, my hand stilling in Otis's fur. "I wasn't trying to tell you anything. I'm just saying maybe we cut her some slack because things haven't been easy."

"There's cutting her some slack, and then there's being irresponsible as a parent."

My left eyebrow inches up, and I wonder if she remembers that's *my* tell that she's provoking me. "You saying I'm an irresponsible father?"

"No, I didn't mean it like that." Yasmen drops the yoga mat and links her hands at the nape of her neck. "I'm just saying we can't ignore her skipping class because we've had a hard time."

"You're sure she skipped?"

"Yeah, she said she was watching a broadcast of some natural hair event."

"The hell?"

"Like I said, you should talk to her."

"What'd she say when *you* talked to her?"

"Just that I overreacted and that she won't do it again."

"Well, if she skipped, there should be consequences. Maybe no posting to social media for a week?"

"That sounds good. We have access to everything. We can shut it down."

"I can tell her today."

"You sure we don't need to do it together? United front kinda thing?"

"Considering how strained things have been between you two, it might go better coming from me."

There's a brief flash of relief on her face, and then she grimaces. "I'm not exactly her favorite person right now."

"Maybe you're being too sensitive."

"What's that supposed to mean?" Irritation slashes her expression. "When am I too sensitive?"

"Um...now?"

"Whatever, Josiah." She picks up her yoga mat and slings it back over her shoulder. "No wonder she thinks I overreact. So do you."

She opens the front door and leans in to yell, "Kids, your dad is here."

With no makeup, she looks young and fresh, her hair gathered to the crown of her head in a coily ponytail. She's as beautiful as the day we first met. She's changing, aging, but to me, only getting better. Like God looked at the feline flare of her cheekbones and the tempting pout of her mouth, the sultry dark eyes flecked with gold and said, *You think she looks good now? I'm just getting started.* I thought I'd see those changes up close, see her grow more beautiful with age, but fate had other plans.

Correction. *Yasmen* had other plans, and I'm still adjusting—obviously not always well—to how things have changed.

"Yas, I didn't mean to—"

"I know what you meant." Her eyes snap to mine. "I always know what you mean. That I'm overreacting. That I'm being too sensitive. That I'm a hot mess."

"I never called you a hot mess, even when you were one."

Our eyes lock, and the hurt in hers spears me right through. I'm an asshole. I'm bad at this. At being with her, but not *being* with her. It makes me come across as terse and impersonal, when I'm really just trying to navigate this new dynamic between us. How do people do this? When the rug is pulled out from under the life they thought they would have forever, how do they pretend it's not seismic? That the roof hasn't fallen in and they're trapped under a concrete beam? How do you breathe when the person you thought you'd cherish forever looks at you the way Yasmen looks at me right now because you've hurt them so much?

"I'll let you talk to your daughter about all of this," she says, the mouth that used to drive me crazy pulled tight. "Kassim needs to be at the soccer field by two. I'll meet you there."

She rushes off the front porch and down the sidewalk toward the park before I can make this any better, not that I would know how even if she stayed. I stare after her for a few seconds, well aware of how badly I mishandled that conversation. I run a hand over my face, tired even though the day just started. Otis stares at me, canine censure in his unblinking eyes.

"Don't look at me like that. Whose side are you on?"

He carefully lifts his head from my lap and turns away, a clear answer to my question.

The door flies open and Kassim speeds out carrying a Frisbee, a duffel bag, and a Pop-Tart.

"Morning, son."

"Hey, Dad," he says around a mouthful of his breakfast.

He keeps right on past me to the Rover, climbs in the back seat, and closes the door, earbuds stuck in his ears within seconds. Odds are he's listening to one of his robotics podcasts. Deja emerges from the house at a much more leisurely pace. Dressed in cutoffs, a TLC T-shirt, and pink high-top Converse. Two braids hang on her shoulders, and she's so pretty. My baby girl is growing up, *dammit*. Soon it'll be boys and all kinds of shit that could give me heart failure. I want to relish the day while she still enjoys hanging with her old man on a Saturday morning because I assume this won't last much longer.

"Dad, why are you staring at me?" Her grin crooks in the exact way Yasmen's does when she's in a good mood.

"You look more like your mom every day," I tell her with a slow smile.

She scowls, rolling her eyes and marching down the steps. "Hopefully I'll grow out of it."

Was Yasmen being sensitive? Because that was...harsh.

Otis races down the steps and past Deja, who takes off with him as soon as she realizes what he's doing. I'm not sure how it started, but they play this game where Otis tries to sit in the front seat only when Deja rides with me. Otherwise, he's content to have me chauffer him in the back.

"No way, Otis," Deja squeals, her face transforming from sullen teen to exuberant kid. "I call shotgun."

When they reach the car, Deja opens the back passenger-side door and points. "You sit back there with Kassim. You get Daddy to yourself all the time."

My irritation disappears. Maybe I'm the one overreacting now and her comment wasn't as bad as I made it in my head. I do acknowledge that I'm at least halfway wrapped around my daughter's finger, but she and Yasmen will be fine.

If there's one thing the Wades have figured out how to be over the last few years, it's fine.

CHAPTER FIVE

∞

YASMEN

Sensitive!"

I fold my legs into the lotus position on my mat at the end of Yoga in the Park. It's the last Saturday of August, and the air is still heavy with humidity. It's Atlanta so we could be in the nineties until October.

"Can you believe he called me sensitive?" I demand, my eyes flicking from Hendrix to Soledad. "Me! Like Deja skipping class isn't a big deal."

Hendrix lies back on her mat, crossing an ankle over one knee, and stares up at the canopy of trees offering shade for our alfresco fitness. "I skipped a class or ten in my day, and I turned out fine."

"Do not defend her, Hen." I resecure my ponytail. "Watching some hair thing instead of going to English? Unacceptable."

"I agree," Soledad says. "I'd freak if my girls started skipping classes."

She sits on her knees and bends forward, curling in to her torso, lifting and pushing her lower body until she's in a perfectly straight headstand...and then spreading her legs into a midair split. Hendrix and I both watch her with jaws dropped. That move is way advanced, and none of us have even attempted it in class yet.

"What?" Soledad asks, head pressed into the mat, upside-down eyes darting between the two of us. "Okay. So I may have practiced a little at home."

"So you *do* think it's a big deal, Sol?" I ask.

"You gonna listen to *her* about what's normal?" Hendrix scoffs. "The woman who goes for extra credit in yoga?"

Soledad brings her legs down carefully, returning to a seated position on her mat. "I'm just saying we have to be clear now with our kids about what they can and can't do. By the time they reach high school, it gets away from you fast. Believe me. I watch *Euphoria*."

Her arched brows and wide eyes say that tells her all *she* needs to know.

"I don't think we're at rehab and cam girls quite yet," I assure her.

"Ya never know." Soledad leans forward and offers in a conspiratorial whisper, "Season one."

"Anyway." Hendrix shakes her head with a good-natured chuckle. "I'm just saying I don't have a teenager, but I was one, and I was a lot like Deja. The harder my mom pulled the reins, the more I bucked. I'm not saying turn her loose, but maybe...loosen up?"

I force a breath through my nose, not a mindful one, and stand.

"I'll think about it." I roll my mat and sling it over my shoulder. "But the decisions she makes now do affect her future. This is part of a bigger pattern. Her grades falling, talking about not needing college and being a hair influencer."

Hendrix stands, too, and picks up her mat. "That wasn't even a thing when we were growing up."

"It's still not," I tell her flatly. "Not as a viable career."

"Folks *are* actually making a living through social media, Yas, but there's plenty of time to figure out her ten-year plan," Hendrix says dryly. "She's in the eighth grade."

"You're probably right, but between her sass and Josiah's...ugh, him being Josiah...my last nerve is barely hanging on." I watch as Soledad collects her mat and bag. "You guys got time for brunch?"

Hendrix laughs. "I was hoping you'd say that."

"Starving," Soledad says. "For once my Saturday morning isn't stuffed. Inez's soccer game isn't until three, and Lupe's recital isn't till five. Where we eating?"

"Anywhere but Grits." The words slip out before I think to *not* slip them.

"Is that because it's your job or because Vashti will be there?" Hendrix asks, eyes narrowed. "We still need more intel on this little development between her and Josiah."

"I got nothing." I fall into step with them as we pass through the ornate park gate to exit.

"But we *do* think they're fucking, right?" Hendrix asks.

I stumble, almost falling, but Soledad catches my arm and searches my face "You okay?"

"Uh, yeah." My heart still trips at the thought. Of course they could be sleeping together. Like I give a damn. "I'm fine. I don't have any claim on Josiah. We're divorced. He can do whatever and *whomever* he wants."

I try to make my shrug a casual thing and change the subject to something I hope they'll find more interesting.

"So brunch?" I ask, pulling out my unbothered smile. "We haven't tried that new place, Sunny Side."

If they watch me a little too closely over our feast of fruit, French toast, and omelets, I choose to ignore the questions in their eyes. They're questions I don't even want to ask myself. Who am I to object to Josiah finding someone new when I was the one who initiated the divorce? They don't know, no one knows besides him and me, how he resisted the idea every step of the way.

Until there were no more steps.

Only papers to sign. Only *relief.*

It felt like the whole world was resting on my chest every morning, and it was all I could do to get out of bed. The divorce was so hard, but it felt like I released a breath after it was done. The house was quiet, and yes, I missed Josiah immediately, desperately, but even in that new loneliness, there was a kind of relief to have only one thing to save. Not my marriage, but just myself.

I take a healthy gulp of my mimosa, thinking they were stingy with the prosecco, and glance up to meet Hendrix's probing stare.

"Okay," I tell her, setting my glass down on the table none too gently. "I know you have questions about Vashti and Josiah, but you can stop looking at me like that."

Hendrix opens her mouth to speak, but I hold up a staying hand.

"I know what you're thinking. That it's natural to possibly resent your ex's new girlfriend."

"Well, actually—" Hen starts.

"And you're probably thinking I need to be a mature adult about this, that it's inevitable that a man like Josiah, strong, tall, dark, handsome, virile—"

"All that," Soledad mumbles. "Damn."

"Charismatic," I continue. "Driven...for example...will attract beautiful women. I'll have to get used to it."

"Right, but—" Hendrix starts.

"And I will." I wag a finger at them. "I mean, I *have*. I *have* gotten used to it already in the two days since I learned that they're—"

"Fucking," Hendrix offers.

"Seeing each other," I say at the same time, frowning down at the remains of my omelet. "So I get it. You can stop looking at me like I might blow at any minute."

"I wasn't looking at you like that at all," Hendrix asserts, gesturing to my face. "I was actually looking at that little mustache you got growing on your top lip."

My index finger flies to my mouth.

"Bitch." I laugh. "It's just a little...stray hair."

"Hmmph." Hendrix cackles. "More like a five-o'clock shadow."

"The women in my family," I tell them, "we're just a little hairy. My great-aunt almost had a full beard when she died."

"Now I rebuke that in the name of Black Jesus." Horror widens Hendrix's eyes.

"Was it an open casket?" Soledad whispers.

"Oh, my God." I bust out laughing. "She was hairy. Not decapitated."

The three of us fall into a fit of giggles, leaning into each other, giddy from food and mimosas and laughter.

"Sinja, the owner of Honey Chile, recommended this honey-infused hair remover that I love," Soledad offers. "It's just a block up."

"That's perfect," I say. "She's doing trivia at Screen on the Green. I can make sure she's all set."

On the walk to Honey Chile a memory slips into my mind, so vibrant it's as real as the jangle of wind chimes over the door when we enter the shop. Josiah and I standing at our twin sinks one morning, eyes meeting in the mirror. Him, the grooves and ridges of his bare chest and abs deliciously distracting. Pajama bottoms resting low at his waist, revealing the carved lines at his hips. He was shaving, the rugged jawline foam-coated, and teased me about the stray hairs on my lip. He'd held me down on the bed, his razor poised above like he was my barber prepared to shave my face. In those days, anytime we got near a bed, we put it to good use, so it wasn't long before my robe was open. Before his head was between my legs. Before he was in my mouth. Before our hands were desperate and searching and everywhere.

"I hope you love it," Sinja says, ringing up the lip wax.

"Uh, oh…yeah," I stammer, heat crawling up my neck and over my cheeks. "Can't wait to give this a try. Thank you."

This is not the time to reminisce about when things were good. When they were scorchingly perfect and I couldn't imagine them any other way because I couldn't imagine the hows or whys of life's irrational cruelty. I can't go down memory lane. There are stretches of it that hurt too much, yes, but there are miles that felt too good.

"So will that be all?" Sinja asks.

"Yes," I say as much to myself as to her, determined to rein in my thoughts and stuff away my memories. "That *will* be all."

CHAPTER SIX

∞

JOSIAH

I'm not sure which of them is happier," I say, watching Kassim and Otis run along the riverbank, both getting liberally splashed. "But I should have waited to get my car detailed. All that mud."

"I got you." Deja grins, patting the small backpack at her feet. "I remembered from last time and packed a towel."

We fist-bump and chuckle as Otis leaps for the Frisbee Kassim threw, only to land in the water and sink out of sight. He breaks the surface a few seconds later, Frisbee gripped between his teeth.

"Show-off," I mutter.

"You love him," Deja teases.

"Whatever." I roll my eyes and clear my throat. "So your mom tells me you're skipping class. What's up with that?"

"Oh, my God." Deja groans and presses a hand to her eyes. "She keeps making it a big deal. It was one period so I could watch an important broadcast. I wish she'd just leave me alone."

"Yeah, that's not exactly how parenting works. No social media for the next week."

"Dad! No. I've already scheduled posts."

"Unschedule them."

"You can take anything else," she pleads.

"Which is exactly why we're taking this."

"We?" Suspicion narrows her eyes. "Did she put you up to this?"

"It was my idea." My brows lift to the level of *now what.* "Your mother's not the enemy. She wants what's best for you. We both do. We're not paying tuition for you to goof off at Harrington."

"Who says I even want to be at Harrington anyway?" she mumbles, kicking at a pebble along the river.

"It's one of the top schools in the state, Day. Do well there, and you'll have your pick of colleges."

"Who says I want that either? College isn't for everyone."

I don't get to respond to that because my phone signals an incoming text.

Vashti: Hey, babe. I'm at the restaurant getting ready for the lunch rush. You coming in?

Me: Yeah. At the river with the kids now. We're leaving soon, but Kassim has soccer at two. I should be in before the dinner crowd. Anthony's there, right?

For so long I did a little bit of everything at Grits. Now that things have settled and we have an executive chef, a sous-chef, and Anthony, a great manager I wooed from one of Atlanta's top restaurants, I have a little room to breathe.

Vashti: Yeah, Anthony's here. Everything's under control. I just want to see you and maybe we can hang after closing?

She's dropped a few hints about wanting to spend the night. We haven't been together long, but the attraction is there, and I like her a lot. I haven't dated anyone in a really long time, but I do remember this is how relationships progress. I'm a red-blooded male. I want this.

Don't I?

Me: I want to see you too. Yas is taking the kids after the soccer match. I'll come by then.

Vashti: So Yasmen's not coming in?

I frown, thumbs hovering over the screen. Despite the tension between Yasmen and me, I'm very clear that our business would not be what it is now had it not been for her ideas and her passion early on. We may not be married anymore, but we're still partners.

Me: She probably won't make it in today. You need her?

Vashti: No, not at all. It just feels a little awkward now that she knows we're together. I want everything to work. I want us to work. I want things to be right here at Grits, and I just don't want to upset any of that. Am I being silly?

Me: No, but you don't have anything to worry about.

Vashti: Okay. See you soon. <3

I stare at the <3 for long seconds before shoving the phone into the pocket of my jeans. It's not even an actual heart, but it gives me pause. I need to be careful with this relationship. I care about Vashti and have no desire to hurt her. I've been up front that I want to see where this goes, but this is the first relationship since my divorce. I'm not trying to get too serious right now.

"Was that Vashti?" Deja asks, not looking up from her own phone.

"Yeah, we were just talking about tonight's shift."

"Come on, Dad." Deja smirks, raising laughing eyes to look at me. "Kassim and I figured it out."

"Figured what out?" I play dumb.

"You." She toggles her head back and forth. "Vashti. Dating. We know."

"What makes you think that?"

"For one, the way she looks at you." Deja bats her lashes exaggeratedly. "Like you so fine."

"I am so fine." I tug one of her braids. "Had to be more than that."

"She's been coming around more even when you guys aren't at work." She shrugs. "I don't know. I can just tell you like her."

"I do," I say, laying the words out with caution. "I wasn't sure how you and Seem would feel about it. You okay with me dating someone?"

"Why wouldn't we be?" She sucks her teeth. "You deserve some happiness after what *she* put you through."

She?

"Um...Do you mean your mother?"

"Of course. Who could blame you for moving on? Mom went crazy and ruined your life and—"

"Whoa, whoa, whoa." I shake my head and look at her full in the face so she'll understand. "Don't ever let me hear you call your mother crazy again. You hear me, Deja Marie?"

"But Dad, she—"

"She was severely depressed, not crazy. Do you understand all we lost as a family in a matter of months?"

"Yes, sir." Deja's throat bobs with a deep swallow. "Aunt Byrd and...and Henry."

Hearing his name turns a screw in my chest. It probably always will.

"Yeah," I reply, some of the heat draining from my voice too. "We all lost Henry, but your mom, she carried him. The same way she carried you and Kassim. And the way she lost him was..."

The inside of my throat burns, and I wish I could swallow the words, wish I could swallow this whole conversation. It's still painful to think about, to talk about, and I realize that I never do. Hell, I never really have.

The memory of Yas, usually bright as a sunbeam, dulled, disheveled, perfectly still in the rocker and staring at the wall of Henry's nursery tortures me for a moment, and I'm back there. Back in that desperate, despondent, enraged place. Not even sure where to direct my fury. Helpless because every day I could feel her slipping away. I knew I was losing her and there was nothing I could do to hold on.

"She had to deliver him, Day," I continue. "Knowing he was already gone, and it was too much. It was so hard."

"I know, but she—"

"No buts. If I ever hear you talk about your mother that way again, you'll have to deal with me." I lift her chin so she can't look away. "You got that?"

Her nod is slow and uncertain, and I feel a bit of remorse. Maybe I was harsh with her, but it pissed me off to hear her talk about what Yas went through, not only dismissively, but with blame. I kiss her forehead to remove some of the sting, and my own words play back. Defending Yasmen to Deja. Trying to understand. There's a voice in the back of my mind wondering if I should have done more of that when I had the chance.

CHAPTER SEVEN

YASMEN

T his is the fourth year of Screen on the Green." I grip the mic and smile to the crowd gathered on the lawn of Sky Park. "And on behalf of the Skyland Association, thank you all for coming. Now, before we start with our feature, *Spider-Man: Into the Spider-Verse*, Sinja Buchanan, who owns Honey Chile right off the Square, is coming to do some movie trivia with you."

I hand off the mic and step down from the small dais, ready to head toward the spot where Hendrix and Soledad are already camped out. I haven't seen them since brunch last week, and my lips quirk with the beginnings of a grin at the thought of an evening with my girls.

"So good to see you, Yasmen," Deidre Chadworth says, stopping me with a hand on my shoulder when I've almost reached my friends.

"Oh, thanks, Deidre."

More than once, a well-meaning neighbor stopped by, ringing the doorbell, waiting on the porch with a casserole or pot of stew. Some days I just ignored them until they went away. Deidre, one of the more persistent ones, hadn't brought food. Being the owner of our local bookstore, Stacks, she always came bearing books.

"I stocked the new Sarah MacLean release," she says, her smile and the wicked glint in her hazel eyes telling me it's a hot one. "And the new Beverly Jenkins."

"I'll try to make it in this week." I touch her arm, speckled with sun spots and decorated with jangling bracelets. "And I never thanked you for all the times you came by when I was..."

I'm not sure how I want to talk about my depression. My philosophy had always been to deal with shit and move on—until the thing happened that I just couldn't move on *from*. It was like waking up every morning on a narrow window ledge and wondering... *Is today the day I fall?*

"Oh, honey," Deidre says, squeezing my hand. "I understand. I lost three before I had my Charlie."

"I didn't realize. I'm so sorry, Deidre."

"Two were miscarriages, and that was hard enough, but that last one." I recognize the kindred pain flickering in her eyes. "Like Henry, he was a stillbirth."

Unless you've been through it, you don't grasp the powerful horror of that word.

Stillbirth.

Entry into a world that child has already departed. The paradox of birth and death swaddled in one soundless moment. Not the first slap on the bottom and cry of new life, but a mother's dirge. A bell that never tolls. I curled into myself in a sterile room with starchy white sheets, hot, silent tears carving grief into my cheeks. Sinking through my pores and infecting the marrow. An inescapable pain shut up in my bones.

"You learn to live with it, ya know?" Deidre says, sympathy, rare understanding in the smile she offers. "But anyone who thinks you ever 'get over it' hasn't lost what we have. I'm just glad you're still here."

Grief is a grind. It is the work of breathing and waking and rising and moving through a world that feels emptier. A gaping hole has been torn into your existence, and everyone around you just walks right past it like it's not even there.

But all you can do is stand and stare.

In the still-bright evening, I blink tears away and return Deidre's smile. "Thank you, and I'll come in this week."

By the time I reach Hendrix and Soledad, I've composed myself, dry eyes and bright smile firmly in place.

At five foot ten sans shoes, and clearing six feet in stacked-heel sandals, Hendrix wears ripped skinny jeans and a cobalt-blue halter top, coupled with oversized hoops and gold hair cuffs woven into her braids.

"You look great," I say, reaching out to touch the silky material of her blouse.

"Thanks. Lotus Ross has this new plus-size line called Mo' Better." Hen chef-kisses. "Perfection."

"Oooh. I need to check her stuff out," Soledad says.

"Yeah, she does have clothes for your little narrow ass too." Hen ducks when Soledad pretends to punch. "Just saying. Mo' Better is for the mo' bigger."

"There may be a lot of things narrow on this body." Soledad slaps her own butt. "But this ass ain't one of 'em."

It takes a few blankets spread on the grass to accommodate Soledad's entire brood. Three girls in varying shades of their mother, with physical flashes here and there of Soledad's wretched husband, sprawl on the grass, grabbing and passing around food from Soledad's picture-perfect picnic basket.

"There's quiche Lorraine," Soledad says. "And a salad I tossed before we left the house. You'll love it. There's olives and spinach and feta. Tomatoes for a pop of color."

"This vinaigrette," Hendrix says and moans, rolling her eyes in bliss and wielding her fork for emphasis. "Omygah. Where'd you get this?"

"Oh, I made it." Soledad shrugs, but a pleased smile lifts the corners of her mouth. "My own recipe."

"Oooh, lemme taste." I sit on the blanket by Hendrix and lean forward, mouth open like a little bird.

"Nawwwww, shugah." Hendrix gives an emphatic shake of her head and nods toward the basket. "This is that 'get your own.' It's too good to share."

"I got you," Soledad says, grinning and passing a plate to me laden with the vibrant salad and a hunk of quiche. "Great job again with this event, by the way."

"Thanks." I accept the proffered plate and go for the salad first. "Oh, Sol. This vinaigrette *is* fantastic. Everything you touch turns delicious. You really need to figure out how to export the Soledad experience."

"I keep telling her I make stars for a living," Hendrix says around a mouthful of food. "If she'd let me get ahold of her, we could brand the hell out of her whole life."

Soledad passes a sandwich and a bottle of LaCroix to Inez. "You're serious, aren't you?"

"As a heart attack." Hendrix taps her plate with her fork. "What do you think I've been saying for the last year? Girl, when you ready."

Soledad's gaze shifts to her three beautiful daughters, giggling, chatting, tossing down cards in a game of War. She sees them as her greatest privilege, raising them as what she was born to do.

"Maybe later," Soledad finally replies, slicing into the quiche and passing a plate to Lupe. "I don't want to lose focus at this stage. Inez is getting serious about ballet and just started middle school. We all know what a hellscape seventh grade is. Lottie is just really digging in with gymnastics, and we're getting her a new trainer next month, someone who sent a few girls to the Olympics."

"Not to be ambitious or anything," Hendrix mumbles loudly enough for only me to hear. I suppress a chuckle and keep my stare trained on Soledad.

"And Lupe starts high school next year," Soledad continues. "Between cheerleading and maybe even modeling, I just—"

"I have no desire to model, Mom," Lupe interjects, lips shiny with Soledad's magic vinaigrette.

"We'll see." Soledad leans forward to whisper to us, "You know I've never paid much attention to the other offers, but a scout from Wilhelmina reached out. Like, who walks away from Wilhelmina?"

"I do," Lupe says over Soledad's hushed comments. She leans

forward, pulls the sheath of dark hair away from Soledad's face and kisses her cheek, leaning her head on her mother's shoulder.

And I get it. The harmony between these three daughters. The quiet confidence each of them wears so effortlessly. The easy, deep affection between Soledad and her girls, it doesn't just happen. I don't believe you only see this with women who stay home, but I understand Soledad's intentions for her family, for her girls, and I respect it.

"Is Deja coming, Mrs. Wade?" Lupe asks.

"Yeah." I swallow a bite of the quiche. "She and Kassim are coming with their father."

"I'm sorry again about..." Lupe looks miserable. "My slipup. I would never want to get Deja in trouble."

"It's fine." I wave a careless hand, like the incident didn't spark a huge fight between Deja and me.

"And you *should* share when one of your peers is doing something dangerous," Soledad says, her delicate brows knit into a frown. "A friend's safety is most important."

"She skipped English," Lupe says dryly. "You make it sound like she was smoking meth and dancing naked down the halls. Mom, you gotta stop watching *Euphoria*."

"But I love those crazy kids," Soledad pouts, amusement glinting in her dark eyes. "Here come yours, Yas."

I turn my head and grin at Kassim walking swiftly across the lawn toward us, Otis close on his heels. Deja follows at the pace of *Do I really have to be here*, but even that doesn't dim my spirits. It's the last breath of summer. I'm back in the groove, working, mentally and emotionally stable, healthy in body and spirit, surrounded by friends. The best friends I've had maybe ever.

I bring a forkful of quiche to my mouth just as Josiah and Vashti come into sight, trailing behind Deja.

Hand. In. Fucking. Hand.

My Zen bubble pops.

I try to take mindful breaths like my therapist, Dr. Abrams, taught me. I reach for the 4-7-8 breathing from yoga class. None of it works. Each breath is chopped up in my lungs and stutters past my lips.

It's been almost two years. You knew this would happen. He'd find someone else and you'd have to see them together. It shouldn't bother you this much.

"Fix your face," Hendrix says from the corner of her mouth. "You look like someone just punched you in the gut."

I glance from the approaching couple to my friend. She lifts her brows and hands me a glass of rosé. "You all right?"

"Uh, yeah. Of course." I gulp the cool drink and school my features into the smooth facade of the unfazed. "I just—"

"Wasn't prepared to see your ex quite so moved on?" Hendrix discreetly glances over my shoulder. "Well, get more prepared. They're almost here, and she does not get to see how much it bothers you. Right now, ma'am, I need you to find your happy place, go there, and bring a bad bitch back."

"Got it. I can do that."

Bad bitch.

Bad bitch.

Bad bitch.

The mantra is still chanting in my head by the time Josiah and Vashti reach us.

"Hey," Josiah greets us all with one word and a cursory glance.

Everyone murmurs a response, but I'm not the only one feeling the tension. A few people around us are staring at the family theater playing out on the lawn like it's better than the movie. This is high drama for our quaint little neighborhood. It's hot news when the couple most likely to make it last forever...doesn't, and the husband shows up holding another woman's hand. Josiah spreads a large blanket in a spot adjacent to ours.

Great. A front-row seat to Vashti sending Josiah disgusting looks of adoration every three seconds. My night can't get any worse.

"Hi, Mom," Deja drawls, sitting at the juncture of the two blankets.

I spoke too soon. I'm sure Deja will find wildly inventive ways to make this night worse.

"This quiche is delicious, Soledad," Vashti says before taking a sip of her rosé. "Thanks for sharing your dinner."

"Coming from you, that's high praise," Soledad says and then sends me a quick look of apology like she offered shelter to Regina George. Josiah and Vashti doing things as a couple with my kids feels so...settled, like they're already this unit completely separate from me. Not quite blended. I'm not angry—Josiah and I discussed this—but it will take some getting used to.

"Oh, incoming." Hendrix elbows me and pinches Soledad.

"Ow!" Soledad squawks, rubbing the reddening skin of her arm. "What'd you do that for?"

"Hot white boy alert." Hendrix subtly tips her head toward some spot behind me. "Heading right for us."

I start turning my head.

"Don't look! Damn." Hendrix taps my thigh. "You'll see him when he gets here because it's obvious he's headed for us."

"Ohhhhh." Soledad grins and leans in, closing our little circle to whisper, "He's not headed for *us*. He's headed for Yasmen."

At that, I can't help but turn to see who is coming. Mark Lancaster, one of Skyland's most successful developers and a newly declared congressional candidate, is crossing the yard with confident steps.

"You know I'm volunteering with his campaign," Soledad says, her eyes already twinkling with something wicked. "He always manages to bring our conversations around to Yasmen somehow. Speaking of the sewers, how's Yasmen doing?"

Hendrix cracks up, but sobers quickly. "Here he comes."

"Evening, ladies," Mark says when he reaches us. He nods to Josiah and Kassim. "And gentlemen. Ready for the movie?"

"We are," Hendrix answers. "Why don't you join us?"

Apparently the self-appointed host, she pats the empty spot on the blanket beside me.

Oh, not obvious at all.

"Don't mind if I do." Mark eases his tall, fit frame down beside me. He's that Ken-doll kind of handsome. Sort of smooth and plastic with movable parts. Blue eyes and blond hair. Even, white smile, a little too *practiced politician* for my taste, but nice enough. There is nothing wrong with Mark, the future congressman, but the faint stirrings of my hibernating libido don't make themselves known around him. I glance surreptitiously at Josiah, who leans back on his palms, muscle-roped arms stretched behind him, the mint-green Lacoste polo shirt straining across his broad chest, contrasting with skin like burnished mahogany. Kassim says something that draws a lazy smile from him, and it flashes across his face. I don't want to examine how "stirring" I still find my ex-husband.

He looks up and catches me watching him. I'm good enough at playing things off to know pretending I wasn't looking is such an amateur move, so I fake a natural smile, waiting for him to return it. Josiah is good at many things. Faking isn't one of them. He doesn't smile back, but flicks a narrowed glance from me to Mark.

I turn back to Mark, my smile a little wider. I *may* bat my lashes the tiniest bit. It's small of me, but my ex is here with our kids and our damn *dog* for all the world to see. Strolling up in here holding *hands*. So, yes, I laugh a little longer and louder when Mark makes a joke that's only slightly funny. I may lean forward an inch more to make it easier for him to check out my considerable above-the-belt assets. I mean... these are the wiles I resort to when backed into a corner. It's one thing to know they're dating. If Hendrix is right, they may be sleeping together already. It just hits different seeing the evidence firsthand of a deepening relationship between Josiah and Vashti. It hits *harder*.

And sometimes I don't handle harder well.

"Looks like the movie is about to begin," Mark says after a few minutes of small talk and light flirting. I'm out of practice with flirting, but I think I do all right. By the warmth of his smile and the way he is completely focused on me, I'd say maybe even better than all right.

"Could I talk to you for a second before the movie starts?" Mark asks, not waiting for my answer, but extending his hand to help me stand.

"Uh, sure." I follow him a few feet away, glancing back to Hendrix and Soledad. Both grin encouragingly. If it wouldn't be so obvious, I suspect Hendrix would give me a thumbs-up.

"So maybe I've been a bit too subtle in expressing my interest," Mark says when we reach the edge of the crowd, out of anyone's easy earshot.

It's not the first time he's tried to flirt with me since the divorce. If he thinks he's been subtle, Pearl Harbor was a day at the beach.

"Subtle?" I ask, blanking my expression. "What do you mean?"

"I like you, Yasmen." His smile is open and genuine, his eyes earnest. "Like...a lot."

I look down at the ground and slide my hands into the pockets of my sundress, suddenly uncomfortable. There's hope in his eyes that I'm not sure I deserve. Not because I'm not good enough, but because I don't *feel* enough. Not for him.

"Mark, I don't want to hurt you."

"Why would you hurt me?" He tilts my chin with his index finger, holding my eyes with his.

I don't want anyone caught in the cross fire between Josiah and me, though Josiah's not playing a game or pretending he likes Vashti to make me jealous. He likes her. He genuinely wants to be with her. I can't drag Mark into the games I might play to make myself more comfortable with that.

"I haven't dated anyone since my divorce," I finally say, looking at him with complete frankness. "And I'm not sure you want to be first at bat. I'm not ready for anything serious or—"

"Look, I'm not asking for anything serious. It can be whatever you want. I'm willing to take the risk of first at bat." He rakes an admiring look from my hair, in coils and running free tonight, over the full dips and curves of my body, down to the sandals on my feet. "I think you're gorgeous, Yasmen. Sexy as hell. Smart. A natural leader. Kind. You're the total package, and I'd like to get to know you better."

The woman Mark is describing is the *before* me. The one who could always push through every setback to get the job done. The one who carried everyone else's burdens, barely feeling the extra weight. Not the one who imploded. The one who fell and couldn't manage to pull herself up. Not the one who hid. It's intoxicating to have someone see me this way again. I've felt like I was coming back to myself, but hearing Mark articulate what he sees when he looks at me, it's bolstering. And after how jarring it was to see Josiah with Vashti tonight, it feels good.

"Okay." I chuckle, flicking an uncertain look up at him. "So first at bat?"

He takes my hand, stroking my palm with his thumb.

"Could be a home run," he teases, dipping his head to catch my eyes and draw a smile from me. "Let me get your number. I'll call and maybe we can do dinner."

We exchange numbers. He gives my hand one more gentle squeeze, and we head back toward the crowd.

I draw a deep breath, steadying my heartbeat. It's not that Mark makes my heart race. I'm honest enough to admit to myself that, while he's attractive and charismatic and all the things a woman could want, I'm just not that into him...yet. But the fact that I'm giving him a chance, that I'm giving myself a chance, feels like a new adventure, when for so long while I recovered, I've had to play it safe.

Mark rejoins the group he came with, and I start back to our blankets and blended families, loving how my little crew and Soledad's are all meshed together. How Hendrix has Deja cracking up about something, and my daughter's face is for once not petulant, but amused and open.

And then Vashti and Josiah sitting together a few feet away. With his sharp jawline and broad shoulders, he's the picture of leashed strength and virility. I know him intimately. Know him beneath his clothes.

Know him beneath the control he imposes on himself. I've seen him break. From pleasure, fury, agony. And I never realized how someone else knowing him that way, seeing him that way, would affect me.

Now I do.

Once I've reseated myself on the blanket, the movie begins and everyone falls quiet.

Everyone except Hendrix, of course.

"So what was that about?" she whispers close to my ear. Someone had the forethought to buy popcorn, bless their hearts. I fix my eyes on the screen, dipping my hand into the popcorn and not answering.

"Yas!" she whispers again. "What did he want?"

I turn on her, abandoning all pretense of watching the opening credits.

"A date," I say more loudly than I intended. A few heads swivel toward us, accompanied by a "shhhhh."

Soledad scoots closer, leaning in.

"What are we talking about?" she whispers, eyes moving from Hendrix's face to mine. "Is she going out with Mark?"

"She should, if only for comparison research." Hendrix laughs. "I've only ever loved Blackly, so the brothers is all the dick I know, but I would assume given the proper girth, length, and velocity—"

"Dear Jesus," I mutter, pressing a hand over my mouth to stifle a laugh. "'Velocity'? What does that even mean?"

"You know," Hendrix says. "The force of thrust."

"That is a blatant misuse of 'velocity.'" Soledad shakes her head.

"But is it, tho?" Hendrix counters, tapping her temple. "It's speed and direction of motion. Girl, that's a thrust."

"She does have a point," I admit grudgingly. "But I have no intention of finding out about Mark's velocity, especially not on the first date."

"Are you going out with Mark because *he*"—Hendrix subtly tilts her head toward Josiah—"has her?"

"No." I wilt under the heat of Hendrix's stare. "Okay. Maybe a little. I don't know. I told Mark I'm not ready for anything serious."

"Mom!" Deja whisper-shouts. "Could you guys be quiet? Like, for real."

The three of us lean into each other like kids, hushing each other, laughter spilling through our fingers. Even as I get my amusement under control, my gaze slides over to Josiah lounging nearby, the long lines of his body, even in repose, powerful and compelling. Vashti leans her head on his shoulder and links their hands in her lap, and I have to hold back a snarl.

What the actual hell?

I have no right to snarl or growl or feel like Vashti is trespassing. I asked for the divorce. I pushed Josiah away. I can't decide I don't want him and then that no one should. The cold reality of this truth settles on my chest like a block of ice, and for the rest of the night, it's easy not to laugh.

CHAPTER EIGHT

∞

JOSIAH

'll be back in about an hour," I tell Anthony, Grits's manager, adjusting my earbuds and scrolling through the messages on my phone. Two texts from Vashti.

"Cool," he says from the other end of the line. "It's crazy-packed tonight, especially for a Wednesday, but we got it."

"Thanks, man." I take a seat in the empty classroom, studying the clean whiteboard and the motivational posters on the walls. "This parent-teacher meeting shouldn't take long. I'll be in as soon as it's done."

Disconnecting the call, I hear the clack of approaching footsteps and turn to find Yasmen standing in the doorway. She offers a tentative smile and enters the classroom. We haven't seen each other much since Saturday's Screen on the Green.

"Hey," she says, taking the desk beside mine.

I remove my earbuds, stealing a glance at my ex-wife. The petal-pink short-sleeved sweater hugs her breasts in a way that, in my objective opinion, is indecent. Yasmen's never been a skinny woman, and with each pregnancy, her shape only got fuller, lusher.

Bigger breasts. More ass. Thicker thighs.

But she always manages to keep it tight, toned. Just *more* of everything.

And I've always been the beneficiary, but now I watch other men follow her with their eyes, knowing if she gave even a sign that she's interested, they'd be after her. Until now, she's never given any signs. At least as far as I know. How will I feel when she does?

Maybe she'll choose Mark. Of course, I didn't miss him spitting game to my ex-wife at Screen on the Green. Hell, every time he comes to the restaurant, if she's there, he makes a beeline for her. Eyes always on her ass. When we were married, if a man had looked at Yasmen the way Mark does, I would have punched that motherfucker in the face.

But...she's not my wife anymore. So he can look at her any way he wants. None of my business. I slowly unclench the fists resting on my knees and unclamp my teeth. Habit. Just habit to feel like pulling his balls through his nose for the way he looks at Yasmen.

"Kids okay?" I ask, training my gaze above her neck since everything below is so dangerous.

"Yeah, they're eating dinner with Clint and then will go over to the house for homework. Clint'll keep an eye on them." She places her oversized bag on the floor and crosses her legs. "Things okay at Grits?"

"Yeah. Anthony has everything under control."

"He was a great hire."

"You were the one who wanted to bring him on."

She smiles, but shakes her head. "I was just happy you asked me to meet him before you hired him."

"I've never hired anyone without you signing off," I remind her with a frown.

"True, but we both know I wasn't around, so I appreciated being involved."

"Well, we made a good call with him." I check my watch and grimace. "I told him I'd be in as soon as this is over, so I hope it doesn't last long."

"What do you think this is about? Ms. Halstead's email was kind of vague: 'I would like to discuss a few things regarding Kassim's progress.' What does that even mean?"

"It can't be anything bad. It's Kassim."

"It's not Kassim's behavior I'm worried about. He's the only Black boy in his class. They better not trip."

"I'm as vigilant as you, but don't go into this being too sensitive. Remember how you *maybe* overreacted to that comment Mrs. Thatcher made about Deja last year?"

"The woman called her *articulate*. That's the most microaggressive bullshit. Like, oh!" Yasmen's face transmogrifies into an uncannily accurate imitation of Mrs. Thatcher's pinched expression. "I'm so surprised this little Black girl can string together two whole sentences using the Queen's English. She's so *articulate*."

Apparently Yasmen's pink sweater is covering a Kevlar vest and she is in fully armed Black Mama mode.

"Yas, we're gonna play it cool, right? Not jump to any conclusions?"

"Oh, was I the one who went HAM when they tried to put Kassim in the yellow reading group?"

"First of all, that was second grade, and it was ridiculous. He was outreading all those other kids and..."

Her smug smile snatches the rest of my sentence, and I have to grin back.

"All right, you made your point, Sistah Souljah."

"I'm glad to hear it, Brother Malcolm."

We stare at each other for a second before breaking the silence with a chuckle. With so much fighting leading up to our divorce and so much tension following, I forgot we make a great team.

Ms. Halstead, a woman with pale, freckled skin, curly brown hair, and hazel eyes, enters and speed walks across the room. "Sorry to keep you waiting."

"No problem," Yasmen mutters with a smile that curves too perfectly while giving me her *She better act right* look from the corner of her eye.

Ms. Halstead turns a desk around until it's facing us. She pushes up the sleeves of her cream-colored cardigan and leans her elbows on the desk.

"It's good to see you both again," she says, her smile friendly and warm. "I mentioned at orientation that I'd heard great things about Kassim, and he has more than lived up to all the compliments previous teachers paid him."

"That's awesome," Yasmen says, her shoulders lowering almost imperceptibly and her smile turning more natural.

"Terrific," I say dryly. "So you wanted us to come just to celebrate how incredible Kassim is doing?"

Yasmen subtly kicks me in the ankle, which I ignore.

"Or was there a concern?" I continue.

Ms. Halstead shifts in the desk, crossing her ankles and clearing her throat. "Kassim is one of our brightest students. So bright, in fact, I think the work may not challenge him sufficiently. If I'm being honest, he could grow bored."

There is so obviously a "but" coming that Yasmen and I share a quick, knowing glance, and I brace myself for it.

"And," Ms. Halstead goes on, choosing a different conjunction, "I would like to discuss acceleration options."

"Acceleration?" Yasmen asks. "You mean like skipping a grade?"

"That's one route," Ms. Halstead answers and nods. "But he would be in need of some emotional and social development before we would consider skipping a grade."

"Clarify," I say, my tone sharper than I intended. "Please."

"Sixth grade is very formative for kids. The leap from sixth to seventh is huge socially and developmentally. To go from fifth to seventh... well, I have no doubt Kassim would excel academically, but we'd have to do some work this year to prepare him."

"What kind of work?" Yasmen asks. "What's prompting this? Because I feel like there's something specific you want to discuss. We like straight talk, Ms. Halstead. We've heard all the good stuff. What are your concerns, because I can hear that you have them?"

Yasmen always gets to the point, especially when it comes to our kids. One of my favorite things about her. Even when depression seemed to push her to the lowest point, she never lost her fierce protectiveness for Kassim and Day.

Ms. Halstead stands and walks to the front of the classroom, retrieving a folder from her desk. Taking a deep breath, she sits back down and flips open the folder.

"Here at Harrington, we're committed to making sure students are not only academically excelling, but also emotionally intelligent," she says. "Students in tune with their feelings perform better, feel better about themselves and the world."

I stop an eye roll just in time, fixing my face into a neutral mask that doesn't give away how yogi–Gen Z that all sounds.

"Go on," Yasmen says, her eyes alert.

She *would* be into this considering all the time she spends with her therapist. Hey, no knock. It seems to have helped her when nothing else did. More power, but I don't need that and I certainly don't think Kassim does.

"With that in mind, we have the students keep a journal of sorts," Ms. Halstead says. "Record their feelings. We also use it as a check to make sure they are not struggling. Kassim has written about his fears, and I think it exposes some issues maybe he hasn't dealt with."

"Meaning?" Yasmen demands, the world sharpened to a fine point.

Ms. Halstead runs her index finger along the edge of the folder. "For example, we asked the class to journal about their greatest fears."

"And?" I ask. "What did he say?"

"First, I want to remind you that the students know we read their entries," she says. "So we are not violating their trust or privacy."

"Got it," Yasmen says, practically sucking her teeth with impatience. "What'd he say?"

"He said his greatest fear is that his whole family will die." Ms. Halstead drags her solemn gaze from my face to Yasmen's. "The way his aunt and his brother died. I believe those two losses occurred close together?"

"Aunt Byrd passed away first," Yasmen says, her voice subdued, her eyes now trained on the hands in her lap. "And my...our..."

She falters, licks her lips, and tangles her fingers into a fist.

"Henry, our son, was stillborn a few weeks later," I say, keeping my words steady.

"I'm so sorry for your losses," Ms. Halstead says, sincerity shining in her eyes. "It makes sense that he would have fears about losing loved ones. He also mentions losing you specifically, Mr. Wade."

"That I would die?" I ask.

"That you would leave," Ms. Halstead answers. "He seems to have a good deal of insecurity around the family structure, based on his entries."

"We divorced about a year after Aunt Byrd and Henry passed." Yasmen says it like a confession, keeping her lashes lowered.

"Did he ever speak with a professional?" Ms. Halstead asks. "A counselor or therapist when that all happened?"

"He and our daughter spoke with a grief counselor here at the school a few times." Yasmen bites her lip. "They probably should have continued. I was so—"

"At the time we didn't see the need to keep on," I cut in. "Are you saying you think he should now?"

"Based on what we've seen in his entries," Ms. Halstead offers, her tone firm yet tentative. "It might be a good idea if he talks to someone again, especially if we'd like to consider him for acceleration next year. If he's not emotionally or socially at a place where it seems wise to skip, then we can build in subject-specific accelerations at his grade level."

"But either way, you think he should see a therapist?" Yasmen presses.

"Have either of you ever seen one?" Ms. Halstead looks from one of us to the other.

"I have." Yasmen clears her throat. "I do. Kassim knows I talk to someone. Both of our children know."

"And you, Mr. Wade?" the teacher asks, turning querying eyes my way. I sense more than see Yasmen stiffen beside me. It was one more point of contention between us, the fact that I wouldn't go to therapy. I saw it then as a waste of time. I was too busy trying to hold our life together, pay our mortgage, save our business, to make time for something I didn't think would actually help anyway.

"No," I reply to Ms. Halstead's question. "I've never seen a shrink... um, therapist."

"If you decide Kassim could benefit from it," Ms. Halstead says, her voice stern for the first time, "it should be presented in a positive light. You can't make it seem like a bad thing, or like something you don't respect."

"We won't." Yasmen levels a pointed look at me. "Will we, Josiah?"

"Of course we won't," I say, as if I hadn't told Yasmen therapy is a load of shit and I'd rather run naked through a hornet's nest. Pretty sure that's an exact quote.

"Good," Ms. Halstead says, breathing out a sigh of relief, her smile loosening. "I'm so glad we got this chance to talk. Maybe you should discuss it and let me know what you decide. As you know, we have school counselors available here, or he could see a private child psychologist."

"And what about the acceleration?" I ask.

"For now, I'll find ways to challenge him where he is," Ms. Halstead says. "He is so advanced in many ways, but we'll leave things as they are. I hope you'll consider having him talk to someone, maybe over the next few months, and closer to the end of this school year, we'll check back in."

Offering her best teacher smile, studded with optimism, Ms. Halstead asks, "Sound good?"

Yasmen and I did always make a great team, but therapy was something we never agreed on. Watching each other warily, we simply nod.

CHAPTER NINE

YASMEN

"Pizza's here!" Deja yells from downstairs.

"It's paid for, Day!" I shout back. "Just get it and you guys can eat."

I shimmy to get the jeans down over my ass. Yoga three times a week, and this booty ain't budging. I cross my bedroom to the walk-in closet, dropping the jeans in the hamper. My closet is huge, as big as the bedroom in our first shoebox apartment. My bags and shoes, slotted into cubbies, take up one wall of the closet. Dresses, slacks, blouses, rompers hang—loosely coordinated by color—on another wall. Wearing just panties and a T-shirt, I sit on the round tufted sage-colored ottoman positioned in the center of the space, eyeing the empty slots and shelves that used to hold Josiah's possessions. For a long time, I left his side completely empty. It felt wrong somehow to "replace" his things with mine when we'd designed this closet together, leaving plenty of room for his massive sneaker collection. I stare at all the empty slots I haven't been able to fill yet. I'll never love shoes as much as Josiah does, but only a small section of what was formerly his side remains vacant. Piece by piece, I'm filling in the gaps with my new clothes, with my new life.

Standing, I walk over to his side, opening a bottom drawer. It's empty, save a pair of powder-blue Air Jordans.

"I can't find my OG UNCs," Josiah said a few weeks after he'd moved out, fresh resentment still marking our every exchange. "You seen 'em?"

"No," I'd lied. "But I'll keep a lookout."

Why am I holding on to this pair of shoes?

I slip them on, my feet swallowed by the size thirteens. You know what they say about a man with big feet. Whew, chile, did Josiah live up to it. A shiver slides down my spine, and that restless ache creeps between my legs, bringing breathlessness with it. My eyes wander to the king-sized bed where, before everything went wrong, we did it so right.

"Stop," I tell the empty closet and the horny girl.

Depending on the day and the website, these shoes would sell for around fifteen hundred dollars, and I know Josiah never wore them more than once or twice. Remembering his excitement when he found them, I caress the tiny orange tag he said proved their authenticity. The leather remains uncreased and that new smell still clings to them. I glance up, startled by the image reflected in the framed mirror at the end of the closet. A half-naked woman with round hips and wild hair and bruised eyes, wearing the shoes of the man she sent away.

Portrait of a fool.

The text message chime from the bedroom drags me out of my own thoughts. I rush from the closet to grab my phone off the bed, half stumbling, losing one of the big shoes along the way.

Josiah: Hey. Be there in about ten minutes. Did you tell him we want to talk, or is it a total ambush?

Me: Total ambush. Thought it would be better just to dive in when you get here. I ordered pizza to put him in a great mood.

Josiah: Save me a slice.

Me: Anchovies. ?

Josiah: Never mind.

Me: Sorry! ? see you soon.

Seated on the bed, I tug the sneaker from my foot, holding and turning it in my hands before rising to scoop up the one I lost. Like a thief, I walk swiftly to the closet and return them to the empty bottom drawer. He'll be here soon, and we'll talk to Kassim about seeing the therapist. I need to be focused on this conversation, not getting lost in the past.

After a day in skinny jeans, nothing feels better than soft cotton lounge pants that skim my tired body and don't constrain. I leave on the fitted T-shirt that stops just short of my waist. A slick of lip gloss, a quick fluff of my hair. Deja's new leave-in conditioner made this twist out look fantastic. I grudgingly admit the girl knows hair, but she cannot make a living on Instagram posts about detangling.

One child at a time. Deal with Kassim tonight, and figure out how to interest my daughter in a viable career later. When I enter the kitchen, both my children are seated at the counter, on their phones and eating their pizza.

"Is it good?" I ask, opening a glass cabinet door to grab a plate. "Thought I'd try that new place called Guido's on the square."

"Yup." Kassim grins, showing all his front teeth. "It's even better than the other place."

I plate a slice, carefully picking off the anchovies. I'm not sure where Deja and Kassim got their love of the topping, since Josiah and I both abhor them.

Aunt Byrd.

I go still for a second, entertaining the memory of Byrd baking pizza and introducing the kids to anchovies. It was love at first bite. For a moment, the pain of missing her is almost too much. When you lose someone that close, the enormity, the finality of it, sometimes hits you full force when you least expect it. When you are least prepared. And your heartbeat stutters and your knees nearly buckle, just like when you first heard they were gone. When you lose someone like Byrd, you never banish the grief completely. I've learned to tame grief, though, so it doesn't run wild and ruin my life. It's in these unguarded moments that the pain hisses and growls, a rabid beast with its face pressed to the bars.

But I hold the whip and chair. I keep the lock and key.

"Your dad's on his way over," I tell them, not looking up from my plate.

Peripherally, I see them both stop chewing and exchange a glance. Josiah is here all the time, but it's always for a reason. He's picking them up and taking them out. He's dropping them off. He's helping with homework. For me to announce Josiah is coming over tips my hand.

"Why?" Deja asks, her eyes narrowed on my face.

"Just to talk." I open the refrigerator and grab a LaCroix.

"Like a family meeting?" Deja presses.

Before I can answer, the doorbell rings. Definitely saved by the bell.

Deja jumps up and leaves the kitchen to answer.

"Is everything okay?" Kassim asks, tearing the crust of his pizza.

"Yes, fine." I lean across the counter to kiss his forehead. "Just talking, baby."

Otis bounds into the kitchen and nuzzles my leg.

"Hey, friend." I smile down and rub his head, silently thanking Byrd again for leaving him with us. Despite my best efforts not to, I do worry about Josiah sometimes. The night Otis made it painstakingly clear he wanted to live with my ex, as irrational as it sounds, I was glad. Not because the dog wouldn't be here as much, but because he *would* be with Josiah. Small comfort, I know, but there it is. Otis lumbers over to the bed we've always kept in the corner for him and lies down, seemingly content. I've often felt Aunt Byrd left him as her very own guardian angel to watch over us. The kind who might piss on your good rug if you forget to take him out.

Deja and Josiah follow closely behind, laughing over something.

Occasionally I envy their effortless rapport. I still can't figure out what Josiah did to escape Deja's vitriol, but I wish he'd share the secret. With me, she's a teen wolf and every day is a full moon. With Daddy? It's all smiles and *yessirs*.

"Pizza?" I ask Josiah, pointing to my plate. "I picked the anchovies off."

"Nah. I have food from the restaurant. I'll eat when I get home." He sits on one of the high stools and looks at me meaningfully, a silent *So what's the plan?* in the brows he lifts.

"Deja," I say, "we want to talk with Kassim for a few minutes. Maybe take your pizza in the dining room for a bit?"

"What's wrong?" Kassim asks, low-grade panic spiking his level tone.

"Nothing's wrong, son," Josiah answers. "We just want to talk with you."

"I want to stay," Deja says, the line of her jaw set. "If you want me to stay, Seem, I will."

"You're making this a big deal unnecessarily," I tell her.

"Oh yeah?" Deja sits back and folds her arms. "The last time you sat us down like this 'just to talk' you said you were getting a divorce. If this is bad news, I want to be here too."

Deja's words transport me back to the night we sat our children down at this counter and told them our lives were about to change forever. The only thing harder than telling the kids we were getting a divorce was asking Josiah for it. The memory swirls around us in the kitchen, and for a moment, the weight of it is so visceral, so real, it suffocates me.

"We need to talk to Kassim about our meeting with his teacher," Josiah says, the deep timbre of his voice even and rich and reassuring.

"Oh. Why didn't you just say so?" Deja grabs her plate. "Good luck, Seem."

She swings her little narrow hips out of the kitchen, sass in every step.

"Am I in trouble?" Kassim mumbles, staring at his plate.

"No." I lift his chin so he can meet my eyes. "The opposite. You've been so amazing, son. We have good news."

I glance at Josiah, who, with brows lifted, inclines his head for me to continue.

"Ms. Halstead says you're one of the smartest kids in the class." I run a hand over his hair, which waves like Josiah's when he needs a haircut, as he does now.

"Yeah." Kassim nods like this is not new information, on the verge of preening. "I am."

I huff a laugh, trading a quick grin with Josiah, whose eyes light with pride and affection.

"Confident, not cocky, son," he reminds Kassim.

"Yes, sir," Kassim replies, though the twitch of his lips marks him as less than repentant.

"You ever get bored in class?" I ask.

He nods. "Yeah, but it's okay. The other kids have a lot to learn, so we have to go slower."

Josiah allows himself a quick grin at that before going on. "Ms. Halstead doesn't want you to get bored. She thinks we need to figure out a way to challenge you more. We aren't sure yet if it's just giving you work from the next grade, or if it might be skipping a grade."

Kassim's eyes go wide and his mouth hangs open. "Go to sixth grade now?"

"No," I rush to clarify. "But maybe next year instead of going to sixth, going to seventh. We aren't sure yet, but we want to talk to you about this. Make sure you're comfortable and ready for whatever is next."

"But if I skip to seventh," Kassim says, the vee between his brows deepening, "Jamal would still be in sixth."

"Right," Josiah says. "Jamal and your other friends could still be your friends, but they wouldn't be in your classes anymore. That's *if* we all agree you should skip a grade. Like we said, we may find it's better to just give you more challenging work in certain subjects. We just don't want you to get bored."

"And to make sure you're meeting your potential," I add with a smile. "We're so proud of you, Kassim."

"You are?" he asks, glancing from me to Josiah.

"Of course." Josiah clasps the back of Kassim's neck and squeezes. "You know we are."

He nods, but a small smile teases the corners of his mouth, and he dips his head, hiding his expression.

"When we met with Ms. Halstead..." I begin, shooting a searching look Josiah's way. He nods for me to go on. "She said if you do decide to skip a grade, we need to make sure you're ready, not just academically, but in every way."

"What's that mean?" Kassim asks.

"A lot of kids are smart enough to skip a grade," Joisah says. "But they end up having a hard time making new friends or adjusting. Ms. Halstead suggested maybe you should talk to someone about what you're...well..."

He looks at me, and I realize he doesn't know how to describe therapy in a way that Kassim would understand.

"Seem," I say, leaning forward and looking directly into his eyes. "You know how I told you and Deja that Mommy needed to talk to someone?"

"Your therapist?" Kassim asks, eyes widening. "You said you were sick and sad."

It sounds so stark and simple put that way, but it was true. There are days it still is. There may always be days like that, and I may be in and out of therapy for the rest of my life.

"Yes, that's true." I hope my smile is natural and reassuring. "But it's also just good to have someone you can talk to about stuff that's confusing or hard to understand."

"Like robotics?" Kassim ventures. "Because there is a new level of—"

"No," Josiah cuts in, chuckling. "Not robotics, though that always confuses me. More personal stuff like about Aunt Byrd passing away. And Henry."

I draw a sharp breath through my nose at the sound of my son's name on Josiah's lips. He's so rarely spoken it. I used to resent him for that, for not saying Henry's name. For not being the sobbing, snotty mess I was every day for months. For holding it so damn *together* when I kept coming apart. Now I know we deal with things in different ways, though there are many things Josiah has not dealt with at all. I'm not his therapist. Hell, I'm not even his wife anymore.

Kassim's expression shutters, and it breaks my heart a little seeing that face, usually so open, even at this age, trying to hide.

"I had to talk to someone about how much it hurt, you know," I tell him. "When we lost them both."

"That's why you stayed in bed all the time and stopped combing your hair and stuff, right?" Kassim asks.

Hot pebbles crowd my throat. I feel Josiah's eyes on my face, but can't bring myself to meet his stare, not sure whether I'll find contempt or compassion.

"That's exactly right," I tell Kassim, forcing a laugh. "I kind of fell apart for a little bit there, but talking to someone helped."

"I'm not sick or sad," Kassim says. "I'm not falling apart."

The statement, spoken in complete innocence and void of any malice, lances through me for a moment. No, I was the only one who fell apart. Those familiar demons of shame and guilt pull up a seat at the counter, running cool fingers through my hair and hissing lies in my ear.

"We all need help sometimes," Josiah says to Kassim, but looks at me. The contempt I feared his eyes would hold isn't there. I'm not sure what is, but Josiah is hard to read in the best of times.

"You need help, Daddy?" Kassim sounds surprised, and his brows shoot up. "Do you talk to a therapist?"

Oh, this should be good.

I don't rescue him. I can't. Josiah has been so adamant in the past that he doesn't need a "shrink," I'm not sure how to help. If I'm being honest, I don't want to.

"I've never talked to one, no," Josiah says, meeting Kassim's intent stare. "But I'll do it if you will."

I nearly topple off my stool.

He will?

"You will?" Kassim asks, surprise evident in his expression. Though Josiah never articulated to the kids, as far as I know, that he thinks therapy is a bullshit placebo to make you feel better and make "quacks" rich, he always seems self-contained, assured and unshakable. So hearing that he might need "help" must shock Kassim as much as it does me.

"I will." Josiah says it smoothly, but his jaw ticks, which tells me Kassim needing him to do this is another form of duress. He'd do anything for our kids, though. I know that. He'd said he'd do anything for me, but therapy was some invisible line in the sinking sand of our life together, and he'd never talked to anyone.

And here we are.

"You talk to someone and I will too," Josiah says, extending his hand to Kassim. "Deal?"

Kassim's face lights up and he grabs his father's much larger hand.

"Deal."

CHAPTER TEN

JOSIAH

What the hell just happened?

Did I just agree to talk to a damn therapist? I don't buy into the idea that just talking to someone about your feelings makes anything better. It may make us feel better about our shit, like we're "taking steps," but it doesn't actually change anything. I know Yasmen thinks it's helped her, but she was also on antidepressants. Drugs? Sure, those can help. Meds are measurable. They're real. The talking shit?

"Hellooooo," Deja says from the doorway separating the kitchen and the dining room. "Can I get another slice of pizza if you guys are finished talking about how brilliant and perfect Seem is?"

She flashes a quick grin at her brother, softening the sharp words, and musses his hair on her way to the pizza box on the counter. They may tease one another mercilessly, and are classic big sister, little brother, but they would do anything for each other. They drew closer when the seams of our family started ripping.

"Yeah, I think we're done," I say, looking at Yasmen and silently asking for confirmation.

"Um, yeah." She glances at Kassim, whose expression is serene as he grabs another slice of pizza. "I think we have a plan."

I stand, jangling the keys in my pocket. "Then I'mma head home. I'm tired and hungry and want to relax for a while. Early start tomorrow."

I pat my leg twice. "Otis, you coming?"

I always ask, as if the dog gets the courtesy of deciding where he'll sleep. He could bounce between the houses like the kids do, but he always stays with me. He stands and walks toward the foyer, head tilted to an imperial angle. Conceited bastard. After a bath, he practically struts at the dog park.

"I'll walk you out," Yasmen says, standing from the stool and following Otis.

I let her walk a little ahead of me. These damn pants she's wearing. The material must be hand-sewn by the devil and shipped from hell the way it hugs her ass and hips. The T-shirt crops just above her waist, gifting glimpses of her stomach—smooth and brown and toned. Beneath the top, her breasts hang ripe and overfull. When we were married, she'd walk around the house with no bra to torture me. I never missed an opportunity to drag her into the pantry or into a corner, tug up her shirt, bare her breasts, and suck her nipples. It was our own kind of foreplay. There were times, if the kids were upstairs or out of the house, when I would take her on the kitchen counter. Spread her wide, eat her out.

Jesus, I'm hard.

Not good. Not good at all. There's no way I can fool myself that this erection has anything to do with my actual girlfriend, who has sent me two texts hinting that she'd like to spend the night. Nope. This is all Yasmen, dammit. I subtly shift in my pants, hoping to rush down the steps and to the car before she notices.

"Hey." She grabs my arm when I move to walk past her on the porch. "Can we talk?"

With a quick glance at her hand on my arm, I nod tersely and sit in the swing. Maybe if I stay seated and the porch light is off, she won't notice the pole stand in my pants.

The motion-sensor light turns on.

Great.

I lean forward and rest my elbows on my knees. She comes to sit by me on the swing, stroking Otis's head. He leans into her palm, eyes rolling in canine bliss.

"That went better than expected." She pulls one leg under the other. "What'd you think?"

"Yeah. It was pretty good. He seems okay with it."

"I think…I'm sure you offering to go to therapy with him helped a lot." She angles a sideways glance at me. "Did you mean it?"

I bend my knees a few times to rock the swing a little. "Damn, Yas. You think I'd say something like that and not follow through?"

"No, of course not. You were just always so adamant about not seeing a therapist when we…when I…well, before, so I was surprised you offered."

"Am I excited about it? No. Do I think it'll do anything for me? Hell, no, but if it might help Kassim adjust, I'll go."

"I see." She blinks, her pretty lips shaping into a wry curve. "So therapy might help children or weak-minded people like me, but couldn't possibly be of any benefit to someone as strong as you."

"You know that's not what I'm saying. Don't twist my words."

"I don't have to." She stands abruptly, the coolness in her eyes not enough to disguise the hurt. "Do you want recommendations? If so, I can get referrals from Dr. Abrams. Or are you just going through the motions to satisfy Kassim?"

Both.

I know saying it aloud would only ratchet up the tension coiling between us, so I blank my expression before I answer.

"That'd be great."

"I'll let Ms. Halstead know we're moving forward," she says, turning to grab the knob of the front door.

"Yas, hey." I stand, and this time, I'm the one who takes her arm. "I really didn't mean to imply I'm too good for therapy or that you're weak or—"

"You didn't have to imply anything, Si." She tugs, freeing her elbow from my grip and looking down. "You obviously see our son's emotional well-being as something worth fighting for, worth going to therapy for. I think it's awesome."

Except it sounds like she may as well have said "I think you're an asshole."

"So we're good?" I ask, even though the tightness in the air, the tightness of her expression, tells me we're not.

She holds my stare over her shoulder, one hand on the door, and I'm not sure if it's disgust or disappointment that darkens her eyes, but it makes me feel slimy.

"Yeah." She opens the door. "We're good."

CHAPTER ELEVEN

YASMEN

You sure you're okay taking Deja, Hen?" I remove bottles of Gatorade from the plastic rings and load them into a cooler packed with ice. "We drove all over the city yesterday, and couldn't find this hair she wants anywhere."

"Oh, I already know this place off Candler Road has it." Seated at my kitchen counter, Hendrix sips her coffee. "Several of my clients get their hair there on the low. When you see it on TV, you'd never know it comes from a shop in the back of a grocery store."

I pause, a bottle in each hand, to stare at her. "The shop is in a grocery store?"

"One of them one-stops you only find in the cut. Get your milk and eggs. Get your nails did. Get your taxes done. Hock a watch and grab four, five packs of hair before you go."

She clasps the long ponytail hanging over her shoulder, lifting it and letting it fall. "That's where I got this silky silky."

"Well, thank you. I can't miss Kassim's soccer match, and Josiah is speaking at this entrepreneurs conference so he couldn't step in." I hold up a bottle of Glacier Freeze and a pack of Go-Gurts. "Forgot I'm snack mom today, so I'm scrambling to get it all together."

I pull a bottle of orange juice from the fridge for Kassim.

"Anyway," I continue, "Kassim's first session with this child psychologist is after the game. Josiah and I did an initial meeting with him and Kassim last week, just to kind of info-gather and for us to meet him, but today will be their first session one-on-one. It was the only slot Dr. Cabbot had available so I don't have time to drive all over, looking for this hair. You're really coming through for me."

"Is Kassim nervous?"

"Am *I* nervous is probably a better question." I pause to lean a hip against the counter. "How did I not know he was so hyperfocused on death? And on losing his family? I'm with him every day, and he's never mentioned anything like what his teacher said is in his journal."

"It's not surprising when you think about it. Do kids really go around confessing their deepest fears to their parents unprompted?" Hendrix shrugs. "Maybe some do, but I didn't when I was a kid. Pat yourself on the back for doing this now instead of condemning yourself for not knowing sooner that he needed it."

"You're right. It's made such a huge difference for me, and I'm really glad Kassim's experiencing it so young. Maybe if he needs it when he's older, it won't hold the stigma it does for so many men."

"Especially Black men. My cousin Bilail has been through so much crap all his life. Divorced parents. Molested by his uncle. Mom was an addict, but you think he's talking to someone about his feelings?" Hendrix shakes her head and turns matte red lips down at the corners. "No, ma'am. That man's twisted tight as a can of biscuits and can't figure out for the life of him why all his relationships have an expiration date before they even start."

"Speaking of Black men and therapy," I say, loading more bottles into the cooler. "Did I mention Kassim is going because Josiah said he would?"

Hendrix's mug of coffee hovers at her lips and her brows fly high. "Wasn't he dead set against it when you guys were together?"

"Yeah." I bend to stuff the last of the sports drinks into the cooler. "He always said it wouldn't do him any good, but he apparently thought him going would convince Kassim, so he will. Just makes you wonder."

"Wonder what?" Hendrix asks.

I glance up, meeting her probing stare for a millisecond before turning my back on her to pull the last of the yogurt from the fridge. "Nothing. So this hair is apparently called Kinky Curly or something like that. Deja—"

"Wonder what, Yas? Why Josiah wouldn't go for you?"

My hand's still halfway between the refrigerator and the cooler, and I have trouble meeting her eyes again when I turn back, but I do.

"Maybe. Not even for me, but for himself when I suggested it. He wouldn't even entertain it, but he volunteered when this came up with Kassim. And I guess I wonder what changed."

I huff out a laugh and close the cooler. "Not that he expects to get anything out of it. He still thinks it's useless, but at least he's willing."

"Therapy can be intimidating, and folks aren't always ready when *we* want them to be. They're ready when they're ready. Josiah thinks he's going because of Kassim, but maybe it's that deep down he's just finally ready. It might surprise him. He may get in there and learn a lot about himself. The right therapist can change everything."

"Yeah, and the wrong one sometimes changes nothing." I roll my eyes. "Thank God I finally found Dr. Abrams."

Footsteps charging down the stairs cut the conversation off, and I'm kind of relieved. I don't want to think about Josiah finally going to therapy, and how that could have impacted what happened with us, much less talk about it.

"Hey, Aunt Hen," Deja says, her smile bright and open. "Thank you for taking me today."

"It's no problem." Hendrix stands to dump the last of her coffee in the sink and rinses the mug.

"And you really think this place will have the hair I need?" Deja asks.

"I already called and confirmed they do," Hendrix says, her smile only slightly smug.

"Eeeeep!" Deja's hands fly in the air approximating a hallelujah. "I've been looking all over, and there's this passion braids challenge I want to do next week, and I have to use this hair."

"Well, I got you," Hendrix says. "And there's a place near the shop called Ruby's. Best neck bones in the city."

"Neck bones?" Deja's skepticism is palpable.

"Wayminit." Hendrix sets her fists on her hips. "You mean to tell me your parents own a soul food restaurant and you never had neck bones?"

"Not on our menu." I laugh, grabbing my purse from the stool. "Byrd hated them, and Vashti doesn't do them either."

Hendrix links her arm through Deja's. "Well, you gon' learn today. We'll have them for lunch if you want."

"Okay!" Deja nods, her space buns bobbing on either side of her head.

"What time you want her back, Yas?" Hendrix asks.

Deja looks directly at me for the first time, her smile fading. I'm like the pin that pops every balloon for her.

"Um, whenever you guys are done," I say, forcing a smile. "Thank you again for helping out."

Hendrix glances between Deja and me, her smile dimming. "You my girl. You already know it's no big."

I walk out of the kitchen, giving Hen's arm a quick squeeze, and head to the foyer, stopping at the base of the staircase.

"Kassim!" I shout up to the second floor. "We're gonna be late. Come on."

He appears at the top of the steps in his red-and-white soccer uniform with his duffel bag slung over one shoulder. I glance at his feet.

"Ankles ashy as a bag of flour." I blow out a breath and tip my head toward the garage. "There's lotion in the car."

"Is Dad coming?" he asks, heading down the steps.

Josiah spent many afternoons and evenings in our backyard kicking the ball around with Kassim. Of course my son loves having me at the games, but it's his father's face and approval he seeks in the crowd every time he scores.

"Not today, but I promise I'll get video for him, okay?"

"So he won't be at therapy either, huh?" Kassim's expression doesn't change, but the flicker of unease in his eyes makes my heart clench.

"He has a convention he has to speak at today, son. I'm sorry. It was booked months ago, and he couldn't get out. I'm sure he'll call tonight to see how it went."

"Okay," he says, shifting the bag on his shoulder. "Do I have time to eat?"

"KIND bar and OJ on the kitchen counter. Grab 'em and go straight to the car. I have the team snacks. We can't be late."

His mouth drops open. "You're the snack mom?"

"Yeah." I grimace. "I forgot."

"Then we gotta go!"

Kassim is definitely "the responsible one" in every situation. He rushes past me, not even breaking stride when he scoops up the breakfast I left out for him. He waves to Hendrix and Deja, but doesn't pause on his way to the garage.

"Guess we'll be going too," Hendrix says, picking up her Hermès bag, a gift from one of those fancy awards shows.

"You be good, Day." I grab the handle of the cooler and start toward the door, dragging it behind me.

"Yes, Mom." The usual exasperation colors her voice, but it can't disguise the undercurrent of excitement. She's been talking about this hair challenge thing for a week, and as much as I disagree that social media hair guru is a wise career choice, I don't want her disappointed.

I give Hendrix a quick kiss on the cheek. "I owe you one."

"We got an open tab," she says, kissing my cheek in return. "You know that."

She and Deja follow me into the garage, then continue down the driveway to where Hendrix's Mercedes G-Class is parked on the street. By the time I back out and the garage door lowers, they're gone.

We arrive at the field just in time. The team is circled up and the coach is starting his pep talk. I place the cooler at the end of the bench and set my folding chair with the other parents on the sidelines. By the end of the second half, the action picks up and Kassim is running the ball down the field.

"Go, Seem!" I stand, aiming my phone just in time to record him scoring the winning goal.

All the parents high-five while our kids shake hands with the other team.

"Mom, did you see me score?" Kassim asks, grinning between gulps of Gatorade, sweat beading his brow and dampening his jersey.

"I did." I hold up my phone. "And I got it all right here."

"We can show Dad!"

"I'll send it to him in a little bit." I check the time on my phone. "But we need to go if we want to make it to Dr. Cabbot's office on time."

The excitement drains from Kassim's face, replaced by something close to dread, and I regret bringing it up.

"Oh, yeah," he mumbles. "I almost forgot. Therapy."

"Therapy" sounds like "firing squad" when he says it.

I grab the cooler and wheel it to the car. Still unusually subdued considering his victory, Kassim carries his duffel bag and takes the back seat. I don't ask him why or pressure him to sit up front like he usually does. If anyone understands those first-time session jitters, it's me.

When we pull up to Dr. Cabbot's office, I park and turn to look at Kassim.

"Hey." I wait for him to meet my eyes. "I know you're nervous—"

"I'm not nervous." He slides his glance away. "I don't think we'll have anything to talk about. There's nothing wrong with me."

"I talk to someone all the time. Do you think there's something wrong with me?"

Wide brown eyes snap to mine. "No. There's nothing wrong with you, Mom. I...I just meant...I'm sorry."

"You don't have to apologize, baby." I reach back, place my hand on his knee. "Sometimes we have a lot of feelings we don't know what to do with. Ya know?"

He hesitates, but then nods, pulling at a thread on his shorts.

"Dr. Abrams says feelings come out one way or another. Like if we're mad, sometimes we take it out on other people. We may snap at the barista at Starbucks or yell at our kids or kick our dog."

"If somebody kicks Otis," Kassim says with a tiny twitch of his lips, "he'll kick them back."

"You're probably right. Otis is not the one to mess with. My point is, sometimes when we don't understand our feelings, we point them in the wrong direction. Or if they do stay inside, they start to make us feel bad. We want you to understand some of what you might be feeling about Aunt Byrd, about Henry, about anything that's been on your mind."

"So I don't kick Otis?" His small smile is still somewhat uneasy, but at least he seems a little more relaxed.

"Something like that, yeah. I just want you to know that the things you feel sometimes about them being gone, I feel them too."

"But you're okay, right, Mom?" The uncertainty in his voice makes him sound even younger than he is, and I wonder how my struggles have affected my kids, how even when I tried to hide my utter inability to deal with the world, they may have sensed it. I could drown in guilt wondering how I may have added to Kassim's fears, or I can do my part now to allay them.

"No one is always okay, Seem." I take his hand. "Life is not about always being okay. It's about getting help when we aren't. About letting our family and friends help us. Letting people like Dr. Cabbot help us. You know what I mean?"

"Daddy's not always okay?"

A part of me wants to scream that *no, Daddy is not always okay*, even though he seems like it. Just because someone never asks for help doesn't mean they don't need it.

"Like I said," I tell Kassim. "No one is always okay, but your father is one of the strongest people I know. He'll always be there for you. We both will."

His face lights up, but before I can congratulate myself on my impressive mommy wisdom, he says, "Dad!"

I follow his line of vision over my shoulder and spot Josiah's black Range Rover parked a few spots away. Kassim undoes his seat belt and scrambles out of the car. More slowly, I follow. I want to give them a few moments together, but I also want time to compose myself. Josiah always looks good, of course, but today he's dressed for the conference. The impeccably tailored suit molds his broad shoulders and fits the powerful muscles of his legs. The unyielding lines of his face soften when Kassim reaches him. He cups our son's neck and bends to kiss his forehead, and there's a part of me at the core that melts. Even at our lowest point, I could never doubt Josiah's love for Deja and Kassim.

"I thought you had to speak at the conference," I hear Kassim say when I'm within earshot.

"Yeah, I do," Josiah says. "I actually have two sessions. One was this morning and the other is in about an hour, so I can't stay long."

He glances from Kassim's upturned face to mine, and his features shutter, the warmth in his eyes cooling. The vulnerability that used to be reserved for the three of us—Kassim, Deja, and me—I don't get that anymore. I lost the privilege of his feelings, his body, his heart; or rather, I forfeited those intimacies when I asked for a divorce.

"Hey." I bite my lip and slide my hands into the pockets of my jeans. "Didn't expect to see you here."

"I had to see my boy," he says, shifting his look back to Kassim and gifting him a dazzling smile. "I figured you'd be fine, but just in case you were a little nervous, I wanted to check on you. You doing okay?"

"Yeah." Kassim angles a look up at me. "But Mom says it's okay not to be okay. She says no one is always okay."

Josiah doesn't hesitate, nodding and bending a little to catch Kassim's eyes. "She's right."

"You too?" Kassim whispers, his voice so low I barely catch it.

In the small silence following Kassim's question, I want to drag Josiah aside and beg him to let down his walls just this once. To at least pretend he hurts like the rest of us mortals so his son doesn't feel alone.

"Me too." Josiah squeezes Kassim's shoulder, that unique tenderness he withholds from everyone except our kids gleaming in his dark eyes. "Remember, I'm gonna talk to a therapist too."

"When?" Kassim's smile is stretched wide with hope and eagerness.

"Monday," Josiah answers. "How about you tell me how yours goes and I'll tell you about mine?"

"Okay." Kassim beams. "Deal."

Josiah glances at his watch. "I have to get back soon, so let's go before I have to leave."

"Oh, you're coming inside?" I ask.

"Yeah." He grins down at Kassim. "You ready, son?"

Still wearing his uniform, Kassim practically skips between us as we walk toward the building housing Dr. Cabbot's office. The waiting area is decorated in warm hues of honey and coriander, spiced with fidget toys, puzzles, and a huge aquarium built into the wall. Kassim is winning a staring contest with a blowfish when the connecting door opens and a man in his late thirties or early forties emerges. His sandy hair is neatly trimmed, and his eyes are still deciding whether they should be brown or green. He extends his hand to Josiah and then me.

"Good to see you again, Kassim." A gentle smile touches his mouth when he looks down at our son.

"Yeah," Kassim says. "I mean, yes, sir."

"We're just gonna get to know each other some today, you and me." Dr. Cabbot gestures to the door he just walked through. "How's that sound?"

Kassim's nod is halting, but he says, "Yeah, okay."

"I have to go, son," Josiah says. "We'll talk tonight, okay?"

"Okay, Dad."

"Love you, Seem," I say, hoping I sound like a perfectly normal person when I really just want to hurl myself at Dr. Cabbot and beg him to take care of my boy.

"Love you, Mom." Kassim walks ahead of Dr. Cabbot and the door closes behind them both.

"Are *you* okay?" Josiah asks, the first strand of amusement evident in his voice since he arrived.

"Barely." I sink to the leather sofa and dig around for the gum in my purse so I can safely gnaw my anxiety. "Thanks for coming. I know that meant a lot to him."

"I knew he'd be nervous, and I wanted him to know I'm living up to my end of the bargain."

"Though you don't actually expect to get anything out of it, right?" I ask, glancing up to search his face.

He quirks one thick brow at me. "I'm not saying therapy isn't beneficial to anyone. I just don't think it's for me."

"Which you'd know based on all those other times you went to therapy. Now remind me how many times that was again." I touch my chin and pretend to think. "Oh, right. Zero times."

His full lips twitch at the corners and he rolls his eyes. "I'm doing this for Kassim, but I have no expectations. Let's talk later to see how his first session went. Gotta go."

No expectations. That's not how I felt with my first session. I had high hopes that first therapist could fix me, could dispel the dark cloud hanging over my head every day when I woke up. Not only did she *not* do any of those things, but in some ways she made me feel worse. I knew the problem couldn't lie with her when, after six weeks of seeing her, I felt no better, so I had to be the problem. And when another two months with a second therapist didn't yield any results, it only reinforced the idea that buzzed in my head like a chainsaw.

I would never be fixed.

I'd never feel happy again.

I'd be a burden and an embarrassment to my family and my friends.

That little voice kept whispering things would never get better. I'd divorced the man I always loved because being with him, fighting with him, *resenting* him hurt too much…and that had not made it better. What a waste. What a failure.

There was nothing wrong with those first two therapists. We just weren't the right fit. Dr. Abrams was, and it took her a long time to help me silence that voice, to turn off that chainsaw cutting me up inside, but when I was able to, what a relief. And that's what I want for Kassim. The assurance that his fears are "normal." That he's okay even when he is not all the way okay.

I stare sightlessly at the fish navigating the fabricated watery underworld, my mind swimming with thoughts of Josiah and what this step might mean for him, but mostly wondering how Kassim is doing on the other side of that door with a stranger poking around in his mind and heart.

My phone rings, jarring me from the swirl of my own contemplation.

"Hendrix, hey." I'm the only one in the waiting room, so I stay seated for the call. "What's up? Any luck?"

"Oh, yeah, we found the hair. We were gonna do mani-pedis. That okay?"

"Oh, well…sure." I lick my lips, fingers tightening on the phone. "That sounds like fun."

"Awesome. And we're still gonna run by Ruby's, if that's all right?"

"Of course. Get that girl some neck bones." We chuckle together, Hendrix's usual cackle sounding easy and natural, while mine feels like it's being strained through a colander. Deja and I used to get our nails done together. We had mommy-daughter days all the time. Now I can't remember the last time she voluntarily spent time with me.

"Thank you, Hen," I say, meaning it. "Really."

"Girl, it ain't nothing." Hendrix pauses. "She's a good kid. I know you two are going through something, but I see you in her so much and you're doing a great job even if it doesn't feel like it."

I close my eyes and let the simple praise wash over me. Let it sink down deep and reach the doubt and guilt that seem to live just beneath the surface.

"Thank you. For everything, Take your time. I'll see you guys whenever you're done."

The door opens and Kassim appears with Dr. Cabbot.

"Hey, Hen. I gotta go. Seem's out. Love."

"Love you, bye."

I stand and cross over to Kassim, cupping his chin and scanning his face, as if I can detect any change in his eyes after one forty-five-minute session.

"How'd it go?" I ask Dr. Cabbot.

"Good." He smiles down at Kassim. "Just getting to know each other today."

"All right," I say. "So what'd you think so far, Kassim?"

He shrugs. "It's cool. Can we go, though? There's a *Halo* tournament this afternoon."

"Oh, of course." I grab my purse from the waiting room chair and give him the key fob. "You go to the car. I'll be right out."

Through the window, I watch him cross the small parking lot. The lights on my car flash when he unlocks it, and he climbs in. I turn to Dr. Cabbot, forcing myself not to unleash a barrage of questions.

"So what are we dealing with?" I ask him.

"It really was just a day to get to know each other," Dr. Cabbot says. "We didn't dive deep, but it is obvious he has a good bit of uncertainty about the future, and a lot of understandable fear about losing people he loves."

"Even if we decide he shouldn't skip the grade, I'm glad we brought him in. I know the value of a safe place to share your thoughts and burdens."

"It's great you got him here to talk things through."

It's so affirming, even that simplest sprinkling of praise. It makes me realize how arid I've been inside, how badly I've needed watering. Dr. Abrams always says I need to be kinder to myself. Based on the way I responded to first Hendrix and now Dr. Cabbot reinforcing that I'm doing a good job as a mom, I think she might be right.

CHAPTER TWELVE

∞

JOSIAH

"S o tell me a little about yourself."

Seriously?

"Uh, what do you want to know?" I ask the therapist seated across from me in a leather recliner identical to the one I'm sitting in.

"The intake form you completed told me a lot about the things that have happened to you," Dr. Musa replies, resting his elbows on the arms of the recliner and steepling his fingers. "But not much about your life if that makes sense."

"If the intake form told you what's happened to me, don't you then know about my life?"

Dark brows rise above his black-rimmed glasses. "Not necessarily. Someone else could have lost both parents at a really young age, lost the caretaker who raised him, lost a child and a marriage, all in the matter of a year or so, and processed it completely differently. There are infinite doors to choose when we lose things and people that are important to us. A million ways to grieve. I'd like to know which doors you chose."

A harsh chuckle rattles in my throat at his unaffected cataloging of my life's shit luck. "So we just diving in, huh?"

"I'm a good judge of people," Dr. Musa says with a smile. "I sense you're a man who likes to get right to it."

The locs hanging to his shoulders are peppered with gray, but the face they're pulled away from is relatively unlined. He's probably not that much older than I am. I take in the African masks and art decorating the walls, certificates and degrees interspersed between them.

"I see you're a Morehouse man." I study his undergrad diploma: Bachelor of Arts in Psychology.

"I am. You?"

"I was there, yeah. Business degree."

"Nothing like it, huh?" he asks, his smile relaxing around the shared experiences specific to HBCUs that others wouldn't fully grasp.

"Nothing like the House, nope." I shift my gaze to his other degrees from Emory and Yale. "Looks like you're a smart man. All these degrees gonna tell you what's wrong with me?"

"Do you think there's something wrong with you?"

"No, nothing's wrong with me." I cross my ankle over my knee, eyeing the box of tissues on the table beside him with amusement. Won't be needing that. "No disrespect to what you do here, but I don't need this. I'm doing it for my son."

"Your son is doing therapy vicariously through you?" He quirks a small grin. "Didn't know that was a thing."

"What I mean is my son was anxious about talking to someone and I wanted him to see he had nothing to worry about. That it's fine for people to go to therapy, so I'm modeling it for him."

"Do you have an attendance card you need me to sign to show him you came? And maybe we can just discuss the Falcons' chances this season or reminisce about homecomings and the good old days on the yard during our sessions since there's no real work we have to do here."

His sarcasm pulls a reluctant smile from me. "I really don't mean to insult what you do. My wife...ex-wife...has benefited a lot from this stuff and swears by it. Whatever helps the people I care about, I'm all for."

"How about we start there."

"Start where?"

"Your ex-wife. You indicated on your intake form that you've been divorced for almost two years. How's that been?"

I stiffen. It's one thing to come here for a few sessions until Kassim feels comfortable, but it's another for this stranger to start digging in caves I've sealed with boulder-sized stones.

"It's fine. She's fine. She's gotten the help she needed." I shift, placing both feet on the floor. "We make a great team. Raise our kids together. Run our business together. It's all good."

"It sounds very progressive and amicable."

"Why wouldn't it be? We didn't want to sacrifice our kids and the business we'd worked so hard to build just because she didn't..." I clear my throat. "Because *we* didn't want to be married anymore."

"So did she want the divorce or did you or was it mutual?" He picks up his pad. "It's rarely actually mutual."

"Do you ask these intrusive kinds of questions with all your clients in the first session?" Irritation prickles beneath my collar, heating my neck.

"I *do* have some kid gloves around here somewhere." He makes a show of searching the office. "I could use those if you'd prefer, but it sounds like you don't plan to come to many sessions. Figured I'd better make the most of the time we have."

We stare at each other for a few seconds in a silence that grows tighter the longer it stretches out. I'm determined not to break it, not to give him anything, because why would I? I don't know this mother-fucker from Adam, and he wants to dig around in my head? Drag out all the shit I store in neat compartments so I can find some measure of peace? He wants to shake all that up, but he wouldn't have to live with the fallout. I would.

"Tell me a little about your ex-wife," he finally says to break our silence. "What's her name?"

I don't relax. Don't take my eyes off him, like he's a hunter setting a trap and I might stumble in if I'm careless.

"Her name is Yasmen." I sit back and fold my arms over my middle.

"Why did you marry her?"

Because she was the best thing that ever happened to me.

It's bad enough I let that thought out of its cage and into the common area of my mind. The hell I'm saying that shit out loud. It's naive, romantic nonsense, and the version of me who first met Yasmen, who fell for her almost on sight, may be able to get away with that sappy bullshit, but the guy who watched her leave in increments every day for a year, who begged her to stay and had to accept that she would go? That guy doesn't get to indulge in soft, squishy thoughts about my ex-wife.

"I wanted to fuck her every day for the rest of my life," I half joke. "She's that beautiful. Is that a good enough reason?"

The answer, though absolutely true, leaves so much out, and I can tell he recognizes an abridged version when he hears it. He huffs a laugh, shaking his head.

"If that's true, and that's all you had together, then I'm not surprised you divorced her. Must have gotten old."

"I know what you're doing. This reverse psychology routine doesn't work on me."

"Reverse psychology assumes that posing the opposite belief will persuade someone to share their actual one. If that were the case, you're saying I believe your marriage was based on more than just how badly you wanted to fuck your wife." He pulls a folder from under his pad, flipping it open. "So did you get tired of her? Maybe she let herself go after two pregnancies."

"Three," I amend automatically. "Three pregnancies."

The reminder of yet another loss, though spoken so quietly, lands in the room with a thud.

"Of course, three," he says, his tone softening.

I don't want to give him even this, but there is something inside of me that fundamentally resists anyone talking about Yas, about what we had, in such dismissive terms.

Even if I did start it.

"She didn't let herself go, as you put it, but it wouldn't have mattered if she had. I wouldn't have cared. She knew that."

"So tell me what happened."

"We, uh, hit a rough patch, which you already know." I wave a hand at the folder in his lap, which flattens a lifetime of pain into a sheaf of paper and ink when it was a bulbous thing that would have consumed my whole existence if I'd let it. It's safer pressed between pages than free to roam and ravage. I've learned over the years that kind of pain must be contained.

"Talk a little about losing your aunt."

Eyeing him warily, I tense in my seat. "What do you want to know?"

"Whatever you want to tell me."

"That sounds like a cop-out," I mutter, but allow half a grin.

He wears the other half of my grin and shrugs one shoulder. "Maybe, but I'd rather you tell me what feels right at the surface for you. If I need to dig, I will."

"Fair enough. She raised me. I was only eight years old when my parents died in a car crash. A pileup on the interstate." I rub my hands across my face. "She was my dad's older sister. We lived in Texas. I'd only met her a few times, but she stepped up right away because there was no one else. I would have gone into the system if she hadn't brought me back to Atlanta with her."

"Wow. That's admirable. How was your relationship with her?"

I can't fight the smile that spreads over my face. Thinking of Byrd brings pain, but I won't disregard the joy she brought not only to my life, but to everyone she knew.

"She was not your typical guardian. She probably gave me so much leeway because she was really independent and hated people telling *her* what to do." My smile peters out, the crushing reality of her absence crowding back in again. "We were family, but we were also friends."

I clear my throat, staring down at my black short boots. "She was there and then she was just...gone. Massive heart attack. I...ummm...I found her."

"I'm sorry, Josiah. That had to be hard."

"Yeah. She was in the kitchen." A hoarse laugh escapes me. "Food was that woman's love language. Best cook I've ever met."

Best person I've ever met.

"She used to carry unopened packs of socks and underwear in all sizes around in her car so when homeless people asked for money like at stoplights, or whatever, she could offer them."

"She sounds fantastic."

"She was. I saw a homeless woman downtown the other day. She didn't have on shoes. Her clothes were...She was obviously on hard times. And all I could think was, *What would Byrd do? How would she help?* Yasmen still rides around with socks and underwear in her middle console because of that."

"They were close? Your ex-wife and Byrd?"

"She was like a second mom to Yas. They were extremely close. First time my aunt met Yasmen she said, 'don't let this one get away.'"

"And what did you say?"

My smile fades, bitterness hardening the line of my mouth. "I said, 'never,' but she did get away, huh? Joke's on me."

"If you don't mind me asking, how far along was your ex-wife when she lost the baby?"

"Thirty-six weeks." I grip the arms of the recliner. "She was in the restaurant alone. Closing up. I told her..."

I shake my head and slam my teeth together to stifle words that may sound like I blame Yasmen for what happened. I don't.

"I asked her to let someone else lock up, but Yasmen was always in the mix. She had such a great pregnancy. No complications. It never occurred to her something like that could happen. Didn't occur to me either. I was away." I roll my shoulders, trying to relieve the tension, wishing I could roll off the guilt. "Shit. Isn't our time up yet? Like, is it time to go?"

"We just started," Dr. Musa says. "You were saying you were away. Where were you?"

"I was at this stupid convention in Santa Barbara."

If ever I could take something back, it would be going on that trip. Yasmen wasn't due yet, and we both agreed it would be best for Grits if I attended, but I had a sick feeling in the pit of my stomach as soon as the plane took flight. I kept texting and calling to make sure she was all right. By then, we'd already buried Aunt Byrd. Maybe it was the fragility of life that made me anxious, having just lost someone I loved so much. Maybe it was a premonition. Whatever it was, it kept me up the first night in the hotel. The next day when the hospital called to say Yasmen had lost the baby, one fire-torched thought ran through my mind.

I should have been there.

If I'd been there, she wouldn't have been closing. The restaurant wouldn't have been empty. She wouldn't have fallen. Those precious moments wouldn't have been lost with her cell phone in another room while Henry wasn't getting air.

And then he was gone.

"Do you want to talk about the trip to Santa Barbara, Josiah?" Dr. Musa asks, his soft, kind voice cutting into the riot of my thoughts.

I swallow past the emotion scorching my throat. *See, this is why I don't do this shit. This is why I leave well enough alone.*

But is it really well enough?

"Do you think the losses you experienced so close together contributed to the failure of your marriage?"

A rough chuckle rattles in my throat. "You could say that. I knew things were really bad, but one night she just…"

I used to alternate between blocking the events of the night Yasmen ended things and playing them over and over in my head, analyzing if there was anything I could have done or said differently that would have changed the outcome. That would have saved us.

"Do you want to talk about that night?" Dr. Musa asks. "We have plenty of time."

Hell, no.

Why would I unpack one of the most painful nights of my life with this stranger? My mouth is open, and the refusal rests on the tip of my tongue, but an image intrudes, shakes my absolute certainty that this dude can't do a damn thing for me. It's Kassim, walking into Dr. Cabbot's office, looking back over his shoulder at his mom and me. Nervous, scared, uncertain, but assured because Yasmen said it was okay not to always be okay.

You, too, Dad?

Me too.

I clear my throat, swallowing the sharp response I had planned for Dr. Musa and look down at my hands gripping my knees.

"*Do* you want to talk about that night?" Dr. Musa repeats, his voice quiet like I'm some skittish animal who might bolt.

"Sure," I finally answer, hoping I don't regret this. "What do you want to know?"

Dr. Musa glances at his watch and smiles. "We may have time for everything."

CHAPTER THIRTEEN

∞

JOSIAH: THEN

I drive home from Grits slowly, barely registering all the things that so captivated us about Skyland when we first moved here. My mind is still buzzing from a day that started before the sun was up and ended long after it was down. I turn onto First Court, our street lined with well-manicured lawns, neatly trimmed bushes fronting seven-figure homes. It had been the perfect setting for all our ambitions. You don't live in the heart of Skyland without paying the price for location, and the price is high. Had things gone according to plan, we'd have no problem paying that price, but things went to shit, and our mortgage has become an albatross hanging around my neck. Mentally drowning in a sea of bills and past-due notices, I almost miss the white paper pinned to the garage door.

"What the hell?" I mutter, taking in our slightly overgrown grass and shabby bushes. The landscaper who services most of the houses on our street was scheduled to come today. I get out of the car and snatch the note.

Check bounced.

It's scribbled on the grass-stained paper, stark and offensive. A muddy trail of shame and fury wends through me. I haven't bounced a check since college, and now that I live on a street of million-dollar homes, it happens?

I pull out my phone to check our balance. Sure enough, our account is overdrawn. To save money while we're finding our footing again in

Byrd's absence, Yasmen and I took pay cuts. It made sense, especially since she's barely been to Grits since we lost Henry. With our reduced revenue, I had to trim fat somewhere, and I wasn't going to reduce pay for our staff. They have families, responsibilities. We can weather this better than they can.

Or I thought we could.

Pulling Deja and Kassim out of Harrington would feel like yet another admission of failure, but we may have to do it.

I crumple the paper in my fist, my emotions as tangled as these bushes. My life as overgrown and unkept. One more thing I'll have to deal with tomorrow.

I walk into our dream house and immediately want to turn right around and leave. The curtains are hung with hurt here. The floors are waxed with it. It lingers heavy and pungent in the air. I'd rather work at Grits fourteen hours a day than do the work of grief waiting in this house. The last few months have been a sinkhole. Of course, we all need time, but there's something so dark and cold and desolate about the place Yasmen's in now. I can't reach her. I want to grab her and drag her back into our life, or what's left of it. I want to beg her to remake it with me. To rebuild this restaurant's reputation with me. We've always been partners. Am I being selfish to want her at my side again? Or am I just lonely? Frustrated? Bitter? All of the above?

Yeah. All the fucking above and I hate myself for feeling this way.

I blow out a harsh breath, shoulders drooping from the day and from what's left of the night. The staircase may as well be Mount Everest. I poke my head into the kids' rooms. Each of them sleeps peacefully. It's hard to protect them from how we're falling apart because if we're not treading in freezing, silent water, we're thrashing in hot springs, screaming the house down. I can't believe this is us. We said we'd ride for each other till the wheels fell off. Lately our marriage feels like a blowout, both of us grabbing at the wheel, tires screeching, spinning out of control, every day narrowly avoiding a cataclysmic crash.

When I check our bedroom it's empty. I know she's in the nursery. My shoes have concrete soles when I take the few steps to the room at the end of the hall we'd used as a home office before we needed it for the baby. I'd suggested we store the nursery furniture until we figured out what to do with it. We need to repaint, move the desk and printer back. Wipe away all traces of what we hoped this room would be, but Yasmen would flip if I even suggested it. I stand in the door to the room, watching her, preternaturally still in the rocker, like she left her body behind and is elsewhere. A carousel lamp we bought after Deja's first ultrasound sits on the table, slowly turning, spreading light and throwing shadows on the walls.

"Babe." Fatigue makes the endearment gravelly on my lips. "It's late. Come to bed."

I honestly can't blame her for choosing any place other than that cold stretch of mattress in our bedroom. In the king-sized bed our bodies don't have to touch, *don't* touch anymore, but it feels like it's not big enough for the two of us and the ghosts who hog the covers.

She doesn't turn her head to look at me, her gaze remaining fixed on the wall. My heart seizes in my chest every time I see the cursive writing—Yasmen's handwriting—a cheerful baby blue against the dark gray paint we selected for Henry's nursery.

I know the plans I have for you . . . to give you hope and a future.

Deja and Kassim each had a nursery rhyme for their wall, but Yasmen saw this verse on a greeting card somewhere, Jeremiah 29:11, and wanted to use it for Henry's.

"Do you ever think about him?" Yasmen asks, still not looking at me, her voice frighteningly steady.

I lean against the wall and cross my arms over my chest, a flimsy guard for a broken heart I haven't figured out how to articulate.

"Of course I do."

"You never talk about him." Accusation steels her soft words. "You've never cried for him."

I have no defense for that because she's right. As much as it hurt to lose Henry, as much as the pain sawed my insides, no tears ever fell. Not even at his funeral with a casket so tiny it broke me in half to think of him inside. No tears. No cracks. At first I convinced myself I was being strong for everyone else, but then I realized I *couldn't* cry. As acutely as I hurt inside, my inability to express it made me feel like a robot. Like a monster.

And that's how Yasmen looks at me now when she finally turns her head to meet my eyes. Like I'm some kind of android who couldn't possibly empathize with her human pain.

She twists her fingers in the silky fabric of her nightgown. Not nightgown. *Negligee.* Something I haven't seen in a long time. No, never. A negligee I've *never* seen. Is it new? Did she *buy* something new? A sexy, new thing? For her? For me? For us? Skimpy and barely covering her generous curves, the silk clings to the swell of her hips and strains at her breasts. She rises, abandoning the rocker and crossing the room to stand in front of me. I will myself to stay on the wall, not pounce on her the way my instincts demand. The carousel lamp casts soft lambent light across her body, touching the gentle slope of her shoulders beneath tiny straps, caressing the full roundness of her breasts and the nipples peaking beneath the silk.

I want to fuck her.

Fast. Right here. So hard and deep we'd dent the wall. I'd come quickly because it's been too long. And then we'd stumble to the bed and do it again. Slow. Savoring each other because I almost forgot the taste and sound of her pleasure. It would take all night to remind me. It's like she can read my thoughts. Promise shimmers like gold dust in her night-dark eyes. She steps so close I smell the scented oil she adds to her bath and runs through her hair. She pushes my arms down and stands flush against me, body to body. Her breasts pressed to my chest. She tips up on her toes, holds my stare, and angles her mouth to capture mine. First the top lip between hers, and then the bottom. Deliberately, she slips her tongue inside, wrenching a groan from me.

This is our ritual, this kiss. A gentle sucking. A slow, licking hunger. I love kissing her. Always have. Not as a prelude to sex. Not with her. Just the act of tasting, touching her lips, loving her one stroke and one breath at a time.

"Fuck me, Si," she gasps into my mouth, the words wreathed in mint and boldness.

Her body is fuller since the last pregnancy. Her breasts rounder, heavier. I test the weight of them in my hands and thumb her nipples reverently.

"Jesus, baby. Yes."

Those are the only words I can manage because this is all I've wanted and haven't been able to make myself ask for. Not when she's been so sad. Not when the world has been on fire and every ship sinking. I knew sex couldn't be the most important thing. Her getting better, feeling better—that was paramount. But I was wrong because this feels urgent. The scrape of her teeth across my lip—essential. The sweep of her tongue inside my mouth—necessary. Every breath feels like a gasp before dying and my heart races, speeds to catch up with the desperation of her hands caressing my chest, of her fingers, sure and steady at my zipper. I drag the silky gown up her thigh, envisioning the firm naked legs wrapped around my waist. I hesitate, knowing where I want to touch her, but still unsure that she wants it. It's been so long and this is the first time she's been interested in sex.

"Yes," she breathes, scattering kisses over my jaw, sucking at my neck. "Touch me there."

I slip my fingers over her and then inside. I pause. I know how she feels when she wants this. She's wet and slippery and slick when she wants me. And suddenly, the heat drains away. The new negligee. The way she is freshly waxed and smooth between her legs. Even the mint of her breath at midnight. It all feels calculated. Deliberate, not desperate. Wrong, not raw.

She pulls back just the smallest bit to study my face in the dim light, a frown pulling between her brows. "Come on."

"Why?" I demand, even though I know. I dread her answer, have avoided this conversation, but knew we'd have to have it. One more fight.

"Why?" She laughs, and it's breathless, nervous. She looks down at the floor, catching her bottom lip between her teeth. "I want another baby."

"No." The word torpedoes from me, startling us both. Her wide eyes meet mine. "No more babies."

No more losses. No more death. No more risk. No more grief.

"Yasmen, the doctor said—"

"What?" She inserts another inch, two between us, her frown morphing to scorn. "That it's a risk? That I might—"

"Die?" It's ejected from my soul, bounces off Henry's nursery walls. "Yeah, is that what you want this family to go through? Another death?"

She ignores that, presses back into me. In the set of her mouth, in the sureness of her hand reaching between us to grab my dick, there is a confidence that my desire, the way I always want her, will override everything else, will obliterate my objections. And there was a time when the soft femininity, the perfect weight of her against me, would have been enough, but when she reaches between us, I know what she'll find.

"What's wrong?" she asks, the smooth, beautiful face lined by consternation. "You want this."

I haven't been hard this whole time. Haven't been hard in a long time. The hungry kisses and searching tongues and ragged breaths— all real. All a cry for closeness, for intimacy, for contact we haven't had since the day she returned from the hospital with empty arms. I wanted to want it, but my body didn't respond. We've always had *this*, the fire that ignites at the slightest touch. At a glance. We've lost even that.

We are a disaster. Her, plotting to seduce me to get a baby we can never have. Me, reaching for the fire that used to spark between us, and finding only ashes. Whatever exists between us now is dry and flaccid.

"Why would you want another?" she asks, her voice climbing. "You didn't even want Henry."

"That's a lie." My anger flares at the injustice, at her well-aimed arrow. "What the hell, Yas?"

"What am I supposed to think? You weren't even there."

"That's not fair. You—" I cut myself off, draw a deep breath. "You told me to go to that convention, and you know it. You weren't due. We couldn't have known—"

"That I would almost die alone? That I would lose him on the floor?" Hysteria colors her voice in shades of sorrow. "That I would—"

I pull her close, hold her the way I wasn't there to do when it counted. She hates me for not being there when she needed me? Not as much as I hate myself.

She jerks in my arms, struggling like I'm constraining her, not comforting.

"Let me go. I don't want you to touch me."

My arms abruptly fall away. "That was fast. A minute ago you were begging me to fuck you."

"I want a baby, Si." Tears water her words even as they grow louder. "Just give me another baby and we—"

"And so I'm what? Your stud horse or your husband?"

"You're being unreasonable. You want to fight. I just want to—"

"To fuck, I got that. So you can have a baby, no matter what I want. No matter the risk. Despite what the doctor said."

"I've talked to the doctor again and she—"

"Without me? You consulted the doctor about having another baby without even discussing this with me?"

I grab her hand and pull her from the nursery, down the hall, the stairs, through the living room and kitchen to the garage. Away from our kids' curious ears, this has become our boxing ring. Where, when our icy silences crack, we come to scream and screech. Yasmen's Acura

MDX sits prettily beside my Range Rover in our garage, in our elite zip code, and it should be the stuff of our dreams. But it's instead a deep freezer, stuffed with metal monsters whose headlights glare at our inadequacies and scowl at how naive we were to think this would ever be enough.

"We're not having another baby, Yas."

My voice comes out hard, unyielding. I can't lose one more thing. One more person. I can't lose *her*. I wouldn't survive it.

"It's not happening," I snap. "And I can't believe after all this family's been through, you'd even consider it."

"We said we wanted a big family. You don't want that anymore?"

"We can have as big a family as you want." I take her hand. "We can foster, adopt—"

"No." She jerks away, removes herself from me, walking around to the other side of her car, staring at me over the roof, incongruous in her gown, surrounded by the leaf blower and the water hose and the lawn mower. "I want...I need..."

She shakes her head, her expression frustrated. I know what she wants. A do-over. A chance to feel a baby kicking, moving inside of her. To see that baby leave her body alive. Not the way Henry came. Still. His soul already fled.

"Having another baby won't fix what's wrong, Yas."

"What's wrong?" Her laughter bites into the chilly air. "You mean what's wrong with me."

"I didn't say anything was wrong with you, but hiding up in that nursery all the time isn't helping. Rushing to have another baby won't help."

"I'm hiding? Who lives at Grits because he doesn't even know how to be in this house anymore? And it's not just Henry. You haven't slowed down since Byrd died. You've been in constant motion. Never even taking the time to grieve. You didn't cry for her either."

"Stop it."

"You need to hear this. Maybe I am stuck, Si. Maybe I can barely leave the house most days, and maybe I am going crazy."

"I never said you were going crazy."

"Well, it feels like it, but at least I'm letting myself feel it all. Every bit of it. They deserve that, both of them. I'm not afraid to mourn, to hurt, to grieve."

"You don't think I hurt?" Anger, disbelief, resentment crack my words down the middle. "Because I don't huddle in the dark every day, barely able to function? I don't hurt?"

"Shut up!" The pain in her eyes slices right through me, echoes around us, absorbed by the shelf-lined walls of the garage.

"We can't afford for us to both break down," I plow on, fueled by my own defenses. "Who do you think is keeping a roof over our fucking heads?"

I slam my hand on the hood of the car between us.

"Me! Keeping the doors of our business open? Me!"

"You've got it all under control, Si! Why do you need me?"

"I don't."

The words come out before I have time to think about the effect they'll have. How they'll land in the cold trapped in these four walls with nowhere to go.

"Right," she says, her laugh void of humor. "Because you have the whole world running like a well-oiled machine."

"A well-oiled machine?" I yank the notice from the door out of my pocket and hold it out toward her, clutched in my fist. "We can't even afford to get our damn lawn mowed, Yas. The restaurant is bleeding money and the mediocre cook we do have put in her notice. I'm working fifteen-hour days."

There's shock in the eyes flitting from my face to the paper crushed in my hands.

"Why did you keep all of this from me?" she asks, her tone hollow. "Because I'm so crazy, so fragile I'd break?"

"Kept this from you? It's been months, months, baby, since you've shown interest in anything," I point over our heads. "Except that damn nursery. Barely paying attention to the kids."

"I take care of my children!" The words ring loud and shrill. "You have no idea what it takes to even get out of bed most mornings, but I do it. Everything hurts, but I keep doing it."

I'm silenced by the sound of her grief, at how deep her pain goes. How encompassing it is. Still.

"And I've tried with you, but you're never here. You're off saving the world, so we'll all be grateful. Well, guess what, Si?" She storms over to the garage door in a flourish of silk and fury. "I'm not grateful. I'm tired."

"Of me?" I demand of her back. "You're tired of me?"

She looks over the smooth brown curve of one shoulder and doesn't answer with words, but the resentment, the anger festering in her eyes, confesses the truth. She walks through the garage door and into the house without a reply.

And it's too much. Her indifference, her bitterness. My body refusing to cooperate, refusing to do what it's supposed to do. It won't cry when people die. It's not erect when my nearly naked wife whom I love like my own breath touches me, kisses me. Fury spikes through my blood. It runs hot and quicksilver from my heart to my hands and feet. I stride to the row of cabinets along the garage wall and jerk open a door, scanning the contents until I find what I'm looking for. A paintbrush—and a can of pink paint left over from redecorating Deja's room. I grab it by the handle, feeling the heft of a half-full can, and charge through the garage door and into the kitchen. Sheer rage and adrenaline propel my tired legs up the steps two at a time and down the hall to the nursery. Sure enough, she's there again, curled up in the rocker with a blanket draped over her scantily clad body. Wordlessly, I walk over to the wall bearing the verse and, with one swift stroke of the paintbrush, slash through the words.

"What are you doing?" Yasmen rushes over, reaching for the brush, which I hold over my head, out of her reach. I quickly slap the brush against the wall, dragging it over the wishes we had for Henry that died with him.

Yasmen cries, heaving against me, beating my chest, slapping at my back. "I hate you. I can't believe you..."

I wrap myself around her, circling her, pinning her arms to her sides, pressing her to the wet wall, heedless of the pink paint staining her negligee, my suit.

"I don't want this anymore," she says, tears streaking down her cheeks. "We can't do this. I want...I need a divorce."

I go completely still, blood freezing in my veins at the word I never expected to hear from her.

Till the wheels fall off.

"You don't mean that." I swallow against the hot lump in my throat. The tears may finally come.

"I only know that I'm so sad all the time. It hurts all the time." Her shoulders shake with sobs, her face twisted with the violence of her emotions. "I wonder if the sad I'd be without you would hurt less than the way I'm sad with you."

"I make you hurt?"

"Yes," she whispers, closing her eyes over the tears trickling down her cheeks.

"You don't love me anymore?"

"I can't find it. I can't find *us.* It's buried under all this pain."

"It's not buried. I don't have to look for it. I don't want a divorce. I love you, Yas, and you love me. We are going through a hard time, but we said till the wheels fall off."

"Look at us," she says, glancing down to where I press her body into the wet wall. "Did you hear us tonight? Is this what we want our kids to see? I said I hated you, but I don't. Not yet, but if we keep on like this, I will, Si. And you'll hate me."

"I could never hate you." I brush my knuckle over her damp cheek. "I will love you until I die. We said till death do us part."

"Death *is* tearing us apart." Her laugh is bitter and short. "We assumed it would have to be our deaths that ended this. Turns out it was theirs."

"We said vows."

"Those are words, not walls. They don't defend. They don't enforce. They don't protect us from life. From pain. From how things change. And I don't want to stay in this just because we said we would. I need to stop hurting, and being with you? It hurts now."

The words stab through me with the sharpness of truth. I hear in her voice that she believes it. Of all the things that hurt her, being with me is what hurts most. She strains against my arms, trying to leave, and I instinctively tighten them around her, holding her to me, pinning her to the wall.

"Let me go," she whispers, the tears thick in her voice and shiny on her cheeks. She doesn't just mean in this moment. She means for good, and as strong as I've been through everything—losing Byrd, losing Henry, the struggle to keep our business—I don't know that I'm strong enough to let Yasmen go.

Our gazes lock, and the sadness in her eyes swallows the gold. I used to think the lighter flecks in her dark eyes meant she could shine even in the darkest night. Now there's no light in the eyes raised to mine. Her bottom lip quivers, and she bites down, fighting back more tears. My arms ache from the tension of holding her, trapping her.

I slowly ease up, step back, giving her room to move. She leaves the circle of my arms immediately, heading for the door. She looks at the wall, and so do I—at the hot pink streaks of obnoxious optimism through the dark gray paint, obscuring the verse. Shame curdles in my belly. Of course, we need to move on, and part of that will be repurposing this room, but the way I did this in a fit of anger, a surge of rage, it feels like I erased him. Paint slides down the wall in clumpy rivulets, weeping along the surface unchecked and staining the carpet. It's a wailing wall. Even this flat, inanimate thing can weep, but I can't.

"I meant it, Si," she says softly, but with enough resolve that the words sink to the very bottom of my heart, chained to an anchor. "I want a divorce."

The room is as still and airless as a tomb, and I can't breathe. The impossible truth of what she's asking me to do, to give up, lands on me with boulder force. I stagger to the rocker, sink into its cushions, aching for the son I never got to meet. I held him once, his little body holding on to the last of its warmth, to the residue of life. My teeth clench against the feral scream caged in my throat, and despite all my efforts—in spite of all the ways I've held things together—I feel myself coming apart at the seams. The very fabric of my life, every part that matters, ripping. I set the rocker in motion, hoping for some magic in the back and forth, but there is no soothing this. Not even a false comfort to be found, so I stop, but can't make myself move from this spot. I sit here, where I've come home so many nights and found Yasmen exactly like this. Immobile and staring at a wall of dead wishes.

CHAPTER FOURTEEN

YASMEN

It sounds like things are going well," Dr. Abrams says, her intelligent eyes peering at me from the screen of my laptop.

We usually meet in her office, but she's out of town this week. Thank God for teletherapy. We only have a few minutes left in our session, and that same sense of peace I usually experience after our time together permeates the brightness of my home office.

"I think so, yeah." I smile and toy idly with a stack of paper clips on my desk. "I forgot to tell you I'm working with the Skyland Association again. We've had two events, and they went well."

"That's so good, Yasmen." She sits back, folds her arms and smiles. "You should be proud of yourself. You've come a long way."

When I first started with Dr. Abrams, I couldn't envision waking up excited or making it through the day without crying at least once. That kind of depression is blunter than sadness. Sharper than misery. It is the impenetrable dark of midnight deepened with the blackest strokes of blue—a bruise on your spirit that seems like it will never fade. Until one day...it finally does. With the help of the woman on-screen, it did.

It is not an exaggeration to say Dr. Abrams—with her always-on-point silk-pressed hair, fashionable blouses and pencil skirts, and watching, wise eyes—changed my life. I trust her implicitly, and she has taught me more about trusting myself.

"How are things with the kids?" she asks. "How's Deja?"

I sigh, rolling my eyes, but allowing a tiny smile. "She's testing my limits and working my nerves."

"That's what they do," Dr. Abrams chuckles.

"I'm trying to be sensitive to all the transition she's experienced, but sometimes she just makes me so mad, and I snap at her."

"You're not a robot. You're human. Let her see that, and just apologize when you should. Move on, but let her know just because you make mistakes doesn't mean she should be allowed to do anything she wants. You're her mother, not a saint. All you can do is love her and try to make things right when you get them wrong."

"I know, but it gets hard sometimes. She's defiant and rude and mean to me and…ugh. I guess lots of parents deal with teenagers acting out, but this feels like more."

"It probably *is* more," Dr. Abrams says. "Your family's been through a lot, and it came during a very formative time of her life."

"So she has a get-out-of-jail-free card for how long?" I joke. "'Cause I'm coming to the end of my patience."

"Just keep the lines of communication open. She doesn't get a free pass, but she should get understanding. You still have to parent her. You still have to set those limits we discussed, and when she crosses them, you still need to enforce consequences." She pauses, canting her head. "And how is her relationship with your ex-husband?"

I lower my lashes, studying the desk at the mention of Josiah. "Um… better than mine. She barely blinked when he started dating someone."

"Josiah's dating?" I glance up to find Dr. Abram's gaze sharper on my face. "How do you feel about that?"

"Fine with me," I say, shrugging, my nonchalance belied by the pen gripped tightly between my fingers.

Her lips part, poised to probe, if I know her as well as I think I do, but she frowns down at the watch on her desk. "I have another appointment, but next time I'd like to hear more about this new phase you and Josiah are entering."

"Of course," I say quickly, smiling my relief. "Next time."

She angles a knowing glance at me, her lips bending into the slightest smile. "Take care, Yasmen."

We sign off, and I slump into my seat. Dr. Abrams has a way of digging past all my protective layers until she reaches the truth. And when it comes to how Josiah dating is affecting me, I'm not sure I want to examine the truth right now.

I stand and stretch, grabbing the watering can from beneath my desk and walking over to the fiddle-leaf fig tree in front of my window. I glance around the office, noting the plants hanging and the ones perched on the edges of my desk. We have plants everywhere in the house now. Dr. Abrams suggested growing them as an activity to help motivate me when I was at my lowest. I had my kids to take care of, and then I had my plants. I'm rubbing a waxy green leaf when my cell phone rings. I walk over and grab it from the desk, glancing at the screen to see who's calling.

"Hey, Seem," I say. "What do you—"

"Mom, I left it at the house," he says in a rush, panic zipping through his words. "Can you bring it? I thought I had it, but I—"

"Kassism, slow down." I grip the phone between my ear and my shoulder, setting the watering can on the desk. "First of all, why are you calling me and not in class?"

"We're in between. The robot I built for my science assignment," he says, breathing as if he just ran to school. "I left the remote at Dad's house. Can you bring it?"

"When do you need it?"

"Now. Like right now, Mom."

"Did you try your father?"

"Three times. It rolls right into voice mail."

"Well, Grits is closed on Mondays, and he has that standing basketball game. His phone's probably in his locker."

"You have a key to his house, right? Can't you go get it and bring it to me?"

I do have a key, and of course, I've been inside the house…when

Byrd lived there, but I don't want to disrespect Josiah's space by going in when he's not there.

"Let's give your father a minute to reply. He always has his phone on him, so soon he'll—"

"Mom, please. I want to test it at lunch before I have to present it in class."

Lawd.

"Okay, Seem. I'll try your dad one more time—"

"But—"

"And if he doesn't answer, I'll go over and grab the remote. Where is it?"

"Yes!" I can practically see his fist pump. "You can't miss it. It's on the desk in my room."

"Got it. I'll text you when I'm on my way. Now get to class."

Once we disconnect, I immediately dial Josiah. Sure enough, it goes to voice mail after a few rings, and his deep voice rumbles over the line. Even in his message he sounds as if you have about three seconds of his attention. Short. Bordering on curt, albeit sexy as hell.

This has to stop.

"Um, hey." My cheeks heat as if I'm standing right in front of him instead of the disembodied voice-mail version. "It's me. Kassim left his robot remote or whatever at your house. He needs it."

I laugh and bite my lip. "You'd think he's Tony Stark and that remote is the key to saving the world or something the way he's panicking, so he wants me to get it. I don't want to roll up in your house when you're not there."

I glance at the top right of my laptop to check the time.

"But he wants to test it at lunch, so I'd need to leave now if I'm gonna get to Harrington in time. Call me if you get this. Otherwise, I'm on my way over to grab it for him."

I run a quick hand over my hair. I've already been out, of course, because I took the kids to school, but it was one of those sunglasses and slap cap days.

"You're not going to see him," I mutter, even as I put on a little mascara and tinted lip gloss.

I grab my purse and keys, walking swiftly to the garage.

"And even if you were," I remind myself in the rearview mirror as I back into the driveway. "It's not like that. You need to get this under control."

What more do I need to see to understand that Josiah has moved on, and it's time for me to do the same?

I pull into the driveway of his stout dark blue craftsman house with the pale gray shutters. It has nowhere near the square footage of our house, but it accommodates a bedroom for each kid and a bonus room in the basement Josiah uses as an office when he's not at Grits. He doesn't have a garage, but just a covered space for his car. The Rover's not parked out front, confirming that he's not home. Instead of ringing the doorbell, I use my key to let myself in. I automatically turn to disarm the system on the wall with the passcode, Byrd's birthday, but it doesn't beep.

"Getting careless in your old age, Si?" I look around the foyer to note the changes. Josiah has, understandably, redecorated the place.

"Very Restoration Hardware," I say as I pass the living room with its sleek lines and textured finishes. A bottle of wine and two glasses sit on the table in the center of the room. One guess who that other glass was for.

"Let me get out of here before my imagination starts filling in the gaps."

Deja's and Kassim's bedrooms are down the hall directly across from each other, so I march in that direction. As soon as I walk into Kassim's room, I spot the remote on his desk.

Grabbing it, I turn to leave, but halt when I catch sight of the photo tucked into the corner, sandwiched between the pristine Rubik's Cube Kassim refuses to touch, referring to it as "vintage," and his Black Panther bobblehead still unopened in its box. It's the last family portrait we ever took. We're outdoors and Kassim looks so young, his smile wide and careless, like now, but with missing teeth. Deja was still in elementary school, and only looking at this photo do I fully grasp her innocence—an emotional purity, something untouched by pain and loss and grief. Deja stares out at the world now with fewer illusions. There's an unguardedness to the young girl in the photo with pigtails brushing the shoulders of her Disney *Descendants* T-shirt.

I want to reach into that photo and hold my children tight, shield them from the pending storm none of us saw coming.

My eyes shift, almost reluctantly, to Josiah. He's standing behind me, and my head rests back on his shoulder in easy intimacy. Our fingers link across my stomach, and there's a secret contentment to us. We hadn't even told the kids yet I was pregnant with Henry, and in this frozen moment, we were the only two people on the planet who knew. We wanted to keep and nurture this secret for ourselves as long as we could. My whole world fit on this four-by-six photo, the boundaries of my happiness inside this frame.

Reminiscing, second-guessing, *remembering*...I don't have the time and I haven't come far enough to look back this way. This day, though years ago, still feels too close. If I close my eyes, I'll feel the crisp autumn air, see the color-splattered leaves, smell the man standing behind me, and taste my future. I swipe impatiently at the tears I hadn't even realized trickled over my cheeks and pull up short to find Vashti standing in the door. We both jump like we've seen ghosts.

"Oh, my God," she laughs, pressing a hand to her chest. "I thought I heard someone. You scared me to death."

"I'm sorry. I..." The words dry on my tongue when I take in what she's wearing.

The hem of Josiah's white dress shirt hits her leanly muscled legs a few inches above her knees. It's unbuttoned just below her bare breasts. She's one of those girls I envied growing up, with the perky tits that barely constitute a palmful and who can go out without a bra.

"I didn't expect anyone," Vashti says, mascara from the night before smudged beneath her eyes and her lips still faintly pink with vestiges of color. "Josiah has a standing Monday morning—"

"Basketball game, yeah."

I want to scream at her that I know his schedule, his life, better than she does. That I know *him* better than she does, but she knew him last night in a way I have not in a very long time. Intimately. Carnally.

Fuckily.

"I'm sorry if I startled you," I continue, not wanting to appear rattled. "Kassim left his remote thingy…um…for the science fair, I mean project. Assignment. It's an assignment, not a fair. Or a project. And so…he called and I came because Josiah isn't here. So…yeah."

Well, that was composed. Not rattled at all.

"Right." Vashti nods slowly, her eyes never leaving my face. "Look, I know this is kind of awkward."

"What? Noooooo." I laugh, scoff even. "Why would it be awkward?"

"Because I'm the first person Josiah's dated since the divorce?"

I hate how gentle her voice is, like I need to be handled with care. Like I'm fragile when she has no idea what I can endure, what I've survived. What I'm capable of.

What I've lost.

The expression on her face is so damn soft, so sympathetic, like this is fucking *Family Feud* and I just got three strikes. Like I'm watching from the wings while she's out there with Steve Harvey playing for a Lincoln Town Car and a trip to Hawaii.

"It's not awkward at all." The habit of lying returns to me easily and just in time. "Vashti, really. I'm happy Josiah found someone so great. And someone the kids love."

"I'm sure he's told you that we've talked about the work dynamic, and if you're worried about it affecting things at the restaurant—"

"I'm not. You're both mature adults, and I know Josiah would never do anything to jeopardize the business."

"Neither would I. If something gets weird, we end it, but I'm just glad right now everything's going so well. You know firsthand how amazing Josiah is."

"Yeah, he's great," I whisper, clutching the remote to my chest like a breastplate in battle. "Well, I better get this to Kassim."

I walk toward the door, but she doesn't move right away, so I have to stand there, smelling him on her. Subjected to his cologne mixing with whatever perfume she favors. A fist tightens around my traitor heart. I'm close enough to see his initials on the cuffs that hang loose past one of her hands. These tiny intimacies feel like treasures she stole from me, but no. I gave them away, and it hits me like a ton of bricks that I have no rightful claim to any of the emotions whirling inside of me. I forfeited my right to be indignant or jealous or resentful. The only feeling I'm entitled to is this hollowness occupying the pit of my belly, yawing in my chest.

It feels like *my* walk of shame as I brush past her and down the hall, averting my eyes so I don't spot a hickey on her neck or further evidence of their night together. The Josiah I remember, before our marriage became an icebox, was one second aggressive, the next tender. He knew when to be gentle, and when to be rough. He used to say he could look into my eyes and know how I wanted it.

What did Vashti's eyes tell him last night?

"I'll let Josiah know you came by," she says, following me to the door.

"I left him a voice mail, but thanks." I don't wait for her response and call out over my shoulder. "Bye!"

I force myself to walk at a leisurely pace to the driveway. I start the car and pull out, careful not to hit any trash cans or mailboxes as I go. I don't know how I get onto the interstate, but I manage to take the correct exit for Harrington. After I've dropped off the remote at the front desk, I text Kassim to make sure he knows it should be there, and I turn out of the school parking lot. My phone ringing through the car's system startles me so badly I almost run a light.

Josiah's name appears on the display.

I inhale and exhale once deeply before answering.

"Hey!" I bend the word to my will, shaping it into a cheerful thing. "How are you?"

"Good. Just leaving the gym. Sorry I missed your call. I got your message about Kassim's remote. I can grab it and take it to him."

"No need. I swung by the house and used my key. I actually just dropped it off to him at school, so all's well."

His pause blares in the quiet as the implications of my words no doubt sink in.

"You went to *my* house?" he asks, cautious, as if there is still a way I may not know he's fucking his new girlfriend.

"I did." My press-play chuckle sounds like a sitcom laugh track, tinny and forced and on cue. "I hope I didn't scare poor Vashti too bad."

"So she was still there when you—"

"Yup." I clip the word, snipping any telling emotion from it. "Look, I've gotta go because I need to turn in these projections for the block party."

"Oh, yeah. Do you need any—"

"Nope. I'm good. I just..." I blow out a long breath through my mouth and blink my stinging eyes. I'm not sure how much longer I can keep my voice steady and my eyes dry. "I just gotta go, okay?"

"Yeah, sure. Look, Yas, about—"

"Sorry, Si. I really gotta go."

Instead of waiting for him to speak again, I hang up. The sign for the interstate looms up ahead, and I know I'd be a mess in Atlanta traffic right now. Do I take a moment to absorb this new development? Or do I do what I've always done? Just keep going, ignore the pain slicing through my middle, and force myself to drive the few miles home. Dr. Abrams often talks about the danger of pushing through my emotions, but I think if I don't push through, don't ignore this, it could get really ugly.

And then God gives me a sign.

It's big, red and white, and shaped like a bull's-eye.

Instead of merging onto the interstate, I pull into the parking lot of Target, turn off the car, press my forehead to the steering wheel, and cry.

I haven't sobbed like this in a long time. Sometimes it's good to cry. It makes us feel better to cleanse our system. This isn't one of those times. Every tear feels like it's being wrung from my body. My heartbeat is the *tick-tick* of a bomb, counting down to the moment when the pressure proves too much and I detonate. I can't pretend that him giving his body to someone else doesn't hurt. It's to be expected, right? It doesn't mean I still love him. This feels like not the end, but the beginning of something. Not for me, but for him. The newness of someone else's head on his pillow. Of her forgetting her toothbrush and using his, not knowing how much he would hate that. Some other woman discovering his coffee is perfect with one and *about* a quarter spoons of sugar. Her fingers, not mine, finding the knots in his neck when he stresses out. Him yielding all the secrets it took me years to discover.

Yes, it hurts that Josiah is sleeping with someone else.

No, I don't want to fully examine why it feels like a betrayal, even though there's nothing stopping him from having someone different in his bed every night should he so choose.

I told myself leaving him would make the hurt stop, so why does this hurt so bad? The pain and the implications of it are too much to process, so I reach for an easier emotion. Anger. He's getting his? I'm getting mine.

I take the cell phone out of my purse, pulling up the text Mark sent me last week.

Me: Hey! You still want to do dinner Thursday night?

I stare at the phone and hold my breath for a few seconds before the bubbles appear.

Mark: I'd love to. What time should I pick you up?

Me: Seven. I'll see you then.

CHAPTER FIFTEEN

∞

JOSIAH

D_ammit._"
 I stare at my phone and resist the urge to punch the locker. That's not how I wanted Yasmen to find out Vashti and I took our relationship to the next level. If I'm being honest, I didn't ever want to discuss it with her. It's not her business what I do. I did want to avoid awkwardness like what just happened at my house. And maybe on some level, I didn't want to hurt her. Not that Yasmen still wants me, but if the shoe were on the other foot...I wouldn't have wanted to be blindsided like this.

I'd be fucked up.

"Why you mad?" Charles "Preach" Hollister, my friend of nearly twenty years, asks. "Your team won, but only because Kevin was sick. He'll be back next Monday and we—"

"It's not the game." I zip my duffle bag and slam the locker door. "It's...never mind."

"The kids?" Preach frowns, leaning against the neighboring locker. "Seem? Day?"

"Nah. The kids are fine. Everything's cool."

Preach, so nicknamed after he went through an intense, albeit short-lived religious phase second semester freshman year, studies my face. I'm not sure the mask I've pulled in place hides anything from him, not after all we've been through.

"I hope this therapist of yours can get you to open up," Preach says, grabbing his own duffel and closing the locker.

I sigh and hoist the bag to my shoulder, still shocked at how much I revealed to Dr. Musa in our first session. There was just something…liberating? Freeing? *Right* about telling this stranger everything. Nothing changed, but somehow I felt better. I don't completely understand it, but after all the shit of the last few years, feeling better is worth something.

"I have another session in a few days," I tell Preach.

"Long overdue, you ask me."

"Pretty sure I didn't, and remind me, what's your therapist's name again?"

"Well, I, you know—"

"Right. You don't have one, so stop talking about all the therapy *I* need."

"I get my stuff out. Me and Liz, we talk about everything."

"We don't all have a wife who doubles as a counselor," I say with telltale bitterness.

Preach winces. "Sorry. I wasn't thinking. You and Yas—"

"Did *not* talk about everything. That's ancient history. You know that, so don't feel bad because you and Liz got it good."

"I do worry about you, bruh, keeping all that shit locked up inside."

"Am I constipated or emotionally stunted?" I ask, managing to crack a smile.

"You keep eating Vashti's macaroni and cheese, you'll be both. That girl can cook," he says and chuckles, leaning against the locker. "This got anything to do with her?"

Do I really want to do this? Crack open this can of worms with Preach, who will keep pressing until my intestines are spilled on the floor? And the hell if I feel like being emotionally disemboweled at the gym.

"That was Yas," I admit grudgingly. "She needed to swing by my house to get something for Kassim's science presentation. She let herself in and…"

I blow out a distended breath. "Vashti was still there from last night."

"Oh, shit!" He straightens from his indolent slump against the locker, eyes alert and a mischievous grin splitting his face. "Like Vashti spent the night, and your ex-wife saw her there? And now she know y'all fucking."

"Fucked, not fucking. Last night was the first time."

"But I mean, you're dating. Not like y'all gon' stop now that the deed's done." His grin widens. "And how was it?"

As close as Preach and I are, I never shared details about sex when I was with Yasmen. He said it was one of the ways he knew how serious it was, because in college, we one-upped each other in our escapades and always jockeyed for bragging rights. Until last night, I hadn't been with anyone other than Yas since college.

How was it?

It had been a long-ass time since I'd had sex, so of course it felt good to have something other than my hand. It was a release.

But after it was over, with Vashti beside me, I stared up at the ceiling and something cracked inside. The last bit of feeling? The last shred of hope that maybe someday…Nah. I stopped thinking Yasmen and I would reconcile long ago. I stopped wanting it. I could never trust her with my heart, with my happiness, again, but maybe some renegade, obstinate sliver of my soul still felt tethered to her. Even though we're divorced, that small, stupid part of me felt like I betrayed Yasmen when I slept with Vashti.

I've been quiet too long, and the eager look on Preach's face turns suspicious.

"It wasn't good?" he asks. "With Vashti? Don't worry. I've heard men fresh out of the joint say sometimes that first time you fuck a woman—"

"Preach, don't be disrespectful. We're too old for that shit. It was fine."

"You know I meant no disrespect. You ain't been with anyone

besides Yas in a long time, so I was asking." His eyes narrow. "And fine? It was *fine*? Vashti's a beautiful woman, and a blind bat can see she's into you, so *fine* sounds a little underwhelming."

"I'm not going into detail with you. I wasn't even gonna tell your crazy ass." I chuckle against my will. Preach has that effect. "I better get going." I dap him up, forcing a smile. "I'm bringing Kassim to the shop soon."

"'Bout damn time. That boy's probably got baby locs it's been so long since he had a haircut."

"Not quite, but Yas'll nag him and me to death if I don't handle it."

"Get him in first thing before the day gets started good. You know the shop be jumping on Saturdays."

"Bet."

And still thinking about the night with Vashti and the awkward call today with Yasmen, I leave.

CHAPTER SIXTEEN

YASMEN

I'm dreading this phone call. My last conversation with Josiah was awkward as hell. I'm cringing, thinking of how Vashti probably relayed our encounter.

"No time like the present," I mutter, pulling my cell phone from the side pocket of my yoga pants and dialing.

"Yas, hey," Josiah says, picking up on the first ring, but sounding like I only have half his attention. "What's up?"

"Um, are you busy? If you're in the middle of—"

"Hold on." There's silence for a few seconds before I hear a door close on the other end. "Sorry. I was out in the dining room. I'm in the office now. You need something?"

"I'm going out tonight, and I thought I'd be fine leaving the kids because Clint and Brock would be home, but Brock has a work thing they have to attend so—"

"I can come over, or the kids can come to my place. Whatever."

"Well, it's a school night, and I'll have to take them in the morning, so maybe just pop in to check on 'em here? Deja's old enough. I just...you know what I mean?"

"It's not a problem. I'll swing by. Another girls' night out? A birthday?"

For some reason, I hadn't expected him to ask. He hasn't demonstrated much curiosity about my social life in the past, what there was of it.

"No, actually"—I walk into the kitchen and take a high stool at the counter—"I have a date."

The silence that follows is how a cigar must feel inside a humidor. Complete quiet sealed in an airtight box.

"A date." It sounds like he's testing the word for its authenticity. "Wow. Who's the lucky guy?"

"Mark Lancaster."

"Figures," he says, the word riding a derisive breath.

"What do you mean, *figures*?"

"Come on, Yas. Dude's up on you every time he comes around. He hasn't tried to hide it."

"Maybe I like bold. I don't have to wonder where I stand or what he wants."

"And what do you think he wants?"

"A date. Obviously."

"With guys like him, nothing's ever obvious."

"Guys like him? I need you to elaborate because I'm not sure what you—"

"Rich guys, Yas. Privileged men used to getting what they want whenever they want all the time."

"Some might argue, considering the car you drive, the neighborhood you live in, the clothes you wear, and the cash you drop on sneakers without blinking, that you're a rich guy yourself."

"You know what I mean."

"You mean white?"

"No. That's not what I mean. I don't want to get in your business—"

"And yet, I'm getting a definite all-up-in-my-business vibe when I have been very careful to stay the hell out of yours."

"So that's what this is? Tit for tat? I start dating Vashti so you go out and grab the first man who shows any interest?"

"Trust me, he is not the first to show interest."

"I only meant that—"

"He's just the first I've accepted. And I *know* you are not insinuating I'm going out with Mark because you're dating now."

A tiny voice in my head reminds me I didn't give Mark's offer much serious thought until I saw Vashti at Josiah's place. But still, Josiah doesn't get to say that to me.

"I didn't mean to imply that, but I know it was obvious Vashti had spent the night and—"

"I'm not doing this with you," I say, taking a rolling pin to the words and flattening them into a tone so even that only I know what it costs me.

He pauses, letting the dust settle on all the things we hurled at each other before going on. "And I don't have time to do this with you," he finally replies, the words clipped by impatience. "What time are you leaving the house? I'll swing by to check on the kids."

"Seven."

"Cool. Gotta go."

I plop the cell phone onto the counter and drop my head into my hands. "Well, that went great."

I don't have much time to dwell on the argument because soon it's time for car pool and fighting traffic to pick the kids up on time. Fortunately, there's no soccer practice tonight. On the way home, I send a sideways glance to Kassim in the passenger seat and watch Deja in the rearview mirror.

"So I'm going out tonight, guys," I say, keeping my voice casual. "But your dad will come through to check on you."

"We'll be fine by ourselves," Deja says, a defensive note creeping into her usual deliberate indifference. "I'm almost fourteen."

"I know." I shift my gaze from the road to meet her eyes in the mirror for a quick second. "But Clint and Brock won't be next door, so your dad'll just poke his head in maybe on his way home."

"Where are you going?" Kassim asks.

I could lie. Skirt the truth. Avoid with a vague response, but why? With Vashti, they've demonstrated they have no problem seeing their parents date other people. Besides, Mark is picking me up from the house, and I don't want the kids thrown off when the guy whose face is plastered all over campaign commercials shows up to take their mother out.

"I actually have a date."

Judging by the shocked silence following my words, you would think I'd said I was joining Elon Musk on his next trip to Mars.

"Who is it?" Kassim asks, his voice tighter, more subdued.

I hazard a glance over at him, and something in his eyes squeezes my heart. Disappointment? Sadness? I don't know, but it's definitely not his usual optimism.

"It's Mark Lancaster."

"The white guy with the goofy signs all over the neighborhood?" Deja snorts, and puts on her best WAVE voice when she parrots Mark's campaign slogan. "*Lancaster Can.*"

"He's very nice, Day," I continue in a measured tone, taking the exit for our house. "He's picking me up at seven, and like I said, your dad will come through."

"What's for dinner?" Kassim asks.

I can't tell if he really has gotten over it that fast, and his usual *eat me out of house and home* trigger has been activated, or if he's redirecting because the topic is too uncomfortable. Either way, I welcome the change of subject.

"Leftover lasagna."

I found one of Byrd's handwritten cookbooks when we cleaned out her house. It's my personal challenge to attempt each dish at least once, starting with her famous lasagna. At first it was just to learn a few tricks in the kitchen, but every time I prepare a recipe she handwrote, I feel closer to her somehow.

"Ewwww," Deja whines from the back. "If Dad's coming, can we ask him to bring something from the restaurant?"

"Oooh, yeah." Kassim's expression morphs into excitement. "Vashti's ribs."

Fuck them ribs.

I'm so damn tired of hearing about Josiah's incredible little chef. I'm not the most accomplished cook, but last night's lasagna was great, and my kids act like I'm reheating dog food for dinner.

"If you want to," I murmur, turning into our driveway and raising the garage door. "It's fine with me. So you'll be okay while I'm gone, right?"

"Sure." Deja opens the door and gets out quickly. "We're not babies, Mom."

I need to go inside so I have plenty of time to get ready, but Kassim hasn't moved. He's just sitting in the passenger seat, fiddling with the zipper on his backpack.

"You okay, Seem?" I kill the engine and turn slightly in my seat to consider him.

"Yeah, I'm good." He draws in a sharp breath through his nose and nods.

"Look, I can imagine it's weird for you, your dad and me dating other people. Divorce is hard on everyone."

"I'm not upset that you're dating other people, and I'd rather you be divorced than fighting all the time like you used to."

I do a double take. We tried to be so careful, always bringing our arguments to the garage to protect the kids from our increasingly antagonistic exchanges. I mean, of course they heard us fighting from time to time, but Kassim makes it sound like a regular occurrence.

"When did you hear us fighting, Seem?"

"All the time." He shrugs, grabbing his backpack by the strap and opening the door. "I used to go to Deja's room and get in the bed with her sometimes because I was scared."

"Scared of what, son?"

"That you guys would get a divorce, but Deja said even if things changed, we'd always have each other, her and me."

"You still have us too." I reach over to caress his hair, badly in need of a cut.

"I know." He gives me a small smile that is much too old and knowing for his age. "But it's different now."

His wide eyes meet mine. "I mean it's fine. It's just different."

"Remember what we said? It's okay not to be okay, and you always have someone to talk to. If not your dad or me, then Dr. Cabbot. Got it?"

"Got it." He gets out, pausing at the open car door and poking his head back in, his eyes, so much like his father's, dark and earnest. "I can, um...I think I'll just have your lasagna if that's okay?"

My sweet boy. My empath.

"You don't have to eat the lasagna if you don't want it. Your dad can bring some of Vashti's—"

"No, I want your lasagna. It was good. For real." He twists his lips. "I know Deja said ewwww, but she was just being...You know."

"Yeah." I grimace, grabbing my purse and getting out of the car. "I know."

I pull the lasagna from the fridge, pop it in the oven, and dash upstairs to get ready. I wish I had more time, but it's the cheap car-wash version, with water flying at my body, hit-or-miss scrubbing and waxing, and a not-so-thorough polish at the end. I give my face a quick jade roll, hoping the cool stone will work its calming magic not only on my skin, but on my nerves.

I frown at my reflection. "But what to do with this hair?"

My regular stylist is out of town, and I didn't want to chance a blowout with someone new. One silk press set to hell degrees Celsius could wreck my curl pattern.

"Mom."

I turn from the mirror to find Deja standing in the doorway of my bathroom.

"Day, what's up?"

"I heard there's going to be a *Hotwives* reunion special filming downtown at the end of the season." She presses her hands together under her chin. "Please see if Aunt Hen can get me in? I wanna go so bad."

"Let's talk to Hendrix. If she can get you in, *and* if she'll be there, then we'll see."

That seems to mollify her for the time being and she nods, but her eyes stray to my head. A frown crinkles her brows. "What's going on up there?"

She twirls a finger in the direction of my hair-nest.

"Carmen is out of town, so I did it myself and..." I reach up to tug on a wayward curl. "You don't like it?"

"I mean, it's aight." Her crunchy face says otherwise. She steps into the bathroom and pulls at a few locks hanging rather limply around my face.

"I'd like to do better than 'aight' for my first date since..." I trail off, not wanting to open a can of worms.

"I get it, but that hairstyle ain't it."

"Any suggestions?" I ask, tying the belt of my robe tighter and propping my butt on the bathroom counter.

She eyes my hair critically. "What are you wearing?"

I point to a burnt-orange jumpsuit, which I found in the recesses of my closet, now hanging on the back of the bathroom door.

She splits a speculative glance between the outfit and me. "I'll be right back."

She returns carrying a large case by its handle. After placing it on the counter, she sets out a spray bottle, several products, and a diffuser.

"Sit." She nods to the stool in front of my vanity.

After dampening my hair and adding a few curl-enhancing products, she pulls some goopy leave-in stuff through, separates the curls, and has me flip my hair upside down while she diffuses. Staring at the final result in the mirror, I gape at how different it looks. Way better than when I do it myself for sure. Actually as good as when Carmen does it.

"Wow, Day." I stretch out one of the curls, watching it spring back. "You did a great job."

"Not done yet." She tilts her head consideringly, before digging into her magic box of hair supplies and extracting studded bobby pins. "Got these from the beauty supply store Aunt Hen took me to."

She center-parts my hair, slicking the front, and then crisscrosses the studded pins all along the flattened sides, leaving a cloud of curls floating around my ears and to my shoulders.

I grab the hand mirror from the counter and examine my hair from all angles.

"This looks fantastic." I glance back to her, a new pride swelling inside for my daughter. "You're really good at this."

"I know." She doesn't quite grin, but her lips do twitch like she's holding it back. "So you like it?"

"I do." I stand and grab the jumpsuit from the door, offering her an eager smile. "Wanna see it all together?"

The pleasure in her eyes withers as if she remembered she doesn't actually like me anymore. "Nah, but will you let me know about the *Hotwives* thing with Aunt Hen?"

I thought we were having a moment. Anytime real connection seems within grasp for us, I say something, do something—I never know what—to ruin it.

"Yeah, sure. I'll check with Hendrix and let you know." I glance at her over my shoulder, managing a smile. "Thanks for your help, Day. I love it."

She nods and turns to leave without another word. Sighing, I sit to do my makeup. The glittering bobby pins paired with gold and green eye shadow, my coppery lip color, and the bronzer on my cheeks make my face a striking palette of precious metals.

I catch a glimpse of myself in the mirror wearing only my bra and underwear. I note the ample breasts that used to feel like a plague when I was younger, the striations of tiny stretch marks around my belly button, and all the subtle and not-so-subtle changes in my body over the years. I've learned not to criticize my thighs for being too round, but to be grateful for how I've been able to stand. I slip on a strapless sculpting body shaper and step into the jumper. It has a structured bodice that lifts my breasts so they're like *hello*. The fabric, a lightweight wool and cashmere blend, hugs and skims the full curves of my hips and ass, falling in wide legs to brush the floor.

In the full-length closet mirror, the woman staring back at me is a stranger, or at the very least a long-lost person I haven't seen in what feels like forever. Confident sensuality wraps around me like an invisible cloak. The burnt orange singes the deep copper-brown of my skin, exposing the strong curves of one bare arm and shoulder. The shaper cinches my waist, making the curve from back to butt and hips more marked, highlighting the dramatic dips and angles.

So many times my eyes in the mirror were vacant or bruised with sorrow. Tonight they are clear and kohl lined, seemingly darkened by mystery and secrets, a cat-eyed stare shining with anticipation. Laughing, I rush to the bedroom and grab my phone from the nightstand to FaceTime Hendrix and Soledad like I'd promised I would. One of Soledad's girls has soccer practice tonight and Hendrix has a huge presentation tomorrow.

"Hey, ho," Hendrix says into the camera, seated at her kitchen counter with an open laptop and a bowl of pho in front of her. "Let's get the full picture."

"Show us!" Soledad says from the front seat of her car.

I prop the phone against the mirror on the bathroom counter and back up, twirling to give them the 360.

"Damn, girl!" Hendrix booms. "What you trying to do? Make the man fall in love on the first date?"

"You look fantastic, Yas." Soledad fans her face. "*Hot.*"

"You think so?" I chew my bottom lip. "I haven't been on a date in forever and I just don't know. Is it too much? Not enough?"

"It's just right," Hendrix assures. "And your hair sets it all off. You did that?"

"Deja." I pat the curls. "You like?"

"It looks great," Hendrix says. "I'm telling ya. Kid influencers are blowing up. She might be onto something with that hair thing."

"Whatever." I roll my eyes. "She needs to be onto those grades. I'm more interested in her midterms than how many followers she has."

"I hear that." Hendrix shrugs. "Just saying she does have real talent and she's great on the socials."

"Okay. Okay." I walk back to the counter and sit. "We'll talk about it later."

"Yes, later," Soledad says. "Tonight is all about you and Mark. Are you nervous?"

"Not really." I meet two sets of disbelieving eyes on-screen. "Okay. A little."

"You'll be fine," Hendrix says.

"Thanks, guys," I tell them. "Lemme bounce, but I'll let you know how everything goes."

When the doorbell rings, I gulp a huge breath into my air-starved lungs. I force myself to walk down the stairs serenely and to the foyer, pinning a bright smile on my face and opening the door.

Josiah stands on the front porch, broad and towering, the light carving shadows under his high cheekbones. Damn my ex for being this fine when I'm about to go on my first non-husband date in a decade and a half.

"Si, hey." I turn back into the foyer. "Thought you were Mark. You're early."

"Between Anthony and Vashti, everything is under control at Grits tonight." He walks in, Otis at his heels, and closes the door behind him, holding up a take-out container. "Plus, Deja texted asking me to bring her dinner."

"Leftover lasagna was good enough for Kassim, but obviously can't hold a candle to Vashti's ribs."

"Fried chicken," Josiah corrects with a faint smile. "You look…"

His eyes take their time assessing the studded pins in my curls, traversing the vibrant pantsuit molding my curves, and the glittering shoes I forced my feet into.

"Nice." He glances away, a line sketched between his brows.

"Thank you," I say, my tone wry. "No chance I'll get a big head from your effusive compliments."

"I'll leave that to your date." He walks to the bottom of the stairs and yells up, "Day, your food's here."

She barrels down to him, her face lit up like Santa just slid from the chimney.

"Dad!" Dejah rises onto her tiptoes to kiss his cheek and takes the food from him.

I can't remember the last time she greeted me like that. I know we're going through a phase, but there is a small part of me that covets the ease Deja and Josiah still share. Something soft and warm brushes my hand, and I glance down to find Otis sitting at my feet, nuzzling his sleek head into my palm.

"Hey, old friend." I scratch behind his ears, leaning down to whisper. "You're always glad to see me, huh?"

I've caught Josiah talking to Otis before. I've even teased him about it, but looking at the steady dark eyes of our dog, I can't blame him for thinking Otis understands every word, because he makes me feel more seen than I have all day.

"You are something else," I tell him with a chuckle.

The doorbell rings, and all conversation ceases, Deja and Josiah both turning their full attention on the door. With perfect timing... or imperfect, from my POV... Kassim makes his way down the stairs and sits on a step halfway down, resting his elbow on his knee and his chin in his hand like he has a courtside seat.

"Are you guys gonna just..." I lift my brows expectantly, hoping they'll scurry and give me some privacy, but no one moves. "Ugh."

Plastering on my first-date smile, I open the door. Mark Lancaster stands on the front porch holding a bouquet of flowers. An immaculately tailored dark suit and slate-colored open-collared shirt contrast with his brushed-back blond hair. Despite the weight of three sets of eyes on my back, my mood lightens with genuine pleasure at the sight of the flowers and at the sight of him. He's tall and handsome and is looking at me like he wants dessert first.

It's me. I'm dessert.

"Mark, hi." I accept the bouquet, lowering my nose to the wildflowers wrapped in paper. "These are lovely. Thank you."

"Hi, Yasmen. You look…" His blue eyes gleam, heating as they roam my face and figure, and then widen when he notices my family congregated behind me in the foyer. "Ummm, great. You look great."

"Thank you." I don't want to invite him in, not with the gang all here and clocking our every move. I turn, unseeingly shoving the flowers at the nearest Wade, which happens to be Josiah. "Could you put these in water for me? Thanks."

After a hesitation, and a long look at Mark that seems to simultaneously probe and warn, he accepts. The man's running for Congress. Does Josiah think he'll slit my throat and stuff me in the trunk of his Tesla? He's not my husband anymore. I know exactly how little he cares about who I'm dating. I also know how Vashti looks wearing nothing except his shirt. With that mental reminder, I check inside my clutch for essentials and turn to the spectators.

"You guys know Mr. Lancaster." I gesture to the tall man on the porch. "Mark, my family."

"Hi." Mark smiles, his gaze spending more time on my children and skidding across the ex-husband awkwardly hovering and holding the flowers he brought for me.

"Hello," Kassim says. "Where are you taking her?"

I cast a half-mortified, half-amused glance up the stairs at my son's serious expression.

"Um, the Rail," Mark replies. "It's this new place a little ways north."

"I read about that spot," Josiah says, interest entering his eyes. He's nothing if not a restaurateur, and the concept intrigues him. "They converted an old train into a restaurant."

Mark's smile loosens at the edges, his shoulders lowering a centimeter or two. "It's getting rave reviews."

"I heard that—"

"I'll let you know what I think," I say, interrupting Josiah. Then I turn back to Mark and nod to the front porch and my escape. "Ready?"

"Sure." His grin widens, and he gestures for me to walk ahead. Sailing out to the front porch, I close the door on the watching Wades and turn to my date with a bright smile.

"Let's go. I'm starved!"

CHAPTER SEVENTEEN

∞

YASMEN

Mark Lancaster could charm the shell off a turtle.

Classic politician, he's got the looks, and the low, smooth voice that lulls you to lean in. Wealthy. Well-dressed.

Well-hung?

Nope. Not going there. Not finding out tonight. Baby steps. Joisah may be ready for sleepovers, but I'm not. Dinner, drinks, conversation, and maybe a kiss if I'm feeling it. A peck or some tongue, I'll decide in the moment. Otherwise, this will be a chaste evening. The only thing I'm falling for tonight is the roasted chicken and garlic mashed potatoes on my plate.

"This food is amazing," I say, glancing around the train repurposed as an elegant dining room. "And this place is beautiful. Great choice."

"As the owner of one of Skyland's best restaurants," he says, his eyes smiling at me over the rim of his wineglass, "you're a hard woman to impress, but I was determined."

"My daughter would say you understood the assignment."

"The assignment?" Confusion wrinkles his brow.

"Sorry." I swallow the food and take a quick sip of water. "It's something the kids say."

"My daughter would be rolling her eyes right now that I didn't know that."

"You have a daughter? What's her name? How old is she?"

"Her name is Brenna, and she's sixteen. She hates being in the public eye for the campaign, so I try to protect her privacy. Her mother's, too, for that matter. Neither one of them signed up for office. My ex likes to say we divorced just in time so she wouldn't have to go through all this campaign stuff."

"How long have you been divorced?"

"Five years," he says. "I wasn't the best husband or father. I generally neglected my family in favor of work. My ambition paid off, but it also cost me everything. I'm still rebuilding my life."

"Is that what running for office is? You rebuilding?"

"Maybe some. My family was gone, and that left me with the business I'd poured everything into. I guess I found it wasn't as satisfying as I thought it would be, and I started wondering what else there *could* be."

"Well, you'll probably get my vote," I say, only half teasing.

"Probably?"

I laugh as he intended and shrug. "What can I say? My vote cost too many people too much for me to just give it away."

"Seriously." He tosses his napkin onto the table and leans forward, holding my eyes. "What concerns would you want to see addressed?"

"Many, but the thing I'm really curious about is how you plan to deal with gentrification."

The same groups bringing money and resources into Atlanta's historically Black communities are the same ones pushing longtime citizens out.

"I think there are solutions that can benefit all involved," he says.

"Don't get diplomatic on me." My smile holds, but stiffens. "People who have lived in those communities for decades have the right to stay there if they want, not be bullied or taxed out of them, and that's what's happening."

"My plan includes affordable housing for those being displaced and protections for most who live in those communities currently."

He grins, a rakish sketch of unnaturally white teeth that's probably been getting him in and out of trouble since high school. "We could spend the rest of the night discussing my plans for the district, but I was hoping for a night off with a beautiful woman."

I huff out a laugh and resume eating. "Sorry. Didn't mean to interrogate you."

"Hey, if I can't take it from my date, I'm not ready for the big stage." He leans back in his seat. "But I can think of a better use for our time."

His eyes wander over my face, moving to my bare shoulder and then, inevitably, as men always do, to rest on my breasts. I resist the temptation to snap my fingers and remind him that I'm up here, but what's the use of dressing to draw his attention if I can't enjoy it when I get it? It's been a long time since a man looked at me this way, not counting wolf whistles and rude comments from random men on the street. This focused, sustained, intense regard heated by desire. I let it warm my skin and I return his smile.

"So I'm your first date since the divorce," he says.

"Yes." I raise my glass and smile at him before taking a sip. "What gave it away? The Wade welcome committee assembled in my foyer? My ten-year-old demanding to know your intentions?"

"I'm pretty sure those flowers are in the trash by now."

I almost spit out my wine. "Why would you say that?"

He hesitates, narrowing his eyes and watching me closely before going on. "Do you mind if I ask what broke you and Josiah up? Everyone was shocked by it. You guys seemed so unshakable."

"We were until we weren't." I laugh bitterly. "There's no Richter scale for the size of our earthquakes, one after the other."

"You loved him," he says it as fact, not a question.

I swallow the sudden heat in my throat. "Very much."

"And he loved you."

I will love you until the day I die.

"Very much," I agree, setting my wineglass down carefully and lowering my eyes.

"I know about all the loss you guys experienced, but a couple as strong as you were, I thought it would bring you together."

"I hoped it would, but maybe we weren't okay enough at the same time to comfort each other. I know I was…not much help with the state I was in."

"Depressed?" he asks, his tone a gentle probe I can handle.

"Yeah." I smile sadly at him. "Very and for a long time. I just couldn't come out of it. Complicated grief. Depression. I've been told both. I was always able to get up and dust myself off, but after Byrd and Henry…I just couldn't. I don't really know why. My therapist says sometimes the people who are always keeping things together are the least prepared when they actually fall apart."

"That would have been a lot for anyone. We all process loss differently."

"Yeah, back then I didn't understand that while I needed to be absolutely still, Josiah had to be in motion all the time, avoiding the pain I was stuck in."

I remember the nights he'd drag himself up the steps and down the hall to the nursery, staring at me in the rocker, his weariness at a stand-off with my grief-induced lassitude. Two shipwrecked souls unable to figure out how to save each other. Both sinking.

How did I turn my first date since the divorce into an autopsy of my marriage? Everything always seems to circle back to Josiah. Not tonight.

"Let's talk about something much more pressing," I say, flashing Mark my sweetest smile. "Dessert."

CHAPTER EIGHTEEN

❦

JOSIAH

"Shouldn't you be getting ready for bed?" I ask, leaning against the doorjamb of Deja's bedroom. She's setting up her light and tripod like she's preparing to record, but it's a school night and it's getting late.

"Shouldn't you be headed home?" she counters. "Or are you waiting up for Mom?"

Smart-ass.

"I was helping your brother with homework."

Deja quirks a skeptical brow. "You were helping our resident genius with homework he could literally do in his sleep?"

"*And* we were also talking about therapy." I step deeper into her room. "He was telling me how things have been going with Dr. Cabbot and I was telling him about my sessions."

"How's it been?"

I weigh my words. Therapy may not be my bag, but based on the conversations I've had with Kassim, he's enjoying it. Thinks it's helping, and I have to agree. It's hard for me to admit even to my thirteen-year-old daughter that maybe . . . just maybe . . . I'm getting something out of therapy too.

And what does that say about me?

"Dr. Musa's cool," I say.

She sets the phone down on her desk and studies me from beneath the lacy edge of her black hair bonnet, which is decked with orange and white ghosts in honor of Halloween next week.

"You guys talk about Henry?" she asks. "And Aunt Byrd?"

My jaws clamp around the answer, and I make a conscious effort to release the words because I've discussed this so little before.

"Yeah." I clear my throat and sit on her bed, wanting to signal that I'm willing to talk more if she needs to. Even a few weeks ago, I probably would have found a way out of here, cut the conversation off at its knees. Something changed after discussing it with Dr. Musa, unpacking how losing my parents at such a young age damaged something in me that I've never acknowledged, much less repaired. It's opened the door for us to go deeper and connect that trauma to how I processed losing Aunt Byrd and Henry.

Or how I didn't process losing them at all, which seems to be the case.

Deja flips the chair at her desk around and straddles it, facing me.

"You were so strong when they died. You held everything together," she says, her young features, so like her mother's, hardening. "And Mom just fell apart. Blew everything up."

"Deja, what did I tell you about saying things like that about your mom? She did her best. We all did. Grief looks different for everyone. You saw her as falling apart and me as strong, when maybe she was doing something I wasn't able to do."

I swallow and look down at my linked hands, elbows on my knees.

"Maybe she was *feeling* it. Accepting that they were gone when on some level I couldn't. Doing what it took for her to heal." I meet the dredges of resentment in Deja's eyes. "That takes strength."

I'm not sure I believed that when we were going through it. Did I make Yasmen feel weak? With my expectations? With my impatience to get our lives back and to move on, with my inability to deal with all we had lost, did I *add* to Yasmen's pain?

"You don't have to defend her, Dad. I was there."

"There?" I frown at her use of the word. "Where? You were where, Day?"

Standing and turning her back to me, she flicks off the tripod light and folds the legs in. "I just meant the divorce and all that happened. I saw it for myself."

She walks toward the bed, yawning and not looking at me.

"You're right," she says, turning back her comforter. "It's late. Night, Dad."

Did my daughter just dismiss me?

She straightens her bonnet and climbs into bed, drawing the sheer canopy suspended over her pillow and headboard, so I'm left seeing a vague shape topped with ghosts and goblins.

"Could you turn off the big light, Daddy?" she asks.

Definitely dismissed.

I don't call her on the avoidance tactic, but make a note to get to the bottom of her resentment toward Yasmen. I can't just put it down to typical teenage angst anymore.

I turn off the light and close the door behind me. I make my way down the stairs, pausing on the bottom step at the sound of Clint and Brock's garage door lifting. With our next-door neighbors home, I can leave without worrying about the kids, but I don't move.

Am I waiting up for Yasmen?

She should be home soon, right? It's a school night.

"Bruh, she's not sixteen," I say as I enter the kitchen. "And you're not her daddy."

I stop by the dog bed in the corner of the kitchen, where Otis lies curled up and drowsing, and pat my leg for him to come. You'd think I asked him to run a marathon instead of walk with me a few blocks to our place the way he breathes wearily through his nose, refusing to rise.

"Let's get out of here before she comes home."

Despite my words, I walk over to the counter where I left Mark's damn bouquet.

"Put these in water," I say, imitating Yasmen. "The hell I will. They'll be compost if you're counting on me to put your shit flowers in water."

It would be so easy to "accidentally" knock the flowers into the trash can, but that would be immature. I glance up to find Otis watching me.

"Judgmental bastard," I mutter.

I look past the flowers to the lasagna Kassim didn't bother putting away. It smells good. Yasmen has many talents, but culinary skills have never been among them, so I'm curious to see how this turned out. I grab a fork from the nearby drawer and scoop up a hearty sample.

"Mmmm," I grunt, chewing through the noodles, cheese, and ground turkey. "It's even good cold."

Otis walks over to see for himself, so tall he can rest his head on the counter. He sniffs, staring at the glass pan and whining plaintively.

"No way," I tell him, tugging his collar until he slides away from the counter. "All the trouble I go to following your fancy raw diet, you think I'm gonna give you lasagna? Then I'll be the one who—"

A small screen coming to life on the wall snares my attention. The security system we installed has a few monitors in various places—living room, our bedroom, and the kitchen. The camera captures any activity on the porch in real time. I know what I'll see when I walk over to the small monitor on the wall.

Yasmen's home from her date. I should leave, slip out the back door and mind my business. It's been a long damn day, and I have a networking breakfast for Black entrepreneurs at 7:00 a.m.

But I can't make myself go.

My feet are bolted to the floor. My eyes, riveted on the screen.

I can't hear what Yasmen and Mark are saying, but it's the classic first-date dance. He's nearly as tall as I am, so she has to tip her head back to laugh up at him, and it exposes the sleek column of her neck. His smile is innocent enough, but his gaze is a torch, singeing her throat, the bare line of her arm and shoulder, lingering on her breasts.

God, she looks good tonight. I mean, it's Yasmen, so she always looks good to me, but when she answered the door, out of habit, I almost reached for her. It used to be a game with us. She'd get dressed, then do her makeup, knowing damn well I was going to smudge it when I kissed her. Knowing there was a good chance my hand would end up down her pants, taking off her bra, cupping her breasts. I couldn't get enough of her. Couldn't keep my hands off her.

Once.

We were once that way, and then...we were what we became in the end. Stiff. Cold. Silent.

Mark steps closer, white teeth gleaming in the warm light of the porch. He twines his fingers with hers, and my hand clenches into a fist. Why don't I just go? This is intrusive. She deserves privacy, but I can't stop watching what could be their first kiss. He pulls her closer, touching the small of her back with his free hand, drawing her to him until their bodies are flush.

My teeth hurt, and I realize I'm biting down hard, a low growl rumbling at the back of my throat. Otis's ears twitch, his senses attuned to the animalistic sound. Mark is touching her in a way that, for years, only I could, and it feels wrong. It feels like I still have every right to charge out to the porch and break his hand if he doesn't move it from the rounded sweep of her hip, the lush curve of her ass.

But I stay where I am, knowing I should leave, but unable to.

The smile they share fades in the same moment, and he dips his head to kiss her, teasing her lips open. And I know what he'll find there. So sweet. I remember her tasting so sweet. Like berries and mint and lust. He dips, deepens the kiss, his hand wandering down to palm her ass, and I think I may lose my mind. Some switch in my head turns over, and it takes all my restraint not to go slam him into the wall. It takes everything not to push him off my porch and away from my wife.

Except she isn't anymore.

None of this life is mine. Sure, I have proximity to her, to this home, but none of it belongs to me and I no longer belong to it. To her.

She decided that, and not for the first time, the frustration, the helplessness of all I've lost, burns in my gut. The chaos of life and how you can calculate and project and plan and save...and then the ones you love die. There can be hope growing inside of the woman you love more than life itself, and in a moment, that hope can be lost. That future, snuffed out. That woman, kissing someone else on the front porch of the house that used to be yours.

And you have no control over any of it.

My phone buzzes in my pocket, so I tear my gaze away from the kissing couple to check the message.

Vashti: Hey, babe.

Me: Hey. You done?

Vashti: Yup. Just finished. I miss you. I'd love to come over. Spend the night?

I glance back to the monitor on the wall. They've separated now, first kiss behind them. I can't see her face, but his eyes are passion-glazed, his hand wandering up and down her back then gripping her waist.

I should take Vashti up on her offer. Lose myself in another woman, and not think of the first time I kissed Yasmen. We ended with me inside her ghetto-ass apartment. I pressed her to the wall, our tongues fucking, our hands frantic. My fingers slipped into her panties and she moaned, pulling her mouth from mine and dropping her head back to the wall, watching me finger her. We didn't look away until she came all over my hand. I watched her fall apart, eyes smoky, that pretty, full bottom lip trapped between her teeth. Big, beautiful breasts straining, heaving with the passion, with the violent churning of how our bodies craved each other.

Of how our souls seemed to lock in a bond that not even time could break.

My dick pokes against my zipper, and I dig one hand into the counter and press the other palm to my erection. Even the memory of that night gets me hard. How, never dropping her eyes, she grabbed me through my pants, pulling gently at first and then, at my urging, harder with tugs that made me groan. That made me come in my jeans like a teenager, and I didn't give a damn. It was messy and hot and it felt like the movies, when the two people who belong together find each other and collide. They combust. They stare at one another in awe because what are the odds that you find this ever in a lifetime?

That was us.

And now she's on the front porch kissing some guy named Mark and I should be on my way home to wait in bed for another woman.

Only I can't. Feeling this and then being with Vashti? It feels wrong. Disrespectful. Selfish. I can hear Byrd's voice in my ear.

Boy, I raised you better than that.

"Yeah, you did," I mutter ruefully, resigning myself to a night with me and my hand.

Me: Hey, maybe tomorrow? It's been a long day. Early start.

There is no response for a few moments, and I can almost see her pretty face wrinkled in consternation while she figures out the perfect way to word her response. She's always careful, measured. Vashti and I are natured a lot alike. Maybe that's why we work.

Vashti: Okay. I understand. Get some rest and see you tomorrow.

Not convinced I won't regret that moment of nobility, I pat my leg again to Otis. He looks up at the view of the porch on-screen and bares his teeth, ears perked, lean body tensed, protective instinct on high alert when he sees a stranger touching someone he deems his.

"Dude, I get it," I say, my laugh slightly bitter when I open the back door. "But we gotta go."

And refusing to look at the tableau on the porch even one more second, I finally do.

CHAPTER NINETEEN

YASMEN

Can't put this off any longer."

I stand outside Josiah's closed office door, the scents and sounds from the kitchen bringing some measure of comfort. Grits became a haunted house once I lost Henry here on the floor alone in the dark, but before that night, this place was my second home. Finally, it's starting to feel that way again.

Drawing a deep breath, I brace to see Josiah this morning. We've been avoiding each other the last few weeks. Ever since his sleepover with Vashti. Ever since my date with Mark. Besides the occasional passing in the hall here at Grits, we've barely been in the same room lately. Even at soccer matches, we haven't stood on the sidelines together. If we didn't have a meeting with our business manager this morning, I'd be at home working on holiday projects for the Skyland Association, steering clear of the man on the other side of this door.

I knock and wait for Josiah's deep baritone telling me to enter. He sits behind his desk, eyes trained on the laptop in front of him. He doesn't look up, but keeps typing. The silence persists, stretches to awkwardness, so I drop into one of the armchairs in the center of the room along with a sofa and coffee table, and set my purse on the floor.

"Harvey's on his way," he says, still not looking away from the screen. "His last meeting ran a few minutes over, but he'll be here soon."

"Oh. Sure. Great."

I run damp palms over my legs, the jeans smooth and cool beneath my hands. Fidgety and looking for something to do, I tighten my top-knot. I got box braids last weekend because I was tired of messing with my hair. This morning they're studded with a few gold cuffs scattered throughout the strands.

All in all, I feel pretty. And confident, and I won't be shook by the pissy mood Josiah seems to have saved just for me. Finally, he closes the laptop and walks over to the sitting area. I study my nails, taking my turn to ignore *him*.

"I like the braids."

Surprised, I glance up to find him sitting on the arm of the leather sofa across from me. I didn't expect him to say anything personal. Definitely not about my appearance. When I meet his eyes, they're cool like they've been for weeks, and his face remains unreadable.

"Thanks." I scour my mind for something else to say. Gone are the days when I couldn't get the words out to him fast enough. We'd watch couples eating dinner in absolute silence and promise each other that would never be us.

"Um, did you see Deja's report card?" I ask.

"Yeah." He frowns. "I can't believe she got a C in English."

"It used to be her best subject. It's not just the grade itself, but I worry she's spending too much time on social media."

"I think she'll find the balance without us having to come down hard. Your relationship with her is already strained enough and—"

"Strained?" I ask, my voice dropping to a quiet warning.

"You've said that yourself, Yas." He crosses his stupid muscular arms across his stupid broad chest. "Let's not fight over how we need to handle things with Day. Have you given any more thought to Kassim playing football?"

"You mean since I said *never* when you asked last time? No. Besides, he has soccer."

"He really wants to play football too."

"A kid can really want a lot of things that aren't good for him, like literally ramming his brain into a brick wall over and over again and risking his life, his mind, for what? A game? With all that's come out about CTE, I just don't think it's worth the risk. Lots of parents aren't doing football anymore."

"Don't you think you're being a little dramatic? I played football. Preach played. Theo's playing."

"I love Preach, but him letting Theo play doesn't mean a damn thing to me. What he and Liz decide for their kids has no bearing on what we decide for ours. Kassim has barely mentioned football to me."

"He hasn't mentioned it," he returns with obvious stretched patience, "because he loves you and he doesn't want to displease you, but he asks me almost daily."

"Of course, because you're the cool parent."

"Well, I'm not the one who says no to everything because I'm too scared or too uptight to allow my kids some freedom to make their own decisions."

"How dare you!"

I surge to my feet, unable to stay seated one more second. I need to move, let this anger circulate, or it will clog in my veins. My steps eat up the space separating us, and before I know it, I'm right in front of him, standing in the vee of his powerful legs. The air sizzles with a lightning strike, sudden and hot and dangerous. Unpredictable. I should take shelter, but I don't step back.

His expression remains inscrutable, the stark beauty of his face unaffected, but his breathing deepens. In response, my breasts rise and fall with the struggle to draw breath as the air between us thickens. This close, his presence overwhelms me and my deprived senses devour him. The way his cologne mingles with his unique male scent. The hardness of his jaw at war with the sensual curve of his mouth. The heat his big body radiates, even at rest, surrounds me.

I lick suddenly dry lips, and he tracks the movement with narrowed eyes. I feel hunted by that look, like I stepped into a trap laid by my own body, devised by my own mind. Something I thought we'd buried long ago rises, encircles us, breathing new life into a connection

I thought was dead. I've known for months that I'm still attracted to Josiah, but right now, with his eyes darkening and his jaw flexing and his hands curling into fists, I can't help but wonder…

Is *he* still attracted to me too?

"Sorry I'm late." Our business manager, Harvey, rushes in and flops into the armchair, dropping his briefcase to the floor.

"Any chance I could get some coffee before we start?" he asks, still not looking at us and pulling a stack of papers from the open bag at his feet.

"Sure," Josiah says. When he stands, since I haven't moved, mere inches separate our bodies. At the heat emanating from him, my heart thrums in my chest, like it's been caged and is ready to claw its way out. He stares down at me for a second, drawing in a sharp breath through his nose before stepping around me and leaving the office in long strides. The air collapses in my lungs, and I clutch the arm of the sofa for support. My mind is spinning, a centrifuge sorting all the emotions those brief seconds stirred.

Anger. Confusion. Exhilaration.

Desire.

"What'd I interrupt?" Harvey asks, not looking up from the papers splayed on the coffee table.

"Huh?" I ask dumbly, sitting on one end of the sofa. "What do you mean?"

"I've been working with you two for over a decade. By now, I can probably tell who had the last word just by looking at you."

"We're fine." I rub my hand over the back of my neck, massaging the new tension there.

Harvey levels a doubtful look at me, but before he can ask more questions I have no reasonable answers to, Josiah returns with a cup of coffee.

"Black, right?" he asks.

"Bless you." Harvey accepts the cup, taking a deep swallow and closing his eyes. "I missed my coffee this morning and the headache has already started. This hits the spot."

"Good." Josiah drags his gaze from the armchair Harvey took to the sofa where I sit. Obviously he has no choice but to join me. Still, he hesitates before taking the other end, stretching his long legs out in front of him.

"First," Harvey says after another long, caffeinated gulp. "I gotta say, it's truly admirable how you guys have managed this transition. Not many couples stay in business together after divorce."

Neither of us replies, but when I steal a glance at Josiah, he's staring straight ahead, his expression blank.

He checks his watch. "Can we get into this so I can attend the staff meeting before we open for lunch? We're already starting late."

"Sure." Harvey's brows lift, but he doesn't seem offended by Josiah's abruptness. By now he knows Josiah is always business first.

Harvey sets the coffee mug down on the table. "I'd like to revisit the discussion about the Charlotte expansion."

Josiah and I both greet this comment with silence. Right before Byrd passed away, business was booming so much we'd dreamed of expanding to another location in Georgia, or even a hot city in another state.

"Before we get into this," I say, studiously avoiding Josiah's gaze. "When we first started talking about expanding, I was the main one pushing for it, but a lot has changed. Si, I know you saved this place when I...couldn't be here. If you don't think we should expand now, I'll defer."

The idea of expanding still excites me, but considering how removed I am from the day-to-day operations, I won't push.

"Grits is just as much yours as it is mine, Yas," Josiah says, angling his head to catch my eyes.

"Thank you for saying that, but we all know that I was—"

"You were taking care of the two things that meant the most to me. My children." His eyes, lit with sincerity, lock with mine. "And yourself. With all you went through, that was all I had the right to expect.

If you hadn't taken care of Day and Seem, I wouldn't have been able to hold it down here."

He laughs, and it's hollow, self-deprecating. "Though I didn't do that great of a job here if—"

"Stop," I cut him off. "It's a miracle that you kept us afloat. I'm sorry if I didn't fully appreciate it at the time. If I ever made it harder for you."

We stare at each other in the seconds elongating between us. After the tension that clotted the room before Harvey came, our words supporting each other feel foreign, but welcome.

"So what are you thinking, Harvey?" I ask, hoping to get back on more even ground. "I mean, things are going incredibly well, but we are just getting back on our feet. What makes you think we should expand now?"

"Opportunity." His mouth stretches into what I like to call his money-eating grin. "There's a restaurant closing in NoDa, North Davidson—one of the most popular areas of Charlotte. We're talking prime real estate."

"If it's so prime," Josiah says, "why they bouncing?"

"Time to retire." Harvey shrugs, turning his lips down at the corners. "They're an older couple who've decided to sell the business and move to Florida."

"Are we in a position to do this if everything checks out?" I ask.

"We are," Harvey says. "The last few quarters, with Vashti's leadership in the kitchen, adding Anthony to management, and you guys making shrewd, strategic decisions, have been very good. The best Grits has ever had."

"True." Josiah cants his head, the look on his face alert and curious. "The space is leased?"

"It's a house they renovated, similar to what you did here for Grits," Harvey replies. "You'd take over the note, but believe me, this place is so hot, you'd have no trouble covering it. Charlotte is like the next Atlanta."

"There is no next Atlanta," Josiah says, smug as the only person in the room who grew up here.

"Charlotte's on the list of best cities to live in, though," Harvey counters. "Banking is big, and folks are prospering. And this part of Charlotte is booming. Lots of artists and great restaurants. They were wondering if you could come check it out after Thanksgiving, before Christmas for a couple of days."

"A couple of days?" I slide a glance from Harvey's eager expression to Josiah's suddenly shuttered one.

"Yeah, I'd want you both to see it, of course," Harvey says. "And they'd like you to hang for a day or so to discuss things, see the neighborhood. And so they could get to know you a little. They don't want to pass it on to just anybody. A quick overnight trip."

Overnight? My brain screeches, setting warning bells off between my ears.

Together?

"Can Yas and I discuss this a little more?" Josiah asks, his gaze fixed on Harvey.

"Of course." Harvey leans forward to grasp a few of the pages on the coffee table, passing some to me and some to Josiah. "In the meantime, here's some promo material of the restaurant and the neighborhood."

I leaf through the photos and find myself smiling, my heart pounding. NoDa is eclectic and charming and a lot like Skyland. The restaurant is a house, smaller than the one we renovated for Grits, but no less quaint. The photos were taken during the summer since everyone's wearing tank tops, flip-flops, shorts. There's a front lawn, and tables are set up on the grass. People of every shade mill about, smiling and eating.

Something about this place tugs at me. Josiah has always been the numbers guy. Show him the data, the facts, and he'll decide. My calculus is...softer. Located farther south, not in my head, but splitting the difference between my heart and my gut. Considering the enmity that has crept up between us, it's easy to forget we made great partners. Between his head and my instincts, we built something pretty fantastic here in Atlanta.

Could we do it again?

"I'll leave this with you," Harvey says, nodding toward the file lying open and spilling glossy color photos onto the coffee table. "I'll email you some figures and specs that may help you decide. My two cents, you'd be crazy if you don't at least go see this place. If they put it on the market, with this location, it'll get snatched, and they won't wait long."

Harvey closes his bag and stands, smiling down at me. I rise, too, and lean forward for the hug and kiss on my cheek I know is coming.

"This place isn't the same without you," he whispers in my ear, hugging me a little tighter. "I'm glad you're back and so is he."

Surprised, touched, I glance up at our old friend and return his smile and his squeeze. "Thanks, Harv."

"I can walk you out," Josiah says, standing too. "You hungry? We can fix you something to go, if you want."

"Oh, I always want," Harvey says, following Josiah to the office door.

Their voices and laughter float into the office from the hall until they're too far away for me to hear. I pick up one of the photos, this one with a man and a woman, a few decades older than Josiah and me, sitting on the front porch.

Merry Herman and Ken Harris, *Proprietors*.

"What's your story?" I muse aloud, staring at the couple who wants to meet us.

A trip overnight.

Together.

Josiah and I would have separate rooms, of course, but still...the idea of the two of us in another city with no kids, no Grits.

No Vashti.

It sends an unwanted thrill through me. That moment we shared before Harvey arrived comes back to mind, and my breath rushes out. Heat liquefies in my veins, moving and burning through me.

I want him.

I shouldn't. It's too late. I won't act on it, but this traitorous ache I'd nearly forgotten roars at me from dusty corners, peers from the shadows and reaches for me through finely spun cobwebs. It's wild and hungry. If I'm smart, I'll starve it, deny it, because unlike before, it won't be satisfied.

CHAPTER TWENTY

JOSIAH

I send Harvey happily on his way, then reluctantly turn back to the office, taking a moment to linger in the hall.

What the hell was that with Yas before Harvey arrived?

I want to scrub my brain so I can't remember those moments when Yasmen stood between my legs, but her scent lingers on my clothes, in my mind. The warmth of her imprinted on my pores. Even though our bodies never touched, I still feel her. But what I recall with absolute clarity is the fire in her eyes.

A fire I haven't seen in years. Anger? Yes. Outrage? Maybe. Desire? Most definitely.

What is worse than admitting I still want her is the prospect that she might want me too.

That shit ain't happening. Not again.

"Harvey's gone?" Vashti asks, stepping into the hall from the kitchen, wearing her standard white chef's attire. She's petite but not delicate. There's a tensile strength to her, a core of serenity that I find calming. I like her a lot. I respect her even more and never want to hurt or mislead her.

"Yeah." I smile down at her. "He loves that chicken potpie."

"Who doesn't?" She laughs, stepping closer until she rests against me. She rises onto her tiptoes, reaching between us to press her palm to my chest, and whispers in my ear. "I cannot wait to get you home tonight."

We're circumspect at work. If you didn't know we're dating, most would never guess from our behavior, but that isn't why I put space between us now. With the memory of Yasmen still tangled in my thoughts, it feels wrong to stand here and talk about tonight with Vashti. I turn my head and kiss her briefly on the lips, but gently set her away from me. Disappointment rises and falls on her expression, gone almost before I detect it.

"I better get back to the kitchen," she says, her smile lacking some of its usual shine. "Today's special has to be prepared just right, or it's a disaster."

"Go kill it." I nod toward the office. "I need to talk with Yas before she has to leave."

I know she wonders about Yasmen and me, but she has asked relatively little about our marriage, divorce, or even our current arrangement. She trusts me to be a good guy, and I will be. I bend down and drop a lingering kiss on her mouth, squeezing the slight curve of her hip. She lets out a little moan, and angles her head to deepen the kiss. A sound at the door distracts me, and over Vashti's shoulder, my gazes locks with Yasmen's. She's standing in the office door, her eyes clouded and the lush curve of her mouth pulled tight. I can't help but think of the night when I watched her first kiss with Mark. Have they kissed again? Had another date?

Fucked?

I don't want to know.

Vashti looks back, unfazed to find Yasmen watching us. She smiles at her, squeezes my hand, and slips back into the kitchen.

"You got a second?" I ask, looking from the purse Yasmen carries to her guarded expression. "I wanted to talk some about what Harvey said."

"Sure." She turns and disappears back into the office.

Vashti is in the kitchen and Yasmen is in the office. Preach would laugh his ass off and say I'm torn between two women, but there's nothing torn about how I feel. I'm very clear. Wanting my ex-wife is not new. Have I ever *not* wanted her? I may want her till the day I die. We'll be eighty years old and my dick will probably still get hard when that woman shuffles into a room using her walker, but I won't let her close again. She has proven she cannot be trusted, and I'd be a fool to ever believe otherwise.

"So what do you think?" I ask, picking up a few of the photos Harvey left. "Worth considering?"

I hope acting like everything is normal will make it so. Considering my conversations with Dr. Musa, apparently, that's my modus operandi.

"My gut says yes." She settles into the armchair. "But I could be wrong."

We both know how reliable her gut has been in the past. Opting to put some distance between us, I sit on the edge of my desk instead of on the sofa across from her.

"I want to see the numbers," I say. "But if it's as good an opportunity as Harvey seems to think—"

"And he's rarely wrong."

"And he's rarely wrong, then it would put exactly what we wanted to do before…"

I stop, holding her stare and letting the unfinished sentence speak for itself. *Before everything.*

"It would put us back on track," she finishes. "I mean, for expansion."

"Right. And you'd be okay going to visit for an overnight trip?"

I ask the question as if it's harmless.

She clears her throat, lifting her eyes to meet mine. "Sure. My mom's coming for Thanksgiving and staying a week. Maybe we could go while she's here so she'd be with the kids."

"Not a bad idea." My smile comes involuntarily. "So Carole's coming to dinner? I hope she cooks chitlings again. The kids still aren't over that."

"Oh, my God. The smell. Remember how they complained about it and refused to touch it? She's determined they'll taste them this year."

Her smile dwindles. "Are you, um...well, we haven't talked about your plans for Thanksgiving."

"I'll be here obviously."

Where else would I go? From the beginning we agreed we wouldn't ask our employees to work Thanksgiving or Christmas Day. We didn't want to ourselves.

"Oh, I wasn't sure if Vashti..." Yasmen looks away and licks her lips. "I thought maybe you might be meeting her family or something."

"Not yet." I cross my legs at the ankle and study her closely. "What about Mark? Is he coming to meet your mother?"

"Are you kidding? Why would I...? No."

"Too soon?" I ask, hoping my tone is light.

"We just haven't even discussed that at all. We aren't there."

"You two been out again?"

She narrows her eyes, tilts her head. "A few times. Why?"

"Just wondering." I shrug nonchalantly. "Let's see if your mom wants to hang out with the kids for a day or so."

"And ask Harvey if the owner would be okay with us coming maybe that Saturday after Thanksgiving?"

"Sounds good."

With that settled, she stands, but doesn't leave right away.

"Um, so about Thanksgiving. Are you eating with us?"

"Why wouldn't I?" I ask with a frown. "It was fine last year, right?"

I don't know that describing the bitter silence that hung over Thanksgiving dinner last year as "fine" is entirely accurate, but it's safer than the truth. It was awkward as hell every time Yas and I were in the same room, but the family was together, dammit. The kids went up to their rooms as soon as they finished eating and I got out of there immediately.

"Yeah, it was fine." Yasmen's stiff smile tells me she remembers it the same way. "I just didn't want to assume anything."

Yasmen's wrestling with something.

Tells: biting her bottom lip, tugging her left earlobe, crease between her brows.

I wait for her to decide if whatever she's working up to is worth saying.

"I mean, you could bring Vashti with you," she says after another three seconds. "To Thanksgiving dinner, I mean."

That I didn't expect.

"Vashti? You're saying I should bring her with me to Thanksgiving dinner?"

Hearing it aloud seems to give her pause. She nods slowly, blinking several times as if she's processing it herself.

"Yes. If you want. It's up to you. I mean, the kids will want you there and—"

"I'll ask what she wants to do and let you know. Thanks for thinking of her."

"Of course," she says, and without any more conversation that could turn awkward, she leaves.

CHAPTER TWENTY-ONE

YASMEN

So let me get this straight," my mother says.

I stop washing the sweet potatoes in the sink to glance at her. If looking at Deja is looking in a rearview mirror to my past self, looking at my mother offers a possible glimpse into my future. Besides a few lines around her eyes, her skin remains taut and smooth and brown. Pretty sure my mother has used Noxzema her whole life. I used to watch her smear the thick white cream on sometimes at night. Nothing fancy or expensive. Everything straight from the drugstore, but her skin is fantastic. I can only hope I look like this when I'm her age.

"You thought it was a good idea," she continues, eyes narrowed behind her red-framed glasses, "to invite Josiah and his new girlfriend to Thanksgiving dinner."

"Mama, it'll be fine." I turn off the water and put the sweet potatoes in a bowl on the counter. "These are clean."

"Peel 'em. What's her name again?"

"Vashti."

She knows this. She's asked three times, and my mother could remind elephants where they left things. Avoiding her sharp gaze, I start peeling the potatoes.

"I told them dinner was at four. That still okay?" I ask.

"Mmmmhhh. She's a cook, you say?"

"A world-class chef, yes." I suppress a smile because I already know where this is going.

"But she knows I'm cooking this dinner, right?" Mama takes a sip of her eggnog. She doesn't wait for Christmas. "She can bring a few sides, but—"

"She did ask if she could bring something, of course, and I told her we'd love that, but that you're cooking the—"

"The turkey, the greens, the yams *and* sweet potato casserole, the neck bones."

"I'm sure we're safe on the neck bones."

"The string beans, the fried chicken, the—"

"Mama, yes. She's bringing a few sides that you are *not* cooking. It'll be fine."

"Are *you* fine?"

"What do you mean?"

Mama leans one rounded hip against the counter and pushes her glasses up to the top of her head. "Girl, don't play with me. I raised you. I know you. How you feel about Josiah dating this woman?"

"Ma—"

"Don't 'Ma' me." She nods to the stool at the counter. "Sit."

"We have people coming tomorrow, and so much to do before—"

"I got this. Why you think I flew in early? Now, sit yourself down and talk to me."

I draw in a sharp breath and release it slowly before sitting. I look at her expectantly, brows lifted.

"Why you looking at me?" she says. "I already asked you a question. How do you feel about Josiah dating again?"

"I'm fine with it." I shrug and look down to the counter, tracing my finger over the granite surface. "She's been great for Grits. The kids love her. Josiah..."

I search for the right words. Does he love her?

"I can tell Josiah cares about her a lot," I finish. "Things seem to be progressing, so I wish them well."

"Progressing? Like you think he might propose or something?"

At the word "propose," I can't help but think about how Josiah asked me to marry him. A rare, impulsive act when both of us least expected it.

"Um, no. At least I don't think so." I frown, because what do I know? "I just…I know they're sleeping together."

I didn't plan to say that, to tell her that, but Mama has a way of getting things out of me I never intend to share. I got away with nothing growing up.

Mama takes the stool beside me. "And you saying that don't bother you…none."

"We've been divorced almost two years. It was bound to happen. Besides, I'm dating too."

"Who?" Mama lifts one brow.

"A guy named Mark. I mean, we're not serious or exclusive, but we've been out a few times. I like him. He's good company."

"So you're both moving on."

"Do you think I could make the stuffing?"

Mama almost spits out her eggnog, whether it's at the abrupt change of subject or at the idea of me cooking the stuffing, I'm not sure. "You?"

"Yeah, me." I force a light laugh and go back to peeling sweet potatoes, training my eyes on my fingers. "I wanted to try Byrd's recipe."

The seconds tick by in silence, and I pause the peeling to look at my mother. Her small smile crooks at the corner.

"I miss that crazy girl," she says softly. "We used to throw down for the holidays."

Byrd was one of the few people my mother would share a kitchen with. Their scandalous stories about the good ol' days, raucous laughter, and undeniable love for their food and their family color so many of my holiday memories.

"Me too." I squeeze her hand and offer a small smile. "I found one of her cookbooks when we cleaned out her house. All the recipes are in her handwriting. I've been trying a few of them."

Using Bryd's recipes somehow makes me feel more connected to her.

I shrug and go back to the potatoes. "We all know I'm not a great cook, but I wanted to try her stuffing this year. If it sucks, you can—"

"It won't. We'll make sure it's perfect." She winks. "Your fast tail should have listened when I was trying to teach you to cook in high school."

It's an ongoing joke that I showed no interest in cooking when I was young, but ended up owning a restaurant.

"Lesson learned." I chuckle. "Guess I'm making up for lost time."

"Better late than never."

"Speaking of late." I glance at my watch. "Kassim's therapy session should have finished awhile ago. I'll text Josiah to make sure everything's okay."

I'm reaching for my phone when Kassim barrels through the back door and into the kitchen, face wreathed in a huge smile. Josiah follows, his pace more sedate.

"Grandma!" Kassim hurls himself at Mama, rocking her back with the force of the hug.

"Kassim, be careful," Josiah says, but his voice is indulgent. "Don't knock her out before she cooks my Thanksgiving dinner."

Mama takes Kassim's face between her hands and kisses the top of his head, then turns her attention to Josiah.

"Well, look who the cat drug in," she drawls, deep affection in her eyes. "You better be glad you so pretty, or I wouldn't cook you nothing."

Josiah's low chuckle rolls out as he takes the few steps to reach Mama and pulls her into his arms.

"I'm not gonna test my luck," he says. "How was your flight?"

"Good." She leans back to look up, searching his face. "You all right?"

His smile fades because he recognizes the question for what it is, evidence of Mama's insight. Byrd made the holidays special, and no one would feel her absence now as acutely as Josiah.

"Yes, ma'am," he says simply. "I'm good."

"Mom, we had Indian for dinner," Kassim says, hanging his backpack on the hook near the back door.

"I wondered where you guys were," I say.

"Sorry." Josiah leans against the kitchen island and plucks an apple slice from the cobbler Mama's preparing. "I thought I mentioned we were gonna eat out after we left Dr. Cabbot's. We went to Saffron's."

Mama slaps his hand and slides the cobbler out of reach.

"It's fine," I say, turning away to wipe the counter down so I don't have to *look* at him. He's wearing a Morehouse hoodie and dark jeans, and I'm not sure I prefer him business fine-ass or casual thirst trap. The man really needs to stop working out. And aging, because apparently that's not helping matters either. His fineness is only getting worse the older he gets, and I can't concentrate. I'll wait until he leaves before I peel these sweet potatoes, or I'll lose a fingertip surreptitiously drooling over my ex.

"Can I play *Fortnite*?" Kassim asks me with begging eyes. "No school tomorrow."

"Sure, but don't fall asleep with that thing on. I know how you and Jamal get."

He dashes from the kitchen and takes a stampede of horses with him judging by the sound of his shoes pounding up the stairs.

"That boy and them games," Mama mutters, turning back to her cobbler. "I'mma get in that closet while y'all in Charlotte. Last time I was here, we reorganized everything, and I bet it's right back where it was by now."

Josiah and I exchange a quick, meaningful glance. Every time Mama comes, she has to organize and deep clean everything within an inch of its life. The kids complain, but it's become our inside joke. They're going to give us so much hate when we come back from Charlotte.

"Four o'clock tomorrow for dinner?" he asks, looking to Mama with brows lifted.

"Yes, and don't be late." She twists her lips. "I hear you're bringing a guest."

"Yes, ma'am."

"And did she get the list of things I'm making and she don't have to worry about?" Mama asks, her look both challenging and teasing.

"Yes, I passed it on." He surrenders a grin and bends to kiss her cheek.

"I'm looking forward to meeting her," Mama says.

"I'm sure she'll love you." The openness of Josiah's look fades a little when his eyes land on me. "I'mma bounce."

"I'll walk you out." I dry my hands on a dish towel. "I want to hear how it went with Dr. Cabbot."

"See you tomorrow, Mom," Josiah says, leaving through the back door.

We walk outside, and he leans against his car. I leave a safe distance between us. Not close enough for his scent and warmth to wrap around me.

"So how'd it go?" I ask.

"Good. Dr. Cabbot's pleased with what he's seeing. He doesn't tell me everything, of course, but he did mention that Kassim's a little anxious about performing well enough to skip next year. He seems to have it in his head that therapy is part of some audition to see if he's good enough to go to seventh grade."

I huff a humorless laugh. "I guess you think that's my fault for expecting so much? You're probably not wrong."

With a gentle finger, he lifts my chin to meet his eyes, surprising me with his touch.

"Don't do that." He grimaces. "I owe you an apology for that comment I made about putting pressure on them. I have no excuse except I'm an asshole sometimes, but it's not your fault."

"I know I'm a lot."

I lean into the rough warmth of his palm. We seem to realize at the same moment that his thumb is tracing the sensitive skin above my chin, below my mouth. I'm sure it was merely muscle memory that made him touch me this way. Our bodies recall things we've chosen to forget. I expect him to withdraw immediately, but the way he watches me in the dimness of the half-moon night, the way his fingers drag across my jaw when he withdraws his touch, almost reluctant, traps the breath in my throat.

My mind rifles through an album of memories I cannot afford to indulge in. For a few heart-thumping seconds I'm transported back to the first time I saw him. The first time I kissed him. The first time we made love, *confessed* our love, voices hoarse in the after-fuck glow of twisted sheets, of tangled arms and legs, of kiss-bruised lips. We had the kind of chemistry that burned everywhere it touched—skin, bed, hearts. Nothing was safe, and if there is one thing I want to be after my last few perilous years, it's safe.

He's in a relationship now. Off-limits.

"So four o'clock, right?" I take a step back. "You and Vashti will be here?"

"Yup." He clicks his alarm, flashing the lights of the Rover. "I better get home before Otis finds something expensive to metabolize. I haven't ruled out that he ate those shoes I can't find."

I choke on my own subterfuge, coughing at the thought of Josiah's tennis shoes neatly stowed away in my closet.

"Yeah, wouldn't put it past him," I agree.

Sorry, Otis.

Josiah glances up at the house, then over to Brock and Clint's, up First Court and all the impressive homes lining our little corner of Skyland, an ironic smile touching the corners of his mouth.

"You ever think how far we've come?"

If I think of that, I have to think of all we've lost too.

"Yeah," I reply, shoving my hands into the pockets of my jeans.

"That first apartment was a shoebox."

"With roaches." I chuckle, shaking my head.

"And no water pressure. I didn't have a good shower for a year." A smile eases its way onto his face. "Remember that first Thanksgiving? We didn't have a pot to piss in."

I surrender to the memory in the grocery store the night before our first Thanksgiving. My usually serious husband picked me up and put me in the shopping cart. He hopped on the back and we coasted down the grocery store aisles, laughing and ignoring the strange looks everyone gave us. I can almost feel the air whipping over my face, hear the clackety wheels on that metal cart protesting our combined weight. Smell his distinctive scent—*clean, male, him*—and feel his warmth at my back.

We'd picked up some basics. Milk, eggs, bread, cold cuts. We had so little money, but as a treat, we each chose one thing we loved. A six-pack of grape Fanta for me. A bag of sweet-and-salty popcorn mix for him.

"We didn't have enough money when we got to the register," he says with a smile, like he's revisiting that night with me in my mind.

"Oh, my God." I laugh, burying my face in my hands for a moment. "All those people behind us with carts full of stuff for Thanksgiving dinner, and we're handing one item at a time to the cashier to put back. Trying to figure out how low we need to go before we can afford it."

"We kept my popcorn," he says.

I frown, but a small smile tugs at my lips. "I'm pretty sure we kept my soda. Remember the power had been disconnected and our shithole apartment was freezing, but the soda was warm."

We could have just gone over to Byrd's, but she always had a full house for the holidays, and we wanted to be alone, so we stayed there. I don't remember once complaining about the cold in that raggedy apartment in the hood. Instead, serenaded by Al Green's "Let's Stay Together" blasting from Josiah's phone, we made the most of the night with lit candles and PBJ sandwiches and lukewarm grape Fanta. When we made love it was frantic, gripping, sinking into each other like he was all I had in the world and I was his everything. Because it was true. To this day, I get a little flushed when I hear "Let's Stay Together." The song belongs to that night and the sweet, dirty things we did to keep each other warm.

Those years, the leanest of our marriage, were somehow also some of the best.

It's ironic that he remembers me sacrificing my soda and I remembered it being him. I wonder if that's true of everything and the truth hides somewhere between what we each remember? Reshaping our memories to be what we thought they should. Did I make it better than it was? Did I ever make it worse?

I take him in, the sharp planes of his face juxtaposed with the fullness of his mouth. His austerity contrasted with his tenderness for the people who mean the most to him. He's an enigma who makes perfect sense to me.

Or at least he used to.

"It was a good night," I say, my throat burning as I try to break our stare. It's like we're in the middle of that tiny apartment again, shivering, huddled under blankets and eating cheap food from the grocery store in the light of candles. Perfectly content. A fist squeezes my heart until it oozes nostalgia and regret.

"I better go," he says, finally looking away, stepping away.

"Yeah, see you tomorrow," I say, my smile hanging on by a thread.

He opens the door and climbs in, starts the Rover, and leaves. I stand in the driveway long after he's gone, shivering in the cold.

CHAPTER TWENTY-TWO

∞

JOSIAH

Wait. Don't ring the bell yet."

I glance at Vashti over the box of covered dishes balanced in my arms, my finger poised at Yasmen's doorbell.

"I'm nervous," she says, squeezing her eyes shut. "I know it's silly, but I can't help it. It feels like I'm meeting your family."

Otis, waiting on the porch with us, looks from Vashti to me and lies down, resting his head on his paws like he's settling in while I calm her nerves.

"There's nothing to be nervous about." I shift my box and give her a reassuring smile. "It's just the kids and Yas, and I think a few people from Grits who didn't have anywhere to go for dinner."

"And your mother-in-law."

"Former mother-in-law," I correct, though Carole Miller never feels like a former anything. She treated me like a son from jump, and that didn't end with the divorce. The fact that she and Byrd loved each other so much only solidified the bond between our families. "You'll love Carole and she'll love you."

"It's really great of Yasmen to invite me. Not many women would be so kind and accepting to their ex's new girl."

"That's Yas for you." I tilt my chin to her own smaller box of dishes. "Besides, you definitely come bearing plenty of gifts with all this food."

"I made sure not to cook anything from Carole's list."

"You're one of the best chefs in the city, so thanks for being cool about Carole's demands."

"Oh, I get it. Just because I went to culinary school doesn't mean I can take over her kitchen. My mother's the same way. Old-school, which I respect."

"I think you'll get along just fine." I lift my brows and inch my index finger closer to the bell. "You ready?"

She takes a deep breath and nods. "Ready."

The door flies open as soon as I press the bell.

"Dad!" Kassim says, practically bouncing. "There's so much food."

"Not for long if you have anything to do with it. Help Vashti with these dishes, Seem," I say, as Otis bounds past us into the foyer like a liberated prisoner. "Otis!"

He stops, obedience in his swift response, but impatience in the twitching ears and swishing tail. I know he's going straight to the kitchen to look for Yasmen, and Carole does not tolerate dogs in her domain.

"Stay in here." I nod toward his bed in the corner of the living room. He huffs disdainfully, but assumes the position, curling up near the fireplace.

Kassim relieves Vashti of a few dishes, and we head toward the kitchen. I expect mass chaos, but I should have known better. Between Carole's prowess as a cook and Yasmen's hostessing supremacy, the kitchen is sparkling clean and filled with mouthwatering aromas. All the dishes neatly line the countertop and the kitchen island. When I peer through to the dining room, the table is set with familiar fine china and silverware. There's an obscene amount of food. My stomach growls, and Carole looks up from adding pecans to the sweet potato casserole.

"I hear that belly talking already." She laughs, gesturing toward a clear section of the kitchen island. "Set the food down."

Kassim and I place our boxes down carefully. Carole slides her hands into the front pockets of an apron with "Not Your Grandma's Grandma" printed on the front.

"And who we got here?" Carole asks, studying Vashti over the rims of her glasses with a friendly smile.

"This is Vashti," I say. "Vashti, Carole Miller."

"So nice to meet you," Vashti says, setting down the dish she's carrying.

"It's nice to meet you too." Carole lifts the top of one of Vashti's pans. "Hmmmph. Salmon croquettes."

"Yes, ma'am. My mama's recipe," Vashti says, some of the uncertainty leaving her voice now that they're discussing food. "For the corn pudding too."

"Corn pudding?" Carole's expression turns alert. "And where is that?"

Vashti lifts the lid on another dish, revealing the golden yellow, sweet-smelling pudding.

"It's been years since I had this." Carole smiles approvingly. "Where your people from?"

"All my family lives in California now," Vashti says. "But they moved out west from Louisiana originally."

"Oh, so you got some Cajun in your blood."

"I do. Look at these." Vashti grins and pulls the lid from a sealed container, revealing beignets dusted with powdered sugar.

"How close are we to eating?" I groan.

"We're ready," Carole replies absently, eyes still feasting on the beignets. "Soon as Yas comes. She went up to shower and change. She'll be down in a sec, and we can get started."

"I'm here."

Yasmen enters the kitchen, ushering in a scent that is the sweetness of vanilla. Gold clamps are scattered throughout the braids twisted into an upswept style. Her black wide-legged pants and fitted kelly green sweater show off the dips and flares of her lush figure. A matte red pout is painted onto her lips. All those details make her look fresh and pretty, but it's the earrings that capture my attention.

"You found them!" Kassim says, walking over to gently tug on the painted turkey earrings dangling from her ears.

"Yes." She grins back at him. "They were in a box at the back of my closet with some other jewelry I'd misplaced. I can't even remember which birthday you guys gave them to me for now."

"Thirtieth," I say, biting my tongue too late.

Yasmen turns her gaze to me like she's just noticing I'm here. Her smile falters for a second before she steadies it.

"Oh, yeah," she says. "I think you're right."

I know I'm right because that's the year I gave her a gold necklace with a tiny wheel charm. "Till the wheels fall off" was inscribed on the back. I'm sure she's lost that, too, but probably hasn't bothered looking for it since the wheels definitely fell off our marriage.

"Hey, Vashti." Yasmen smiles, lifting the lids on a few dishes. "Thank you for coming and bringing so much food."

"It was nothing." Vashti's nervousness seems to have vanished, and her smile is wide and natural. "Thank you for having me."

"Of course." Yasmen's gaze skitters over me and to Carole. "We ready, Mama?"

"All them hungry folks in the living room hope so." Carole chuckles. "Like six of your staff from Grits actually showed up."

Pleasure brightens Yasmen's expression. That woman loves a party. The more the merrier. "Then let's do it."

It's good to see so many familiar faces from the restaurant around the table as we load our plates and dive in. Milky ends up seated on one side of me and Vashti on the other.

"How's your daughter, Milk?" I ask, trying to decide where to start on my plate loaded with everything from macaroni and cheese to Carole's famous cornbread.

"She's good." He bites into a roll and chews a little before going on. "She and her family went to spend Thanksgiving with her husband's people in Memphis. They'll do Christmas here."

He pauses and looks at me. "I sure do appreciate y'all having me over. The holidays is when we miss the ones we've lost the most, ain't it?"

It strikes me that I'm not the only one missing Aunt Byrd today.

Trying to figure out how to make it without her. Harsh lines bracket Milky's mouth and dent his forehead. For the first time since I've known the man, he looks his age.

"I'm glad you're here, Milk," I say softly. "You know you're always welcome."

Before things get awkward, we both slice into our turkey, which Carole always seasons perfectly. I scoop up some of the stuffing. As soon as the food hits my tongue, I freeze, fork suspended between my mouth and the plate. I put the fork down and take my time, savoring the stuffing for another moment, testing it.

"Carole," I say, frowning. "Your stuffing is delicious. It tastes like..."

Byrd's.

I don't say it aloud because I don't want reminders of loss today, but a wave of nostalgia washes over me. Not accompanied by grief, but wrapped in joy. The flavors explode in my mouth, exactly as only Byrd's ever tasted, and she could be seated here, glowing with the pleasure of cooking food for those she loves.

"I didn't make the stuffing," Carole says.

"Wow." I shift my eyes to Vashti. "You did a great job, V. I haven't had stuffing this good in a long time."

"I didn't make it either," Vashti says a little stiffly. "And what about my stuffing on the menu? You said you loved it."

"Oh, I do, but if you didn't make this, then who—"

"I made it," Yasmen says from the other end of the table.

"You?" I ask disbelievingly. Her mouth tightens and she casts a self-conscious look down the row of people half eating, all listening. "I didn't mean it like that, Yas. I just...it tastes exactly like Byrd's."

The tightness around her mouth eases, and a small smile lifts the corners. "I used her recipe."

"You have it?"

"When we were going through her things," Yasmen says, piercing a mound of macaroni and cheese with her fork. "I found a notebook with some of her recipes. Handwritten."

Everyone is listening and I should probably save my inquisition for later, but I need to know. There are some recipes Byrd didn't use for Grits but reserved for family and friends, almost like she kept something special for us. This particular version of her stuffing is one of them. Vashti has since reshaped Grits's menu into her own creation, so the food we serve now doesn't truly reflect Byrd's. I have photos and keepsakes and all kinds of things Byrd left for me to remember her by. Hell, I even have her dog, but her food? I can't ever have that again. Not quite the way she prepared it, so anything even close is something to be treasured. And to see the recipes handwritten— priceless.

Yasmen shrugs, lowers her gaze to her plate, and smiles ruefully. "It just made me feel closer to her, I guess. We all know I'm not a great cook, but—"

"It's delicious." I ignore everyone else at the table and hold her eyes, trying to convey my gratitude from all the way down here. "I'd like to see the notebook sometime."

I slowly realize everyone's stopped eating, and they're all looking from Yasmen to me with varying degrees of curiosity. Everyone except Vashti, whose eyes are fixed on her lap, back ramrod straight.

"Anyway," I say, hoping to dispel the sudden tension. "This turkey is great, too, Carole, as usual."

"Thank you," Carole answers, flicking a searching gaze to her daughter.

"Now that you mention it," Milky says, taking a forkful of the stuffing. "It does taste like Byrdy's. I'mma need to see them recipes, too, Yas."

"Anytime." Yasmen laughs, her eyes warmed from Milky's approval. "Now, Kassim, Grandma made your favorite. How's that sweet potato casserole?"

With that pivot, everyone returns to their plates, grunts of satisfaction punctuating the hum of conversation at the table.

"These salmon croquettes are so good," I tell Vashti in a low voice, reaching under the table to take her hand. It feels disingenuous somehow, like I'm only touching her to reassure her of something, but she squeezes my fingers back and lifts her head to give me a half-hearted smile.

"Thank you." She takes a sip of the sweet tea at her elbow. "Now tell me more about this trip to Charlotte."

"We leave Saturday," I say, keeping my tone flat and neutral. I've deliberately not given much thought to the trip. "It's really quick. We'll fly back Sunday afternoon."

" 'We' being you, Harvey, and Yasmen? You're all flying out Saturday?"

I eat a stalling scoop of mashed potatoes, taking my time chewing and answering. "Harvey has family in Charlotte, so he's already there for Thanksgiving and we'll meet him."

Vashti puts her fork down and angles a narrowed look my way. "So it's just you and Yasmen traveling?"

"Yeah," Deja pipes in from beside Vashti, her mouth full of something. "Grandma's staying with us. She'll make us clean every-thing. I hope she doesn't cook chitterlings again. Have you ever had them, V?"

Vashti tears her eyes away from mine to answer Deja. "What? I'm sorry. Have I ever had what?"

"Chitterlings." Deja covers her mouth, eyes twinkling. "They stink so bad."

"I wash 'em in Clorox," Carole interjects, laughing at both Deja's and Vashti's horrified expressions. "All the poison boils right off. Ain't nobody ever died eating my chitlings. Y'all don't know what's good. I'll save you some, Vashti."

"Um, that's okay. No, thank you." Vashti manages a small laugh, but her sober eyes return to me and I know she's still thinking of the implications of Yasmen and me traveling together. There shouldn't be implications. We're two adults who are no longer married and have moved on, even dating other people.

And yet . . . I hadn't mentioned it to Vashti because I feel some type of way about it myself. It waffles between dread and anticipation. I squash it because it's irrational and dangerous and useless.

"It's such a quick trip," I remind her, squeezing her hand again.

"I know. I just wish you had told me." She jerks her hand away, ostensibly to take another sip of her tea, but I can't help but feel it's a gesture of censure.

"I would have if it was important," I say, loudly enough for only her to hear. "But it's not. It's just business."

The look she levels on me holds irony and a tiny chip of concern. "Okay, Josiah. If you say so."

She goes back to eating and chatting with Deja beside her. I hazard a glance to the other end of the table, where Yasmen is chatting with Bayli, one of our best hostesses, head thrown back, the long expanse of her throat working with one of those laughs of hers that fills the room and makes you want in on the joke. The tacky, brightly colored turkey earrings swing when she leans forward to grab her glass of water. Her dark eyes are lit with amusement, cheeks lifted in a smile that makes her look happy. Happier than I've seen her in a long time. Actually, that's not right. She's been looking happy for months now, and the realization is a tiny pin pricking my chest.

She's back.

The woman I married, who ran the world around her without breaking a sweat, took care of our kids, of herself, of everyone—she's back.

The woman I loved is back. Therapy, medicine, time. The hell if I know everything it took to bring her back to us, as beautiful and bright and confident as ever, but it's happened.

Vashti tugs my sleeve, and I glance over, forcing my mouth to match her smile. Her tranquil expression tells me she's dismissed her concerns about Yasmen and me traveling alone. She believes it will be fine. She believes me.

I hope I deserve her trust.

"Are we gonna say what we're thankful for?" Deja asks once there is more conversation happening than eating.

I glance at her, surprised, but pleased. She's obviously going through some stuff, but at her core, she's still that girl who loves being surrounded by her family and geeks out over holidays.

"That's a great idea." I smile at her and then at Kassim, whose face lights up at the suggestion.

"We always go around the table and say what we're grateful for," Deja tells everyone.

"Glad you remembered, Day," Yasmen says, linking her hands under her chin. "You want to start?"

"Oh, sure," Deja says. "I'm grateful for all my new followers. You can find me at Kurly Girly on the Gram and TikTok."

Everyone laughs as expected, and Deja's grin takes over her whole face.

Charmer.

We go around the table, each sharing what we're grateful for. It's good to hear from the Grits employees about things that are important to them, glimpses into their lives, especially Milk. He and I don't talk much about Byrd, but if there's anyone who misses her nearly as much as Yasmen and I do, it's Milk. I'm not sure why I haven't reached out to him more. Maybe on some level, he reminds me of what I've lost. Even the few therapy sessions I've had with Dr. Musa have helped me realize that when I'm hurt, I shut down and bury myself in work, which I knew. But I'm also realizing how much I isolate, lick my wounds alone. Maybe subconsciously, because I've lost so much, I'm afraid that someday I *will* be alone.

If I were in front of Dr. Musa, I'd laugh with him about his psychobabble bullshit rubbing off on me.

"What I'm grateful for?" Yasmen tilts her head. "Wow. I'm not sure where to start. I'm gonna have to cheat and say more than one."

She drops her eyes to the remnants of the meal on her plate, biting her lip and toying with her fork.

"My kids. They're honestly the reason I'm even still here." She looks up with wide eyes, like she's said something she hadn't intended to. "I just mean, everyone knows it's been a hard couple of years. Deja and Kassim, you guys mean everything. I'm grateful for friends who feel like sisters. And I think I'm most grateful for time, which doesn't always heal all wounds, but teaches us how to be happy again even with our scars."

Her words drift over us, landing with some even more than others. Carole blinks rapidly, toughing out the threat of tears. Even she couldn't reach her daughter when Yas was at her lowest point. Seeing Carole here, laughing with Yasmen again, makes this holiday even more special.

"Kassim," Yasmen says. "Your turn."

Kassim sits up straighter, and you'd think he was at the head of a class preparing to give a report. I'm not sure where the overachiever gene was strongest, me or Yasmen, but Kassim must have gotten a double dose.

"I'm grateful for therapy," Kassim says without hesitation. "Dr. Cabot's cool. I like having someone to talk to."

It's so simple, but so profound, this kid saying he's in therapy and that it helps him. How many adults never admit they need help? Need someone to talk to? Never get the help I've begun to understand therapy can offer? A quick dart of shame pierces me. At ten years old, my son is braver with his feelings than I've ever been. I look up to find Yasmen's eyes not on Kassim, but on me. Pleasure, pride—there's some mixture of them clear in the small crook of her smile.

After dessert, some guests leave, some camp out in front of the television for football.

"This has been so great," Vashti whispers to me. "I loved it."

"I'm glad. You ready to head out?" She nods and I look around, but there's no sign of my kids. "Let me tell Kassim and Deja we're leaving."

"Tell them goodbye for me. I'm headed to the car. I was up late *and* early cooking. I'm exhausted."

"And I told you there was nothing to be nervous about," I tease. "Carole doesn't even bite."

"She's wonderful. I'm gonna tell her goodbye and thank her for everything."

I head up the stairs, pretty sure I know where Deja is. Sure enough, she has her phone and tripod set up, along with an array of hair products. With promises not to spend the whole night on her phone, she kisses me and pushes me back out. Kassim is also in his room, wearing his headset and playing video games with Jamal. Otis drowses at his feet.

"Hey, Dad," he says, eyes never leaving the action on-screen. "Can Otis stay with me tonight?"

I glance down at Otis. It's not unusual, especially on holidays, for him to stay here instead of at my place, though sometimes he whines to come home. Dog can't stand to sleep away from me.

"Sure, but I'm not coming back if he starts crying to come home."

"He'll be okay," Kassim says, rubbing the dog's head. "Won't you, Otis?"

Otis drops his head to Kassim's lap, which is sign enough for me.

"You and Deja have to walk him early in the morning," I remind Kassim. "It's still dark outside, so you can't go alone."

"I know. I already asked her. She said it's fine."

I reach down to scrub behind Otis's ears, and he leans into my palm for a second before returning to Kassim.

"Okay then," I tell him, dropping a quick kiss on Kassim's head. "Love you, kid."

"Love you, too, Dad."

Carole stands at the bottom of the stairs, lines of fatigue bracketing her mouth and eyes. She's not as young as she used to be, and two days of cooking for so many may be catching up to her.

"I was hoping I hadn't missed you," Carole says, looping her elbow through mine. "It was good seeing you."

I give her a side hug, and it feels like a hundred other times our family gathered and she stood with me, but everything's different now.

"Good seeing you, too, Carole. Amazing job as usual."

"It was great meeting Vashti. She's very sweet." She looks up at me, her smile in place, but eyes narrowed. "I'd hate to see that girl get hurt."

"Why do you say that?" I ask, even though I think I know.

"Boy, you ain't dumb, and I ain't either." The smile fades. "I *know* you, Josiah, and I know my daughter."

"Well, maybe that's who you should talk to," I tell her, rounding out the sharp edges of the comment. "Because that ship has sailed, and she was the captain. That's over."

"Doesn't feel like it to me. Not the way you look at Yasmen when another woman is sitting right beside you."

The last thing I need with all the conflicting emotions rioting inside of me is Carole making things worse.

"Vashti's waiting in the car," I say, putting a nail in the conversation. "I better go."

"I didn't mean no harm. I love you like a son. You know that."

"I know." I bend to kiss her cheek.

"Oh! I think Vashti left one of her dishes in the kitchen. Could you grab it on your way out? And thank her again for them beignets."

When I walk into the kitchen, it's shockingly clean after such a huge meal with so many dishes and so many people, but Yasmen, grinning down at her phone, is the only one here.

"Did you do this all alone?" I frown at my inconsideration for not thinking about cleaning up. Carole had assured us they had everything covered, but was it just her and Yasmen doing all the work?

Yasmen's smile falters a little when she looks up from her phone.

"Oh, no. Mama and Bayli helped. Mama even wrangled Deja's sassy tail for a few minutes to help load the dishwasher. It didn't take long."

"Oh, good." I nod to her phone. "Boyfriend?"

It's none of my business and the look she shoots me says as much.

When did I lose all control of my brain-to-speech function? I didn't mean to ask that. I don't care if she's texting Mark.

"I don't have a boyfriend." She slides her phone into the pocket of her pants, meeting my eyes with a slight smile. "But if you mean Mark, no. Hendrix and Soledad were just checking in."

I nod and glance around, searching the clear counters for any stray dish. "Your mom said Vashti left one of her dishes?"

"I don't think so." A frown puckers Yasmen's brows. "She double-checked before she left."

I hesitate, knowing I have no reason to linger, but feeling compelled to speak. "It was good, what Seem said today, huh?"

She swooshes out a breath, touching both hands over her heart. "I don't think I've ever been prouder of him. No perfect score or prize he's ever won compared to what he said at that table today for me."

"Yeah." I lean against the counter beside her. "He's something else. He just came right out with it. No embarrassment. Most guys I know wouldn't do that, even if they are in therapy."

"That's the young man you're raising," she says, slanting a look up at me from a curl of long lashes. "I know you've had your issues with therapy, but you're going for him. You've modeled for him it was okay, and he'll be healthier for it."

"I modeled it?" I scoff. "I think we both know you've done a lot more to demonstrate the merits of it than I have."

"We did it then," she says. "We still make a pretty good team, huh?"

A new tension circulates in the air, coiling around us. It tugs on me until, though neither of us has moved an inch, it feels like we're only a breath apart. Like the space separating our bodies disappears and we're close. The coolness of her breath, the intoxicating scent of vanilla warmed on skin I know from memory is soft to the touch. My senses absorb her in long draughts until it feels like I can't breathe one more second if I don't—

"I better go." I push away from the counter and stride over to the back door, opening it, hoping the bracing cold air clears my head of her.

But I'm not sure it can. Not sure anything ever will, even though I have to try because she made her choice. It wasn't me. Isn't me. I can't stay here. Not in this kitchen and not here, still wanting her.

"Josiah," she says from behind me.

I don't face her, but turn my head, giving her only my profile. "Yeah?"

"I'll, um, see you Saturday morning, right?"

Shit. Charlotte.

"Yeah. Car will pick us up at ten."

"Great. Um…" It feels like we share a held breath as I wait for her to say what she has to say. "Happy Thanksgiving."

I nod, not looking back, and walk toward the car, where Vashti waits.

"Idiot." I shove my hands into my pockets, frustration gritting my teeth. "You never learn."

CHAPTER TWENTY-THREE

JOSIAH

Vashti wants me to spend the night.

Of course she does. It's a holiday. We've had very little time alone lately since things have been so busy. And if I'm honest—and I need to be with myself and with her—ever since that charged moment with Yasmen in my office, I've been avoiding this. Maybe even since I watched her kiss that wannabe congressman on the front porch. My response to seeing her with someone else was unreasonable, out of proportion, and disturbing. I really need to unpack this shit with Dr. Musa next week, but he's not here to help navigate this conversation that is probably long overdue.

"Dinner was really cool," Vashti says, stacking Tupperware in her refrigerator. "Everyone was great, and Yasmen's mom is so sweet."

"Yeah." I take one of the high stools at the counter in the kitchen of her apartment. "Carole's one of a kind."

I'd hate to see that girl get hurt.

My ex-mother-in-law's words looped in my head the whole ride to Vashti's apartment. I didn't want to hear what she had to say, and God knows I don't want to deal with it, but she's right. I can't hurt Vashti. My mind won't release the image of Yasmen at the other end of the table today, head flung back, husky laugh floating down to me. Those stupid turkey earrings whispering against her neck. It's been hard and cold and lonely since the divorce, and I really needed to move on. On some level, wanting to move on from what was the most painful season of my life, I hoped this relationship with Vashti would make it hurt less. If I wait to feel *nothing* for Yasmen, I'll be standing in this same spot forever.

But maybe I need to stand still until I feel less for her than I do right now.

That's a hard, lonely pill to swallow. It's going down straight, no chaser, but the longer I think about it, the more this seems the right thing to do.

Once the leftovers are put away, Vashti walks over to stand between my legs at the island and looks up to me with clear eyes. She trusts me, but I don't trust myself. I'm not saying I'll do anything about wanting Yasmen, but I can't be in a relationship with someone else while I feel this way.

Vashti's fingers wander up, over my shoulder, to caress my neck.

"Vash," I begin as I put my hand over hers, stopping her from going any further, "we need to talk."

"Sure." She leans up to kiss me behind my ear. "After?"

I stand, carefully moving her back a step and crossing around to the other side of the kitchen island, leaning my elbows on the granite surface to face her.

"Now."

"Okay." Her short laugh holds a note of nervous uncertainty. On some level, does she see this coming? Certainly at Thanksgiving dinner her suspicions surfaced, even if she quickly tucked them away. Maybe she's been in just as much denial as I have.

"Do we need a drink for this convo?" she half jokes, walking over to grab a bottle of wine from the counter.

"Uhhh...I'm good, but thanks."

"I think I will." She fills a wineglass almost to the top and sets the bottle down between us on the counter before hopping up onto the high stool. "Because 'we need to talk' does not usually bode well."

I can't even reassure her on that point because I'm not sure how to make this *not* hurt. I do know the longer I wait, the worse it will feel.

"I don't want to hurt you, Vash."

"Then don't," she says, her voice a thready whisper, the light in her eyes dimming a little.

"I don't think we should see each other anymore." I rush to fix that because I know how much Grits means to her. "Outside of work, of course. I'm saying—"

"You're breaking up with me."

Our gazes lock over her untouched glass of wine and I draw a deep breath. "I think it's best if we end it now."

Her lashes drop, covering whatever is in her eyes, and she takes a long gulp of wine, setting the glass down carefully.

"Yasmen?" she asks.

At her question, so stark and straightforward, I want to be the same, but it's more complicated than that.

"Yes," I reply. "And no."

At her lifted brow, I press on.

"Yes, I have some unresolved issues from my marriage. No, nothing's going on between Yasmen and me. I don't plan for there to be."

"Then why can't we just—"

"Because it's not fair. You don't want a guy who's thinking about someone else when they're with you."

"Oh." She blinks rapidly and bites her bottom lip. "So she's been in your head this whole time?"

"It's not like that."

"But you think about her and you *feel* about her." Vashti seems to be holding her breath waiting for my response, tension across her shoulders and in the fingers gripping the fragile stem of her wineglass.

"If I waited until I don't have feelings for Yasmen before I moved on," I tell Vashti as gently as I can, "I never would."

The truth of my words sinks in for both of us. There it is. As much as I don't want it to be the case, getting over Yasmen is not a thing I may ever be able to do. That doesn't mean I can trust her or even be with her again. I'm not sure I can do either of those things, but I can't root these emotions out of my heart. They're woven into the fiber of who I am. It's an emotional impasse I need to resolve for myself, and until I have, I can't involve anyone else.

"I know you care about me," Vashti says, tears glittering in her eyes. "I can give you time. We can keep trying to make this work."

That sounds exhausting. Fighting what I feel for Yasmen has become a full-time job. Moonlighting to make sure I'm giving Vashti what she needs is not fair to her, to me, not even to Yasmen.

"You deserve everything from the man in your life, Vash," I say, reaching over to hold her hand. "I hoped that could be me. I really did, but I don't want you to settle for less."

A tear slides down her cheek and plops onto the back of my hand, and I feel like an asshole. I wanted so desperately to move on, to eradicate Yasmen from my system, that I entangled someone else in our quagmire. Guilt gnaws at my insides, and I want nothing more than to bring this to the kindest close possible, so I sit in the uncomfortable silence, giving her space to process it.

"We never said this was love, right?" she murmurs with a choked little laugh.

I've never told her I loved her. I've always known that wasn't true. I've given those words and my heart to exactly one woman ever, and that backfired on me in a shit bomb of pain and regret. The next time I say those words, it will be because I've somehow managed to tear Yasmen out and, by some miracle, let someone else in. But that time is not now.

I clear my throat. "At work we—"

"I'll be fine," she cuts in, eyes going harder and chin set to a defiant angle. "I've worked too hard for too long to let a relationship derail my career. Grits is one of the hottest spots in the city. I'm not giving it up."

"Good. Then we agree."

"I think we just tell people if they ask. Don't make it a big deal." She huffs out a tiny breath of a laugh. "I mean, it wasn't a big deal."

"Hey." I wait for her to look up. "I wasn't toying with you. I legitimately wanted to move on. I hoped I was ready for something with someone I cared about. That's what this was. I hope you believe that, and that I never wanted to lead you to think it was something else."

"You never did, no." She offers a teary smile. "But you're right. I deserve a man who is as wild about me as you are about her."

"I'm not..." I cut off my words at the disbelieving look she aims at me. "I hope you get everything you deserve."

CHAPTER TWENTY-FOUR

YASMEN

Yasmen!" Mama yells from downstairs. "The driver's outside to take you to the airport."

"I'll be down in a few minutes," I shout back.

I inventory the room. A few minutes seems pretty ambitious since my clothes are scattered on the bed, beside the suitcase instead of in it. I've showered, but am in my robe, a scarf still tied over my braids.

"Of all mornings to oversleep," I mutter, trying to organize my thoughts and figure out what to do first.

I tiptoe over to the window and peer through the curtains. A black Suburban idles in my driveway. Maybe I could send the driver to get Josiah if he hasn't picked him up yet, and then come back for me. There's a firm tap at the door before I have time to execute this excellent plan.

"Come on in, Mama." I toss my robe onto the bed. "I could actually use some help."

"I figured, since we've been waiting outside for ten minutes," Josiah says, his tone curt, irritation sketched into his features. "We're gonna miss this flight if you don't hurry up. What do you need me to do?"

When his eyes meet mine, we both freeze. Me, standing stock-still wearing only my bra and panties.

"What I need," I grit out, grabbing the robe again and shoving my arms through the sleeves, "is for you to get out of here."

Josiah doesn't budge, but fixes his stare somewhere over my shoulder.

"Carole said she was busy and couldn't help right now, but sent me to check on you."

First Mama sent him into the kitchen for a dish Vashti did not leave behind. Now this.

I see you, Mama.

Matchmaking your daughter and her divorced husband should be a punishable offense.

Matricide?

"She should have known better than to send you up to my bedroom when I'm still getting dressed," I tell him, gripping the collar of the robe at my neck.

"Maybe she realized it's nothing I haven't seen before." His tone is deliberately casual, but there was nothing casual about the way he scoured my body before he looked away. "I think I can be in the same room as you without losing control."

What about my control?

"We need to get out of here," he says. "What do you need help with?"

I sigh grudgingly and nod to the clothes scattered on the bed. "I've showered, so just toss those into a suitcase."

"All this for an overnight stay?" He cocks a brow and starts folding.

"A girl has to be prepared for anything." With a forced grin, I leave the room to enter my closet and dress, only to realize I left my clothes on the bed. When I step back into the room, a lacy black thong dangles from Josiah's index finger.

"Gimme that." I snatch the underwear and stuff it into the suitcase. "You know what? I got this. It's not much. Go to the car and I'll be right down."

"I'm just trying to help your slow ass." He chuckles, shaking his head.

"I can be ready in no time if you just leave me be."

I roll my eyes and push his arm, urging him toward the door. Without being tight, a navy blue sweater molds the sculpted muscles of his arms and torso. I'm hyperaware of the tiny sliver of space between his chest and mine. Conscious of the fact that my breasts feel fuller pressed against the robe. My bra, a silken cage brushing my sensitive nipples. My heart, a wild beast, pounding to get out. I'm barefoot. Broad and tall, he towers over me in a way that used to make me feel safe when we stood together. I don't feel safe right now, though. Every stunted breath, every second of this silence throbbing between us feels perilous. I'm threatened, but the enemy is within. The danger is in my own traitorous responses to a man who used to be mine. He looks down at me, dark eyes hooded, watching me closely, and makes no move to leave. My fingers clench around his arm, and finger by finger, I release my hold.

"Give me ten minutes," I say, my voice smoked over and husky. I'm desperate to get him out of this room and out of my vicinity.

"Make it five." He tosses the terse words over his shoulder as he walks out the door.

It takes seven. Zipping around the room like the hounds of hell are nipping at my heels, which isn't far from the truth, I toss the clothes and toiletries into my roll-on and stuff my makeup bag into an over-sized purse. I dress and tap at Deja's bedroom door, waiting for her invitation to open. When I enter, she draws back the sheer curtains encircling her bed. Poking her head out and blinking at me sleepily. A leopard-print silk bonnet covers her hair and she's wearing Marvel pajamas. Storm's chalk-white eyes watch me almost as intently as my daughter's do. Like this, she looks young and vulnerable, with no time to raise her guard.

"Hey." I smile, leaning against the doorjamb.

"Hey." She stretches and yawns. "What time is it?"

"Early. You can go back to sleep, but we're leaving for the airport. You guys behave for your grandmother."

She falls back into her pillows and pulls the cover over her neck and shoulders. "Deuces, Mom," she mumbles from the depths of her bedclothes. "We'll be fine."

"We'll call when we land. Grandma is here, but look after your brother."

"Always do." Her voice drowses into oblivion, the last syllables trailing off as she drifts back to sleep.

I close her door and crack open Kassim's. He's still sleeping peacefully, covers kicked off and arms folded beneath his pillow. I don't wake him, but drop a quick kiss to his hair before tiptoeing out and down the stairs.

The smell of coffee and bacon greets me in the foyer. Leaving my bag at the door, I walk to the kitchen. Mama glances up from the dough she's shaping into biscuits.

"You leaving?" she asks.

"Yeah." I walk over to her and lean a hip against the island. "I know what you're doing, and you need to stop."

She stretches her eyes into wide innocence. "I have no idea what you mean."

"Thanksgiving night, you sent Josiah to me in the kitchen for the dish Vashti did *not* leave behind. This morning you send him upstairs to my bedroom to 'help.'"

"I was busy." She waves flour-covered hands at the expanse of dough. "These biscuits won't make themselves."

"Mama, we're divorced. Not taking a break. Not separated. It's over and Josiah's with someone else."

"And I really like Vashti," Mama says. "Such a sweet girl."

"She is."

"Much too sweet to be caught in the middle of two people who obviously belong together."

I stare at her unblinkingly, frustration twisting inside of me.

"Mama, don't—"

"You think other people can't see it? That you still want him, and he still wants you?"

"He doesn't want me," I answer flatly.

"I see you didn't deny that you still want him." The triumph on Mama's face is galling.

"Will you just stop?"

The words come out louder and more forcefully than I intended, powered by all my frustration and irritation and anger. All focused on myself, but directed at her. Mama doesn't even flinch at the sharp edge of my voice, but holds my gaze.

"Do you want him back?" she asks, not giving me the chance to respond. "Because if you do, you have a rare opportunity here. A weekend alone with no distractions. Just the two of you. Maybe you can really talk and figure out how two people who loved—excuse me, *love*—each other as much as the two of you do end up not together, because I'll be darned if I know."

Her question pings off the walls in my head.

Do you want him back?

Even if I did, he's taken now. Found himself a woman who doesn't make him feel like he's living in the spin cycle.

An obnoxious honk sounds from the front yard, cutting her diatribe blessedly short. I know Josiah put the driver up to that honk.

"I gotta go." I kiss her cheek. "You have our numbers, of course. Call if you or the kids need anything. We'll be back tomorrow night."

"I got this, but you need to think about what I said, Yasmen. It's not too late *yet*, but what if he marries her?"

I freeze at the word "marry," my fingers clawing around the handle of my suitcase. My heart is beating in my shoes because it dropped to my feet at her question. Of course I've always known Josiah could remarry, but the possibility never had a specific face and body and person attached to it. Now it does. And she's a beautiful, talented, confident woman who would probably never lose her hold on life so badly that getting out of bed felt like an Olympic sport.

"Bye, Mama," I say, rolling my bag out of the kitchen and toward the foyer. "I gotta go."

Josiah is leaning against the passenger side of the Suburban when I step onto the porch. Pushing away from the truck, he takes a few steps forward and grabs my suitcase to load in the trunk.

Traffic is light and the ride is uneventful while I do my makeup and Josiah responds to emails on his phone.

"Kids were still sleeping when I looked in on them," he says.

"Yeah." Small mirror balanced in my lap, I dot concealer under my eyes and on a few uneven spots. "I talked to Deja briefly, but Seem didn't even stir."

"We'll check on them when we land."

"How was Vashti this morning?" I ask, cursing myself as soon as the question leaves my lips, but managing to keep my hand steady as I sponge-blend my foundation.

Josiah turns his head to look at me. "We haven't talked today, but I assume she's fine. She and Anthony will hold the restaurant down until we get back if that's what you're wondering."

It's not.

After seeing her at his house that morning, I guess I assumed she spends the night all the time. My curiosity about their relationship is endless. They are, admittedly, very discreet at work, and they aren't a PDA couple. I've seen them hold hands occasionally, but they're never all over each other. Not how Josiah and I were when things were good. Though more reserved than I am, Josiah was always unabashedly affectionate and readily demonstrative. Does he hold back with Vashti when I'm around to spare me discomfort? Or are they always that restrained? How are they when they're alone?

How are they in bed?

My hand slips. A line of dark brown pencil streaks beneath the bottom row of lashes.

"Dammit." I lick my finger and carefully wipe away the offending mark.

"You okay?" Josiah asks, eyes not leaving his Apple watch.

"Yeah. Just a bump in the road."

I go back to my smoky eye. With eyeshadow done, I apply a little Trophy Wife highlighter to my cheeks and chin. If Rihanna never records another song, I'm fine as long as Fenty keeps on giving. It's a fair trade.

Our phones ding simultaneously with an incoming text message. I'm midstroke filling in my brows, so I leave it for Josiah to check.

"Harvey," he says, reading the message from his watch. "Asking if his assistant sent us the hotel itinerary."

"I got it." I spare him a sideways glance. "The Hardway, right? That boutique hotel not too far from the restaurant?"

"Yeah, it looked really nice online."

Pulling his phone from his pocket, he types out a response.

By the time we pull up to Hartsfield-Jackson departures, my makeup is done and I've removed the scarf from my braids so they hang down my back. Josiah grabs both our bags and rolls them toward the airport entrance.

Over the next few hours, I wish a dozen times that Harvey were traveling with us so he could act as a buffer. When it's just the two of us, we seem to err on the side of saying too much, or not enough. The wrong thing instead of the right. I can't wait to get to Charlotte, check into my room, and interact with Josiah only when absolutely necessary. Seeming to have the same idea, he puts in his earbuds as soon as we take our seats. I close my eyes and pretend to sleep the entire flight.

Once we land, Harvey has arranged another car for pickup, which takes us to the Hardway. Lack of sleep and the early morning are catching up to me, and all I can think about is the possibility of resting in my room for an hour before we meet the couple who's selling the restaurant. The parking lot and lobby are a hive of activity. We wait for a few minutes in the line of guests checking in. By the time we reach the front desk, my feet ache and I'm longing for my more comfortable shoes. I'm so fixated on the pain in my pinky toe, the front desk manager's words barely penetrate my haze.

"What the hell do you mean, there isn't another room?" Josiah snaps, a line forming between his brows. "I have the reservation right here."

He shows her the confirmation number from the email Harvey's assistant sent.

"Yes, sir," Amanda, according to her name tag, says with exaggerated patience. "I've given you the key for room 428."

"Yes, but you also just gave me a key for her," he says, tilting his head toward me. "For room 428."

"Yes, your reservation is a king-sized bed," she says, consulting her screen. "Two occupants. Josiah Wade and Yasmen Wade."

"We're supposed to have separate rooms," I nearly screech.

"This is obviously a misunderstanding," Josiah tells me. "They'll give us another room."

"I'm so sorry, but like I said, there *are* no other rooms." Amanda divides her apologetic look between the two of us. "There's a huge women's conference in town. A church thing, and all the rooms around here are booked. Room 428 is all we have."

"I'm calling Harvey. He'll get this sorted out," I say, a note of desperation in my voice as I fumble for the phone in my purse. There's no way I'm spending the night with Josiah and a *bed*.

"There's a pullout in the living room," Amanda offers, not helping. "Maybe you can—"

"No," I cut in, my heartbeat ticking up with every ring of Harvey's phone.

"Yasmen," Harvey says, finally answering. "You guys here? How's the hotel?"

"The hotel," I say, "has us booked in one room."

I let that sink in so he can absorb how disastrous this situation is.

"Oh, my new assistant must have mixed that up. She's been making a lot of mistakes lately. She has this—"

"Harvey, forgive me for not giving a *damn* about your new assistant, but do you have a solution?"

"They don't have another room available?"

"No, some women's conference is happening all over the city and the rooms are booked everywhere. You have to fix this." My voice rises as the reality of our situation bears down on me. "We can't—"

"Yas," Josiah interrupts, his tone calm, even. "It's not a big deal. I'll take the pullout in the living room. It's only one night."

The world has been shaken in a matter of a day. One event can fundamentally change the course of our lives forever. I know it's one night, but it will be our first time under the same roof overnight in more than two years.

I stare at him, and his expression is implacable, but it feels like a deliberate control he's imposing on himself and, by extension, also on me.

And maybe it would work, would reassure me if the memory of that moment in the office hadn't been haunting me the last few weeks. Standing between his legs, the strength of our wills clashing, emotion boiling in the air. As much as I try to disregard it, to believe it meant nothing, I'm not convinced.

Nothing has ever meant nothing between us.

"It'll be fine," he says, pocketing the key. "Trust me."

How can I tell him it's not him I don't trust?

It's me.

CHAPTER TWENTY-FIVE

∞

JOSIAH

"Harvey, you gotta fix this."

I pace the hall in front of room 428, clutching the phone to my ear with one hand, gripping the back of my neck with the other.

"I thought you said you could sleep on the pullout," Harvey says, clearly confused. "And it would be fine."

"I lied."

"What—why would you lie?"

"Obviously," I say, lowering my voice, "because I don't want Yasmen to know it's not fine."

"That makes no sense."

"You're not listening."

"Yeah, I am. It sounds like you're scared to be in the room for one night with your ex-wife."

"Scared?" I stop pacing. "Pfftt."

Great rebuttal.

"You'll be in the living room on the couch, and she'll be in the bedroom. I don't understand the problem."

There shouldn't be a problem. I know that, but I can't shake the feeling that if we spend the night in that room together, everything will change... again.

"You don't seriously think anything will happen, do you?" Harvey asks. "I mean, between you and Yasmen?"

It's already happening.

The ground has been shifting by inches ever since that day in my office. Maybe even before. Being in the same room overnight? One wrong move, and this shift could turn tectonic.

"You think you'd cheat on Vashti. Is that what you're worried about?"

"That's irrelevant." I squeeze the bridge of my nose and force out a long breath. "Vashti and I broke up."

The small gasp from behind me makes me turn slowly to meet Yasmen's wide, startled eyes.

Dammit.

I wasn't planning to tell her yet, and certainly not like this.

"Harvey," I say, eyeing her warily, "I gotta go. We're due for lunch at one o'clock, right?"

"Yeah, I'll meet you guys there," he says. "It'll be fine."

I hang up without responding, sliding the phone into my pocket and schooling my expression into absolutely unfazed.

"You and Vashti broke up?" Yasmen asks, a frown puckering her sleek brows.

"Yeah."

"When?"

"Thanksgiving."

"Oh, I'm..." Her eyes drop to the floor. "I'm sorry to hear that."

"Are you?" I ask, my voice soft and devoid of any real curiosity.

Her expression when she looks back up tells me nothing. She turns back into the room, not bothering to answer. I hesitate at the threshold before following her in, closing the door behind me.

It's broad daylight. We have a meeting in less than an hour. Business to handle. I know nothing will happen, but lately every time we're alone, that cord that always seemed to draw us together, the one I thought had been permanently severed, tugs on me.

"I think this may be a little too casual, what I'm wearing. It was fine for the plane," she calls from the bedroom. "But I'm gonna change."

I settle onto the couch and pick up the room service menu. I haven't eaten since breakfast, and my stomach is making monster noises.

"I hope their restaurant has good food," I say loudly enough for her to hear in the other room.

"I'm so hungry, forget good food. I'll settle for anything cooked."

I look up, and my response stalls in my throat. The door is slightly ajar, revealing a sliver of the bedroom. Yasmen stands in her bra and underwear. The view only affords flashes of pink satin and lace and smooth brown skin, but my imagination can fill in the gaps. It was bad enough seeing her half-naked and stumbling across her thong this morning. I should have known better than to listen to Carole when she sent me upstairs to "help" Yasmen. But didn't I know better? Didn't I recognize the danger of going to her bedroom—formerly *my* bedroom—when she was getting dressed? Seeing danger and running headlong into it is foolish and reckless. Two things I can't afford to be. Two things I'm usually not, but the unusual has always happened with this woman.

"Uh, yeah." I deliberately avert my gaze from the tempting view. "I'm starving."

She opens the door and pokes her head out. "You need to get in the bathroom? I'm done in here."

Braids cascade around her shoulders to her elbows, making her look even younger. The red knit dress she changed into loves every curve of her body, and the black belt cinching her middle exaggerates the line from breast to waist to hips and ass.

"Nah. I'm good." I clear my throat and look away, back to the menu. "I'mma eat this menu if we don't get some food soon, though."

"Guess what I got?" Her smile is sweet and familiar and contagious, and I find myself smiling back.

"What?"

She dashes into the bedroom, emerging seconds later with her oversize purse.

"Ta-da!" She tosses a small bag to me.

I catch it, my smile faltering when I look down at the package. Chicago-style popcorn, my weakness.

"Wow." I hold the bag for a few seconds without opening it. "Thanks."

"You still like it, right?" Her smile shrinks. "I was just grabbing some snacks for myself last night at the grocery store and saw the popcorn. If you don't—"

"Still addicted," I admit, opening the bag and eating a handful of the sweet-salty crack corn. "Thanks. This'll hold me over till we get some lunch."

"You already requested the Uber?"

"I'll do it now."

She gathers front sections of the braids and raises her arms to twist them into a top knot, leaving the rest loose down her back. The motion lifts her breasts, pressing them tight against the form-fitting dress. I grind the popcorn between my teeth. I'm being tested. Obviously. I have to pass. Failing would be disastrous and stupid. I'm not a glutton for rejection and I'm nobody's fool. I'd have to be both to even consider giving in to this gut-punch, dick-hardening lust I've never been able to squash. I'm not oblivious. Pretty sure the attraction is mutual, that she still wants me, too, on some level. But she doesn't want me for the rest of her life, and that is the promise we made to each other. The one she defaulted on. That's not completely fair. I know what she was going through, but understanding how you got hurt never makes it hurt less.

I set the popcorn on the low table in the sitting room, then grab my phone to order the Uber, giving me something to focus on besides how good Yasmen looks in that damn dress.

Once we're in the car, I relax some, safely seated on my side, the width of the back seat separating us. No sooner have I closed my eyes, determined to shut her out for the ten-minute ride to the restaurant, than she finds another way to torture my senses. This time with her scent.

"What is that damn smell?" I snap, turning my head to study her face.

"Oh, sorry, sir," the Uber driver says, flicking an apologetic look to me in the rearview mirror. "I had garlic knots for lunch. You may still smell—"

"Not you," I tell him, eyes still fixed on Yasmen. "You."

She sniffs under her arms, frowning. "You don't smell me."

"It's a good smell," I admit. "But it's new. Not the one you used to wear."

"Oh." She presses one wrist to my nose. "This?"

She has no idea how close I am to pulling her wrist to my lips and sucking the pulse throbbing there, tracing the veins with my tongue like some thirsty vampire. This is getting worse by the second.

"Yeah, that's it." I push her wrist away and turn my head to look out the window, not really seeing the charming neighborhood already decorated for Christmas, wreaths and lights on the street poles.

"I got it from Honey Chile. Vanilla. You like it?"

"It's fine, yeah," I say abruptly.

"'It's fine' must be one of the best compliments anyone's ever paid me," she says with a dry laugh.

"Is that what you want?" I swivel my head back around to stare at her. "Compliments? You need me to tell you how good you look and smell? Mark not pumping up your ego enough?"

Why did I say that?

The smile withers on her lips and her eyes narrow. Her anger and irritation are much easier to deal with than when she's sweet and tempting.

"I don't need compliments from anyone," she says, her voice knife-sharp. "Least of all from you when I know you don't even mean them."

I shake my head and huff out a self-mocking laugh. Don't mean them? If only she knew.

"Look, Yas. I'm sorry." Coward that I am, I address the apology to my window instead of to her face. She's so damn perceptive, and I don't need her knowing what's really going on in my head and in my pants.

"There's a lot happening," I say. "But I shouldn't take it out on you."

"No, you shouldn't," she replies, the heat already draining from her voice. "Is it anything I can help with?"

"No." *Not when you're my problem.* "Thanks, though. Looks like we're here."

The Uber stops in front of a white Victorian house with dark red shutters. Flower boxes flank the short flight of steps leading to a dark red door. Christmas lights twinkle on the front porch and wreaths hang on the windows.

When we enter HH Eatz, Harvey stands from the bench in the waiting area to greet us.

"There they are," he says. "Right on time. Sorry again about the rooms. My assistant was distraught about her mistake."

"So are we," I mutter.

"It'll be fine," Yas says, shooting me a pointed look. "These things happen. We'll make the best of it, right, Si?"

"Sure we will." I glance beyond the hostess podium into the restaurant, noting the decor mostly comprising dark leather and weathered wood. "Please tell me food is part of the program."

"Oh, yeah. Merry and Ken have something special prepared for you," Harvey says and motions for us to follow him into the restaurant.

It's smaller than Grits, a little cozier. We really lean into the highlife down-home vibe, and our decor reflects the come up. The dishes may be homestyle favorites, but Grits's luxurious decor and first-rate presentation elevate the experience. At least that's what we're going for. Here there's a warmth and intimacy that could be a function of the smaller city, but is probably a deliberate calculation by the owners.

"They're already waiting for us," Harvey says, leading us to the couple seated at the large booth at the back of the restaurant. "Josiah and Yasmen Wade, meet Merry Herman and Ken Harris."

Yasmen extends a hand and a friendly smile. "Nice to meet you."

"We've been looking forward to this," Merry says, taking Yasmen's hand and then mine into hers. "So nice to meet you both. We have prepared our most popular dish, but if there's something else you prefer on the menu, just let us know."

"Maybe we should tell them what their options are, baby," Ken says, a white man of medium height with graying hair and alert hazel eyes. I'd put him between sixty-five and seventy, but it can be hard to tell sometimes.

"You're right." Merry is a woman of average height with pale skin whose hair was probably once blond but now blends with gray, and her blue eyes sparkle when she laughs up at her husband. "Let's sit and then we'll get into it."

Yasmen and I scoot into one side of the curved booth, Harvey sits in the middle, and Merry and Ken face us. I flinch when the long line of Yasmen's thigh touches mine.

"You okay?" she asks, watching me with a concerned frown.

She leans over a little and her breast presses into my arm.

Dammit. This whole meal will be torture if I can't get my head in the game.

"Yeah. Fine." Out of habit, I push down my lust, call up a smile, and turn it on the couple. "I'm starving. What we got?"

CHAPTER TWENTY-SIX

YASMEN

Merry and Ken are couple goals. Over a potpie stuffed with perfectly seasoned pulled chicken and tender vegetables, we get to
know the older couple. They can't keep their hands off each other. Not
in a salacious way. When they're not holding a fork, they're holding
hands. He toys with her earring while he's talking. She leans into the
crook of his arm, rests her head on his shoulder. They share an easy
intimacy that's as tried and warm as a blanket you've had for years and
still treasure.

"That was one of the best meals I've had in a long time," Josiah says,
sitting back when the last morsel disappears from his plate. "And our
chef is one of the finest in Atlanta."

Vashti.

I've barely had time to process that they aren't together anymore. A
dozen questions batter my mind, and now isn't the time for answers
to any of them. He doesn't owe me answers or explanation. They were
dating. Now they're not. It doesn't change a thing between us, but
watching Merry and Ken, I can't help but think of how Josiah and I
used to be. Ironic that when we were younger we had this zeal for each
other, and now we sit across from a couple twice our age whose love
still burns hot, while ours lies in ashes.

"We have an excellent chef," Ken says. "But she's moving to Paris
once this place shuts down."

Surprisingly, it's the first time we've broached the subject of the sale, which is why we're here. They've told us about their kids, and we've shown them pictures of ours. We swapped starter stories, how our businesses came to be. They met through a large catering business where they both worked and decided to strike out on their own.

"We'd have no problem finding a great chef to guarantee continuity between the Atlanta location and this one," Josiah says, sipping his water. "Should it come to that."

"You've seen our numbers," Merry says. "You know how profitable our business has been here. We've done our homework, too, and we know a little about Grits. There's a lot of similarities between what we do and what you do. NoDa is one of the hottest parts of the city. It's a boom within a boom. Charlotte's star is rising fast, and this neighborhood is one of its most sought after."

"It's eclectic," Ken picks up. "There's a community of artisans here, along with some of the best food in the city. Makes for great foot traffic. We can barely keep up with our weekend crowd."

"It's impressive," I offer with a smile. "What you've done here."

"Well, we're impressed by the two of you," Merry says. "We love all the parallels between our journeys and yours. Finding another couple to take this on would be amazing."

"We, uh, aren't a couple anymore," Josiah says, tracing the wood grain of the table with the tip of his finger. "We're divorced."

"Oh." Ken's brows rise. "Then I'm even more impressed. It's hard enough to be in business with your life partner, much less your *former* life partner. That's what I get for assuming. Sorry about that."

"No problem," I assure him. "We've put our business and our kids first. They're most important. We've managed to remain friends."

I hazard a glance up and find Josiah watching me. Our eyes lock and won't let go for a few seconds. Heat crawls up my neck and spatters my cheeks. I finally drag my gaze away to the linen napkin in my lap.

"Friends, huh?" Merry looks between us, a wry smile etching fine lines around her mouth. "I can see that. Well, we never bothered with the marriage part, but we did everything else."

"What?" My head pops up and I latch on to her words. "You two aren't married? But how long have you—"

"Thirty years we've been together." Ken kisses the top of Merry's head. "One successful business and two successful kids, but no rings."

"That's . . . unconventional," Josiah says.

"We are that," Merry says and laughs. "But it works for us. We didn't need the paper or the hardware. Most of the marriages I saw growing up were traps, a means to keep women minimized. Not that I think my Ken would ever do that."

She lifts his knuckle for a kiss.

"We just don't really believe in it as an institution," Ken adds. "But we believe in each other forever. We've made a life together on our own terms."

"The only thing holding us together," Merry says, looking at Ken with affection, "is our love, but that is the proof of it. That we could leave at any time."

"But neither of us ever would. Never have. I would argue that what we've made is stronger, truer than most marriages because of the freedom it allows us."

"So you have an open relationship?" Harvey asks. "I didn't know that."

"It's not open. We're monogamous." Ken slides Merry an amused glance. "At least I think we've always been."

"Always." Merry chuckles, settling deeper into the crook of Ken's arm. "We chose each other, and our minds have never changed."

A server walks up to our table with a tray of desserts, redirecting the conversation, but I can't shake what they've said. If Josiah and I had taken that route, we never would have divorced. We would have just parted ways, but I think the hurt and bitterness would have still followed us. The piece of paper doesn't define your commitment, but neither does its absence. I suspect what Josiah and I once had would have been just as strong had we chosen not to marry, and it would have hurt just as much when we fell apart. My thoughts wander to the simple gold band and chip diamond ring Josiah gave me, all he could afford at the time. It's in the same jewelry box with those turkey earrings and the wheel necklace he gave me for our anniversary. A crypt for diamonds and demons and ghosts.

"Chocolate?" Josiah asks, jarring me from my maudlin musings.

"Huh?" I look from him to the plate of desserts.

"The chocolate is delicious," Merry says. "But the pear turnover is sublime. I recommend everyone try it at least once."

"Pears are my favorite fruit," I tell her with a smile. "I haven't had any in forever. I'll have the turnover."

"The pear trees are out back," Ken says and slides the pastry onto my plate with his knife. "They were here long before we were. We just keep them going. Some of the best pears in the state."

"They've won contests," Merry adds, pride in her smile. "You won't regret trying it."

"Oh, dear God," I moan, turning the warm pears and flaky crust in my mouth. "This has to be a deadly sin."

Merry laughs. "Told you."

"Taste," I say, heaping some of the gooey dessert onto my fork and bringing it to Josiah's mouth. It's habit. We always used to share our food. He opens immediately, his eyes closing in appreciation.

"Wow," he says, forgoing the chocolate cake to reach for a turnover of his own from the tray. "Does the recipe for this come with the business?"

"Perfect segue," Ken says. "You've seen us on paper and now you've met us in person. Seen our operation."

"Eaten our food," Merry says with a smile. "Are you interested?"

"You have a great place here." Josiah sets his fork down on the plate in front of him. "Beautiful space. Great neighborhood. Yasmen and I need to discuss it before we make any solid plans."

"It's not just what could happen here," I tell them. "But making sure expanding won't compromise what we're doing in Atlanta."

"I've got all your numbers," Harvey interjects.

"She doesn't mean money," Josiah says. "We'll need to oversee this expansion. We're in a boom, too, and it demands a lot of us. We don't want to spread ourselves thin."

"Our kids come first," I say. "We need to make sure we won't be cheating them, missing things we should be there for if we take this expansion on."

"We respect that." Merry twines her fingers with Ken's on the table. "How old are they again?"

"Deja's thirteen," Josiah says.

"And Kassim's ten," I add.

"We were in the thick of building this when our twins were young," Ken says, exchanging a rueful smile with Merry. "We missed a lot."

"And we paid dearly for it." Merry sighs, her perennially cheerful expression darkening some. "Thank goodness we realized they were getting off course before it got too bad."

"So you weigh the pros and cons, keeping them first," Ken says. "And let us know, but don't take too long. We'd love knowing this place we put so much into is in great hands when we leave. You seem like exactly the kind of people we'd want to see here, but either way we'll be putting this place on the market come the new year."

"And as soon as that happens"—Merry snaps her fingers—"it'll be gone."

We finish dessert and walk the property, touring it in more detail than when we passed through the dining room to the table. In the back, there's a large room with bottles of wine and all varieties of liquor lining the walls. Ken grabs one from a high shelf and holds it out to Josiah.

"I wanted to give you this as a token of our appreciation," Ken says. "The two of you coming up here to view the place, taking time to see what we're about, means a lot."

"Wow." Josiah reads the label on the square bottle, a note of admiration creeping into his voice. "Yamazaki. Nice. Thank you very much."

I've heard Josiah talk about the expensive Japanese whiskey, but haven't actually tasted it myself. We end the tour in a small courtyard where, when it's warm, diners can eat at wrought-iron tables. It's exactly the kind of thing I could see us doing for our customers. This is a great spot, and a second Grits would thrive here. I recognize the gleam in Josiah's eyes. It was there when we first started in Atlanta. The man loves a challenge.

"It was so nice meeting you," Merry says, leaning forward to give me a peck on the cheek while we wait for the Uber. I move to pull away, but she squeezes my arm gently, bringing me closer.

"It's not too late," she whispers in my ear.

I lean back to peer at her face. She subtly tips her head toward Josiah and Ken saying their goodbyes just ahead of us.

"I don't…" I glance at Josiah, too, my heart skipping traitorous beats at how handsome he looks, a broad smile creasing his lean cheeks. "I don't know what you mean."

Merry releases a sly, low laugh. "I watched the two of you all through lunch stealing glances at each other when you thought no one was looking. Maybe a second chance?"

My eyes stray to Josiah's wide shoulders, the powerful lines of his back beneath the impeccably tailored jacket, the striking profile and flash of white teeth in a panty-melting smile.

"I was no walk in the park, Merry."

"Who wants to walk in the park? I think that man would run wild with you."

Her words settle between us on the cool air, and I don't know what to make of them. Don't know if there's any truth to what she says, or that I'd be willing to risk my pride to find out.

Do you want him back?

Mama's question sifts through my thoughts, disturbing and titillating. How much longer can I ignore the attraction simmering between us? Now that he's no longer with Vashti, should I press? See if he'd even be interested in…what? I demanded a divorce, and now that my libido wants to come out and play, I want *what* with him?

"Thank you for everything," I tell Merry. "We'll be in touch."

She gives me a knowing smile, but lets me go and waves goodbye.

The Uber pulls up to the curb and I climb in gratefully. When we were in the restaurant, time seemed to fly by, but now that we're done, the long day is catching up with me. We spent more than four hours with Merry and Ken. Once we reach the room, I don't want to move until we have to fly back.

The room.

Meeting Merry and Ken, checking out the restaurant, distracted me from the clear and present danger waiting in room 428. I have to sleep with Josiah mere feet away.

"Let's talk about it when we get back, yeah?" Harvey leans into Josiah's window, brows arched questioningly.

"Okay." Josiah gives a little salute and rolls up the window. Harvey pats the car twice and strolls back into the restaurant as we pull off. I let my head loll against the seat.

"So what'd you think?" I ask, watching him through the slits of my lashes, eyes growing heavy with fatigue.

Josiah rests his head on the leather seat behind him, linking his hands across the tautness of his stomach. "I think it's a great opportunity."

"Agreed."

"We have to weigh what it will cost financially, of course, but also what it will require of us." He turns his head to look at me. "I would have to be here a lot in the initial stages. If I'm not around as much, more falls on you with the kids."

"I'd be fine with that, I think. It'd only be for a season." I catch his eyes in the dimming light of early evening. "It could be great for us. Help us set up the kids well."

"Yeah. I did think of that, of course. College fund, money to help with their first car, first house."

"Mama couldn't afford any of that. I was lucky to get a partial scholarship, and paying back those student loans was rough in the beginning. I want better for them."

"Byrd definitely didn't have the money to help me with my car, that secondhand Honda."

"Secondhand?" I laugh. "That was more like fourth- or fifth-hand."

"Hey." He fake frowns. "I worked at a car wash all summer saving for that thing."

I bend forward a little, giggling. "And had the nerve to pick me up for our first date in that death trap. I should have gotten a tetanus shot after sitting in that tore-up front seat. Literally tore up from the floor up."

"I can't believe I drove you around in it." A smile bends his lips, and his shoulders shake with a silent laugh. "Or that there was a second date."

"Remember we had to rig the seat belt?"

"And we got stopped by that cop?"

"Um, we didn't get *stopped* by the cop," I remind him. "We were parked behind that fried-chicken spot that caught fire over off Moreland."

"Shit." He runs a hand over his head, laughing. "You're right."

"He banged on the windows with that flashlight because they were all fogged up and we were…"

Fucking.

Steam-drenched memories waft around us. Me on top in the front seat, thighs spread over him, dress pooling at my waist, panties pushed aside so he could get in. We couldn't make it home. Josiah had pulled into the abandoned lot when it was late and there was no one around because we *had* to have each other. Urgent heat had burned through common sense and caution.

My heart hammers a frantic beat and my lungs are breath-starved. I lick my lips, and he tracks the movement, heavy-lidded eyes smoldering from the memory or from this moment, I'm not sure.

I cough and sit up straight. Josiah turns away to look out the window, effectively shutting down the conversation. The last few minutes of the ride we spend in silence, the city a whir of bright lights and holiday optimism strung through branches and suspended from the stars like tinsel.

CHAPTER TWENTY-SEVEN

JOSIAH

"So room service for dinner?" I ask Yasmen, poking my head into the bedroom.

In the last few hours since our meeting, we've both been chilling in our own corners. She's lying on her side, one pillow beneath her head and one between her knees. The braids splay out around her, rippling over her shoulders and down her back. She's changed clothes since our lunch meeting and scrubbed her face free of makeup. In her sweatpants and Aggie pride T-shirt, socked feet tucked under her, she could be that college girl I fell for practically on sight.

"Yes, please." She rolls onto her back, staring up at the ceiling and groaning. "I don't care if you bring the food to me in a trough, as long as I don't have to leave this room."

I walk in and sit on the edge of the bed, handing her the room service menu. "The steak looks good."

"Already had steak. I'm trying not to eat red meat more than once a week. I may have to make an exception because you know I'm trash for a good mushroom sauce."

"Still medium-rare?"

"Yup."

"All right. Well, lemme get this order in."

While we wait for the food to arrive, I change clothes, too, putting on sweatpants and one of my Morehouse hoodies. When I leave the bathroom and reenter the bedroom, Yasmen sits propped up against the pillows.

"I'd love for the kids to have the kind of college experience we did," she says wistfully.

"An HBCU?"

"I'd settle for anything with Day at this point. She keeps saying she doesn't need college at all. Kassim will probably end up at MIT or Harvard or somewhere."

"You may be the only mom I know who sounds disappointed that her son will most likely attend an Ivy League school."

She rolls her eyes, allowing a small smile. "You know what I mean."

Her phone rings on the bed beside her.

"Speaking of our amazing children," she drawls, picking up the phone. "It's them. FaceTime."

I sit down beside her, leaning back on the pillows and smiling at the screen when their faces pop up.

"Mom!" Kassim says. "Dad, hey!"

"Hey, son," I say. "What you been up to today?"

"*Madden* with Jamal." His face lights up. "But guess what Grandma did?"

"There's no telling." Yasmen laughs. "Made you clean out your closet? Scrubbed your shower with a toothbrush?"

"Yeah, like she always does," he says, practically bouncing in his eagerness to spill it. "But she cooked chitterlings again."

Yasmen wrinkles her nose. "She smelled up my whole house?"

"No!" Kassim's smile grows impossibly wider. "She cleaned them with bleach before she cooked them and you can't smell 'em at all."

I share a quick panicked look with Yasmen. "Don't eat that."

"I tasted a little." Kassim grimaces. "It wasn't that bad."

Deja pokes her head into the shot. "But then I reminded him she cleans them so much because chitterlings are literally full of sh—"

"Deja Marie," I warn. I know she curses, but it would be great if my ten-year-old didn't follow suit quite yet.

"Well, they are." She grins, flitting a glance from me to her mother. "Where are you guys?"

"In Charlotte," Yasmen answers. "You know that. We'll be home tomorrow."

"No, I mean, where are you right now?" She frowns. "Are you in bed?"

Oh, damn.

In the FaceTime preview, I see Yasmen and me sitting shoulder to shoulder, propped up by pillows, our heads nearly touching as we both try to fit into the shot.

Yasmen straightens, leaning a few inches away from me. "We're, um, just waiting for room service."

"We were in meetings all day," I add. "And didn't feel like going out, so we're eating in your mom's hotel room."

"Cool," Kassim says, not questioning. Deja's eyes, however, remain on us, fixed and suspicious. "Guess what Grandma told Deja today."

"Oh, Lord," Yasmen says. "What?"

"She said," Deja begins and laughs. " 'You so hardheaded, you don't believe fatback is greasy.' "

"It *is* greasy!" Kassim pipes in. "She fried some and there was grease everywhere."

"And she started playing her music while she was cooking," Deja goes on. "But stuff I've never heard like 'Merry Christmas' by the Temptations and 'Jesus Is Love' by the Commotion."

"The Commodores," I correct.

"Put your grandmother on the phone," Yasmen says after a few more minutes of them relaying all the weird things Carole did with chitterlings and bins from the Container Store.

"Okay," Kassim says, running from the room and holding his phone. "Grandma!"

"I'm gonna take this into the sitting room," Yasmen says, standing and leaving the bedroom just before I hear Carole come on to greet her.

She doesn't want her mother asking the kinds of questions Deja did, doesn't want her to realize we had to share a room. Carole and Yasmen are still chatting when our food arrives. I tip the server and set our tray down at the small table in the dining area.

"Mama says hey," Yasmen offers, sitting at the table across from me.

I lift the lid from my dish to reveal the chicken piccata I ordered. "They haven't driven her crazy yet?"

"Not yet." Yasmen laughs, lifting the lid from her dish too. "Ooooh. This steak looks delish."

She eyes my chicken covetously. So predictable.

"And yet," I say, my smile knowing, "you want to taste mine."

"I mean, just a little." She holds up two fingers, squeezing a tiny bit of space between the tips.

I slide my plate across to her, and she slides hers across to me. We always shared our food, sampling whatever was on the other's plate.

"Oh, this is so good," she moans.

I bite into the steak, which seems to dissolve in my mouth, it's so tender. "Damn, that is good."

"Halvsies?" A hopeful grin crooks the corners of her lips.

Wordlessly I slide my plate across the table, and she divides her steak and puts half onto my plate and then does the same with my chicken. She passes the plate back to me and we dig in, grunting at how good it is.

"Not bad for hotel food." I wipe my mouth with the linen napkin and lean back in my seat. "Want dessert?"

"What I want," she says, "is to taste that Yamazaki."

"Seriously?"

"Break it out. You'll just take it to your house and let it molder for the next half century."

I retrieve the bottle of whiskey from my bag, grab two glasses from the bar, and meet her in the adjacent sitting room. She takes the couch and I sit in the armchair directly across.

"It's strong," I warn and pour a glass for her.

"I could use strong." She takes a long draw of it and gasps, lightly bangs her chest. "You weren't lying. Good, though. Tastes like pure gold."

"It costs about that much. Slow down." I take a more measured sip and nod. "This is the good stuff. You gotta savor."

"Mama's having the best time. I wouldn't be surprised if she moves here after she retires."

"The kids would love that."

"So would I. I sometimes wonder if…" Yasmen shrugs. "I don't know. If maybe I would have handled things better if she'd been around."

I'm silent, processing that and giving her room to go on if she likes.

"With distance and the right medication," she continues wryly, "I can appreciate how much I isolated myself then. How it only made things worse."

I have a proven track record of saying the absolute wrong thing in situations like this, so instead I take another sip and remain silent.

"Do you mind if I ask how things have been going with Dr. Musa?" she asks.

"It's good." I set the glass on the side table and link my hands behind my head. "He's good. He has a way of making me consider things I haven't before."

"Like what?"

"Man, where do I start? Like how I never came to terms with losing both my parents at such a young age. How it affected me. I don't think I had the tools to deal with losing Byrd and Henry so close together that way."

My laugh comes out, a breath of self-deprecation. "Who am I kidding? It probably wouldn't have made a difference. I probably wouldn't have handled it any better if they'd been years apart."

"We did the best we could in extraordinary circumstances. At least that's what Dr. Abrams says I should tell myself." She takes another sip from her nearly empty glass. "She has this thing where she encourages me to be my own gentle observer."

"What does that mean?"

"It means seeing myself clearly—good, bad, beautiful, ugly, faults, mistakes—acknowledging what I really think and feel, and not judging those emotions. Understanding myself. Not censoring it. Having compassion for myself."

"I like the idea of you being gentle with yourself," I reply, not looking up even when I feel her eyes land on me.

"It's harder than you might think. Between the expectations society imposes on us, shit we inherit, and mom guilt, which is the worst, it can be hard."

I lean back in the armchair and chance a sideways glance at her. "Can I ask *you* something?"

She folds one leg beneath her, eyes both wary and open. "Sure."

"You said something at Thanksgiving." I reach for my drink and take a fortifying sip because I'm not sure I want to know the answer to my question, but I have to ask. It's been bothering me ever since dinner that day. When she said it, I didn't want to think too deeply about what she *wasn't* saying, but I'm learning not to ignore hard conversations. Hard feelings.

"What'd I say?" she asks, brows drawn together.

"You said you were grateful for the kids because you didn't think you'd still be here if not for them."

The words throb in the silence of the room. We could be the only two people on earth, it's so quiet. Like we're in a temporary time capsule, sealed from reality and the world beyond these walls.

"What did you mean by that?" I ask when she doesn't answer right away.

"What do you think I meant?"

"Did you ever…" I pause before finishing the question in case her answer confirms my worst, most terrifying suspicions. "Did you ever think of hurting yourself?"

"Hurting myself?" Her brows lift, nostrils flaring with a sharply drawn breath. "If we're having this conversation, ask me what you really want to know, Si."

"Did you think about ending your life?"

I ask it the softest way you can ask such a difficult question, and it still stirs panic in my belly while I wait for her response. Her throat moves with a swallow, and she finally lowers her gaze to the floor.

"In my first session with Dr. Abrams, she asked me that same question."

A bear trap closes in my throat, and for a second I can't free the words. "And what did you say?"

City lights twinkle through the window, and the only illumination comes from the lamps on the sitting room tables. In the dim light, her eyes fill with shadows and tears.

"I told her it wasn't that I wanted to take my life," she says. "But that I didn't want to *live* it. I'd wake up disappointed that I wasn't still asleep and think, *Oh, my God. I have to do this again. I have to be here again.* The only thing that got me out of bed was knowing I had to take care of my children, even though I had no desire to even take care of me. All day I had to remind myself of how much they would miss me if I was gone. Of what I would miss if I wasn't here, even though here was the last place I wanted to be for a long time. I ached every moment of every day."

"And when you were reminding yourself," I say, trying to unclench my jaw, "that your children needed you, that they would miss you, did it ever occur to you once that I needed you? Did you think about what you would have missed with me? Or did I not factor in at all?"

She scans my face, searching, wary before she answers. "Dr. Abrams has this concept of radical honesty. It's being as honest as you can possibly be. I want to do that with you, but I'm not sure that I should."

"You don't think I can take it?"

"I'm not sure I can."

"Try."

She pulls her legs up, wrapping her arms around them and resting her chin on her knees. "I was so mad at you."

"For Henry." I bite the inside of my jaw, punishing myself in the most undetectable way I can think of. "For not being there. I know. I don't think I'll ever forgive myself for it either."

I wasn't there, so I've built my own memories to torture myself. How many times have I envisioned Yasmen alone on the floor while I was hundreds of miles away?

She shakes her head. "I wasn't mad at you because you weren't there when I fell. I was mad at you for after."

"What are you talking about?"

"I heard someone say once that when you try to fix people's hurt, you're controlling it instead of sitting with them and connecting. I didn't have the words for it then, but I have language for it now."

"And what is that language?"

"This is not me saying you were wrong and it was all your fault. It's me understanding how completely incompatible we were in our grief."

"Incompatible?"

"In every way possible. I needed to stop. To process, and maybe I stayed in that space too long. I'm sure I did, but I felt like you didn't stop at all. It felt like you were running from everything I needed to work through. And we didn't talk about any of it."

"You're right. I thought I was doing what I should. I was keeping the roof over our heads and trying to save the business. After talking with Dr. Musa, I realize I used work so I didn't have to deal with all the loss. I wasn't equipped for any of it, and I need to feel capable."

"You're the most competent man I know," she says with a sad smile. "It must have driven you crazy not to be able to make it work. Not to be able to make me better or convince me to get up and move on."

"It's only recently that I realized the one I really couldn't fix was me."

We stare at each other for long seconds. I usually make myself look away, but tonight feels like a room with no rules. I can look as long as I want and see whatever lies behind her eyes, the mysteries I haven't been able to decipher in a long time.

"We were so messed up," she says, sliding to the floor, knees pulled up and her back pressed to the sofa.

"Were? I still got so much shit to work out."

"We both do, but we're better, right?"

"We're divorced, Yas. Don't see how we could get worse."

She looks up at me, and I don't know if I see regret, sadness, or relief. For once, I can't read her at all. I knock back half the glass of whiskey, relishing the way it burns my throat.

"Where did you go that night?" she asks, her voice soft and awash with curiosity. "The night we fought."

The night she asked for the divorce.

Besides that first session with Dr. Musa when I spilled all my guts, I've avoided discussing or even thinking about that night if possible. Talking with Yasmen about it seemed like a can of worms not worth opening.

I walk over to sit beside her on the floor, taking the liquor with me. We're separated by a few inches and a half-empty bottle of Japanese whiskey. This conversation, long overdue, may require what's left.

CHAPTER TWENTY-EIGHT

YASMEN

Where did I go that night?" Josiah tosses the question back to me, his dark brows gathered over eyes clouded by memory and liquor. Half a smile, void of humor, crooks the corner of his mouth. "I crashed with Preach. Got drunk and passed out at his place."

"You never get drunk."

"I think your wife asking for a divorce is a good enough excuse."

I wince, balancing the glass of Yamazaki on my bent knees, cupping the coolness of it between hot palms.

"That night when I threw it in your face that you weren't there when I lost Henry . . . that wasn't right," I say. "I was in such a dark place, but that's no excuse. I'm sorry."

"It was true." His voice is subdued, laced with misery. "I wasn't there."

"You have to forgive yourself, Si, even though it wasn't your fault. You were right when you said I told you to go on that trip. I did. We could never have known. So many things conspired against us that we couldn't have predicted or controlled."

"I knew something was wrong even before the hospital called. As soon as the plane landed, I wanted to get right back on and fly home. Something just felt off. I should have come home. It would have changed everything."

"Do you have any idea how many times I replay you telling me not to close Grits that night? To go home early?" Tears thicken my voice.

"Or how I hated myself for not getting that loose board repaired the week before, when it was on my list of things to do?"

I tripped.

Alone at Grits, rushing to set the alarm, my shoe got caught in the tiny space created by a loose floorboard, and I fell so hard right on my belly. I'd sent Milky home because he was sick and exhausted. And there, alone on the floor with a bad ankle sprain in the long minutes it took to reach my phone in another room, I lost Henry.

Placental abruption.

I knew it was a bad fall, a hard fall. I didn't catch myself, so my stomach took the brunt of it, but I didn't have any idea Henry wasn't getting air. So many days I would sit in the rocking chair and stare at the words on his wall, think of him unable to breathe, and hold my breath, deny myself oxygen for as long as I could, until black spots appeared before my eyes. A tiny punishment that never changed a thing.

"He was always so active." I force the words from my throat.

A rueful smile touches the strong line of Josiah's mouth. "We used to say that boy kicked you like he was trying out for the Cowboys."

"Right?" I manage a short-lived smile that comes and goes like vapor. "But after I fell, nothing. He didn't move at all, and I knew..."

My water broke, tinged pink with blood and panic. On the frantic drive to the hospital, I knew I was losing him. Tears floated in my throat while the doctor did the ultrasound, waiting for a heartbeat. The ill-disguised horror in the nurses' wide eyes. The doctor's professional mask of compassion when he confirmed Henry was gone before he ever came.

"A part of me did die with him," I tell Josiah, my voice scratching to get out. "And it took a long time to learn how to live without that piece."

I sat in the chilly, sterile room, numb and only half hearing the doctor say a C-section would be the best option in a case like mine. My body, which for eight months had been the source of life for my baby, had become a tomb.

"Some nights," I whisper, eyes fixed but unseeing, "I feel this phantom pain. It's not from falling on my stomach, though. It's my ankle. How it twisted when I went down. How long it took me to get up, and I wonder what those minutes cost him. Should I have called the ambulance instead of driving myself to the hospital? If I could have... if I had never..."

Tears streak my cheeks as I bury the unfinished thought with all the other what-ifs and unfulfilled prophecies that plague me. Josiah pulls me over to him, wraps his arms around me. I huddle into his warmth, into an embrace so familiar it makes me ache that I haven't had it. With our past coming back to haunt us, he's tethering me to this night, keeping me from drifting back into a black hole that some days doesn't feel far away. His hands are big and warm on my back, stroking from shoulder to waist in long, reassuring sweeps. He smells so divinely the same, and I burrow into the crook of his neck. I grip his arms with trembling hands, feeling fiercely possessive of this moment and this man. He is mine tonight. This is a conversation so long overdue, and this is just for us and no one else. Only ours. The intimacy of sorrow for the life we made together and lost.

My tears slow and dry, but he doesn't let go and the world would have to be on fire for me to move. He's no longer stroking my back, but his hands stay on me. I'm afraid if I move an inch, he'll let go, so I lie against him, holding my breath. But when he kisses the top of my head, all the air whooshes out of me. I tip my head back until I can look up at him. God, he's beautiful like this, the lines of his face so rugged, but him, so vulnerable. His mouth, not tightly held like when he's in control, but a relaxed sensual curve. His eyes, drowsed and heavy-lidded instead of sharp. I could stare at him in this private corner of the world until the sun comes up.

We're so close that I'm unavoidably attuned to him. To how his heartbeat accelerates. To the tightening of his muscles around me. To the way his breathing speeds to match mine, ragged and rough and fanning over our lips. If I move even a centimeter, we'll be kissing. So close, if I lick my lips, I'll lick his too. I want to taste him again with an intensity I'm not sure I can govern.

"Si." I push his name out, and my chest rises and falls with upheaving breaths. "Ask me again if I'm sorry you and Vashti broke up."

His eyes darken, narrow, the long lashes curling and tangling at the corners. "Are you?"

I grip the back of his neck, pull him closer to leave the truth on his lips.

"Hell, no."

We crash together and our first kiss in years burns from the beginning. His lips are hungry and desperate and familiar. It overpowers me, the *you-thought-you-knew-ness* of it. The *you-had-no-idea* of it. The hot novelty of a man I've known for so long kissing me with first-time fervor. The taste of him overtakes everything with the speed and intensity of wildfire. I can't see or hear or even feel. Every sense convenes between our lips, and all I can do is taste the whiskey and want on his tongue.

"Yas," he expels my name on a labored breath and presses our foreheads together. "We gotta stop."

"Why?" I drag my lips across the abrasion of his shadowed jaw.

"It's not a good idea. I can't...I can't go there with you again." The wildness of passion in his eyes is overlaid with resolve and caution.

These old feelings, stirred by alcohol and nostalgia into a witch's brew, went to our heads, but don't wash away my mistakes or erase all the ways we've hurt each other. I was a fool to think they could. His lips brush my temple for the briefest second before he pushes to his feet and walks across the room. He runs both hands over his face, the kickstand in his pants leaving no doubt that he wanted it as much as I did.

Until he remembered.

The air cools, but my heart still thunders in my chest. My lips throb from the thoroughness of his kiss. I'm still wet between my legs. Shame pools in my belly, and I stand quickly, needing to get away from this and from him.

"I'm sorry," I mumble, rushing to the bedroom and closing the door, slumping against it and biting my lip to stifle a scream of frustration. Yes, because my body is humming, revved with nowhere to go, but also frustration with myself for forgetting that I did this. It's my fault and there is no second chance.

I can't go there with you again.

I don't even bother undressing, but slide between the cool sheets wearing my clothes. Turning my head into the pillow, I feel the sting of tears but refuse to let them fall. Not with him in the next room regretting the kiss that breathed so much life into me. I'm kicking myself a thousand different ways when a noise at the door stops me. I turn onto my back, easing up onto my elbows to watch Josiah's imposing frame fill the doorway.

"Once," he says, his voice hoarse but controlled, eyes hot and unwavering. "We do this once, get it out of our systems, and forget this night happened. That's the only way it works."

Can I do that? Can I live with having him just one more time, knowing I'll probably always want him? With the promise of pleasure we've always found together, my body screams *yes*. My mind and my heart ask if I'm sure. I hurt him. I know that, but does he have any idea how much he could hurt me? That if I give him my body, my heart can't help but follow? I wish we'd talked sooner. Wish we'd gone to therapy. Wish I'd found the right therapist, the right meds, the right everything in time. It would have made a world of difference. Maybe it would have saved us, but none of those things happened and this is all that's left.

His body, tonight and no more.

I'll take it.

I sit up, sheets pooling around my waist, then pull the T-shirt over my head. He's always loved my breasts, so I take my time showing him. I reach behind my back, unlatching my bra. His eyes flare in the lamplight as the straps slither down my arms and my hard nipples come into view. His sharp, indrawn breath fills the room. I push the covers away from my legs and tug my pants down, past my knees and over my feet. When I toss them to a corner, he crosses the room to tower over me. I crane my neck back to look up at him, fingers twitching at my sides with the need to strip him and explore every hard muscle and the warm skin hidden beneath his clothes. Before he can start talking, rationalizing, laying out conditions or changing our minds, I reach for him.

Our second kiss is more explosive than the first. There's nothing tentative about the way he plunders my mouth, groaning into the kiss and gripping my arms. He cups my breasts, thumbing the nipples, and I arch into his touch. I'm starved for this. I haven't had sex in a very long time, but it's not just the physical release I crave. It's the complete focus of his eyes on me, the reverence in his touch that, despite all the hell we've gone through, somehow survived.

His hand coasts from my breasts and down my stomach to rest between my legs, touching me through drenched panties. Our eyes lock and he presses his thumb to my clit, nudges aside the silk and flattens his hand against me. As his eyes burn into mine, fiercely possessive, he cups my pussy.

"This is mine tonight, Yas." His voice is half growl, half groan.

No one has touched me there since he last did and doing this with another man has not seriously occurred to me. He wouldn't believe it, looking down at me with his doubts hovering just beyond his desire. He sees the woman who sent him away. He wouldn't understand how my body has felt hollow since the last time he was inside of me. That I miss him so much, sometimes I wear his shoes to feel close to him. That at night, alone in my bed, I hear echoes in our room of him gasping my name like he did all the times he lost himself in my arms. He wouldn't understand that, so I just nod my agreement. Tonight I'm his.

My breath quickens when he slides the underwear down and off. He turns me so my legs hang over the side of the bed and goes down on his knees. I stare at the top of his head, the deep waves of his hair and the strong line of his shoulders. He leans down to kiss the skin inside one thigh, repeating the intimate gesture on the other, before lifting my legs and resting my heels on the mattress. This position exposes me completely and my knees drop together with involuntary modesty.

"Open," he says, pushing them apart. "I want to see you. I've thought about this pussy so many times."

He runs a knuckle between the lips, brushing my clit, stealing my breath and making the muscles in my legs go tight. He dips his head, drawing a deep breath through his nose.

"God, yes," he rasps and lowers his mouth to me.

I writhe under the assault of lips and tongue and teeth. He grips my hips, dragging me closer and holding me in place for his mouth. The deep rumble of his groan vibrates through the center of my body and I'm head-to-toe shaking, on the verge of shattering. When he adds one finger, two, three, all the while sucking on me and licking at me like he's afraid to miss one drop, my hands claw at his hair. I can't help it. I push his head, his mouth deeper into the vee of my thighs. Shameless, I grip my knees, pressing them wider, holding myself open for him as my hips buck and my chest heaves. I come like crashing waves, wet and hard, drowning every rational thought.

"Oh, God. Oh, God. Oh, God." It's a chant, a prayer, a litany that falls from my lips over and over as my head tosses back and forth on the bed. The orgasm clenches the muscles in my stomach, in my legs. My toes curl and I fist the sheets. He runs his fingers over my pussy, locking his eyes with mine. We both hear how wet I sound, and he licks his fingers clean as I slowly come back to myself.

I'm still a trembling mess when he gently turns me back onto the bed. My mouth is slack and my eyes are hungry as I watch him strip. He jerks the sweatshirt over his head, revealing a slab of muscled abs and precisely cut biceps. I've always loved his chest, the pecs carved and smooth, his nipples dark discs in the rich brown of his skin. His pants and briefs follow, and I literally lick my lips. I want him in my mouth. I had always been squeamish about blow jobs, much to former boyfriends' dismay, but from the first time I wrapped my lips around Josiah, I loved it and gave him head eagerly and often.

"Don't look at me like that," he says with a rueful chuckle and climbs onto the bed. "I promise I wouldn't last long in your mouth."

I almost say, "Next time then," but remember there will be no next time. Only tonight. The desire to have him inside of me right now, fast and hard, wars with the need to slow everything down so I can savor this one-night reprieve.

He puts on a condom, and I almost laugh and ask him why. We haven't used condoms since our early dating days. I was always trying to get pregnant, or definitely *not* trying and on birth control. That was in a monogamous relationship founded on complete trust. We aren't that anymore. We're both...single. He was in a relationship with another woman and can't assume I haven't been with anyone else.

When he settles between my legs, I expect him to thrust inside, but he dusts kisses over my jaw, down the curve of my neck and opens his mouth on my nipple in greedy suction. I clutch his head to me, tangling our legs while he worships my breasts. He braces his weight on his elbows, and I reach between us to take him in my hand. I stroke, at first slow, and then fast, tightening and loosening my grip. He releases a harsh breath, dropping his forehead to mine.

"You better stop," he says. "Unless you want me to come all over you."

With a wicked smile up at him, I guide him inside. I'm not prepared for this moment, the reunion of our bodies after so long. Every part of me gasps at the feel of him. Not just my body, but my soul clicks with his again. His fingers play over me like tumblers on a safe and I open for him. Only ever for him this way. He goes still, and instead of moving, lowers his head to kiss me. He's hard, but the kiss is so soft, my eyes water. I caress his shoulders, his back, his ass, rediscovering the ways he's always been beautiful and noting how he's changed. He's as big and hard as I remember. The fit is just as tight and if possible, more perfect. My body moans a welcome as he starts to move.

"Fuck, Yas," he groans into my hair and grips my thigh, bringing my knee up to bracket his hip. "This don't make no sense."

I love how his voice, his language, roughens during sex. The completely controlled, always polished front collapses when he loses himself in me. I stifle a whimper when he hits the spot that always makes my eyes roll back in my head. He doesn't have to fumble or search or guess. His body knows mine. Our skin, our hands, our breaths find a familiar rhythm that is as exciting as the first time. He pounds into me, our grunts and groans mingling as the bed moves and the headboard bangs into the wall. I close my eyes and give myself over to the primitive dance of our bodies and the feral sounds we make as we *take and take and take* and *give and give and give* until he reaches between us, stroking my clit so I come again before he does. He drops his head, kissing our temples together, one hand braced above on the wall behind us, the other gripping my thigh.

"Baby." It rushes out of him on a long breath as he tenses over me.

I go still at the endearment he probably didn't even notice slipped. I want his body, but I yearn for this intimacy, his affection, just as much. Clutching him close, I map the muscled terrain of his back with desperate hands. I suck at the taut skin of his throat, sink my teeth into his shoulder, clench around him reflexively as he lets go.

My heart pounds so hard, I swear I should hear it, but the only sound in the room is our ragged breaths. It is the quiet shock that follows an earth-shattering event. We watch each other mutely as all the pieces fall around us, reordering the world as I had come to know it.

In the middle of the night I awake with his strong arm holding me from behind, his grip possessive, his hands wandering. He cups my face in one large palm, his thumb brushing over my cheek, eyes blazing in the lamplight, and he kisses me. We said once, but he fucks me again, and it's even better the second time. It is slower and more tender and more heartbreaking because I know this time...it *is* the last.

CHAPTER TWENTY-NINE

YASMEN

"Mom, what's for dinner?" Kassim asks, peering through the French doors of my office.

I glance up from an email from Harrington's boosters about new uniforms for the band. You wouldn't catch Deja dead in a band uniform, but Kassim keeps threatening to take up trombone, so I may get involved.

"What's for dinner?" I lean back in my chair and tease him with a smile. "Why am I the only one in this house cooking all the time?"

Kassim looks abashed, his eyes going wide and his mouth dropping open a little. "Um...well...'cause I can't cook?"

"You telling me you can assemble a robot from scratch, but you can't follow a simple recipe?"

His brows lower, furrow. If something is "simple," Kassim assumes he should be able to do it.

"Maybe spaghetti?" His voice evens and his shoulders square with determined confidence.

Today, spaghetti. Tomorrow, the world.

"I already ordered Indian." His features relax with what looks like relief and I laugh. "But thanks for the offer."

My cell phone rings on the desk, and Mark's contact flashes up at me on-screen. I frown, tempted to ignore the call. We were never exclusive or serious. I was completely honest with him about that, but it still feels wrong talking to him when I can't move without long-unused "screwing" muscles aching from my night with Josiah. That man still puts it *down*. I've been shoving away memories...okay *fantasies*...spawned by that night in Charlotte ever since he dropped me off from the airport yesterday and headed home.

"You gonna get that?" Kassim asks, flopping into the chair across from my desk and pulling out his phone.

"I guess privacy's too much for a mother to expect," I mutter, knowing he's oblivious.

I grab the phone on the fourth ring. "Mark, hey."

"Yasmen." A pleased note runs through his voice. "Glad I got you. Thought for a minute it was gonna roll into voice mail."

"Sorry. I was..." I glance at Kassim, engrossed in his game. "Busy. How are you?"

"Good. I've missed you."

I'm not sure how to respond to that in a way that is honest and also not hurtful.

"That's so sweet." I wince at my not-exactly-enthusiastic reply. "It's good to be home. What's up?"

"I wondered if you've got your Christmas tree yet?"

"Christmas tree?"

I regret the words as soon as they leave my mouth. Kassim's eager eyes flash up to meet mine. We'd usually have our tree up by now, even though Thanksgiving was only days ago.

"My family owns a tree farm," Mark says. "That lot off the square that sells trees all month? That's my dad's."

"Oh, those are the best trees in Skyland."

"That's what the sign says," he chuckles. "I just grabbed a great one from the lot. I could bring it by if you wanna take a look."

Kassim's stare has been fixed on me since "tree." He and Deja love Christmas, and I *did* have getting the tree on my list for this week.

"If you don't like it," Mark continues, "I'll just take it to my sister.

She's a single mom of four and works full time. Knowing her, she hasn't thought of a tree yet."

"Why not just take it to her then?" I ask, keeping my tone light.

"Because I'd like to see you, and this seemed as good an excuse as any."

It's just a tree, but when he puts it like that...

"Oh...okay." I agree after a beat of silence. "Why not?"

"And maybe we could grab dinner after the tree's up? Or a drink?"

"Um...it's a school night and my kids—"

"Right. Sorry. I wasn't thinking. I can just drop off the tree then."

The man *is* bringing me a tree.

"I ordered takeout," I force myself to offer. "You're welcome to stay for dinner."

"You sure?" he asks, but I hear his *yes* poised and waiting.

"Of course. I hope you like Indian."

"I hope you like this tree."

Thirty minutes later, Mark stands on my front porch with one of the biggest Christmas trees I've ever seen.

"You weren't kidding." I laugh, my gaze climbing the branches to the top. "It's massive and beautiful."

"Is this our tree?" Kassim asks, poking his head from behind me to the porch. "Whoa!"

"If you want it." Mark raises querying brows at me.

"Yes!" Kassim shouts before I can confirm.

"Of course, we want it." I step back so Mark can come in and maneuver the tree with him.

I'd already set the base up in the family room in front of the window we use each Christmas. Mark makes quick work of getting the tree in the stand and upright, its branches brushing the ceiling.

"Day!" Kassim bellows from the base of the stairs. "Come see our tree!"

At the top of the landing, the door to Deja's room opens and she sticks her head out. Half her hair is loose and held in clips on one side. The other half is in braids. Blue this week.

"What tree?" she asks, her eyes settling briefly on me before shifting to Mark behind me in the foyer. "Hey, Mr. Lancaster."

Her tone is studiously polite considering she mocks him as "the goofy guy with the signs" any time he's mentioned.

He returns her greeting with a smile, and an awkward silence settles over the four of us. The sound of the doorbell saves the situation from getting even more weird.

"Food's here." I rush over to the door and take the bags of savory-smelling food from the delivery man.

"I guess I should get going," Mark says, his eyes drifting up the staircase to Deja's face set in lines of careful impassivity.

"No, stay." I tilt my head toward the kitchen. "I told you we'd love to have you for dinner. It's the least we can do after you brought us that amazing tree."

"They make the best butter chicken," Kassim tells him.

"Did we get chicken masala?" Deja asks, fully emerging from her room and coming down the stairs.

"Yeah." I hand her the bag. "You guys get started."

With a quick look between Mark and me, she takes the bag, bumping Kassim with her shoulder. "Come on, freak."

He practically skips around the corner to the kitchen ahead of her. *Boy loves him some butter chicken.*

"Like I said, we've got plenty," I tell Mark and slide my hands into the back pockets of my boyfriend jeans.

"I'd love to stay." He steps closer, glancing in the direction my kids just took. "There's only one thing I'd love more."

He leans down to press his lips to mine, and I freeze. We've had a few dates. A few kisses, and though I haven't exactly burned with passion, it was fine. Pleasant. This isn't pleasant. After the night I spent with Josiah, this feels like a betrayal. I know how stupid that is because Josiah warned me it would never happen again. *We* would never happen again. And yet...Mark's mouth presses more firmly to mine, seeking something I can't give. Not now.

"Mark," I mumble into the kiss and pull back. "I...no."

His brows gather into a confused frown. "I was hoping—"

"I don't think we should see each other again. At least, not like...that." I lower my gaze to the small patch of hardwood floor between our feet before forcing myself to look him in the eyes again. "You're great. You really are, but I'm not ready even for a casual situation."

"I see." Understanding clears the frown from his face but clouds his eyes. "Is it that I'm not the one or that he still is?"

A grin-grimace is all I can manage, his insight and straightforward question taking me by surprise. "I guess both?"

A wry grin pulls up one corner of his mouth. "You *did* warn me that I was first at bat, huh? Not the first time I've struck out. Won't be the last."

I search his blue eyes—intelligent and kind in his classically hand-some face. He's successful, ambitious, principled. Maybe one day I'll regret letting a guy like him get away, but the kisses, the touches, the whispers in the dark I shared with Josiah are too fresh. My feelings for him too visceral, for me to consider anyone else right now. Apparently I need to put down these feelings for my ex before I cultivate any for someone else.

"You, Mark Lancaster," I say, taking his hand in both of mine, "are someone's home run."

He nods, bending to drop a quick kiss on my head and turning to the front door. I follow, standing on the porch as he takes the steps down and heads for the Tesla in my driveway.

"Oh, and, Mark!" I call, causing him to turn just as he opens his car door. There's disappointment and acceptance in his expression as he waits for my parting words.

"You've got my vote."

A slow smile works its way onto his face. He gives me a jaunty salute, climbs into the car, and drives away.

"Mr. Lancaster didn't want to stay for dinner?"

I turn to find Deja standing in the foyer studying me, a LaCroix in one hand, curiosity scribbled on her pretty face. Arms folded against the chill, I go inside and close the door behind me.

"No, it was time for him to go." Sniffing the air, I walk past her toward the kitchen. "Let's eat."

CHAPTER THIRTY

JOSIAH

"How was school?" I ask Kassim as we pull out of Harrington's parking lot.

"Good." He turns around to pet Otis, who lounges in the back seat, before pulling out his phone. I know he's going straight for *Roblox*.

"Hey. Talk to me for a minute before you get lost in that game."

He lays the phone in his lap. "Yes, sir."

"How's class been? You're not getting bored?"

"Ms. Halstead has been giving me some extra stuff to do. Like, different from the rest of the class."

"And how do you feel about that?"

Damn. I sound like a therapist. Dr. Musa would be pleased to know he's rubbing off on me.

Kassim shrugs. "It's okay. Some of the kids tease me, like I think I'm so smart."

"You *are* so smart."

"I don't want to rub it in, though."

"Good. Don't be that guy. You're not better than anyone else. Ms. Halstead just recognizes you need more of a challenge than the classwork was offering. She sees your potential and wants to make sure we're doing all we can to fulfill it."

"Yeah. Jamal says it's kinda cool that I do stuff nobody else can do yet, and that I might get to skip a grade, as long as we can still hang out and play *Madden* and stuff."

"Great," I say, recognizing the significance of the Jamal seal of approval. "Well, let's get that bush cut down so you can get home and do your homework."

I reach across and tug the textured 'fro he's growing.

"And decorate the tree!" Kassim answers with a wide smile.

There's a small pinch in my chest. We used to make a big deal of choosing the tree together. Usually the Saturday after Thanksgiving, and then we'd head someplace like the Laughing Latte on the Square for hot chocolate with marshmallows. Things have been so fractured the last few years, and it's one of the traditions we let slip through the cracks.

"You guys got the tree already?" I ask.

"Yeah, Mr. Lancaster brought it over."

This poor steering wheel. I'm practically choking it when Kassim mentions that man's name.

"Mark Lancaster?" I ask casually.

"Yeah, Mom's new boyfriend."

Boyfriend?

The hell he is. She wasn't thinking about her boyfriend when I fucked her *twice*.

The thought rears up before I can whip it back. She made it seem like there was nothing serious between them. Are they more committed than she let on?

My imagination floods with visions of the blond politician leaving our bedroom wearing nothing but pajama bottoms, strolling down the stairs and making himself a cup of coffee in my kitchen with my kids after a night fucking my wife.

She's not yours.

For one night she was. I haven't talked to anyone the way we did in Charlotte since Byrd and Henry passed away. Or ever. Maybe therapy made it easier to talk about my shit when before it felt so damn hard. Holding Yasmen like that, being inside of her again, her heart pounding when she was pressed into me, breathing in the scent of vanilla and her unique essence. She was soft, her curves fitting like she was made for me. And me alone. We've both stuck to our bargain. It's like that night never happened. If anything, things are better between us since we cleared the air.

I just have to keep pretending I don't think about that night all the time, that my body doesn't crave another and another.

"It's a good tree?" I ask.

"It's huge," Kassim gushes.

Of course it is.

"He owns one of those Christmas tree farms. He asked Mom if we still needed one and brought it over."

My steering wheel won't survive any more talk about the wannabe congressman.

"So we keeping it simple today for this haircut?" I ask. "Or you want some of them lines and arrows?"

He laughs like I knew he would and describes a pattern he and Jamal agreed they'd try next time they went to the barber. When we pull up to Preach's shop, The Cut, I'm proud of how well my friend has done. We both graduated with business degrees and knew what we wanted to do. Well, Byrd and Yasmen conceptualized Grits, but I knew I didn't want to work for anybody else. Preach cut hair out of his dorm room and then his off-campus apartment all four years. He paid his dues working in other shops and doling out booth fees until he could afford to open The Cut in Castleberry Hill, which, last I checked, has one of the largest concentrations of Black-owned businesses in the country.

"'Sup, fam?" Preach smiles a greeting over the hair he's cutting. "Look at all that hair, Seem. You been avoiding me, li'l man?"

Kassim grins and leads Otis over to the corner where he always curls up and behaves himself. I take the empty barber's chair in the station beside Preach's.

"You up, Seem," Preach calls, brushing hair from the neck and shoulders of the customer he just finished.

Kassim settles into the seat and describes the pattern he and

Jamal came up with. Preach sets the clippers in motion, his smile indulgent.

"Missed you at the gym yesterday," Preach says.

"Sorry I didn't call." I stand to select a magazine from the stack on the counter in the station where I'm sitting. "I was out of town and been catching up ever since. Lot going on."

"We won...again." Preach smirks and glances up from Kassim's hair. "Where'd you go?"

"Uh, we're reconsidering that Charlotte expansion." I flip through a few magazines on top, trying to keep my voice casual because this dude's spidey senses be tingling. "So Yas and I went and scoped a spot."

The questions and commentary practically pop up in bubbles above his head, but with Kassim in the chair, he settles for a speaking glance that demands details later.

He ain't getting any.

I need to put what happened in Charlotte behind me, not explore it. I block out the questions in my head and tune in to the customers chopping it up. The conversation skids from the Falcons' chances this season to the usual GOAT debate: MJ versus LeBron.

"Bruh, you gotta give it to 'Bron," a customer getting his locs trimmed asserts. "All he do for the community."

"What the hell that school he set up got to do with that rock?" Rick, the barber beside Preach, asks. "He ain't got that killer instinct like Mike and Kobe."

"I put Kobe over 'Bron," the guy in the last chair on the row says.

"Shiiiiiit." Preach shakes his head as he finishes shaping up Kassim. "Rest in peace to Mamba, and he in my top five, but not over 'Bron."

"Who you got, Kassim?" Rick asks, smiling encouragingly.

"Um..." Kassim looks panicked, like he's taking a pop quiz and is afraid he might give the wrong answer. "Jordan?"

I lean forward and fist-bump him, winking. "That's my boy."

Kassim beams and sits up taller in his chair. It's crazy how he flourishes under the slightest praise I give him. His confidence is so easily bolstered. I guess that's what a father's unconditional love and acceptance should do for a boy. My father was a military man and a hard-ass, but I had his love and acceptance until I was eight years old. According to Dr. Musa, maybe I never got over losing it.

"Whatcha think?" Preach asks Kassim, giving him the hand mirror so he can check out the back of his hair.

"Wow!" Kassim grins. "I bet Jamal's won't look this good."

I pay Preach and pat my leg. "Otis, come on."

Otis lumbers to his feet, yawns and strolls over, passing me to wait at the door, like I'm the holdup. I roll my eyes and brush a few stray hairs from Kassim's shirt.

"Hey, I need to ask you something before you go, Si," Preach says.

"Aight. Seem, go wait with Otis. Do not go outside. Stay in here."

"Yes, sir," he says, heading for the door.

"And did you tell Preach thank you?" I ask.

Kassim turns back around. "Sorry. Thank you."

I let him get a few steps away before turning to Preach, who steps closer.

"What's really real, bruh?" he asks in a low whisper. "Last time we talked, Yasmen was up in your house with Vashti and we had sleepover drama. Now y'all going on overnights. What's up?"

"Nothing." I lie easily. "Vashti and I broke up. Me and Yas went on a business trip. Simple."

"When you and Vash break up?"

"Thanksgiving. It just wasn't working."

"Hey, it was your first time out after the divorce. Better luck next time." He searches my face. "Unless you don't want a next time and realize you ain't all the way over your ex."

"Nah, bruh."

I laugh like it's ridiculous. Preach saw me completely undone the night Yasmen asked for a divorce. Even as close as we are, I don't want to tell him I not only still want her, but gave into it for a night that I can't forget.

"This is me." Preach places his hand on my shoulder and looks directly in my eyes. "You and Yas had that once-in-a-lifetime shit."

"Well, we don't anymore," I say, shaking his hand off. "How'd Erykah put it? Maybe next lifetime."

"I wouldn't be your friend if I didn't make sure."

"She wanted a divorce. She got it. It may not have worked with Vashti, but I've moved on. Stop digging into this old shit, Preach. Even if we could start something back up, how could I ever trust Yas not to push me away at the first sign of trouble?"

"You're both in different places now than you were then. I mean, she in therapy. You in therapy. Who would've guessed that? You the most tight-assed, repressed nigga I know."

Hands in pockets, I rock back on my heels and let out a chuckle. It's funny because it's true.

"We don't all get second chances, Preach."

"Well, make another chance, and this time don't fumble the bag."

"Fumble the bag? I didn't..."

The taunting smirk on his face tells me he's messing with me.

"Asshole. I ain't got time for your shit. I'm out."

"Think about what I said." He daps me up. "And if you won't talk to me, maybe at least talk to your doc now that you all in touch with your feelings."

In touch with my feelings is one way to put it.

I *feel* hard every time I'm near my ex-wife.

I *feel* rage at the thought of Mark Wannabe bringing my family Christmas trees, nose all wide open for Yasmen.

I *feel* frustrated because the one night that was supposed to get her out of my system has backfired, and after tasting her again, having her again, holding her again, dammit, she's embedded even deeper.

In touch with my feelings? My feelings are a hot stove I want to test, even knowing the last time how it burned.

CHAPTER THIRTY-ONE

YASMEN

It's my favorite night of the year.

Or at least it used to be. On New Year's Eve, you stand at the juncture of before and after. I know a new year doesn't actually deliver a clean slate. That past-due rent? Still past-due at the stroke of midnight. That dead-end job? Still not going anywhere. The ailing marriage doesn't heal itself by the end of "Auld Lang Syne." This I know firsthand.

But the feeling of newness, the sense of possibility, can spur you to transform your circumstances in significant ways. Other than the last two years, I've planned every New Year's Eve party Grits has ever had. Last year Josiah and I were barely speaking, and I left the planning of the party to Bayli and a few of the staff. Tonight we're on better terms, though a different kind of tension has crept up between us. We may not have discussed our two-fuck, one-night stand, but too often I wake up sweating and panting and wet between my legs because Josiah roams around naked in my dreams.

"Party's hype," Hendrix says beside me. "Good job as usual."

"Thank you. The whole staff did their part."

Surrounded by partygoers halfway to their New Year's buzz, we're seated on Grits's second floor at a huge table on the landing that leads out to the roof and overlooks the main dining room. Deja, along with Soledad, her three girls, and—for once—her husband, Edward, round out our group.

"I love the decorations," Soledad says, peering over the side and scanning the Christmas lights and holly still suspended from the ceiling and hanging on the walls. "Everything looks fantastic."

"That special bunting you made is chef's kiss." I grin at her and sip my French 75. "You really need to consider turning these talents to dollars, girl."

"What's that mean?" Edward asks, eyes lifting from his phone maybe for the first time tonight. "Dollars? What's she talking about, Sol?"

Soledad clears her throat and rerolls her silverware in its linen napkin on the table. "Yas and Hen think I could turn some of my ideas into a business."

"No doubt about it," Hendrix chimes in. "Joanna Gaines got nothing on Sol."

"Except a billion-dollar empire," Edward scoffs, knocking back his scotch.

"Only a matter of time." Hendrix's smile is tight and her eyes are sharp. "Given the opportunity to focus her energies on it."

Edward laughs. "You've got good friends, honey."

"I really do," Soledad replies, deliberately taking his sarcasm at face value. "Maybe I should listen to their advice."

The glass on its way to Edward's mouth freezes midair. "You can't be serious. We've got the girls."

"Joanna Gaines has five kids," Deja interjects from across the table, chewing on an appetizer of fried green tomatoes.

"Doesn't seem to have slowed her down," Lupe adds, blinking long lashes innocently at her father. "I don't want to be the reason Mom doesn't do all she's capable of."

I glance between the two confident, composed thirteen-year-olds making more sense than the only grown man at our table. The next generation is scarily fierce if these girls are any indication.

"You aren't," Soledad tells Lupe firmly, taking time to look all three girls in their eyes. "None of you are. Raising you is exactly what I want to do. It always has been."

"What about when we're gone? I'm starting high school next year, and these rug rats"—Lupe grins, gesturing to her sisters—"aren't far behind."

"Yeah, Mom," Inez adds. "We aren't babies anymore."

"Running our home, raising our kids," Edward says, a frown puckering his brows. "That's always been your dream."

"One of them," Soledad says, her words soft, but laced with a bit of steel I'm not used to from her. "Things change, right?"

A long look passes between husband and wife, and they are definitely holding a silent conversation the rest of us aren't privy to. Hendrix kicks me under the table. I grunt and shoot her a glare.

"You guys want refills or more of anything before I go?" I smile like all is sunshine and lollipops. "I need to go make sure we're ready for the midnight toast."

"I'm good, but thanks," Edward answers, lifting his phone to resume staring down at the screen.

Soledad fixes a stony look on the phone in her husband's hand, her mouth set into a flat line. After a second, she glances away from him and catches me staring. Her expression brightens, shifts to the usual sweetness. What is she hiding? What's she holding? I recognize the strain of keeping things together in public. It only works for so long before you fall apart. I speak as someone who fell apart rather spectacularly and publicly the last few years. I take her hand under the table and squeeze. Even if she isn't ready yet to share what's going on, I hope she knows Hendrix and I will be here when she is.

"All right." I push my chair away from the table and stand. "I'll be back, but if I get caught up and don't make it before midnight, toast without me."

"Can I still sleep over at Lupe's?" Deja asks. "Kassim's staying at Jamal's."

"If it's okay with you, Sol?" I raise my brows in query.

"Oh, fine with me," Soledad says.

"I can take all the girls home with me right at midnight," Edward offers. "If you want to stay behind and hang with Hendrix and Yasmen, Sol."

That seems awfully magnanimous from the man who usually does the bare minimum to help out. The thought must also occur to Soledad because her eyes narrow with suspicion.

"Sure," she says, the word sprinkled with saccharin. "How kind of you to offer, honey."

"You work so hard," he tells her. "I always want to make sure you have time for you."

"Bullshit," Hendrix coughs into her hand. "Sorry. Something went down the wrong way."

Them lies he's telling.

Hendrix and I both know. I just hope Soledad does too. I've never liked him. Something tells me we shouldn't trust him either.

"Well, if it's gonna be grown girls only," Hendrix says, "let's crash at my place. All this drinking I'm planning on doing, I didn't even drive here. I walked, so we can hightail it together back to my spot and swing by the fountain on our way."

"Oh, yeah. I haven't done the New Year wishes in a long time," Soledad says.

Every New Year's Eve, people gather around the fountain to toss in their coins, hoping for a great return in the coming year.

"I got my coins ready," I say. "Let me make sure everything's okay, but we'll hook up."

I step carefully down the circular staircase to the bottom floor. The party is alive, the music pulsing like a heartbeat through the speakers, the crowd swelling as more people pass through the doors. We are wall-to-wall, and I make a note to check capacity. Last thing we need on the biggest night of the year is to get shut down. Knowing Josiah, he's on top of that. I haven't seen him tonight, but he's probably in the kitchen more than usual. With all the preparations for the party, the long hours here with the holiday crowds, and moving forward on the Charlotte expansion, we've barely seen each other since he came over on Christmas Day. That morning lingers in my mind, though. The two of us eager, watching our kids tear into their gifts and squeal and scream their pleasure. Him at the stove with sweater sleeves pushed up over his forearms while he cooked Byrd's famous sweet potato pie pancakes. We'd eaten our weight in breakfast, laughed and talked, Josiah at one end of the table, me at the other. It felt like old times. Even better in some ways. It felt right...until he went home and I slept in my cold bed alone.

When I reach the main floor, Cassie, wearing her chef's uniform and a New Year's party hat, stands at the bar chatting with the bartender.

"Happy New Year, Boss," she greets with a warm smile.

"We got..." I glance at my watch. "Another thirty minutes before the year goes new. Don't rush it now. How's everything going?"

"Smooth."

"Everyone seems to be eating up the specials. You and Vashti did a great job with the menu."

"Glad they like 'em," Cassie replies, nodding her satisfaction.

"Well, lemme go make sure we have enough champagne for the big toast. See you later."

I thread my way through the thickening crowd, but I get stopped every few steps. The whole neighborhood seems to be happy I'm back this year. That careful look they used to give me when I first lost Henry—when I fell and couldn't get back up, not just here with a loose floorboard, but during the long months that followed—that look is gone. I clear the dining room and stand at the threshold of the hall. I pause.

It's a night for new beginnings. I pull out the necklace tucked beneath my dress and stare at another relic. My wedding ring looped onto a chain with the wheel charm Josiah gave me for our anniversary. I flip over the charm, reading the inscription on the back.

"Till the wheels fall off."

Foolish woman, wearing it tonight. Wearing it ever, but especially tonight, when I have to see Josiah. I tuck the necklace and charm back beneath my dress. It's not a night to look back, but somehow I hadn't been able to help myself.

The dining room is all laughs and music, but the kitchen is contained chaos. Vashti is running things, barking instructions, her usually soft voice rough with use and urgency. For the people who attend, it's the biggest party of the year. For our waitstaff and kitchen crew, it's the busiest.

"Everything okay?" I ask her. "You need anything?"

"We're good," she says, sparing me a quick look and wiping sweat from her brow.

I've had very little interaction with her since she and Josiah broke up. We never really vibed or hung out, but I've been avoiding her, and I suspect she's been avoiding me. I glance around the kitchen, filled with steam and buzzing with activity.

"Have you seen Josiah?" I ask.

She tilts her head toward the rear of the kitchen, her expression serene minus the telling tightness around her mouth. "Cellar."

"I'm gonna go make sure we're ready for the toast," I tell her. "Happy New Year, Vashti."

Her eyes glint with something that in anyone else I would take as resentment, but the glass over her emotions is opaque. I can't be sure what I see. She nods and turns back to the team pulling down orders and preparing food.

We don't have a true cellar, not with the two-story house we renovated for Grits, but we made do, creating a large space dedicated to the liquor at the back of the kitchen. Inside, Anthony, Milk, and Josiah are loading bottles of champagne from a cooling station onto carts. The three men glance up when I enter, and I smile, only looking long enough at Josiah to see he's fine as hell in his impeccably tailored slacks, white dress shirt, and suspenders.

Suspenders. He never used to wear them. My new favorite thing could be divesting him of them.

"Gentlemen," I say, walking in farther. "Getting ready for the big toast?"

"Yeah," Anthony answers. "We're close, so loading up the champagne."

"You look mighty pretty tonight, Yas," Milk says, stepping over and wrapping an arm around my shoulders.

I glance down at my bright pink dress studded with sequins. The neckline is high enough to hide my necklace, but it's not modest. Not on me, clinging to my breasts the way it does like a sparkly second skin. The hem hits midthigh. I splurged on Tom Ford padlock sandals. Hendrix said they make my legs look like they should be wrapped around either a pole or a man. I take that as a compliment.

I hug him back and kiss his cheek. "Happy New Year, Milk."

"Wanna take these out?" Anthony directs the question to Milky. "And come back for the next batch?"

"Yessir." Milky releases me with a final squeeze and helps Anthony wheel out the first cart of champagne bottles.

Leaving Josiah and me alone. We stare at one another in the secluded space, and for a breath, I forget the revelry beyond this room and all the people gulping down their sorrows and sloshing good times in glasses. It's just us again. Everything we built together lies on the other side of this door. The flourishing business, all the friendships we fostered, even the children we brought into this world, none of it existed before this right here. The you and me of Josiah and Yas. I fight back the ludicrous urge to bolt the door and trap him here with me until the New Year dawns.

"I could help." I gesture toward the second cart partly loaded up with bottles.

"Nah. I got it." He runs appreciative eyes over my appearance. "Besides, that dress is much too pretty for hard labor, and those shoes ain't ever seen a day of work."

I laugh, fisting the high ponytail Deja gave me for the night and tossing it over one shoulder. "You right about that."

His deep chuckle rumbles in the quiet of the room, and I shiver, absorbing the low, sexy timbre. His cologne, the one he's worn for years that seems to smell better than ever, fills my nostrils. I'm having a visceral reaction to my ex-husband in a confined space.

"Um, are we okay on code?" I ask, as much to distract myself from dry humping the man as the need to know the answer.

"Yeah. Bayli's counting. When we reach our maximum, she stops letting people in. Pretty sure that was about an hour ago."

"It's a packed house." I lean one hip against the counter. "Everyone's loving it."

"You did an outstanding job." He loads another bottle onto the cart. "Seem's at Jamal's, right?"

"Yeah, and Deja's spending the night with Lupe."

"So empty house. Free night. Big plans with Lancaster?"

"Mark?" I laugh and shake my head. "No. I heard he's doing a fundraiser to ring in the New Year."

"And he didn't want to show his girlfriend off to all the Black folks he needs votes from?"

Hurt prickles behind my breastbone. I turn down the corners of my mouth. "So that's the only reason a man like Mark would want to date me?"

He runs a glance over me from the top of my ponytail down to my shoes, lingering on the ample curves in between. "I think we both know he has plenty of reasons to want a woman like you. The question is whether he deserves you, and I say hell no."

Tension blooms between us with each second we don't look away from each other. With every hammering beat of my heart and every stuttering breath, I want to pull those suspenders down, off, unbutton that shirt, and press my lips hard over his heart. A kiss that would imprint him as mine again.

"It's not like that with him," I say.

He pauses loading bottles to watch me for a few seconds before resuming the task. "It's not?"

"Nope. I haven't seen him since he surprised us with that Christmas tree."

He shakes his head in mock chastisement. "Using that man for his trees."

"I told him..." I trail off and run my finger along the edge of the counter, avoiding his eyes. "I told him we're better off as friends."

"Like us."

My head pops up and I stare at him. His gaze is steady, but seems to be searching for something. Whether he's actually looking at me, or inside himself, I can't tell.

"Not exactly." I laugh dryly, struggling to regulate my breaths. "He never got further than a kiss."

"Is that true?" He leans against the counter and folds strong arms over his chest.

"Yes." My voice comes out like froth, light and airy.

"We haven't talked about..." He stares at the floor and then meets my eyes directly. "That night in Charlotte."

I'm shook that he's the one bringing it up. It's been like a specter between us, never mentioned but rippling beneath the surface of every interaction.

"We said we wouldn't," I remind him, my breath shortening.

"Yeah, but it did happen. I just want to make sure you're okay with everything and it didn't make things weird. You know I cherish your friendship. I wouldn't ever—"

"We're good," I cut in, having no desire to hear him wax poetic about what a great friend I am when I fuck him in my fantasies. Does he really think I can forget what happened? It was fantastic, mind-melting sex. It was like old times, but even better. Apparently absence makes the heart grow horny.

Cross-stitch that on a pillow.

"Um, Soledad and I are spending the night with Hendrix," I say before he can tell me more about what a great platonic buddy I am. "So that's what I'm doing with my night of freedom while the kids are gone."

"They asked me to take them to the Old Mill before they go back to school."

And just like that we're back to the mundane, back to this life where we don't kiss or fuck or spill secrets in the dark. Our one night has been washed away. Our frank conversation about the issues that destroyed our marriage left a new openness and understanding.

Affection, respect, friendliness.

All there, but the passion we shared—gone. That's the price I paid. He told me it would be this way, and I know it's for the best.

You can pretend it never happened.

You can be his friend, business partner, co-parent without having more.

You can stop wanting him.

Dr. Abrams says honesty is medicine to the soul. I'll have to ask her the remedy for a lie.

He takes another two bottles from the fridge to the cart.

"Is that a new brand?" I ask, nodding toward the champagne in his hand.

"It is." He shoots me a sly glance. "Wanna try it?"

I giggle, but walk closer. "Isn't it bad luck to pop bottles before midnight?"

"We make our own luck." He reaches for a wine key and gives a *dare me* look. I nod, grinning like a kid smuggling chocolate from the candy store.

Pop!

The sound makes me laugh, as does the stream of fizz pouring from the bottle, so bright and bubbly in the dreariness of the cellar.

"We don't have glasses," I gasp, stepping forward to catch some of the cold liquid on my fingertips.

"Who needs 'em." He hoists the bottle high. "Here's to a new year. May all your pain be champagne."

"Did you come up with that?"

"Nope. Otis."

"Our dog?"

"No, the song "Otis" from the *Watch the Throne* album. I play it when I work out at home, and Otis does love it. He probably thinks it's his anthem."

"Well, then may all your pain be champagne."

He chugs straight from the bottle, his stare never unlocking from mine, heating, gentling the longer he looks at me. Wordlessly, he passes me the bottle, and I wrap my lips around the rim where his just were, the closest we'll come to a New Year's kiss. I gulp as long as I can before coming up for air, gasping as the effervescent bubbles caress my throat and invade my bloodstream.

"Happy New Year." I laugh, tipping up to hug him with one arm, the crook of my elbow looped around his neck while I still grip the bottle. He stiffens for a second before relaxing against me, his hands coming to my hips, his nose dropping to my neck. He draws in a deep breath of me and exhales, his warm sigh breezing across my skin. I shudder, pressing even closer, turning my head at the same moment he turns his. Our noses are separated by mere inches. Our faces so close I can almost taste the champagne on his lips.

"Happy New Year, baby," he whispers, his breath misting my mouth.

The air between us feels clear and yet fogged with lust and affection, like it always did before everything fell apart. In his arms, I feel like his girl again. The one who wanted him wildly and promised to love him always. To love him until the wheels fell off. These few seconds, spiked with effervescence and champagne, feel more real to me than anything has since our night in Charlotte, but a sound at the door shatters the illusion.

Vashti.

"Oh." Her wide eyes watch us standing in each other's arms. "Sorry to interrupt. Anthony thought...well, I—"

"You're not interrupting," I say, taking my time stepping away from

Josiah, making sure it doesn't look like we got caught doing something wrong. "We were just loading up the champagne."

"Yeah." Josiah places the last few bottles onto the cart and pushes it toward the door. "The waitstaff can start taking bottles to each table so we're ready at midnight for the toast. Did you need something?"

"Yeah." She darts doubtful glances between the two of us. "Just had a question."

"I better get out there," I tell them, my smile coming through for me. "It's almost midnight."

I leave them together and a little anxious knot forms in my belly. I never asked Josiah much about their breakup, but took him at face value when he said it wasn't working out. I haven't seen them together much over the last month. It's clear to me, though, that she still has feelings for him. What if they find a way to work it out after all?

What demon prompts it, I don't know, but I tiptoe back to the cellar to stand outside the door. There's no sound, no conversation coming from inside. Back pressed to the wall like I'm in a spy movie, I lean my head just the slightest bit. It's only for a split second, but long enough to see them in an embrace. She's so petite, her head fits neatly under his chin, his arms linked at the small of her back. I jerk back immediately, rushing as quickly and quietly down the hall as possible.

What's stopping him from going back to her?

Are they sleeping together again?

Have they reconciled and he just didn't tell me? Because why would he tell me? He doesn't have to. We had one night in two years of not trusting each other and nothing more between us than business and our kids. It was one night, but nothing has changed.

Tears burn my throat as I zip past the kitchen and lean against the wall before I reach the dining room.

"You ready, Yas?"

Startled, I look up at the question, brushing hasty fingers under my eyes. Cassie's gaze fills with concern.

"You okay? We can get someone else to do the toast if you—"

"No." I straighten and flick my ponytail over one shoulder, smile plastered on my face—all balls and bravado. "I'm ready."

After the last few years when I wasn't able to plan this or to be here, the night has been a success. I won't let anything ruin it. Not even a possible reconciliation between Josiah and Vashti. It's a new year, a new day. If anyone needs to leave the past behind, it's me.

Bayli passes me a glass of champagne, and I take my spot onstage by the DJ's booth. With microphone in one hand and bubbly in the other, I survey the capacity crowd. The booth is positioned so that I can not only see the entire bottom floor, but look up and see most of the tables on the landing above too. There are speakers on the roof so those diners can hear the music all night, and they also will hear my toast.

"May I have your attention," I begin, my broad smile firmly in place. It's too many people for me to know everyone, but so many of the faces are familiar. Peripherally, I note Josiah and Vashti at the bar together, but I don't allow myself to linger on them. There are parents from Kassim's soccer team. Members of the Skyland Association. Sinja from Honey Chile. Regular customers who sent cards and flowers for weeks when word got out that we'd lost Henry. Deidre, who never stopped coming by with her casseroles and stacks of romance novels, is tucked into a corner across the dining room. Clint gives me a thumbs-up, while Brock holds their beautiful baby girl on his chest. My eyes drift up to the landing, where Soledad and Hendrix, my friends who keep my secrets and soothe my hurts, smile down at me.

"I'm supposed to make a toast," I say. "But I first want to thank you all for coming tonight and for your support throughout this year. Grits couldn't keep on without you."

I search my mind for something meaningful to say. If I'd prepared, I would have crafted something safe that felt sincere, but didn't reveal too much. I didn't, though, so I'm only left with this real thing I'll probably regret saying tomorrow.

"I wasn't at this party the last couple of years," I say. "It's been a tough time for me, as many of you know. If you don't, just think of a time in your life when you felt you'd lost everything. That was me, and I couldn't bring myself to show up and pretend otherwise."

My words seem to fall into a vat of silence. I'm self-conscious, and the smile that comes to my lips is genuine but faint.

"If any of you are in that place tonight, I encourage you not to give up. To give yourself time to heal, to grow, to find joy again. What a difference a year can make, and in just a few minutes, we get a brand-new one. As long as you have a new year, you have another chance."

I lift my glass, and a sparkling wave of glasses rises along with mine.

"So here's to another year, another chance. Make the most of it." I look around the room until my eyes collide with Josiah's, which are fixed on me. "And may all your pain be champagne."

People all over the room lift glasses to their lips, sip, gulp, get the bubbly down just in time for the countdown.

"Here we go, everybody!" I laugh into the mic. "Ten, nine, eight."

I stop counting, letting the crowd take over and look up to the landing, where Hendrix, Soledad and her girls, and Deja still sit. I raise my glass and blow a kiss to the table. They all return the salute, except Deja, who stares at me unsmiling, but not in that resentful way. She stares at me like I'm a riddle, something she's still trying to figure out. I'm trying to figure her out too. Maybe this year we'll decode each other.

"Three!" the crowd yells. "Two! One! Happy New Year!"

"Auld Lang Syne" blasts through the sound system, party horns squawk everywhere, and lovers turn the page with a kiss. I accept hugs from every direction, and allow my eyes to stray across the room, where Vashti tips up to kiss Josiah's cheek. I've imagined them kissing. Hell, after seeing Vashti at his house, I've imagined them doing a lot more than that, but seeing her back in his arms tonight was an unbearable reality.

"Time to go." Hendrix appears beside me, brandishing a bottle of champagne. "After-party at my place."

"Yeah," Soledad says. "Edward's taking the girls home. Let's make the most of the night."

"Okay." I hazard another look over to the bar, but Josiah and Vashti are no longer there. "Let's get out of here."

I grab a bottle of my own from a passing server. I don't alert anyone that I'm leaving. I've spent the last few weeks planning and making sure everyone knew exactly what to do before, during, and after this event. They got this.

Outside, I'm unprepared for the cold's blustery greeting when we step onto the sidewalk.

"These shoes were not made for cobblestones," Hendrix complains, pointing to her stilettos.

"'We'll walk home,' she said," Soledad reminds her in a pitch-perfect imitation of Hendrix. "'It's not that far,' she said."

"My apartment *is* around the corner." Hendrix shivers, pulling her cape around herself more tightly. "But Mama's too pretty for frostbite. I ain't losing toes for y'all, so come on. Let's go toss our coins into the fountain so we can kill the rest of this champagne at my place."

I haul in a long draught of wintry air, allowing the cold to clear my mind from the disturbing image of Josiah and Vashti in the cellar.

"You okay?" Hendrix asks softly.

"Yeah." I turn to look at her. "Why wouldn't I be?"

"You just seemed a little..." Soledad side-glances me. "I don't know, sad at times tonight."

"Everything's fine." I offer them a wry smile and point to the fountain at the center of the Square, ringed with people tossing in their coins. "Let's wish."

"Remember," Soledad says. "You can't tell us your wish or it won't come true."

The three of us stand at the rim of the fountain, each staring into the gurgling water with sober expressions. Soledad tosses in her coin and then Hendrix follows suit. I reach into the silk-lined pocket of my dress and finger the coin I brought specifically for this moment, but my hand wanders instead to my neck. I pull out the gold chain with the wheel charm and my old wedding ring. Lifting it over my head, I cup it in my palm. Still warm from my skin, it's heavy with the dead weight of old wishes. It's time for a new start, right? So why hold on to this symbol of an old love from my former life when it's so obvious Josiah has no interest in looking back? Without thinking too hard, I toss it to the center of the fountain. It's not a night for wishes. It's a night washed in my mistakes and haunted by the things I cannot change. Tomorrow may be for resolutions, but tonight is doused in regrets.

My eyes sting, and I hope my friends will assume the tears are from the wind and cold. We don't ask one another what we wished, but turn away from the fountain in silence, each of us holding a bottle of champagne and our own counsel. We've only taken a few steps when the chilly wind carries a whisper to my ears.

Happy New Year, baby.

He didn't take it back. He didn't stutter. What if that moment with Vashti in his arms was innocent? What if the most right moments tonight were the ones we shared alone in that cellar when our lips almost met? When our hearts beat like talking drums through our chests? It hadn't felt like nothing, hadn't felt like things were over and done between us, even though that night was supposed to be the end. Could it be that what I thought were ashes were actually embers, waiting to be rekindled?

Do you want him back?

I've been afraid to answer Mama's question, but with my face wet from tears and my heart heavy, aching, I can't avoid it anymore.

I do.

I want Josiah back in my life as more than a friend, more than just the father of my children. I want him back in my bed.

I want him *back*.

Was I the one who asked for the divorce? Yes.

Did I make mistakes? God, yes.

Does it feel insurmountable? I have to admit it does.

But he was *maybe* jealous of Mark tonight. He called me baby. He looked at me with desire and affection. I can work with that. I can build on that. I have to try. Before I let go of the past and grab hold of a future without him, I have to be sure. I don't know when or if I'll get a second chance, but as long as it's possible, I'll hold on to hope.

I stutter-step back to the fountain in my heels, not even checking to see if my friends are following me. I return to the spot where I stood, where I tossed the past into a well of wishes, and I lean over to peer into the water. The lights in the fountain floor illuminate piles and piles of coins, but no necklace.

"I was standing right here," I mutter, propping a knee on the rim of the fountain, leaning over and peering in. "It has to be here."

I have no right to hope my happily ever after with Josiah will come around again. It's irrational. It's unfair. I did this to us, to him, to myself. I don't deserve a second chance, but is it worth fighting for?

Is he?

Before I talk myself out of it, I take off the heels and step into the icy water, shuddering from the cold. People around me gasp, some laugh. I ignore them and step through the shallow water, eyes peeled for the glint of a diamond among the copper coins.

A small splash to my right distracts me from the search. Hendrix stands with me, the legs of her pantsuit rolled up past her knees. Soledad joins us in the middle of the fountain, barefoot and shivering. We triangulate a look between the three of us, and, in unison, bust out laughing.

"What are we looking for?" Hendrix asks.

"A gold necklace," I tell them, resuming my focused perusal of the fountain floor. "With a tiny diamond ring and a wheel charm."

After a few minutes of fruitless searching, panic grips me. As irrational as it sounds, it feels like if I can't save that necklace, I can't save us. I bend, pawing through mounds of coins, trickles of tears warming my cold cheeks. I'm about to give up, when a stream of gold catches my eye. I reach for it, scooping up the chain with the charm and ring suspended from it.

"I got it!" I tell my friends, who are still searching the fountain floor. A whoop goes up from the people gathered around the fountain watching me make a fool of myself. The necklace is still cold and wet, but I slip it over my head and back around my neck, tucking it into my dress again.

The three of us make our way to the rim of the fountain, gingerly stepping over and out.

"Do we get to know what that was all about?" Hendrix asks, unrolling her pant legs and picking up her shoes.

"Can I just thank you now and tell you later?" I ask, not prepared for where my confessions will lead us for the rest of the night. I want to rest and sleep, and being up all night unpacking my feelings won't allow for either.

"Yes," Soledad says, leveling a pointed look at Hendrix when she says, "No," at the same time. "You'll tell us when the time is right."

"I will." I link my arms through each of theirs and guide us back onto the cobblestone walkway leading to Hendrix's apartment. "For now just know I don't need wishes as long as I have hope."

CHAPTER THIRTY-TWO

YASMEN

I messed up."

I pace back and forth before Dr. Abrams, linking my hands behind my neck. Sunshine from the window filters through the leaves of hanging plants suspended all around her office. Her desk sits in the far corner, neat and orderly, a few stacks of papers dotting the surface. She gestures to the chair where I usually sit—where we face each other in the comfortable armchairs by the windows, sunbathing our conversations in light and warmth. I've worked through so many of my emotions there. It's the very spot where I came to terms with so many hurts and wrestled my demons to the ground. But this time, I don't think there is an affirmation, meditation, or journal entry that can help me live with the consequences of what I've done. In the stark cold of morning, realizing I want Josiah back was as much a curse as a blessing. It's waking up in a nightmare of my own making.

"Be more specific," Dr. Abrams says once we're both seated. "How did you mess up?"

I pull the fluffy pillow from behind me and place it in my lap, toying restlessly with the tassels edging it.

"My ex. I think I still love him."

"Oh, that." Her lips curve into an indulgent smile. "Based on a few of our conversations, I suspected as much, but you needed to come to it for yourself."

My breaths chop up in my throat and I can't get enough air. I grip the chair's armrest and fight off a wave of panic. Not a wave. A tsunami. It crashes over my head, submerging me in every possibility that I've screwed this beyond unscrewing.

"Calm down, Yasmen," Dr. Abrams says. "Breathe in long. Breathe out slow."

This shouldn't work. The mere act of drawing air into my lungs should not calm me down, should not make me feel better, and yet it usually does. The stream of cool air swelling inside, reaching my brain and oxygenating the air-starved pockets, never fails to help. I go through that a few times until my heart stops stammering and the dots clear from my vision.

"I've ruined everything." I shake my head, tears slipping from the corners of my eyes. "My daughter hates me. My husband...ex-husband is done with me. What was I thinking? How could I..."

My voice breaks on a sob, and I bury my face in my hands, shame and guilt and frustration seizing me by the throat, squeezing until my breath shortens again and my head swims. It's been so long since I had a panic attack, but I'm on the verge of one now.

"Let's say you did ruin everything."

The alarming words crooned in such a soothing tone coax my eyes open. Dr. Abrams's kind stare holds me in place when I would dart back behind the protective shield of my eyelids.

"This happens, Yasmen. Depression is an altered state of mind. Not just feeling sad, but the chemistry of your brain, your hormones. Your body is a participant, held hostage to depression just as much as your mind."

We discussed all of this before I started the antidepressant. Revisited it as we fiddled with dosages to find the right mix for my body, my brain chemistry.

"Depression," she goes on, "is a liar. If it will tell you no one loves you, that you're not good enough, that you're a burden or, in the most extreme cases, better off dead, then it can certainly convince you that you're better off without the man you love, and that, ultimately, he's better off without you."

I know depression deceives, but how this illness warped truth, how it manipulated my emotions and turned my fears on me, takes my breath for a moment. The magnitude of what I've lost, what I surrendered, lands on me with the weight and heat of a meteor.

"While believing the lies depression tells us," she continues, "sometimes we make decisions and do things we wouldn't otherwise. Part of the process of healing from depressive episodes can be dealing with the fallout of things we did and decided in that altered state of mind."

"Fallout? Is that what you call something as irreversible as divorce?"

"Oh, divorce isn't irreversible. It's not the worst regret you could have as a result of decisions you made when depressed or grieving," Dr. Abrams says. "There's a documentary about the Golden Gate Bridge. A documentarian left a camera on the bridge around the clock for a year. Filmed twenty-four jumps."

"Oh, my God." I clasp my hands tightly in my lap and hold her stare. She knows the truth of how I grappled with my darkest thoughts. Though I never tried to end my life, the thought became something the untried, pre-tragic version of myself never imagined it could be: tempting.

"They talked to a survivor and you know what he said?" She pauses, waiting for me to shake my head, breath bated. "As soon as he jumped, he changed his mind."

I blink at her owlishly. The weight of that sinking through my bones and flesh and digging into my heart.

"That," she says, "is an irreversible outcome. Divorce may or may not be. Broken relationships may or may not be. You may never repair those completely, but you're still here to try. Do you recognize what an amazing gift that is? To still be here to try?"

I blink back hot tears and nod.

"You're right. I'm grateful to still be here," I say. "I look back and read my journals from when I first started therapy, and now I can see how warped my thinking was, how I swallowed the lies depression fed me. They became so much a part of me until they felt like truth. I don't know that person. It feels like someone else was in charge of my life. Like someone else made those decisions and now I'm back and have to live with the consequences."

"You have to make peace with that woman, Yasmen, because she is you. She's not someone you banished with therapy and meds. *She* is *you*. You cannot dissociate from her. Until you reconcile that, you won't find true peace. Until you have compassion for her instead of judgment, you cannot fully heal."

She grabs her pen and pad from the side table, lifts her head, and stares me down. "So let's set a date."

"A date? For what?"

"We need to put it on the calendar, the day you're going to forgive yourself and get about the business of living your life."

"Um, pretty sure it doesn't work like that."

"It *can* work like that. You can't change what has already happened. What you did or decided. So you have two choices. Wallow in it, stay in the chokehold of guilt and shame that holds you back from the next phase of your life"—she taps the pad with the pen—"or decide you've punished yourself long enough for things you can never change and set a date when you'll forgive yourself and move forward."

How could it be that simple? My chest tightens and my breath shortens and my head starts spinning again, and I understand.

It's a cycle.

It will come back around, this crippling guilt, this enormous shame, as long as I let it, but nothing will ever change. The futility of it angers me because while I'm sitting here unable to breathe, punishing myself every day, my life is waiting for me. I must embrace the necessity of finding joy in the borders of my own soul, sketching the parameters of contentment along the lines of my heart and myself. Not because everything is perfect with my kids. Things will never be perfect. I have to let go of perfect. Not because I'm guaranteed a happily ever after.

Maybe one day I can get Josiah back. Maybe, against all odds, he'll give me another chance. Or he may never love me again. Even if he doesn't, I can't live like this. There is a corner of my heart, a room in my soul, where I must choose joy just for me and just because I want to be free of this. I want to heal, to be the best, most complete version of myself for my children, for my mother, for my friends.

Most of all, for *me*.

So when will I forgive myself and be about the business of making the life I deserve, even when I don't feel I *do* deserve that life?

I lift my head, swipe at the tears lingering on my cheeks, and nod to the pen poised over Dr. Abrams's pad.

"Today," I say. "Write down 'today.'"

CHAPTER THIRTY-THREE

JOSIAH

It's Deja's fourteenth birthday, and I'm surprised by how emotional I am about it.

I blame Musa.

He may have me a little too in touch with my feelings because when I woke up this morning, I pulled up photos of the day my daughter was born. Starting with the trip to the hospital. Yasmen insisted we capture everything, so I have dozens of pictures documenting her labor progression, going from a tight smile in the first, to an irritated scowl, to finally a full-on-wrath photo with her mouth stretched open on a bellow. I can laugh about it now, but it was our first pregnancy. I was scared shitless. What did I know about being a father? I'd had so little time with mine, I just knew I'd screw it up. That I'd fail Deja, disappoint Yasmen. I hadn't been able to express it then. So I basically grunted my way through that nine months, sure that I would break out in hives, my anxiety was so high by the end.

I can't take all the credit for the beautiful young woman bouncing down the staircase, hair big and curly, lips pink and shiny with gloss, but I didn't ruin her.

Not yet at least.

"Daddy!" Dejah practically hurls herself down the last two steps and into my arms.

The air whoofs out of me as I absorb the impact of her small frame. My arms tighten around her and pull her even closer. She's precious.

Defiant. Strong-willed. Hardheaded and sometimes downright petty, but she's mine, and anyone who wants to fuck with her has to go through me first.

"I can't breathe," she fake chokes.

"Brat." I give her a shake before releasing her. "Happy birthday, squirrel."

Her surprised eyes lift to mine. "You haven't called me that since I was a kid."

"News flash. You're still a kid. Fourteen ain't grown."

She's right, though. I haven't called her that in years. She used to be so quick as a toddler, scampering from place to place. Before we could reach her, she was off to some other life-threatening adventure. At least to me, as a first-time dad, everything felt life-threatening.

"It's cute," she says. "But please don't call me that in front of my friends."

"I'll try not to. What's the plan here? What's happening?"

"Just a few girls from school sleeping over. Did Cassie send the food I asked for?"

"Yeah. I just dropped everything off in the kitchen." I hesitate, not wanting to cast a cloud over her day, but needing to discuss something with her. "Hey, for your cake—"

"I know." She rolls her eyes. "Mom told me she wanted to make it. Should I warn everybody it probably won't be any good?"

My irritation spikes. Yasmen wasn't in the kitchen when Kassim let me in to drop off the food, but the cake she baked was on the counter under glass. I knew immediately what she had done.

"Day." I catch and hold her eyes, touching her shoulder gently. "She made limoncello pound cake."

"She did? That's my favorite. Aunt Bryd's the only one who ever made it for me."

"I know, but I'm sure your mom found the recipe in Byrd's notebook and wanted to try."

"Oh." She bites her lip. "Okay."

"Can you just be kind to your mother for me?"

"Even if it tastes like crap, you mean? Just fake it?"

"You remember that ashtray you made when you were in second grade?"

"Yeah." She grins up at me. "It's on your desk at work."

"It's hideous."

Her smile falls and her eyes narrow.

"If you so grown," I say, lightening my tone, "you're old enough to know the only reason that thing is on my desk is because you made it. I don't even smoke. It's not about how much I love *it*, but about how much I love *you*."

She nods and I push thick curls away from her face, leaning down to kiss her forehead.

The doorbell rings, and she beams like sunshine.

"They're here."

She runs down the hallway to the foyer to open the door just as Yasmen descends the stairs. The braids are gone and her natural hair is out in a curly Afro. She's added some color, brownish-gold highlights, and it's a bright contrast with the deep copper of her skin.

"Hey." She takes the last few steps until she's standing in front of me.

"Hey." I stuff my hands into my pockets because she looks good enough to grab. "How you doing?"

"Good." She glances over my shoulder to the foyer, where Deja's squealing friends spill into the house. "You ready?"

"If you are."

Over the next few hours, the house is overrun by a pack of thirteen- and fourteen-year-old girls. They eat their way through all the food Cassie sent. A mound of wrapping paper and boxes grows as Deja opens gifts, shouting and laughing with every present revealed. She specifically told Yasmen and me she only wanted money from us because we "have no clue."

Once the games have been played, it's time for the cake. Yasmen seems relaxed enough as she distributes slices of the yellow cake with its ivory icing on plates to everyone. She finally makes her way over to me, offering a huge slice, not quite meeting my eyes.

"It's delicious," one of the girls says, slicing her fork into the cake for another bite. "You made this, Mrs. Wade?"

"Yeah." Yasmen's smile is hesitant, her cake on the plate in front of her untouched. "Glad you like it."

"It tastes just like Aunt Byrd's," Deja says, chewing the cake and looking at her mother, no laughter in her eyes, but no malice either. "Thank you, Mom."

Yasmen nods, smiles, and finally slices into her own piece. She looks up to find me staring and freezes, darting a look at my untouched cake.

"Scared it's poisoned?" she teases, taking her bite.

"Nah." I pierce the corner of my slice with the fork and bring it to my lips. "The anticipation is the best part."

"Hmmm." She chews, eyes never leaving my face. "Enough anticipating, Wade. Eat the cake."

I used to watch Byrd bake this. While delicious, it was never my favorite of hers. Her chocolate cake holds that honor, but as soon as I bite into this cake, I remember why it was always such a hit. The lemon zings on your taste buds, and it's so moist, it practically melts in your mouth. The sweet icing blends into the just-right sourness. It's perfect.

"You're getting pretty good at this, huh?" I lift another forkful.

"I be trying." She laughs and uses her fork to toy with the bright yellow crumbs on her plate.

Most of the girls leave, but a few stay and head upstairs for all the teenage-girl stuff I'm afraid to think they do behind closed doors, including Soledad's daughter, Lupe.

"Where's Sol today?" I ask, throwing out the clear plastic plates we used for the cake.

"Lottie had stuff going on all day," Yasmen says, washing a few dishes. "So she dropped Lupe off and ran."

I nod, pulling the trash bag out, tying it off, and taking it to the bin in the garage. When I come back, she's still at the sink. I stand beside her, reaching for the soap to wash my hands. Our shoulders brush, and a current of electric heat runs between us. Well, I can only speak for myself, but what I feel at the contact, it's electric and hot, skittering across my nerve endings. I glance over at Yasmen, paused in washing the dish, hands submerged in water, her breath hitched.

Yeah, she felt it.

"I needed to talk to you about something," I tell her.

It's true, but I also need a distraction from the tension that keeps sparking between us.

"What's up?" She turns to face me, leaning one hip against the sink. Water from the dishes has splashed onto her dress, and the material is nearly transparent and clinging to her breasts. It's driving me out of my mind. I drag my eyes to her face.

"It's about Vashti."

Her expression shutters, but her gaze goes alert. "I think I know what you're going to say."

"You do?" I doubt it, but I'm interested to hear what she *thinks* she knows.

"I, um, saw the two of you on New Year's Eve. After I stepped out of the cellar. I looked back and the two of you were…" She blinks down at the hardwood floor. "Hugging."

I lift my brows, not sure where she's going with this.

"I assume you want to tell me that you two are getting back together," she says in a rush. "I know you still care about each other and—"

"She wants to go to Charlotte."

Shock flares the gold flecks in her eyes, but there's something else. Before she has time to disguise it, relief flashes across her face like a neon sign.

"When you saw us hugging on New Year's Eve, she had told me she wants to take the position as head chef at Grits Charlotte, and I said that would be fine." I watch Yasmen for more clues to how she really feels. "She'll spend the next few months making sure Cassie is ready to take over here, which shouldn't be a problem because—"

"Cassie's great," she cuts in absently. "She won't miss a beat. How do you feel about this?"

"You mean do I think we'll be okay here in Atlanta? Yeah, I think we'll be fine as long as—"

"Not about Grits. About Vashti leaving."

"It's what she wants to do," I say, shrugging, but not quite meeting her eyes.

"But she loves it here. She's always said she wants to be here."

"Not anymore."

"Because you two broke up?"

"Because she thinks you and I will eventually get back together, and she doesn't want to see it."

I didn't intend to say it, to tell her the root cause of Vashti's departure, or maybe I did. Like a chemist in a laboratory pouring the truth all over litmus paper. I want to see what color Yasmen turns.

"She-she does?"

"Yeah." I lean against the counter and grip the rim of the sink. "She thinks it's only a matter of time."

"Did you tell her that's ridiculous?" Yasmen asks, eyes fixed on my face, and her breaths coming out shaky. "That you don't want me anymore? That you wouldn't touch me with a six-foot pole?"

I'm a glutton for punishment and a fool for lust because despite going weeks convincing myself one night would have to be enough, I cup her jaw and lay my hand at her waist, drawing her into me.

"I'm touching you now."

CHAPTER THIRTY-FOUR

∞

YASMEN

This is what they call a moment of truth.

Ever since my last session with Dr. Abrams, I promised myself if I got the chance to show Josiah how I felt, I would. What was the use of retrieving that necklace from the fountain, of not letting go of hope, if I don't seize the chance to fulfill it?

"And I," I say, pressing into his hard body, "am touching you."

He towers over me, looking down through a long sweep of lashes, the muscle in his jaw tensing under the taut brown skin.

"Yas," he says, the baritone of his voice lower, huskier. "Be careful. Unless you—"

I raise up on my toes and kiss the words right out of his mouth. I'm done being careful and quiet. That route almost lost me this man for good. I plunge my tongue into his mouth, licking into him—hungry, thirsty, parched, starved—and he groans into our kiss. He grips my back, flattening my breasts to his chest. His hands meet at my spine and slide down to my waist and then cup my ass. Without breaking the kiss, he lifts me higher until our hips are flush, and the steel of him presses through the cotton of my dress. I can't resist slipping my hands between us to feel it for myself.

When I grip him through his pants, he releases my mouth and drops his forehead to mine.

"Yas," he breathes. "I can't... You don't want—"

"I do want." I nip at his neck with my teeth. "I know what we said, but not one day has gone by when I haven't thought about that night."

He goes still, catching my eyes with his and tracing his thumb across my mouth. "Me too."

Hands encircling my waist, he hauls me up to sit on the counter, legs spread. Standing between my thighs, he pushes the dress up until my legs are bare under his fingers.

"Touch me," I breathe into his ear and link my wrists behind his neck. "I'm so wet."

His fingers slide up my thigh, investigating, shoving aside my panties and slipping inside to stroke me. I brace my palms on the counter behind me and let my head fall back. When he pushes one finger in, I cry out, biting my lip to quiet myself. I drop my chin to watch him, meeting the molten darkness of his eyes. Desire is written so clearly there. No guessing. No wondering. He strokes in and out, and brushes his finger over me.

"Oh, God." I eject the words at the persistent stroke of his fingers.

"You have to be quiet." He dips to rub his lips over my breasts, and they harden through the layers of my bra and dress.

"I don't think I can." My hips roll hard into his touch, and I reach up one hand to grip his neck. "Garage."

With a terse nod, he pulls me down and drags me by the wrist into the garage. I don't hesitate, opening the back door of my SUV and climbing in, stretching out. I lift and spread my legs until the dress falls back. With a guttural sound in his throat, he pulls me to the edge of the seat, drags my panties down and off. The air is cool against my heat, against my wetness, and I shiver from the cold air and the anticipation. His head disappears beneath the hem of my dress, and the first swipe of his tongue makes me twist and buck against his mouth.

I brace one palm against the leather seat and stretch to cup his head with the other, spreading my thighs wider, offering him everything. Not just my body. My pain, my sorrow, my contrition, my past and all that lies ahead. Whether he knows it or not, I'm giving it all to him. He laps at me like a man dying of thirst.

"I want you," I gasp. "Si. Please."

"Not yet." He licks me top to bottom, peeling me back and sucking. "So damn good. God, I missed this, Yas."

The orgasm storms through me, and I can't hold the sobs back. They shake my body, and it's not just a physical release. It frees my soul, my heart. Everything locked away, imprisoned, flies loose, takes off. I bite my fist to keep from screaming.

"Please fuck me. Si, please."

He answers with the jangle of his belt, with the hiss of his zipper, with the blunt pressure at the entrance to my body. He pauses, lifting up the slightest bit, catching my eyes in the car's interior light.

He cups my face in his hand. "Are you sure you want to do this?"

I wrap my legs around him, link ankles at the small of his back and pull him closer. He eases in, feeding himself into me by inches, and it's excruciating and perfect, giving my body time to know him again. My muscles clamp around him, and he hisses through his teeth. Once he's in to the hilt, our hips flush, he rests his weight on his elbows, breathing labored.

"I can't go slow," he pants over my lips. "I want you too much."

"Don't go slow. Don't hold back."

My words snap the chain restraining him and he braces one hand on the window behind us, and grabs my leg with the other, pushing my knee back to my shoulder, drilling in deeper, his pace so ferocious, the car rocks. The force of it with every thrust knocks the air from me. I'll feel this when we're done. He wasn't lying. It's rough, a deprived man's possession. And I take every bit of it as my due. He's mine, and even as he's plowing into me, sweat on his brow and dampening his back through the shirt, I'm sweeping my hands over the slope of his shoulders, the dance of muscle and sinew under taut skin, the ridges in his abdomen. Reminding each part to whom it belongs. The slide and squeeze of our bodies creates the cadence *home, home, home, him, him,*

him. It's an overwhelming intimacy, and tears gather at the corners of my eyes because he feels so right inside me again.

"Shit, Yas." He dips his head to scatter kisses at my neck. "I'mma come."

He starts pulling out, but I grab his ass and won't let him go.

"I'm on birth control," I whisper. "Don't pull out."

He stills, looks down at me, and a frown puckers his thick, dark brows. "I've never been raw with anyone else. I promise."

"I believe you." I reach up to brush my fingertips over the fullness of his lips. "Give it to me."

He groans, closing his eyes tightly and dropping his head for a consuming kiss that steals all thought and makes me forget where we are and what day it is. It is a kiss cloaked in mist and memory. Cold puffs of air surround us in the garage, licking at my cheeks. He holds me like forever was never promised and like nothing is inevitable. With arms that take not one thing for granted. The heat of his release floods me, and I kiss him in a chaos of tongues and swollen lips and ragged breaths. For long seconds, our hearts pound through our clothes, our labored breathing the only sound in the world.

"Mom!" Deja calls from inside.

"Oh, shit." Josiah pulls out, scrambles off me and through the back door of the car.

I'm not far behind, sliding my bare butt across the cool leather seats and searching the garage floor for my underwear.

"Crap," I groan. "If Deja sees us..."

"Or her friends." He zips up and belts his pants hastily. "She'll kill us."

Her footsteps pound down the stairs, coming closer. My nipples are still hard, poking shamelessly against the bodice of my dress. I feel a slight burn on my neck where Josiah's stubble scraped the sensitive skin. His cum is leaking down my leg. I'm a mess. Not just the scramble to hide what we've been doing, but inside. Blood is singing through my veins and I'm floating. I'm unraveled by the fact that it happened at all.

He pulls me against him for a quick kiss, taking a precious second to look at me, his eyes going gentler even in our race to set our clothes to rights. "We'll talk tomorrow, okay?"

"Okay."

I want to tell him I don't care if Deja catches us and pull him to me again, crawl in the back seat to cuddle and relish his bare skin against mine. But I do care. It's not just us. It's our kids and their expectations. The changes they've been through. Whatever is happening between Si and me, we have to navigate it carefully for their sakes.

He has barely escaped when Deja jerks the kitchen door open and pokes her head in.

"Day," I say, super casually opening the car door. "What's up?"

"I was calling you." She glances around the empty garage. "What are you doing out here?"

"Just looking for something I left in the car." I fumble around in the center console, pretending to search for said imaginary item. "You need me?"

She presses her hands together beneath her chin. "Can we please go to the movies?"

"It's your birthday. Whatever you want."

"Yes." She turns to go back into the house, but slowly faces me. "Oh, and thank you again for the cake. It was perfect. Everything was."

My heart warms, and I'm so glad she didn't walk in on us a few minutes before. I have no idea how Deja would respond to what's happening between Josiah and me. I don't even know what it *is* yet, but I know I want it. I want whatever we can have, but I also want to restore the tattered relationship with my daughter.

"Good. I'm glad, baby. Happy birthday," I say, smiling. "You guys get ready and I'll drive you to the movies."

Once the door closes behind her, I slump against the truck. That was a close call. But also...oh, my God. That was so damn hot. If he were still here, I'd fuck him again. I'd do anything to chase the high of our bodies together, the drugging emotion in his eyes when he looked at me. The way my heart strained to get to him.

When I walk into the kitchen, my phone vibrates on the counter with a text message.

Josiah: All clear?

Me: Barely. You were just through the door when Deja came in.

Josiah: That was amazing.

Me: Agreed.

I bite my lip, thumbs poised over the keys, hesitant about my next words.

Screw it.

Me: Can we do it again?

Josiah: I want to, but we need to talk.

Me: Okay.

Josiah: Oh, and by the way... I got your panties. ☺

CHAPTER THIRTY-FIVE

∽

JOSIAH

Thanks for seeing me on such short notice," I tell Dr. Musa. "And so early."

"You said it was urgent." He eyes me walking back and forth in front of his desk. "You should sit."

I force myself to take the seat across from him, even though my body hums with pent-up energy. I should not be energetic since I barely slept last night. What the hell was I thinking? Fucking Yasmen in the garage like some horny teenager? With Deja's friends upstairs? Fucking Yasmen *period*. Who better to tell me I've lost my mind than my shrink?

"I slept with my ex." The bald words barrel out of me. "Twice."

"Okay." Dr. Musa adjusts his glasses, his professional demeanor unshaken. "Before we go there, let's—"

"Naaaaaaaaw, Doc. We need to go straight there. I don't need no deep breaths. No affirmations. And I for damn sure don't need that feelings wheel. I know exactly how I feel."

"Then tell me how you feel."

"Like an idiot."

"That's not a feeling."

"Dammit. Gimme the wheel."

Lips pressed and holding back a smile, he hands me the sheet of paper with the bright colors and emotions listed on it. I look at them, struggling to find myself in the sea of words swimming on the page in front of me.

"Uh, I guess I feel confused." I study the circle further. "Anxious. Sensuous. Definitely sensuous, that shit was..."

I clear my throat and frown at the words leaping out at me.

Excited.

Hopeful.

Scared.

I can't bring myself to say those out loud, not even to Dr. Musa, but by the way he watches me, he probably already knows.

"Why did this constitute an emergency?" he asks.

"We're divorced. That's not what you do. When you divorce, you stop that. It shouldn't have happened, but..."

I swallow, draw a deep breath as my heart races with the memory of our frantic lovemaking. No one has ever felt like that before or since, and I suspect no one ever will. Not just how it felt being inside of her, but how it *felt*. How it felt like coming home and running wild at the same damn time.

"Are you sure it shouldn't have happened?" Dr. Musa asks softly. "Or are you just afraid of what it means if it happens again? If it *keeps* happening?"

"Yeah, that," I mumble. "That might be it."

"Do you want her?"

A scathing laugh slips out and I cannot stay in this seat. I spring to my feet and start pacing again, adrenaline and panic and desire sprinting a three-man race through my body.

"Of course I want her. I've always wanted her, even when I couldn't..." I swallow, floundering at the prospect of discussing something so shameful I've never even revisited it in my own private thoughts. "There were times when I wanted her, but my body wouldn't...well, when I didn't..."

Despite all the secrets I've divulged to this man, the words about the times my body didn't respond lodge in my throat. I give up on saying that shit out loud.

"A lot of men experience grief-induced impotence," Dr. Musa says after a few moments of awkward silence.

"I wasn't...that," I grit out. "It was just a couple of times. I couldn't—"

"Josiah," he says softly, waiting until I meet his steady gaze. "There's nothing to be ashamed of here, ever. Least of all over your body expressing grief in the only way it could."

I'd never thought of it that way, and something knotted in my chest loosens.

"Well, it's safe to say I don't have that problem at all now." I laugh harshly, eager to leave this most vulnerable point. "I can't stop thinking about sleeping with her, but that doesn't mean I should give in to it."

"Why shouldn't you give in to it?"

"How do I trust her?" I stop to stare at him. "I can't do it again. I don't think I'll survive it."

And there it is, the truth. It took everything I had and some stuff I didn't know was there to live through Yasmen leaving me. Through her pushing me out of her life. Through her telling me she didn't even know if she loved me anymore. Maybe dating Vashti wasn't the best idea, but I needed to move on. At least I tried to make a life for myself that didn't include *her*. Isn't that what Yasmen wanted me to do? To leave?

"If this is just some phase she's going through," I continue, taking my seat again. "Some closure she needs for recovery or whatever, I can't do it."

"If this is something you want," Dr. Musa says, "and you obviously have very strong feelings for her, lay some ground rules. Agree on your expectations. Articulate what you think this relationship will give you both, what you want from it, what's acceptable, the grounds for ending it. All of it. Be up front and protect both of you in the long run. If you want it as badly as you seem to..."

He raises querying brows, silently asking if I do indeed want it.

"Yeah. I want it."

I want her.

"Then do what you should have been doing all along," he says. "What you should have done the first time around."

"And what's that, Doc?"

He smiles, not unkindly. "Talk to her."

CHAPTER THIRTY-SIX

YASMEN

By the time I pull up to the house after dropping the kids off Monday morning, Josiah is already parked out front. I wave at him as I pull into the driveway, my heart double-Dutching at the sight of him. Once the garage door lifts, he ducks under, walking in behind me. I lower it and sit in the driver's seat for a few seconds, even though I know he's waiting for me to get out. He has that *we need to talk* look on his face, and that could mean several things. With some time and a little distance, he may have thought better of what happened Saturday, and he's come here to tell me it's really over.

Or maybe he's here to blow my back out again. This time in our old bed upstairs.

Options.

He motions for me to lower the window. I do, and watch him warily, scared that if I say anything it'll be the wrong thing, and I'll ruin our lives all over again.

"Get out of the car, Yas," he commands softly, stepping away from the door. "We need to talk."

I do as he asks and walk into the house, taking one of the high stools at the kitchen island. He sits on the stool beside me and leans his elbows on the granite surface.

"What happened Saturday," he starts. "We—"

"I don't regret it."

He stares at me, a line stenciled between his dark brows. "That's good to know, but I talked to Dr. Musa this morning and—"

"Already? It's only nine o'clock."

"It was scheduled... early. So we talked about what happened."

"You told Dr. Musa we slept together?"

"Yes."

Maybe I should be self-conscious about it, but I'm just so damn proud. Look how far he's come. From being basically a clam when it came to communication about real shit, to telling his therapist we slept together, presumably seeking guidance?

Training wheels off.

"And what did your therapist have to say?"

"He asked if I wanted to do it again." His hot stare melds with mine, and the kitchen suddenly feels very small, the air between us charged and steaming.

"And you said?" I ask breathlessly.

"I said I did. I do."

Relieved, I relax a little, licking my lips and sending him a searching glance. "So what do we do about it?"

"If we're going to keep doing this—and I do want to, Yas—then we need to set some ground rules and be clear about our expectations."

"Okay. Shoot."

"This is not a reconciliation."

Of course I knew that, but the words spoken so clearly, so easily, like it doesn't cost him anything, the idea of living the rest of his life like this, still burns.

"I know that," I answer. "It's just fucking."

He shakes his head, a breath of a laugh breezing past his full lips. "It could never be just fucking, not with us. You know that. It will always feel like more, but I want to be very clear that it can't be."

"Got it. What else?"

"We need to keep it from the kids, from everyone for that matter, at least for now," he says. "Not because I'm embarrassed. Who gives a damn what people think? But our kids? They've been through enough. All the fighting and uncertainty leading up to the divorce. Then adjusting to us being apart. Then dating other people. It's a lot and I especially don't want Kassim getting his hopes up."

"And Deja?"

"I don't know how she would respond, but we don't even know how long we'll want to do this. For something that could be temporary, is it worth further complicating what's already been a difficult transition?"

"I agree."

"And if I'm honest," he says, taking my hand, "I want us to have this without the pressure of other people's expectations or judgments. It's already sticky enough without folks putting their noses in it."

"Sticky?" I ask, rubbing my thumb across the back of his hand. "Why is it sticky?"

"How could it not be? We were married. We're still connected in so many ways. Still in each other's lives. What happens if you meet someone you want a relationship with? Or you decide we need to stop? Whenever this no longer works for one of us, it's quits."

"Got it." I tilt my head, scanning his face. "Are those all your terms?"

"*Our* terms. We should be on the same page."

My only term is that I'll take him however I can get him. I said if I ever got a second chance, I would take it. I'm grabbing it by the horns.

"Okay. Our terms. Are those all of *our* terms?"

"Yes." He tugs on my wrist and pulls until I'm standing between his spread legs, his hand wandering down to cup my ass, his fingers resting in the divide between my cheeks.

"Good." I loosen the top button at his throat. "Because you're off today. Grits is closed."

He dips his head and leaves kisses at the base of my throat. "Correct."

"And I don't pick up the kids until three."

He brushes his thumbs over my nipples, and they pebble through my sweater. My sharply indrawn breath is the only other indication I feel any response. I keep my voice even and my expression unchanged. But when he takes both breasts in his hands, testing the weight and shape of them, lifting the sweater and sucking them through the silk one by one, I can't even pretend to be unaffected. My fingernails dig into his shoulder as I struggle not to scream. He slowly peels the sweater over my head, tossing it and unsnapping the bra, freeing my breasts. It feels so decadent. His breathing changes and he lays his face between them, inhaling the scent of vanilla I spritzed there in hopes we'd come to this very moment.

"Upstairs?" I whisper, holding my breath waiting for his response.

Is that too intimate? Does he only want quick and frantic, or could we take our time? Rediscovering each other through gasps and moans and orgasms, and, if I'm lucky, lying in each other's arms. His kiss is sweet, the way he licks into me, bites at my lips, holds me by my chin while he ravages my mouth. Finally he pulls back, collects my sweater and bra. Grinning, he takes my hand and leads me toward the stairs.

"I remember the way."

CHAPTER THIRTY-SEVEN

YASMEN

This is long overdue," Soledad says, setting the large charcuterie board on her dining room table. "I can't believe how long it's been since we got together."

"What's wrong with us, bitches?" Hendrix asks, picking up a spear of olives, brie, and pepperoni. "Oooh. I love a good charcoochie board."

"Charcuterie," Soledad corrects.

"You stay cute with yours," Hendrix says and winks. "But it's the coochie that brings the boys out."

"Well, it's a girls' night," I remind her. "So no coochie. I mean, unless we want to talk about coochie, but no boys."

"I'm just glad we finally got some time," Soledad says. "The year started off so hectic."

"Yeah, spending the last couple of weeks in LA with my client was exhausting." Hendrix pops a grape into her mouth. "But commission off that seven-figure deal makes it worth it."

"Okay, Black luxury," I say, high-fiving her. "I see you."

We all laugh while Soledad fills our glasses with white wine.

"I needed this." I take a long sip, letting it cool my throat and relax my nerves. "Kassim is playing basketball, and that is eating a chunk of my free time. Getting him to practice early *and* late, being there for games, but that was the compromise we reached. Since I wouldn't budge on football, he negotiated basketball."

"My girls are in everything." Soledad takes a healthy sip of her wine. "Lupe's actually taking acting classes."

"She chose that over modeling?" Hendrix asks.

"She chose it for herself," Soledad emphasizes. "I'm not encouraging her to trade on her looks. I'm teaching her to use every gift in her arsenal."

"And when do you plan on taking your own advice, ma'am?" Hendrix asks, only half jokingly. "We been telling you about *your* arsenal forever. What will model that lesson for her better than seeing her own mother max out her gifts?"

"Ugh, I hate it when you're right." Soledad rolls her eyes. "I'm so busy, I haven't given it much thought, but I will."

"I've been slammed too. Work just keeps coming," Hendrix agrees. "I haven't even had time to get on Tinder, Match, Bumble, nothing. Not even BlackPeopleMeet.com. I need to go to church, where the Black people *do* meet. Sometimes that's where you find the best men, chile. Horny and highly favored!" Hendrix lifts one hand and waves. "Hallelujah."

"This whole conversation"—Soledad waves her hand in Hendrix's direction—"feels sacrilegious."

I'm still choking on a laugh when my phone buzzes in my pocket. I pull it out and grin at a new text from Josiah.

> **Josiah:** I think I pulled something this morning. I'm not ashamed to admit I can barely keep up with you in bed.

I giggle and type out a quick response.

> **Me:** I got one word for you. 69.

> **Josiah:** That's not a word.

> **Me:** Whatever you want to call it, it was your idea.

> **Josiah:** I seem to remember you approving.

My cheeks heat, and I feel like a teenager passing notes in math class. When I glance up, Hendrix and Soledad both watch me with identical curiosity.

"Who got you biting your lip all dirty?" Hendrix imitates me biting my bottom lip in what I hope is not even close to how I look.

I slip the phone back in my pocket. "No idea what you're talking about."

"You got a man?" Hendrix demands. "'Cause if you been holding out on us—"

"Is it Mark?" Soledad cuts in. "He seems very happy lately."

"He's doing well in the polls," I answer. "Nothing to do with me. Besides, I told him I thought we should remain just friends."

"Well, who is it then?" Hendrix asks. "We'll find out one way or the other."

"It'll have to be the other," I tell them with a smug grin. "Because it's nunya."

"Oh, I got your nunya." Hendrix stands and tackles me to the floor.

"Get off me," I huff. "Oh, my God. What are you . . . Get off."

"Get her phone, Sol!" Hendrix orders, pinning my arms and legs to the floor with her entire body laid on top of me.

Soledad, traitor that she is, squirms into our writhing pretzel of womanhood and manages to fish my phone from my pocket.

"I got it!" she squeals, leaping up and taking off to the living room, holding my phone over her head triumphantly.

I finally manage to shove Hendrix off, scrambling to my feet and pursuing Soledad, but it's too late. By the time I reach her, she's sitting on the floor, back pressed to the couch, reading my text messages with wide eyes, mouth hanging open.

"Oh, my stars." Soledad tosses her head back and cackles. "You're not gonna believe this, Hen."

I snatch my phone and fall onto the couch with a groan. Here we go.

"Lemme see," Hendrix says, extending her hand for my phone.

"No." I shake my head and release an exasperated breath.

"You let Sol see," Hendrix complains, settling onto the floor beside Soledad.

"No, she took my phone." Staring up at the ceiling, I sigh and accept the fact that it's no use trying to hide it anymore. "I slept with Josiah."

A holy hush falls over the room…for about two seconds, and then both women explode into giggles. I sit up and narrow-eye them both.

"When?" Hendrix asks, mirth still all over her face.

"Um, you mean when did I *last* sleep with him?" I ask, my voice pitching higher at the tail end.

Soledad's eyes round. "You're having an affair with Josiah?"

"Is it really an affair if it's your husband?" I ask.

"Is he really your husband if you're *divorced*?" Hendrix counters. "Spill."

I tell them about the first time in Charlotte and then the second time in the garage. I get hot and bothered recounting it, confessing that for the last month, we've been sneaking around.

"So you set ground rules?" Soledad asks, walking the charcuterie board in from the dining room and setting it on the coffee table in the center of the living room. "Well, that was smart."

"His therapist said we should," I brag.

"He told his therapist?" Hendrix laughs. "Wow. He's come a mighty long way from the guy who wouldn't go near one before."

"Right?" I smear cream cheese and a bit of jelly onto a cracker.

"I know it's hot and all," Hendrix says, some of the humor draining from her expression. "But real talk. Where are you with this whole thing?"

"Oh, me?" I bring the white wine to my lips, taking a sip. "Help-lessly in love."

"And how does he feel?" Soledad frowns.

"He's…he doesn't…" I shake my head, frustrated and not sure how to articulate what's going on with Josiah despite the ground rules we laid. "He says it could never be just fucking with us, but at any point if either of us says it's over, no hard feelings."

"That's a far cry from 'helplessly in love,'" Soledad says.

"I want this." I swing a sober look from one friend to the other. "For as long as I can have it. I want him. Do I secretly hope he falls in love with me again? Yes."

"Girl, fall?" Hendrix scoffs. "You can't tell me that man ever fell *out* of love with you. Vashti was him *trying* to get over your pretty ass. I do believe all's well that ends well, and you will get your man when all is said and done, but you need to take care of yourself."

"Yeah," Soledad agrees. "Are you guys exclusive?"

"Yes." I frown. "I mean, I didn't ask, but yes."

"On *your* end, yes." Soledad pops an olive into her mouth. "But you haven't asked if he's sleeping with anyone else?"

"I know he's not. I mean...Si has never...he wouldn't—"

"Of course not when you were married," Hendrix says. "But ain't no ring on your finger or his. What's stopping him from smashing somebody else? And is that a deal-breaker for you?"

Absolutely. The thought of him with someone else...I drop the hunk of Gouda to my plate. Feeling sick, I take a gulp of wine.

"It didn't take superb investigative skills to figure out you two had unfinished business. The man can't keep his eyes off you, and vice versa," Hendrix says. "I know he cares about you; I just don't want you to get hurt."

"I don't believe he would sleep with anyone else while we..."

While we...what? What are we doing? Conducting an affair with no strings and no guarantees. Meanwhile, I'm in love with him.

Did I ever really get over the Josiah who, down on his knees, set fire to caution and asked me to marry him? The Josiah who pushed aside his reserve to hop on a shopping cart and laugh with me, riding through the grocery store? The one who rubbed my feet when I was pregnant, held my hand through labor, matched his breaths to mine as I gave birth to our children?

No, I probably never got over that man, but I've fallen in love all over again with the Josiah who shepherds our children through hard times, always checking their hearts to make sure they're okay. I'm in love with the man who, despite his misgivings, ventured into therapy for our son, but then learned to use it to heal himself. I'm enamored with the passion that burns even brighter between us than it did before. When we make love, the past and present collide in a scorching intimacy that consumes us. The man he was, the man he is, the way he'll mature and evolve as the years go on—I'm in love with every version of Josiah I've ever known, and I'm certain the man he'll become will also hold my heart.

"I'll talk to him," I finally say. "Just to be clear. We did lay out guidelines, but other people never occurred to me. I don't think it occurred to him either, but you're right. I should make sure we're on the same page."

From the couch, I reach down and grab one of Sol's hands and one of Hen's. "I'm sorry I kept it from you guys, but it was just ours, ya know? I'm glad I told you, though. You're the closest thing I've ever had to sisters, and I don't want to keep anything from you."

"I think Edward's having an affair," Soledad blurts.

Hendrix and I exchange wide-eyed stares, and I slip off the couch, landing between the two of them on the floor.

"What makes you say that?" I ask.

Her laugh is the most caustic, biting thing I've ever heard from Soledad. "Him saying her name in his sleep every night?"

"What's that heifer's name?" Hendrix asks.

"Amber." Soledad blinks at tears. "I told him he said her name in his sleep, and he said Amber's his new assistant, and that things are so stressful at work, he's probably just taking it into his subconscious."

"Does that man think you were born yesterday at two o'clock?" Hendrix rolls her eyes. "Don't gimme that bullshit."

"What are you gonna do, Sol?" I ask.

"I'm not sure yet." She shrugs. "It hasn't happened again for the last week, but I can't just turn a blind eye."

"No, you cannot," I agree. "What can we do?"

"Right now?" Soledad begins and sighs. "Nothing. I'll figure it out. I'm watching him to see if there's actually a devil behind this bush. After I just forced your secret out, Yas, I didn't want to keep this from you."

"Speaking of keeping things from you," Hendrix pauses, splitting a look between Sol and me. "There's some shit with Mama I haven't told you."

"Hen, what's going on?" I ask, squeezing her hand.

"Remember Mama's famous German chocolate cake we had on New Year's Eve?" she asks. "I made it. Mama tried, but the eggs were still kind of raw and there were clumps of flour in it. She just...she can't remember her recipes. She's forgetting more and more, and now seems to be having delusions about someone breaking into the house. She's called the cops several times. They..."

She stops, swallows, blinks furiously.

"They called me and said we can't leave things as they are, and that I may need to consider finding a place for her."

"Oh, gosh, Hen," Soledad says. "I'm so sorry."

"I think it's just starting to sink in that there's no going back, ya know?" Hendrix offers a watery smile, and it's the closest I've seen her to tears. "It's a debilitating disease, and things will only get worse. I'm not sure which part is harder. Losing her or watching her lose me."

Hendrix hiccups, letting out a shoulder-shaking sob. We gather her into our arms, the three of us huddled together, unique in our challenges, but twined in our love, our support for one another. Maybe if I'd had this when everything fell apart, I could have held it together, but I want to stop what-iffing my life. Little by little I'm learning to do the best I can and live with the consequences. To love fiercely and to forgive myself when that's not enough.

It's not the lighthearted girls' night we anticipated, but a night when we confide our deepest fears and shine light on the things we've kept hidden in the dark.

CHAPTER THIRTY-EIGHT

YASMEN

Slumping in the cushioned seat, I force myself to watch the presentation on the large screen. The lights in Harrington's auditorium are down, and Dr. Morgan, the headmistress, is saying something about a new wing for the library. Just when my eyes start crossing and I'm on the verge of nodding off, a large hand grips my thigh, squeezes. I straighten in my seat, an indrawn breath loud to my own ears. In the dark, I cast a sideways glance at Josiah, seated beside me, watching the screen with narrowed eyes and a furrowed brow like it has his full attention. Slowly, he lifts the jacket from his lap and places it over mine. Beneath the jacket, his hand inches up my thigh and comes to rest between my legs, his touch burning a hole through my jeans.

I clutch his wrist, stopping his progress. He looks over at me in the dim light, one eyebrow cocked. He leans over to whisper in my ear.

"Are you telling me no?" he asks, his breath on my neck eliciting a shiver.

I lean up to his ear. "I'm telling you not now."

"Why not?" His smile is devilish. "I'd love everyone to hear how you sound when you scream my name."

I don't remember being a loud lover during our marriage, but every time we have sex, it feels like a three-alarm fire and I scream like a siren. I can't help it. This time around, I feel freer than I ever have. We always had extraordinary chemistry, now it feels even hotter. Every touch, every time, like walking across the sun. When I think it cannot possibly get any better, we reach some new level, climbing clouds to reach the next high.

I gasp when his palm presses hard between my legs, moving beneath the cover of darkness and his jacket to rub me through the denim. My breath shortens and, involuntarily, my legs spread wider, making room for him. I give in to it, lying back in the seat. I turn my head to look at him, and he's watching me. Our gazes lock and wrestle in the barely there light of the auditorium. I want to beg him to stop and I want to jerk my jeans down so I can feel his fingers. He licks his lips, his eyes dropping to my lap, where, beneath his jacket, my hips roll into his touch. I swallow a moan, bite my lip, and squeeze my eyes shut as I release breath in short, tight gasps. I grip the armrest and press my heels into the cement floor, silently begging my body for control, but unwilling to ask him to stop.

Just when I think I'll go full *Harry Met Sally* orgasm wail, the lights come up. The jacket and Josiah's hand are abruptly removed from my lap. I was so close. I would have bitten my lip in half to come quietly. Now my body rebels, a throb between my thighs, the pulse insistent at my throat and wrists, perspiration boiling at my temples, and the blood racing through my veins at autobahn speed.

"And that concludes our budget plans for next year," Dr. Morgan says, smiling out over the crowd of parents assembled in the auditorium. "We couldn't do any of this without you. We raised enough money last year for a new Olympic-sized pool and to offer more scholarships to qualified students unable to afford tuition."

Exchanging discreetly heated glances, Josiah and I join in the smattering of applause. When you pay as much as these parents do for your child's tuition, sometimes raising money for swimming pools and other kids to attend doesn't inspire much enthusiasm. Fundraising rarely does, but Dr. Morgan's great at it. I'll give her that, and helping students who can't afford the outrageous price tag—I'm all for it.

"We're a little over halfway through this year," Dr. Morgan continues, pushing her glasses up with one finger. "It's been amazing so far. Let's make this second half the best yet."

She clasps her hands under her chin, signaling a shift in the agenda.

"Now our teachers are eager to discuss your students' progress," she says. "Some of you met with them over the last few weeks, but if you have not, they'll be in their classrooms for the next hour. Thank you again for coming to parents' night. Have a good evening."

I want to drag Josiah through the parking lot, find a secluded spot in the woods, and fuck him against a tree, but several people make a bee-line for us. I suppress my frustration, even out my breathing, and try to focus on each conversation, profoundly aware of the tall man beside me smiling easily like he didn't just have his hand shoved between my legs. Some of the parents own businesses and ask about the Skyland Association. A few are basketball moms I've seen at practices and games. Josiah is at every game and spends a lot of time working with Kassim on fundamentals. We've kind of found a new group of parents to socialize and commiserate with. They usually watch us with varying degrees of fascination and curiosity. They know we're divorced, but we're always together at parents' nights and games and any of Kassim's or Deja's activities. It feels like basic good parenting to me. Set your shit aside so you can put your kids first... 101.

While we're laughing with the parent of one of Kassim's teammates, Josiah's hand creeps to the small of my back. It's a casual touch, innocent to anyone watching, but it may as well be a poker, blazing through the cotton of my blouse.

While one of the PTA committee heads drones on about some fundraising idea to a few of us, I hazard a glance at Josiah. He grins, leaning down to whisper in my ear.

"You really want to fuck me right now, don't you?" he asks, the words singeing the sensitive skin of my neck.

My smile stays fixed, plastered on my face, but I barely hear the conversations going on around me for the next fifteen minutes, and couldn't tell you a thing anyone said. I grin and nod, but have trouble focusing on anything other than this fire Josiah started and won't get to extinguish.

"That's really generous of you, Yasmen," the PTA committee head says. "I appreciate it."

"Huh?" I'm jarred by the sound of my name. "What?"

"I was just saying we really appreciate you volunteering to take the lead on the spring dance."

What the . . .

That's what I get for checking out and fantasizing about forest sex.

"Um, oh." My startled gaze pings from her smiling face to Josiah's knowing smirk. "Of course. Of course. Anything for the kids."

"I'll email you this week," she says, glancing at her watch, "but I really need to go."

I look around, surprised to find that we're the last ones in the auditorium. Other parents have left to see their kids' teachers, or maybe have already spoken to the teachers like we have, and headed home.

"You ready?" I ask Josiah, breathless and still turned on, but resigned to a date with my vibrator tonight.

"Not quite." He casts a look around the empty auditorium and grabs my hand, walking me up the aisle and toward the stage.

I snicker, looking over my shoulder to check for any bystanders. "Where are we going, Si?"

"My tongue would like some quality time with you, and my dick requests the honor of your presence."

He pulls me up the steps and backstage. We venture deeper into the shadows, past costumes and props and stage lights and finally into a dressing room nestled at the very end of the corridor. He closes the door behind us and flattens me against it, muscled forearms on either side of my head.

"I'm still mad at you," I whisper, biting into an irrepressible smile. "For doing me like that during the budget presentation."

He slips his hand into the waistband of my jeans, plunging his fingers into my panties and rubbing my clit.

"You feel mad." He laughs, pulling wet fingers up to his mouth and licking them clean. "You taste mad too."

Our laughter dies, and he lowers his nose to my neck, inhaling and kissing his way down, nudging the collar of my blouse aside to suck the top curve of my breast.

He palms the indent from my waist to my hip and grinds his erection into my stomach. My body autoresponds, melting into the unyielding line of his tall frame. I grab his neck and draw him down to me. When I suck his tongue, he groans and sends his hand back into my pants, into my panties. Without prelude, he fingers me, rubbing his thumb over my clit, pulling back to watch desire splash across my face. It's so erotic, looking into his eyes while he plunges into me over and over.

My arms fall to hang loosely at my sides. I'm addicted to his touch. Nonsensical sounds spill from my lips. He palms my throat, his fingers tightening until I can barely sip air, somehow the struggle to breathe and the sensations taking hold of my body intensifying the pleasure. The heat of his hands, his eyes, burns rational thought to the ground. I grind against him mindlessly, no shame, all hunger.

"That's right." His gaze is riveted on my face. "Ride my hand. Come all over my fingers."

A sob explodes from me, and he clamps his hand over my mouth, shaking his head.

"Quiet."

I'm falling apart, and spilling onto his fingers, tears leaking through my lashes. I bite his hand covering my mouth.

He laughs and dips his head to the curve of my neck. "You're vicious. Don't stop."

He drops his hand from my mouth and kisses me instead, swallowing my cries. He thrusts and rubs, strokes until my body weeps for him. The release quakes through me with core-racking shudders. I slump against him, overtaken by sensation, spent. He lifts my chin to kiss one corner of my mouth and then the other, dotting more kisses over my wet cheeks. I rouse myself to reach for his zipper, but he stays my hand.

"You don't have to," he says. "I wasn't gonna leave you hanging like that. Plus, I just wanted to kiss you."

He has always loved kissing for the sake of kissing. My heart constricts. This is how he won me all those years ago, and this is what still holds me. On the surface, he's often hard edges and curt cynicism, but with me, those layers dissolve and I'm left with a romantic. A man who pulls me into the shadows to kiss me and wants nothing in return. It means so much that he shares those parts of himself with me, and something withers inside at the thought of him divulging these vulnerabilities to anyone else.

"Si, do you…" I falter, not wanting to squash the tenderness that has sprung up between us, but needing to know. "Are you…seeing anyone else?"

The granite line of his body stiffens.

"Are you asking if I'm seeing anyone else, or if I'm sleeping with anyone else?"

I let my head fall back to rest on the wall, considering him with clear eyes and rapidly cooling passion.

"Both." I hold his stare. "I mean, if you are…well, we said no strings. And if we find someone else, then it's fine. That it's quits so—"

"Have *you* found someone else?" His expression darkens, brows dipping into a deeper vee.

"No. I'm messing this up." I let out a sigh of frustration. "Hen and Sol saw some of our texts. They found out about us, but they won't tell anyone."

"Okay." He shrugs. "It's fine."

"Well, they…they asked if we're exclusive, and I—"

"Do you want to be?"

I force myself to look at him, jaw tensed, teeth clenched. It's a risk, confessing even this secret of my heart when I'm holding so much else in reserve, but if this is my second chance, if it can *become* our second chance, then I'll *take* a chance.

"Yes," I breathe the word out, braced for whatever he says in response.

"I do too." He lifts my chin, holds my gaze. "I don't want anyone else, Yas."

This thing between us is a living organism that keeps twisting, evolving, remaking itself. It has since the day we met. There was no iteration I ever envisioned where he was not in my life, and I was not in his, but I thought that had, admittedly by my own hand, been damaged irreparably. But it surprises me again, regenerating, starting as something that has no strings, but sprouting strings and wrapping them around my heart.

And his?

I'm not brave enough yet to ask, but I pray he's as tangled in this as I am.

CHAPTER THIRTY-NINE

JOSIAH

I never thought I would have this again, waking up with one arm flung across Yasmen's hip, our naked bodies spooned together in bed. Early morning sun glares through the blinds we forgot to close in our haste to have each other. The worst part is that I could get used to this...again. Not just the sex, though *damn*. It's gotta be said. The sex is better than it's ever been, and that's saying something because it used to be fantastic. Is it the illicit nature of this that makes it feel so incredible?

Or is it just that good?

That addictive *thing* that used to draw us together is back with a vengeance and making up for lost time. There's a hook in every kiss and I've stopped trying to get loose.

But last night was the best so far. Kassim is camping with Jamal's family. Deja slept over at Lupe's. On that stealth tip, I parked in the garage and spent the night. We weren't rushed and could take our time, not just with the buck-wild sex. We made a meal together. Broke open a bottle of wine. Talked over dinner lit by candles. It felt like a *date*, and that is treacherous behavior I need to check.

I watched her nightly routine, something I used to love doing. Watching as she wrapped her blowout and tied a brightly patterned scarf around her hair. Washing her face and all the stuff that goes into her skin care routine. All these rituals performed while she wore a lacy see-through gown revealing her breasts, the dark nipples poking through a bodice barely equipped to handle all that Yasmen. The plump-peach ass. Glimpses of her long legs through hip-high slits. All of it laid a brick between my legs by the time she climbed into bed beside me.

Between the memory of last night and this morning wood, I'm hard again, and let her know, pressing into her from behind.

"Wow," she mumbles in a scratchy-sexy voice colored with humor. "Well, good morning to you too."

"I wanna fuck you," I mutter into the satiny skin of her neck, sliding my hand from her hip up to cup her naked breast. When I pluck the nipple with my thumb, her breath stutters and she rolls her hips into me.

"Well, come get it."

Say less.

I lift up on my elbow and gently roll her onto her back. Sunlight bathes her face in amber, painting her lashes as shadows on her cheeks. Her mouth is extravagant, the bow finely sketched, the bottom lip juicy and kiss-swollen because I can't ever stop kissing her once I start. The stubble from my jaw and chin left faint marks on her collarbone, the slope of her shoulders. I pull the sheet away, searching for more evidence that I've been there, claimed her last night. She wanted it hard and I gave it to her. It was by turns feral and tender, rough, right. So damn *right.*

"You just staring all day?" she asks, reaching up to trace my eyebrow with her thumb. "Or you doing something about it?"

I trail a finger down her chest, over her stomach, ending between her legs, parting her, rubbing her. I slip one finger in, finding her hot and slick. Give her another. She licks her lips and twists her hips, coaxing me even deeper. I brush the underside of her breast, sending my hand on a slow journey down her rib cage. Dropping my mouth to her breast, I set a rhythm of licking and sucking that has her grinding onto my hand.

"Si, it's so good."

I can't stop watching her get hers. The way her pretty face goes slack and she bites her lip and sometimes, when it's really good, a tear might slip down her cheek. Sometimes I wish I could cry as easily. That's one release I haven't experienced in years. Having this again when I never thought we would—yes, it feels hot and frenzied and wild.

But it also feels like a gift.

I can't help but wonder...when will it be taken away from me?

It's like she's mine again and I don't know what to do with that. Shouldn't trust it. Do I feel like hers? Is she turned the hell out? Because I am, and I have no idea where this is going or how it ends any way other than me wrecked like I was when she left me the first time.

She's loud when she comes. She grips my wrist, winding her hips, dropping her legs open when I brush my thumb over her in rapid strokes that push her over the edge. I'm transfixed watching her, wanting to stretch it out as long as I can, despite the urgent demand of my own body. Her laugh is husky, her chest heaving with the last of her orgasm.

"What are you looking at?" she asks.

"You."

I pull my fingers out and paint the silky skin inside her thigh with her essence.

"Don't look too close." She chuckles and pulls the sheet to cover herself. "Morning light is harsh."

"You're as beautiful as you've always been." I tug the sheet away, exposing the long, curvy, brown length of her body again.

"You do see the lumps and stretch marks, right?" She grins, and it's the perfect mix of confidence and modesty she's always had.

"Know what I see?" I ask, kissing between her breasts and down to her belly.

She looks at me through her lashes, cupping my head and caressing my neck. "What?"

I kiss her hip, brushing my lips over the small rings of Saturn etched into her skin by her first pregnancy. "I see Deja."

I lick at the concentric sunburst around her belly button. "I see Kassim."

I caress the slightly raised C-section scar stretched between her pelvic bones. "I see Henry."

When I look up her eyes have sobered, saddened a little, but still burn hot watching me worship her.

"This body gave me my children," I tell her, sliding down to lift her knees over my shoulders. "And it will always be beautiful to me."

I drop my mouth to her, losing myself in her taste, her wetness on my lips and cheeks, clutching her ass to bring her closer. She's a luxury I can't bring myself to sip. I slurp, uncouth and uncivilized in my need for as much as I can get.

"Jesus, Si." Her hands frame my head, urging me closer. "Baby, I already came."

"Come again." I chuckle, sucking her into my mouth, gripping her thighs, torn between spending the whole morning here pleasing her and pushing into her right now to satisfy myself.

When she's limp, head scarf off and tossed across the room, I kiss my way back up her stomach and find her mouth, feeding her the taste of her own pleasure. She opens greedily, sucking my tongue into her mouth, nails digging into my ass, urging my hips between her legs, reaching between us to pull on me.

"Want you on top," I mumble against her lips, shifting until I'm lying on the bed, pulling her up to straddle my hips.

"You just wanna watch my titties bounce." She laughs, cupping them, pushing them together because she knows it drives me insane.

"You ain't wrong. Now stop playing."

She widens her legs over me, holding my eyes with hers as she guides me inside. It's a tight, hot, slick channel. I bring my knees up to her back. She presses her palm to my chest and rolls her hips, twisting me in deeper.

"Yas," I grit out. "Keep doing that."

I sit up, framing her hips with my hands, kiss her breasts. She links her ankles at the base of my spine, bracing one hand behind her on the bed and hooking her elbow at my neck. Our eyes lock as a storm of lust rolls in between us. Her expression wrenches almost like she's in pain. Moments like these feel so good they *do* hurt. Hurts that it's this perfect and that it has to end; that it's fleeting, yet indelible. That the feel of her will be tattooed onto my skin the way I hope that mine will be on hers.

That's how it is with us.

I come, gripping her hips, pushing up into her, flooding her with a stream of heat and bliss that leaves me spent and breathing hard. Her hair is everywhere, spilling around her shoulders, strands clinging to her cheeks. She brushes her fingers over my chest, traces the muscles in my arms.

"You just keep getting better, don't you?" she asks, a slight smile curving her lips.

"Trying." I laugh, running my palms down the smooth plane of her back and squeezing her ass. She caresses the stubble on my chin, traces my cheekbones.

"I'll miss you when you're in Charlotte."

"Don't remind me. At least it's a quick trip. I'll be back Tuesday." I pull myself up to sit straighter, resting my shoulders against the headboard with her still straddling my lap. "You sure you can't come with me?"

We both know she can't. The kids have school and Kassim has basketball and she has commitments for the Skyland Association.

"You and Harvey got it." She leans forward and kisses down my cheek, down my throat. "Give Ken and Merry my best."

"It feels full circle in a way, right? Us expanding to Charlotte the way we wanted to years ago?"

She pulls back to watch me closely, because the expansion isn't the only thing we've come back to. We've come back to each other. Not with rings and vows and promises. Those proved to be flimsy, but we've come back to *this*. To the heat we've only ever found together. To the burn of our bodies. The singe of our skin. Every time I'm in bed with her it feels like I leave pieces of myself in the sheets. That's not what this was supposed to be, but I don't know how to resist the deep, volatile pull that always draws us inexorably together.

"I'll make sure to check on things at the restaurant while you're gone," she says.

"Don't stress. You got enough on your plate. Anthony and Vash got it."

A frown sketches between her brows and her smile fades, lips tightening. I link our fingers across my chest.

"What is it?"

"Nothing." She drops her eyes to our hands, shaking her head.

"Yas."

She closes her eyes, biting her lip. "I don't like to think of you this way with...her."

Well, damn. Didn't expect that. "You mean with—"

"Vashti." She opens her eyes, but they're clouded with emotion. "I understand I have no right to feel that way. We weren't together. We're divorced. I get it, but the thought of her being with you like this drives me a little crazy."

"I'm sorry," I say, my throat constricting.

"You have nothing to be sorry about. You didn't do anything wrong."

"I know, but I'm sorry it hurts you." I choke out a laugh. "If it makes you feel any better, I nearly lost my mind watching you kiss Mark on your first date."

Her startled eyes meet mine. "How'd you see...Huh?"

"Security camera. Kitchen feed."

She searches my face for a beat before glancing down.

"Nothing more ever happened with him. He was..." She shrugs. "I guess I just needed to feel like I was moving on since you were, but there was never any chance of more with him."

I nod, letting that soothe my savage thoughts a little bit.

"Do you want to ask me anything about my relationship with her?" I squeeze her fingers until she looks back to me. "You can."

"Did you love her?"

Her question is instant, as if springing from a brooding curiosity. Not if the sex was good or about how we were together or asking me to make comparisons, which I couldn't do. No one has ever compared to Yasmen. I'm assuming no one ever will.

"No." I can give her that. "I told her from the beginning it was my first try at dating since our divorce, and I wasn't ready for anything that serious."

"Could you have? Loved her, I mean."

Maybe if I'd never had you.

I don't say it aloud, but surely she knows she's ruined me for everyone else.

"I don't think so," I settle on saying. "It wasn't... like this. Nothing's ever been like this."

"No." She shakes her head, passing her thumb across my mouth, her eyes possessive. "Nothing's ever been like this."

We stare at each other, soaking in the afterglow of our lovemaking, relishing the abandonment of our bodies and the stark truth of our words. We both know this has gone way beyond the casual thing I thought we could reduce it to. God, I was a fool to think anything with Yasmen could ever be tamed.

A sound downstairs shatters the silence. The door opening and footsteps in the foyer entrance.

"Crap," Yasmen says, eyes going wide and panicked.

She scrambles off me, falling on the floor completely nude, but grabbing for the sheets. I leap from the bed, reaching for my jeans, stuffing my legs in as fast as I can. It happens so quickly. Footsteps pound up the stairs and Deja's voice reaches us just before she does.

"Mom! It's me," she yells. "Lupe got sick, so I came home. I didn't have breakfast. I'm starving."

We were here alone and didn't even bother closing the bedroom door. My daughter stands there, rooted to the spot, eyes like saucers, darting between me—shirtless, in jeans that are zipped, not buttoned, belt hanging loosely around my waist—and Yasmen, draped toga-style in love-mussed sheets with actual hickeys visible at the top curve of her breast and scattered along her neck and shoulders.

"Dad?" Deja's voice squeaks up an octave. "Mom? Oh, my God."

"Day," I say, surprised at the evenness of my own tone. "Close the door."

"But, you—"

"Go wait for us downstairs." I give her a look that won't tolerate back talk, nodding to the door. "Close."

She scowls, outrage or some intense emotion on her face before she slams the door behind her.

I walk over to Yas, cupping her face, tipping her chin up with my thumb. "It's okay."

"It's not." She drops her head to my chest and releases a long breath. "Did you see her face? This is bad."

"Get dressed." I grab my T-shirt from the floor and pull it over my head. "I'll go talk to her."

"But—"

"Babe." I dip to bring our eyes level. "We aren't doing anything wrong. This isn't how we wanted her to find out, but it is what it is. We'll talk to her. I would have liked more time before we had this conversation, but if we're together, this was inevitable."

We're together.

Her head lifts at my words and something melts in her eyes.

I drop a quick kiss on her lips and slap her butt, hoping to ease some of the tension. "Come down when you're ready."

When I enter the kitchen, Deja's foraging in the pantry. Gripping a box of cereal, she glances over her shoulder. We stare at each other for long seconds until it feels like the moment will snap if one of us doesn't speak.

"You hungry?" I ask, nodding to the box of cereal.

"Lupe was sick," she explains again in a rush instead of answering my question. "So I walked on home early. It's just a couple of blocks. I didn't call because..."

Because she hadn't expected to come home and find her divorced parents in bed together.

"All right." I walk farther into the kitchen, the hardwood floor cold beneath my bare feet. "Pancakes?"

Apparently taking her cue from the unnatural calm I found from God knows where, she answers.

"With blueberries?" She puts the cereal back on the shelf and takes out pancake mix instead.

"If we have 'em." I open the fridge, check the crisper, and spot a container half full of blueberries. "You're in luck."

She sets the mix on the counter and reaches up to grab a clear glass bowl. In silence I assemble the ingredients, feeling her eyes on me, but taking time to gather my thoughts while she perches on the stool at the island, setting her elbows on the granite surface.

"I'm sorry you found out this way," I tell her, glancing up from the ingredients I'm stirring in the bowl. "About your mom and me. We would have told you eventually."

"When?" she demands, brows snapped together. "And why? Why is this even happening? How long has it been going on? Are you planning to—"

"Let me be very clear about something, Deja Marie." I push the bowl aside and face her, arms folded across my chest. "Your mother and I don't owe you explanations, but I'll answer some of your questions because I love you and want to be as open with you as possible."

"But, Daddy—"

"This is grown folks' business. This is *our* business. We didn't tell you because we don't have to." I pause to let that sink in before going on. "And we know you and your brother have experienced a lot of transition. We didn't want to confuse you unnecessarily when this between your mom and me is..."

I let the sentence trail off because what *is* this Yas and I are doing? I think about her constantly. I want to be with her all the time. I think she feels the same way. It's as good as, no, better than old times, but without the words that sealed everything in emotion. In commitment. I knew, though, as soon as Deja walked in and discovered us that I wasn't willing to give it up. I won't give Yasmen up. I'm willing to endure the indignity of having this damn conversation with my fourteen-year-old to keep Yas for as long as this lasts.

"Are you guys getting married again?"

"That's not what this is." *I can't risk that.*

"I don't understand." She shakes her head. "Why would you even want her after what she did? After what she said?"

"What she *said*?" I key in on the word. "When?"

"I heard her, Daddy." Fury fires her eyes, so much like Yasmen's. Her lips thin with youthful disdain. "In Henry's room she asked for the divorce. She said she couldn't do it anymore. You begged her not to do it, but she did. She did all of this to us."

Tears streak her face and rage mottles her clear complexion, pinkening the tip of her nose and tightening her eyes at the corners.

"She doesn't deserve you! It's all her fault! Everything is her fault."

A gasp from the kitchen door draws our attention. Yasmen stands there, devastation all over her face.

CHAPTER FORTY

∞

YASMEN

It's all her fault.

Every demon I've been trying to exorcize screams at me in the voice of my daughter. I'm horrified that she overheard me in one of my weakest moments on one of my worst days. *What's really the use of forgiving myself if the people I love most never will?* But looking at my daughter, her face contorted by rage and hurt, I recognize her anger laid out like a rug covering her pain. I used to do that, too, and I know a fight won't fix that hurt. I want peace for her even more than I want it for myself.

"Deja," I say, willing my voice not to tremble. "I'm sorry you overheard that. We didn't intend for you to."

"No, you wanted everyone to think it was Daddy," she spits back. "When he still loved you. He wanted to keep our family together. But it was you, Mom."

"It didn't matter who initiated it." Josiah's words come soft, but firm. "We weren't working, so we were getting a divorce. That's all you needed to know."

"You were protecting her," she says.

He frowns. "No, I—"

"Yes, he was," I say, looking at him and letting all the love I still haven't voiced again flood my eyes. "He didn't want you to blame me."

"I didn't want them to blame you," Josiah agrees. "But at the time, I blamed you too. Dr. Musa's helped me see that what I did was really no different. You couldn't move and I couldn't stop moving, but neither of us was handling our grief in a healthy way. What went wrong, it was my fault too."

"Bullshit," Deja snaps.

"Watch it." Father and daughter stare at one another in the tight silence following her harsh curse.

"I'm not a baby." She folds her arms across her chest. "You want me to pretend I am? Pretend I don't curse? Pretend I don't know what really happened between you?"

"What happened," I say, "is that Byrd died and Henry died, and I fell down and could not figure out how to recover. Every decision from that season of my life was made through the lens of my depression. If I could go back, I would. But I don't know what would change because that's who I was. That's how I coped."

I release a huff of humorless air masquerading as a laugh. "Or didn't cope. We were fighting all the time, your dad and me. I could barely get out of bed most days. Everything hurt so much, and I couldn't make it stop. You and your brother kept me going, but it was hard."

"I remember..." Deja's voice peters out before resurging. "I remember tears on your face when you picked us up in the carpool line and hearing you cry in your room through the wall sometimes."

It's quiet in the kitchen, but the demons whisper that I failed my children by letting them see me that way. The poisoned vines of condemnation wind around my heart and squeeze, showing no mercy even when I cannot breathe.

"I remember you and Daddy shouting," Deja goes on, eyes fixed on the floor. "Sometimes you'd go into the garage and try to hide it from us."

"Kassim said he would come to your room when you heard us fighting," Josiah says.

"Yeah," Deja says. "We knew something was wrong, but I didn't think you'd actually split up."

She glances up at me. "Then I heard you arguing that night and knew you would because *she* wanted to."

I swallow hot emotion and clear my throat. "You're right. My actions did set the divorce into motion. I can't change what happened or how I responded, so I'm asking you to forgive me for my mistakes."

"So you think divorcing Daddy was a mistake?" she demands.

I've never felt more exposed than in the harsh light streaming through the kitchen window. Than in my bare feet under my daughter's watchful stare. Than in the held breath between her question and the answer that will tell Josiah the painful truth secreted in my heart.

"Day," Josiah says. "She doesn't—"

"Yes," I interrupt, forcing myself to meet her eyes and not look into his, which I feel trained on my profile. "I think it was a mistake."

I walk deeper into the kitchen and stand right in front of her, not touching her, but looking her squarely in the eyes, praying she sees my sincerity and regret.

"People don't become perfect when they become parents," I tell her. "If anything, parenthood gives us more chances to screw things up, just with higher stakes. We all mess up. Sometimes we have to live with that for the rest of our lives. I can't promise I won't mess up, but I promise I will love you even when you do. Unconditionally. That means even if you can't find it in your heart to forgive me, even if you hate me—"

"I don't hate you," she cuts in softly, eyes on the floor.

"It means I'll always love you no matter what. And we can go on like this, not getting along, you resenting me and me not understanding you."

I tip up her chin with my finger, waiting for her tear-drenched eyes to meet mine.

"Or we can decide today that we want something else. We can decide we've already lost too much to waste another day. I lost Byrd. I lost Henry." Tears roll down my cheeks and my voice breaks. "I don't want to lose you, too, Day."

She may reject me, but I'm willing to risk that. I'll *keep* risking it to win her trust back. To earn a second chance. Knowing she could very well roll her eyes and walk away, I extend my arms. They tremble. For a perilous second, I think she'll reject me for the spite of it, to hurt me the way my actions hurt her. But she doesn't walk away.

She moves *toward* me, her face crumpling and tears streaking her cheeks. She walks into my arms, burying her face in my neck, the wall she's erected between us for so long collapsing. Like a cracked dam, the emotion, the tears crash through. I cry, too, but it's as much relief as anything else. That after so much time of cutting remarks and frozen silences, I have something real with my daughter, even if it is her tears.

CHAPTER FORTY-ONE

YASMEN

"No school!" Kassim runs through the house delivering the news. "Mom, there's no school!"

I walk over to my bedroom window and watch the steady drift of snow to the ground. Otis, here with us while Josiah's in Charlotte, yawns from the foot of my bed.

"It only takes an inch for Georgia to cancel school," I say. "Or even the *threat* of an inch."

"Won't hear me complaining," Deja says, entering my room, still in her pajamas, and coming to stand beside me at the window. There have been awkward moments since she caught Josiah and me on Sunday. I imagine you never forget the image of your parents having sex. Not that she actually *saw* the act, but close enough. A few minutes earlier, and she would have seen her mom riding her dad like a roller coaster.

Even Mama's Clorox couldn't have scrubbed that from her brain.

But in between awkward moments, there's been an ease, a loosening. I don't expect her to forget overnight what she heard when Josiah and I argued or the anger she's felt about it, but it seems like she's trying. Like she heard me, believed me when I said I wanted things to be right between us and am willing to work on it.

"What do you want to do today?" I ask her.

"Eat? Watch TV. There's a marathon on."

"What kind of marathon?"

"*A Different World*? I've heard about it, but never seen it."

"How have you never seen it? It's one of my favorite shows of all time." I hesitate, glancing at her from the side. "You wanna watch...together?"

Deja turns to look at me, her expression somewhat guarded, but not unpleased. "Sure, but can we make breakfast first?"

"Breakfast, yes," Kassim says from the door, peering at us through the slits of a Captain America helmet. "Can we do sweet potato pie pancakes like Dad made?"

Deja and I share a quick look. We told Deja we would explain our "arrangement" to Kassim when Josiah returns from Charlotte. I'm not looking forward to it.

"I can't guarantee they'll taste like your dad's," I tell Kassim. "But I'll try."

They don't taste like Josiah's, but they aren't awful. A few notches above merely edible. Kassim eats four, so I'm counting it a win. After breakfast, with the snow still falling outside, Deja and I crawl into my bed and turn on the television. The marathon is already underway, so we come in on season three and lose ourselves for hours on the campus of Hillman College.

"Is this how it was for you and Dad?" she asks, dipping her hand into the bowl of popcorn we brought upstairs. "Is this what it's like at an HBCU?"

"I mean, this is fictionalized, of course, but yeah. It's definitely inspired by real traditions and experiences like the ones I had at A&T and your dad had at Morehouse."

She cradles a handful of popcorn, watching the students gather in the Pit to eat Mr. Gaines's greasy food and digest his sage words.

"I want that," she finally says.

My heart springs into action. "For college, you mean?"

"I don't know. I'm still not sure college is for me, but I could have it now, right?"

"What do you mean, *now*?"

"I don't want to go to Harrington for high school."

My stomach sinks and I pause the episode, turning to give Deja my full attention. "It's one of the best schools in the state, Day."

"It's the Twiwhite Zone. I want to be around more people who look like me."

She gestures to the flat screen mounted on my wall. "Isn't that one of the things you loved about attending an HBCU?"

"Well, of course. There's nothing like it, but you..."

Wow. It hits me, the irony of my success being so shaped by my experience at an HBCU, and me thinking my daughter should only thrive at a place like Harrington.

"You're serious?" I probe. "You really don't want to go to Harrington?"

"I really don't."

"Where would you go?"

"The high school for our district is in walking distance. Lupe and I talked about it. She's gonna ask her mom too. She doesn't want to go to private school next year either."

"Well, I do," Kassim says from the door, holding a jar of peanut butter and a spoon. "I love Harrington."

"You would." Deja rolls her eyes. "They think you're the second coming."

"What can I say?" Kassim preens. "I keep it hot in these streets."

"Pretty sure being on the robotics team doesn't constitute keeping anything hot in nobody's streets," Deja says.

The three of us laugh, and Kassim brings his peanut butter to the bed. I scoot over so he can take one side and Deja the other. We pick back up with the marathon, but I barely follow the story line. Contentment covers me. Tucked beneath this duvet, inside this bed, is my whole world. These are the people who matter most.

Only one is missing.

"I'll be back," Deja whispers, glancing covertly at Kassim, who has fallen asleep after two episodes. "My cousin's in town. I need to hit the bathroom and make that change."

"Okay. I'll pause it until you..."

Her cousin is in town. When was *my* period? Shouldn't it be...last week? I calculate in my head, shocked that my cycle is more than a week late and I hadn't even noticed. A few months ago, I wouldn't have thought anything of it. But a few months ago I wasn't having sex with my ex-husband like it's FreakNik circa 1998.

In a daze, I stumble from the bed to my closet, pulling jeans and a heavy sweatshirt over my pajamas. I'm slipping my arms into a full-length puffy coat when Deja pokes her head in.

"Where are you going?" she asks, eyeing the Hunter rain boots I'm stuffing my feet into.

"Um, to the drugstore. I need to get something."

"Now? The roads are icy. You gonna drive?"

"No." I grab a beanie and scarf from one of my drawers. "It's just a block or two. I'll walk and be right back."

"Okay," she says, skepticism clear in her voice. "If you're sure."

"I am." I kiss her forehead on instinct, braced for her to jerk away. She doesn't, though, just leans into it. Even that small victory is invigorating. I know we have a long way to go, but maybe we'll be okay.

I appreciate the freezing air biting through my layers of insulation and the flurry of snow dusting my cheeks. It makes me feel when my insides have gone numb, head spinning at the possibilities. I'm more than a week late. I got the shot, so I shouldn't have to worry about birth control for another few years. Nothing's foolproof, though. What if I really am, by some unlikely accident, some twist of fate, pregnant? My doctor clearly laid out the risks. Women who have placental abruptions are less likely to have a successful pregnancy later. When the baby didn't survive, the likelihood of another abruption also increased. It was a point of contention between Josiah and me. He wanted to get a vasectomy, but I didn't want him to. He wanted me to consider getting my tubes tied, but I could never take that step. What if...

I can't finish the thought, but push open the door of Skyland's drugstore, greeting the young woman at the register with a half-hearted smile. I speed walk past the bodywash and supplements and adult diapers until I reach the section I need.

My heartbeat stutters and the row of pregnancy tests blurs in front of me. It's not until I taste salt that I realize I'm crying. I tug the beanie lower and glance around the store self-consciously. Because of the weather, there's almost no one here, but I've been that woman who loses her shit in public places.

Public grief is tricky to negotiate. At a certain point, and it varies depending on the person and circumstance, there comes a time when you should be "over it." You should have moved on by now. And you're so aware of the fact that you have not, that you *cannot*. You don't want others to see your past-due tears or sense the pain that has outstayed its welcome. You protect *them* from feeling awkward because you're still in pain. When the facade fails and you lose it, the stares soaked in sympathy are as bad as the ones filled with contempt. I know the aftertaste of such meltdowns well, have experienced firsthand the violent vulnerability a broken mind and desecrated spirit can use against you.

There's a civil war raging inside of me right now. I'm a city of unfortified walls and it feels like any moment everything could be laid to waste. If I'm pregnant, the list of implications is a mile long. Implications for my health, both physical and mental. After my ravaging battle with depression, can I even trust my body with those hormones? Could I carry another baby without constantly revisiting the one I lost, especially given the likelihood that it could happen again? I believe I could, but I also always assumed I was Teflon, only to find I was papier-mâché. My happiness, my wellness, feels like a tenuous ecosystem made up of therapy, coping mechanisms, and a precise dosage of meds. If something disrupts it, what would happen?

Only... is that the truth?

Papier-mâché is easily crushed, yet here I am still whole after a series of debilitating losses.

And tenuous? I've laid a foundation for my mental health: habits and practices that keep me well. If I feel unwell, I know what to do. When I can't solve it on my own, I have people in my life now who won't let me stay down. Dr. Abrams, Soledad, Hendrix.

Josiah.

I haul in a panicked breath. Josiah has been very clear that he doesn't want another baby. Doesn't want me taking the risk of carrying another child. Hell, this isn't what he wanted at all. Obviously we've evolved from the no-strings, easy-exit arrangement we started with, but who's to say he would want *this*? He's too good a man to turn his back on me, but *want* it? Want something else that ties me to him even longer, even deeper?

Would Josiah move back in with us if I was pregnant?

The warmth of that thought penetrates the residual cold from my walk in the snow. A fierce desire thaws the icy fear in my heart. I want him home. How could I have ever thought he belonged anywhere else?

A young girl, maybe sixteen or seventeen, walks up beside me. Without a word, she grabs one of the tests and resumes her perusal of the vitamins farther down the aisle. Barely older than Deja and she grabbed it and went on her way like it was nothing. When I pick up the box it seems to solidify two things I refuse to shy away from.

One—if I'm pregnant, I'll deal with the risks and the hormones and the doctor's orders. I have the tools and I know how to use them.

Two—I want my husband back, and I want him to come home. I miss him. A specific longing for touch and connection that, no matter how many girls' nights or parties I attend surrounded by people, only he dispels.

"No time like the present," I mutter to myself, rushing to the front to buy the test and then walking back out into the winter cold.

CHAPTER FORTY-TWO

JOSIAH

I'm home.

Not sure if I ever really stopped thinking of the house on First Court as home, but after days of not seeing my kids, not holding Yasmen, they're here, so this feels like home. I didn't even bother going to my place first, but drove here straight from the airport. Over the last few weeks of clandestine hookups, I've gotten in the habit of not knocking, but walking right in. With the kids home, I hesitate. We said we'd tell Kassim when I got back from Charlotte, but what are we telling him exactly?

Mommy and Daddy still like to fuck, but that's as far as it goes.
Got it? Good.

Is that even true? *Is* that as far as it goes? I hid it well, but when Yasmen told Deja our divorce was a mistake, it tore something inside of me right down the middle, something still hanging in raggedy shreds. The implications of her admitting that? Tectonic. Shaking and shifting the very ground under our feet.

We didn't discuss what she said. I didn't spend the night. Even though Deja knows now, it would have felt weird being in Yasmen's bedroom with our daughter under the same roof. Our whole situation feels like it's occurring in a time warp, trapped between cycles. There are moments when we feel like the people we used to be. That passion. That connection from before. And at times this feels completely foreign, like we're strangers discovering each other for the first time. It makes sense, though. I'm one person made of two strands. The things from my past that continue to shape me, and the person I'm slowly becoming.

My finger still hovers over the bell when the door flies open.

Deja stands there, draped in sass and a BTS onesie. Her smirk is disturbing. Knowing. Like she has something on me. She caught me postcoital with her mom, so I suppose she does.

"What happened to 'Daddy! Daddy!'?" I ask dryly. "Aren't you usually squealing and hurling yourself into my arms when I come home from a trip?"

Her brows lift and her smirk deepens. "Seemed to me your arms were full last I checked."

Smart-ass. How is she only fourteen? Just how bad will this become the older she gets?

Without a word, I step past her into the house.

"How was Charlotte?" she asks, closing the door and leaning against it.

"Good. Lot of work to get the operation up and running, but we'll make it happen." I hesitate, shooting her a searching look. "Vashti's moving there to be head chef."

"She wanted that?"

"Yeah. She asked and Cassie's more than prepared to take over here. We're looking for a sous-chef to take her place."

"I'll miss her."

"We all will. She's been great." I keep my tone neutral, my gaze wandering up the staircase. "So where is everybody?"

She folds her lips in on a sly smile. "You mean where's Mom?"

"Kassim's not here?" I ask, ignoring her question.

"Basketball practice. Jamal's mom is bringing them home."

"Where's Otis?"

"In the kitchen asleep." She rolls her eyes. "Lazy dog's been sleeping ever since I got home."

And your mother?

I don't ask the question, but the little minx knows I want to, grinning and canting her head in expectation.

"Anyone else you want to know about?" she asks innocently.

"Brat." I hook my elbow around her neck and pull her in for a noogie.

"I'm too old for this," she squeals, but leans into me instead of pulling away. "She's upstairs cleaning out her closet or something."

"Okay." I look down at her, sobering some. "And how's it been with you two since—"

"Since I was scarred for life seeing you in bed with my mother?" Wicked delight dances in her dark eyes.

"You didn't see nothing. Don't even try it." I grimace. "For real, though. How's it been?"

She shrugs, leaning deeper in to me. "It's been okay. We hung out yesterday when it snowed and we talked. It was cool."

It will take time to repair what broke between them. Hell, it'll take time to repair what broke in us all.

I kiss the top of her head and release her. "I'm gonna go catch your mom up on the Charlotte trip."

"Oh, is that what you call it, Daddy?" She air-quotes and quips, "'Catching her up?'"

I huff out an exasperated laugh. "You too grown for your own good."

"I know," she says, proud.

I climb the stairs, forcing myself to go slowly, with my daughter's eyes burning a hole into my back. As soon as I hit the landing, Yasmen's voice reaches me, raised and off-key, singing Hendrix's Tony! Toni! Toné! anthem "Feels Good." I walk into the bedroom, but the a cappella singing is coming from the closet. I lean against the doorjamb for a few seconds watching her back turned to me as she pulls items from the hangers and tosses them into a pile on the floor. She's wearing black yoga pants and a Minnie Mouse sweatshirt she got the first time we took the kids to Disney World.

And earbuds.

Which explains the concert for one she's got going on, accompanied by rolling hips and…random…a crip walk. I creep up on her, grabbing her from behind by the waist.

"Oh, my God!" she yelps, arms flying and eyes wide. When she faces me, her face softens and she pulls the earbuds out and places them on a closet shelf.

"Hi." Reaching up she cradles my face and kisses me hard, deeply. Though it's only been days, this feels like a reunion. It's not just this kiss. Lately, I always feel parched. Thirsty like I've been without her for ages. Because I have. And it feels fragile, having her again. It *is* fragile. Every kiss, every touch, every moment placed in a bell jar. Preserved, protected, but only by a thin sheet of glass. Our conversation backstage confirmed that we're exclusive, but we still have easy exits. As soon as one of us feels it should end, it can. My arms tighten around her.

What the hell I was thinking when I proposed that?

"You're home," she says, smiling against my lips. "I'm glad."

"So am I."

I flop onto the oversized ottoman, bringing her down with me and onto my lap.

She snuggles into me, muttering against my neck, "I missed you."

"Missed you too." I shift her higher on my lap so she feels how much.

"Oh." She pulls back, peering into my face and laughing. "Don't think we have time to take care of that, kind sir, especially with your daughter downstairs."

"Don't remind me," I groan into the textured curls fanning out around her face. "She's not gonna let us live it down anytime soon. Walking in on us."

"Small price to pay," she says. "For this dick."

"You're not making this any easier." I give her a little shake. "Change the subject, or it's happening and Deja will straight up blackmail us if she hears. Reach into my coat pocket."

She grins, wiggles on my lap, reaches into the pocket of the coat I haven't bothered taking off yet, and pulls out a cheesecloth bag tied with gold thread. When she peers inside, a smile breaks out on her face.

"You brought me a pear." Judging by the way she beams, it may as well be a diamond bracelet. "Is it from Merry and Ken's pear tree?"

"It is." I plant a kiss behind her ear. "I remember you saying they were the best you'd ever had, so I—"

"Thank you." She leans down and takes my bottom lip between hers, holding my stare. I swallow hard and grip her hips, groaning when she grinds down on me. I want her so much, but Deja downstairs is a serious cockblock.

"How were they?" she asks.

"Good. Said you have to come with me next month when I go back." I pause. "Vashti will probably want to go soon to see the space and start getting a feel for everything."

To her credit, Yasmen doesn't even stiffen in my arms, but simply nods. "Makes sense. She should."

"So what happened here while I was gone?"

She does stiffen this time, looking up at me for several seconds, like she's weighing her words. She traps one corner of her bottom lip between her teeth and draws in a sharp breath.

"Hey, what's up?" I frown. "What happened?"

"I had a kinda weird experience, I guess." She lowers her lashes and clasps her hands together.

I shift her off my lap and onto the ottoman beside me so I can read her expression better. Lifting her chin, I scan her face. "What happened?"

"I realized my period was over a week late." She says it so softly, but it hits me with the sonic force of a rocket launch.

"Your...what?" I'm dazed. Confused.

Scared.

My heart pumps blood to roar in my ears, and a starting pistol sets my pulse to racing. I wanted a vasectomy as soon as the doctor told us the risks. Yasmen begged me not to get one, and her grief was so deep, I didn't press. Now I wish I had.

"What the...but you're on—"

"Birth control, yeah. I'm not pregnant. I just thought...being so late, I had to make sure. My cycle actually started last night."

Air whooshes from my chest in a rush, relief slumping my shoulders. "Damn, babe. You had me 'bout to lose it."

She smiles faintly, licking her lips and training her gaze on the hands in her lap. "I know it's for the best that I'm not, but those few minutes from the time I peed on that stick to when the negative sign popped up, I was..." She looks at me, uncertainty written on her face, in her eyes. "Hopeful. I wanted it, Si. So bad."

I'm quiet, not sure how to respond. This—her having more kids—was an impasse we never found a compromise for.

"It made me realize," she goes on, her tone careful, measured. "I mean...I knew this...have always known it, but it reminded me how much I want more kids."

Tension creeps across the line of my shoulders, tightening the muscles in my back, balling my hands into fists on my knees.

"With you." Her gaze is steady, sure now. "I want more kids with you."

Her words land on me like bricks, and I have to force myself to stand under the weight of them. I walk to the rear of the closet, rubbing my mouth. Facing shelves of shoes and purses instead of facing her.

"I know what the doctor said," she continues. "I'm not saying I have to *carry* children. Adopt? Foster?"

"You weren't open to that before."

"I wanted a replacement for Henry, hoping it would help take some of the pain. I thought I needed that, and anything you said to the contrary felt like you just didn't understand, but I'm open now."

She touches my shoulder, and I turn to face her.

"This isn't really about us making more kids," she says. "It's about us making a life together...again."

"This isn't what we agreed on," I remind her quietly. "We said this isn't a reconciliation."

"I don't know what the hell we're doing anymore." She breathes out a laugh, her eyes searching my face. She bites her lip in the way that always precedes something she's hesitant to say out loud. "But we don't have to remarry for you to come home."

Home.

The word startles a humorless laugh out of me. I grip the back of my neck with one hand, angling an incredulous look at her.

"Home?" I ask, acid creeping into my tone. "This home? The one you threw me out of?"

She flinches like the words are a slap in her face, and I guess in some ways they are, but I won't take them back.

"I deserve that," she says, her voice flattened, but still puckered with hurt.

"It's not about you deserving anything, Yas." I drop my head back, staring at the closet ceiling. "I don't want to make you feel bad, but it's true. I left this house because you told me to. We divorced because you wanted that. I didn't, but I've come to terms with it. Now that we're sleeping together, you want to wave a magic wand that wipes all of that out because your uterus is twitching?"

"That's not it."

"Nah." I shove my hands into my pockets. "Doesn't work like that. You sent me away. It's not as simple as me just coming home."

Even as I say it, I can't deny that I came straight here from the airport because I couldn't wait to see her and the kids. How that word "home" beat though me like a pulse the whole ride here. How, if I'm honest, this is where I want to be more than anywhere else. It's always been. A year ago, I would have sold my soul to hear her say these things. So what's holding me back?

"It *can* be that simple." With a flurry of quick blinks, she swallows deeply, the muscles of her throat moving. "I think on some level, I knew it was a mistake as soon as you left. On some level, even though we were fighting all the time, I still wanted you here."

"Yeah, right."

She strides over to a row of drawers on the far wall of the closet and opens the bottom one, pulling out a pair of shoes. She throws them to the ground like a gauntlet.

"Are those my..." I squint, my brain catching up to the evidence of my eyes. The UNCs I searched months for. "You found them?"

"They were never lost. I kept them."

"So you lied to me when I asked you about them?"

"Surely lying to you about a pair of sneakers is low on the list of things I did wrong."

"Why lie about it? Why keep them in the first place?"

"I don't even know." She shrugs. "It was instinct. I just...did it. I think I needed to keep a part of you here with me."

"A part of me?" A scoffing laugh booms from my chest. "Keep a part of me here? *All* of me was here, Yas. My kids, the house we built, our life together. My *wife*."

I point through the walls in the direction of Byrd's house.

"The man who lived two streets over? That was a shell. Everything that mattered was still here. You exiled me, so don't talk about keeping parts of me. You had it *all*. You took custody of our whole life. And you toss a pair of shoes at me like it's proof you still wanted me?"

"Do you think I need you to tell me again how badly I fucked things up? I'm well aware it's my fault that we're in this situation. My fault that Deja resents me. My fault that Seem's in therapy."

"You know his issues aren't all about the divorce. He has a fear of death. Losing so much at a young age, I get that. It's normal to feel those things. It's only in therapy myself that I realized what's not healthy is refusing to deal with them."

I meet her eyes, remorse sifting into my anger and frustration.

"And I don't blame you for everything that went wrong. I told you that. It was unhealthy the way I dealt with the shit that happened. And to make matters worse, when you asked me to go to therapy, I refused."

We stare at each other, the hard-learned truth of my words lingering in the air.

"But what I didn't do," I say, setting my jaw, "was give up on us. You didn't try to save us."

"I did try," she says, emotion clogging her voice. "I tried and tried, but I couldn't save us *and* save myself."

"What does that even mean?"

"I was losing both battles, Si." Tears trickle down her cheeks. "The fight for us and the fight for me. I didn't even want to live."

She clamps her hand over her mouth like the words barged out of her without permission. Her eyes are smudges of agony in her face. She alluded to this in Charlotte, but seeing her now, her misery, I realize I didn't know how bad it was. Didn't fully grasp how dark it got.

"The way we were with each other," she says, looking tired and sitting on the ottoman. "The coldness, the fights, the pain—I was already fighting myself just to *be* here, to stay here. I didn't have the energy to do both. Losing our marriage hurt in a way I can't even describe to you, but losing the other battle? For myself? That would have been fatal."

The word "fatal" hangs in the air like a noose. A sharp pain serrates me, leaving uneven cuts and bleeding memories of just how bad things were at the end. If I listen closely enough, I can still hear echoes of the clashes we had in this very room, in this closet. Angry words trapped between these walls. Miserable, enraged, helpless. I was all of those things and so was she.

And yet.

Here we are again. Arguing in this house. Didn't I learn my lesson? I can't stop thinking about her. I want to be with her all the time. The stupid grin I wore when we were dating and I knew I would see her— it's back, dammit. I haven't tried to stop these feelings because I knew it could only go so far, but now she's asking for more.

After everything we've been through, when it comes down to it, I'm still the idiot who wants to give Yasmen the world. But to trust her again, enough to come home? To hand her that much of me again? I'm not sure I can give her that.

She thinks she barely survived the first time? I'm not sure I *did*. Am I intact? Or just a pieced-together version of myself fooling everyone?

"I know I said I couldn't find the love," she continues, fresh tears sliding from the corners of her eyes. "But I promise it's still here. It wasn't your love I couldn't find under all that rubble. It was *me* I had to find. I had to dig myself out."

You don't love me anymore?

Her answer that night shattered me in a way nothing else ever has, and as emotionally obtuse as I am sometimes, even I recognize I never recovered from that conversation.

"I know it's a lot," she says, voice trembling. "But I've learned to be honest with myself. I love what we have, Si. You know that, and I thought I could live not knowing where this would lead, or if it would ever lead anywhere, but I don't want that."

"What are you saying?"

"I want it to lead you back to me. Back here. I want to earn your trust again. I want to talk openly and do it better this time. To do it right."

She stands and crosses the space between us, stopping just short of touching, but her warmth and scent tempt me.

"I'm not saying we have to get married." She licks her lips and stares down at the tennis shoes on the floor between us. "But I want us to build our lives together again, and not because it's what's best for the kids or because it makes sense for our business."

She presses her hand to my chest, spreading her fingers over my breastbone, her eyes filled and brimming over with so much love, my throat catches fire. "I want you back."

My heart stops when she says it, and I step away from her touch as if I've been burned. I'm torn between walking out that door and fucking her against a wall, *locking* the door so she can't ever get away. Making her say it over and over again.

I want you back. I want you back. I want you back.

My emotions are rioting.

Confusion and frustration.

Hope.

Fear.

I don't need Musa's feelings wheel to know I'm scared shitless and angry as hell, but I'm not sure I fully understand why. Not the surface reasons, but the insidious ones that hide behind my traumas and settle into the cracks of my past.

I stare at her and bark out a laugh. "So you had a pregnancy scare with a side of epiphany and I'm supposed to believe that changes everything? That night when I asked if you loved me, when it mattered so damn much, you weren't sure."

"Here's what I can't do." She counts them on her fingers. "I can't go back to that night and change what I said, what I felt. I can't undo the time we were apart. I can't unbreak your heart."

Tears roll down her cheeks, into the corners of her mouth.

"I can't unbreak mine, either, because whether you believe it or not, as soon as you walked out that door, there was a part of me right here"—she bangs a fist over her heart—"that wanted you back, and I've been fighting it ever since."

"And it had nothing to do with seeing me with Vashti?" I ask dryly, probing. "Rediscovering that you actually did want me?"

"Did it jar me to see you with her? Of course it did, but every time I was in a room with you, I wanted you. I've never not wanted you. I think I couldn't imagine saying I wanted you back because I didn't believe you'd forgive me."

She twists her fingers together at her waist.

"How could you forgive me when I couldn't forgive myself? I used to tell Dr. Abrams I just wanted to feel like myself again."

"What did she say?"

"She said I would never be that person again. Not exactly the woman I was before. I was fundamentally changed by what happened. It took time and therapy and the right meds before I could learn to be happy as the person who remained after I lost so much."

Her eyes blaze with sincerity and passion and everything I used to fantasize I would see there again.

"I'd like for you to trust that the person standing in front of you has done the work to get better and to understand how I lost myself. I've developed the tools to cope when I inevitably lose more, because losing things you love is a guarantee in this life."

She takes my hand and presses it over her heart, her lashes spiked with tears. "Ask me again if I love you, Si. Ask me now."

The words wait on my tongue, but there's a gate set over my mouth, like if I let them loose, despite all my fears and reservations, I won't be able to resist her.

There is a part of me that knows this is where I belong. There's another part, though: the self-preserving part that remembers she gave up on us and it ruined me. The woman standing in front of me is the fighter I needed then.

How could I *not* love her?

She curls her fingers into a fist over my heart, and if she asked, I would carve it out of my chest and give it to her. Maybe that's the problem when you love a woman and want to give her everything, only to lose it all.

I still haven't asked the question when she closes the last few inches between us and leans up to my ear. Reflexively, my hand goes to her hip, possessive, anchoring her to me in case she decides to run.

"Yes, Josiah," she says in a watery whisper to the question I couldn't make myself ask. "I love you."

CHAPTER FORTY-THREE

JOSIAH

There's a crack in Dr. Musa's professional inscrutability when I arrive at his office. I was so disoriented after leaving Yasmen that I got on the interstate instead of driving the short distance to my house. Before I realized it, I was en route to his office. When I called him from the car and asked if we could talk, he'd had a cancellation and could squeeze me in. He sounded unbothered, but when I enter his office, he watches me with a strange expression.

"Are you..." I tense, narrowing my eyes. "Are you laughing at me?"

It's definitely humor in his eyes, however mild, and in the faint curve of his lips.

"Not really," he says. "Just pleased you're using therapy to help process life. Considering you showed up to our first session like it was detention, we should least acknowledge how far we've come."

"Yeah, I guess so." My smile fades as I remember what I need to discuss. "Thanks for seeing me on such short notice...again."

He nods toward the two leather seats. I take one and he takes the other.

"So what's going on?"

"Yasmen thought she was pregnant." I rush to clarify. "She's not, but it made her realize she wants more than the current arrangement we have offers."

"The one where you have sex without commitment or any pressure," he says. "Those were the terms, right?"

It sounds so sterile when he says it like that. I guess that's essentially what I told him when we discussed my relationship, but I don't recognize it as what Yasmen and I have had.

"Right," I say. "It made her realize she wants more kids at some point and she says she wants them with me. She says she wants to build a life with me, even if we aren't married. She doesn't want to continue our current arrangement not knowing where it's going, or if it will ever go anywhere. She wants me to come home."

"Sounds like a woman who knows exactly what she wants."

"Now," I snap. "She wasn't this sure when she asked me for the divorce."

"Did you ask her about that? What's changed?"

"She says she's changed, and that through therapy she's come to understand why she responded the way she did when Byrd and Henry died, and she's developed tools to cope better."

"But you don't believe her?"

"I'm scared to."

A few months ago, I couldn't have imagined sitting across from this dude and confessing my fears so easily.

"Let's play this out." He places his elbows on the armrests and steeples his fingers beneath his chin. "If you believe her and she actually has matured, grown, and you go home, restart your life together, and it all works out, how would that feel?"

"I'd be the happiest motherfucker on the planet," I admit with a wry smile.

"And if the two of you try again and it doesn't work out?"

A sinkhole opens in my stomach, sucking down my smile.

"That's the thing," I say, gritting my teeth until my jaw aches. "I can't imagine going through that again. Losing her again. If you've been run over by a bus, you don't go stand in front of another one as soon as you can walk again."

"So losing her again would be too devastating."

I nod.

"And she's not worth the risk," he says calmly, like he doesn't know how that would set me off.

"I didn't say she's not worth it. I just—"

"Don't want to lose anything else?"

"It hurts too much."

"We've never really talked much in detail about when your parents died, which was your first major loss. I know you were young, but could you tell me what you remember about that day?"

I've so rarely talked about this. I told him they both died in a car accident, but I've never unpacked that *day*. Not with anyone. My fingers twitch on the armrests. Everything in me wants to squirm, wants to run, but I force myself into stillness and draw a deep breath.

"I got off the bus," I start softly. "My mom was always home when I got there, but that day she wasn't."

The image crowds my mind, me sitting in the porch swing, rocking back and forth with a backpack at my feet. I was huddled into my coat, putting on gloves when it got colder and started getting dark.

"And then the cops came." I draw a deep breath. "A police officer said there had been an accident and my parents weren't coming home."

I laugh shakily. "It's amazing how vivid it is in my mind. Every time I've lost someone, it's captured in Technicolor, and slowed down so every detail is engraved on me."

"Go on," Dr. Musa says. "This is good."

"Then Byrd came and took me home with her."

"You said before that you found your aunt when she passed away. Do you mind telling me a little about that?"

I clear my throat. "When I found Byrd, all the ingredients for her limoncello cake were on the table. The kitchen smelled like lemons." I rasp out a brief laugh. "I've never told anyone that."

"Not even Yasmen?"

I shake my head. I've never shared the losses, and I see now that was a mistake because it gave them even more power over me. I never told anyone that Byrd was wearing her favorite pair of earrings, and one had slipped halfway out. I carefully pushed it through the small hole in her ear. Never told anyone that Henry had my mouth. I held him, light as a ball of cotton, dark hair plastered to his little head, and I traced his lips. He had *my* lips and I wanted to cry because I would never hear *him* cry, but the tears wouldn't come. And I can still smell the paint mingling with Yasmen's perfume in the nursery when she told me to go. When she delivered the greatest loss of my life. When I lost her.

Our traumas, the things that injure us in this life, even over time, are not always behind us. Sometimes they linger in the smell of a newborn baby. They surprise us in the taste of a home-cooked meal. They wait in the room at the end of the hall. They are with us. They are present. And there are some days when memories feel more real than those who remain, than the joys of this world.

"Live long enough," Dr. Musa says softly, "and you'll lose people, things. We just need to learn how to deal with it in ways that aren't isolating or destructive. You have to decide if being *afraid* of losing Yasmen again is worth never *having* her again."

Since that night, I haven't allowed myself to trust her. I thought she razed my life, but now I know she did what she did to save her own. Now I know I played a part. Now I understand that everything I saw in black and white was shaded, nuanced in ways I wasn't in touch with my own pain enough to grasp. Now my feelings rise, unwilling to be denied.

Do people remember the exact moment they fall in love?

I've learned it's not one moment, but a million of them.

I fell in love with Yasmen dreaming of our bright future over cheap Chinese food in a raggedy-ass apartment with no heat and shitty water pressure.

I fell in love with Yasmen a little more, a little deeper, every time she took me into her body, showed me how passion burns your tongue when you taste it.

When she rolled up her sleeves and poured her creativity, her match-less energy, into building a business together we can be proud of.

When she gave me our children and became a mother who made magic, who held up everyone else, carried the world on her shoulders with infinite grace. Even when she fell, she *stayed*; when everything urged her to give up and go, she *stayed* for us, and she fought until she found herself again.

I've fallen in love with the warrior woman who walked through fire, the one who came through stronger, reshaped by sorrow, reformed by grief, reborn in joy.

I think of her today with her small fist over my heart. She stood bravely in front of me asking that I take her back. Offering me the chance to have everything that really matters again—my home, my family, my *wife*. She offered it all to me on a platter, and I basically tossed it back in her face.

Panic rings a bell in my head and the sound of my own blood rushes in my ears like an alarm. The walls I've built to contain my feelings are falling. It's not a wrecking ball that starts the demolition. It begins with a tremor, a realization that love happens in the fragile context of our mortality. That love and life occur just beyond the reach of our control. There is only one letter of difference between *love* and *lose*, and somewhere along the way, for me they became synonymous. I understand now that something broke in me after my parents died that somehow healed wrong, and I started measuring how much I loved people in terms of how much it would hurt to lose them.

Once the first brick topples, they all begin to loosen and collapse. It feels like every hurt, all the grief of a lifetime, falls on me in one landslide of emotion. In seconds, I'm standing in the ruins of all the things I thought would keep me safe from ever losing something precious again. It's cathartic, this release and relief. It hollows out a trench inside me for waves of dammed pain to pass through.

The tissue Dr. Musa thrusts in my direction like a white flag startles me, and I look at him, confused.

"What's that for?" I ask, my voice emerging like gravel.

He nods to my face with a faint smile. "For the tears."

CHAPTER FORTY-FOUR

YASMEN

In the kitchen alone, I assemble the ingredients for Byrd's homemade mac and cheese. The uneven scrawl of her handwriting on the page of her old notebook blurs through the scrim of tears over my eyes. I don't think I've gone ten minutes without crying since Josiah walked out the door a few hours ago.

"Dinner," I say, swiping my cheeks with an impatient hand. "I'm going to make a meal for my children that they probably won't eat because that's just the kind of masochist I am."

Haven't I had my share of humiliation for the day? Or do I think I might top throwing myself at my ex-husband, begging him to move back in, declaring my undying love for him…and watching him storm from the room without a word? Because I suspect that will take the prize.

"Elbow noodles, cheese, milk, eggs, salt and pepper to taste."

I mutter the ingredients under my breath over and over like an incantation I wish could summon Byrd here. Or at least call on her wisdom, because I've messed things up so badly, I don't know what to do. If the ingredients are the prayer, the steam rising from the boiling pot of noodles is the incense and this kitchen a temple where I would sacrifice just about anything to have her here with me right now.

"I miss you so much, Byrd," I say, licking the tears from my lips. "Still."

On my wedding day, she said, "I love you like a daughter, Yasmen, but if you hurt my boy, I'mma whoop your ass."

I laugh through my tears, leaning my elbows on the kitchen island and dropping my head into my hands.

"Sorry I let you down," I whisper. "I'd take that ass whooping just to have you back for a little while. I promise I'm trying to fix it, but it may be too late. You know how he is, though. As stubborn as I am."

I close the recipe notebook. At this rate, we won't eat before ten o'clock. Delivery then. I grab my phone and pull up a delivery app, hoping to find something we haven't eaten recently. I'm ordering Mexican when a key turns in the lock of the back door and it opens. My jaw almost unhinges when Josiah fills the doorway. We stare at each other in elastic seconds that stretch into an endless silence. I'm mummified. Wrapped in a dozen reactions at once that paralyze me. I can't move or speak.

"Hey," he finally says. "Sorry I left like that."

I blink at him and nod because it's okay. He's here and it's okay.

"Just wondering," he says, dragging a suitcase in behind him and into the kitchen. "If your offer still stands."

"Yeah," I croak out. "You mean my offer to...that if you want...we can...you could—"

"Come home," he says, saving me from babbling for another twelve seconds. "I just grabbed the one suitcase. Figure I can get the rest later, and I know I have at least one pair of shoes here."

"Oh, my God." I cover my mouth, but hysterical laughter spills through my fingers. "I cannot believe I told you that."

"I'm glad you did. You put all your cards on the table and held nothing back. I needed that from you, but I'm just sorry that in the moment I couldn't do the same. I had a lot to process."

It's surreal that he's here and saying he'll come home. As the reality of him being here sinks in, my stomach somersaults and my heart beats so loud and hard, all the blood rushes to my head. My knees literally go weak, and I collapse onto the stool at the counter. My shoulders slump with what feels like years of relief. He crosses the room in a few steps, coming to stand between my legs, gripping me by the waist. He frowns and frames my face with his hands, thumbs skimming my damp cheeks.

"Your eyes are puffy," he says, leaning down to drop a kiss on each eyelid. "I'm sorry I made you cry."

I look up to study his face with the red eyes and the slight puffiness around *his* eyes. I palm his face, feeling fresh tears spring up.

"You've been crying too?" I ask.

"Courtesy of Dr. Musa." He glances away and to the floor for a moment. "He sends his regards, by the way, and looks forward to meeting you."

"You went to see him?"

"I needed to think things through, and he...well, he helps me do that."

"I'm glad," I whisper, so very proud of him and how far he's come. How far we both have and for how far we still have to go...together.

"I know I didn't want to do couples counseling before," he says. "But I think it might be a good idea if we give it a try."

I nod, almost scared to say much in case this is a dream and I wake myself up.

"I still have so much to work out on my own too," he admits. "I'll probably always want to fix things, to hold it all together. But I can get better."

"I know you need to be strong for the people you love." I angle my head so I can catch and hold his eyes with mine. "But I want to stand with you when it rains, when the wind comes. When it's hard and the odds are stacked against us. We didn't always do that before, but I believe if and when trials come, we will stand together."

He presses his forehead to mine, palming my neck and bringing my lips to his.

"You have me," I whisper into our kiss. "And I know you may not trust that. I can't blame you, but I mean it. I'm not going anywhere."

"That's good." He pulls back to push the hair away from my face. "Because I'm apparently not very good at losing things, and I'm really bad at losing you."

I lean in to kiss him again, but the sound of paws on the hardwood floor makes us both turn our heads. Otis trots into the kitchen and walks up to Josiah, leaning his head into his hip, obviously angling to be touched.

Josiah rubs the huge dog behind his ears. "Whaddya say to coming home?" he asks.

Otis barks as if in complete support of this idea and we laugh.

"Byrd knew what she was doing leaving him with you," I say. "She saw in you what I do. That you'll do whatever is necessary for those you love."

"And I do love you," he says, the truth of it blazing clearly in his eyes. "I'm sorry I didn't say it back before."

"Don't be. We have a lot to work out." I laugh. "Hey, Merry and Ken have been shacking up for thirty years. I think we can take our time. I love you and there's no rush."

He angles my face up for another kiss. Compared to all the hot stolen moments we've shared lately, it's chaste. A mere press of his lips to mine, but there's such tenderness to it. It feels like it did before, inlaid with commitment and devotion, but laced with a new appreciation. Maybe we took what we had before for granted, didn't know it was fragile because *we* were fragile in ways that had never been tested. Now, though, this thing between us is a tensile thread that I truly believe won't snap when life jerks. His arms tighten around me, possessive, protective. It will take time for him to be sure I won't slip away, so I'll just keep standing still, held by him.

The kiss deepens, probes like he's seeking answers in the touch of our lips, in the tangle of our tongues. We break apart, breathing hard, our foreheads bunting as I slip a hand behind his neck, anchoring us together.

"Ewww."

Deja's voice jars us both, and I can't help but laugh at the disgusted look on her face as she enters the kitchen.

"We eat here," she says, pointing to where I sit and he's pressed to me. "Not anymore. That counter is officially suspect."

I breathe out a laugh and Josiah's chuckle vibrates through me at the places where we touch.

"What's going on?" Kassim asks from just behind his sister. His wide eyes flick from us to Josiah's suitcase standing by the door.

"It's a lot to explain," I say. "And we'll talk through everything."

Josiah clasps our hands together on the counter for our children to see.

"But long story short," he says, his openly loving gaze set on me, setting me on fire, "I'm coming home."

EPILOGUE

∞

YASMEN

"Why are you cast down, O my soul…Hope."
—Psalm 42:5

New Year's Eve is always one of my favorite nights of the year, though one of the busiest. I made the midnight toast, as I usually do, ringing in a new year at the Grits celebratory bash. Bottles popping. Champagne flowing. The place, pulsing with possibility and jubilation an hour ago, is starting to clear out. By one o'clock, everyone should be gone. The DJ was great, a new guy I found by chance. He played "Feels Good," and Hendrix did lose her mind the way she does every time that song comes on. She's still slightly sweaty and breathless when she and Soledad find me on the roof wishing the diners Happy New Year and thanking them for coming.

"Great party," Hendrix says, coiling her waist-skimming braids up into a messy bun. "Once again."

"Thank you," I say.

"How are things going in Charlotte?" Soledad asks. "With their first New Year's Eve bash?"

"Great," I reply with a smile. "Our new manager there, Charles, sent us some pics. Everyone looked like they were having a ball. The place looks fantastic. Thanks again for your help decorating it, Sol."

"It was nothing," she says.

"I'll have to check it out next time I'm visiting Mama in Charlotte," Hendrix says.

"Yeah, you can kind of keep an eye on it for me." I smile, grabbing an unopened bottle of champagne from a nearby table. "One last drink to toast another year? I wasn't with you tricks when the New Year rang in, so shall we?"

"Oh, we shall." Soledad takes a seat at the table.

"Lemme get us some glasses," I say as Hendrix sits too.

I walk over to the bartender on this level, who's shutting down for the night, and snag three shot glasses from the bar since there's probably not one clean flute in the building.

"Pour it up!" I hold the glasses triumphantly, returning to the table to take my seat. "These are the best I could do."

"That's about as much as I can take anyway." Hendrix laughs. "I'm *lushed*. You hear me?"

"You really went for it tonight," Soledad agrees with a smile. "If you weren't drinking, you were dancing."

"Lots to celebrate." Hendrix winks. "It's been a very good year, and this one will be even better."

"Oh, that's right. You signed that new client," I say. "Lucrative, huh?"

"Yeah." Hendrix pours champagne into the three shot glasses. "If she keeps pulling in seven-figure deals, me and that commission will get along just fine."

"Edwards's firm has had one of the best years too," Soledad says, her smile a little stiff. "This new partner has been shaking things up, but Edward says he's not sure about some of the changes."

Hendrix and I share a quick glance, treading lightly by tacit agreement where Edward is concerned. As far as we know, he hasn't been sleep talking about other women lately, but we don't trust him as far as we could toss him.

"Oh, wow," Hendrix murmurs. "How nice for Edward."

"He's home with the girls tonight?" I ask.

"Yes," she says. "Well, not Lupe. She's at that same sleepover Deja's at."

I pull my phone from the pocket of my skirt, smiling down at the screen. "Deja sent me like five text messages. I told her it's not cool to text your mom from a slumber party, but she wanted me to see these braids she did for one of the girls."

"We did the right thing letting them leave Harrington, right?" Soledad sighs. "I mean, we jumped through hoops, robbed Peter to pay Paul so we could get them in, and they walk away from it."

"It's their second year in public, and they're both doing great. Deja's definitely happier." I shrug. "Each of our kids needs different things. Kassim is still thriving at Harrington."

"And skipped a grade," Hendrix interjects, fist-bumping me.

"Showing out too," I say, proud Mama preening. "All As. Both of them are actually doing really well."

"The whole family *is* in therapy," Hendrix says wryly. "So y'all better be doing well."

"Literally!" I laugh. "Deja wanted her own therapist because she didn't want to be left out, and of course, we're in family counseling."

"It's all still working, though?" Soledad asks, lifting her perfectly threaded brows delicately. "The arrangement?"

"Yes, but I kinda enjoy folks' confusion when they realize Josiah lives with us and he and I are together...again, but still not married."

"Keep doing you," Hendrix says with a big grin. "You're happier than I've ever seen you."

"I'm happier than I've ever been."

It's true. Our life, our love, didn't follow the path we thought it would, but that makes it no less true. I often think back to the day we met Ken and Merry, who said they didn't believe in the institution of marriage, but they believed in each other forever.

The only thing holding us together is our love.

I still believe in marriage, and Josiah does, too. Our love is the only promise binding us, but whenever Josiah is ready to seal it again with vows, so am I. For now, we've taken time to grow, to heal, and as Ken and Merry said, to make a life together on our own terms.

I pick up my shot glass of champagne. "Are we gonna do this, or what?"

"We doing it," Hendrix says.

With a smile as bright as the sequins on her dress, Soledad picks hers up. "Who's got the toast?"

"I've already done one toast tonight," I say. "You got it, Hen?"

"Ever ready." She raises her glass. "Here's to sex that cracks our backs."

"Oh, Lord," Soledad murmurs, lips twitching.

"Adventures that snatch our edges," Hendrix continues, her smile melting into a rare, sweet curve. "And friends that stick like you."

"You mean stick like glue?" I ask, chuckling.

"I said what I said," Hendrix booms.

"To friends that stick like you," we chorus, clinking glasses and knocking back our champagne.

"Well," I say, slamming my shot glass to the table, "Kassim is at Jamal's, so Josiah and I have a rare night with no kids. Later for you, bitches. I'm gonna find my man and get outta here while the getting is good."

Soledad looks over my shoulder, quirking a smile. "Looks like he found you."

I turn in my seat, and my heart skips that beat reserved specifically for this man, a rhythm that only he has ever inspired. Josiah crosses the roof to us. He's the kind of handsome that grabs your attention, cloaked in the brand of sex appeal that holds it. His smile is weary, just a tilt to one side of his mouth, but his eyes are alert on me. I don't have to wonder if he loves me. He tells me every day with his words and with that look fixed on me right now.

"Ladies," Josiah says when he reaches our table. "What are we drinking to?"

He nods to the bottle of champagne and the incongruous trio of shot glasses.

"New Year shit." I don't even check my goofy grin up at him. I haven't had enough champagne to be drunk, but the thought of a night in the house alone with him is intoxicating in itself.

He tugs me up, sits in my seat, and pulls me back down to his lap. I nuzzle into his neck, lost in the familiar scent of him, the warmth of his hard body, the affection in the hand stroking my thigh, sending tingles even through a thin layer of silk.

"Okay," Hendrix says, standing. "I think that's our cue to leave, Sol. They might start screwing on the table right here in front of us."

"That's probably a good idea." I link my fingers with Josiah's across my stomach and press my back to his chest. "Wouldn't put it past us."

The low rumble of Josiah's chuckle vibrates along my spine; I was joking, but my belly somersaults at the unyielding bone and muscle beneath me. The way this man makes me feel, we may not make it home. Wouldn't be the first time we made good use of the cellar.

"Guess I'll live vicariously through you," Soledad says, a touch of bitterness in her smile. I know it's not directed toward us, but to her husband. Grasping her hand for a squeeze, I offer a sympathetic smile.

"Y'all still coming to my place tomorrow?" Hendrix asks, tucking the half-empty bottle of champagne under one arm. "I'm doing a New Year's lunch with greens and black-eyed peas. Get our luck right for the New Year."

"As long as lunch is not before noon," Josiah says, "count us in."

"Then I'll see you at noon. Come on, Sol."

"Night, lovebirds," Sol says, her smile warm this time.

"Love you guys." I give a little finger flurry wave and watch the two best friends I've ever had take the stairs down.

I'm so blessed they're in my life. The absolute truth of that has me blinking back unexpected tears...again. I'm emotional tonight. I'd wonder if I might be pregnant if it weren't for Josiah snipping that possibility away with a vasectomy a few months ago. It gave him peace of mind knowing we wouldn't accidentally end up with a high-risk pregnancy, and it solidified a new direction for our family.

"Did you see Brock and Clint tonight?" I ask, shifting a little on his lap to look into his eyes.

"I did. I told them we're starting the adoption classes next week. They're hyped for it."

We're adding to our family, and it feels like just one more step in the right direction for us. Kassim and Deja are happy and secure. We communicate with them openly about our relationship and our commitment to them and to each other. We leased Byrd's house out a few months ago, to a sweet family, and that felt like cutting one last thread to the painful time we spent apart. We're stronger than we've ever been before. Tender wrapped in tungsten. The most vulnerable parts of me sheltered by rock devotion.

I turn my head to look at him, bringing our lips close enough to kiss... so we do. How a man you've kissed a million times still has the power to make you weak in the knees, I don't know, but clinging to him under a cathedral sky with an audience of stars, I know I'll never take it for granted. We've been through too much, and what burns between us shines brighter and hotter for having been tried.

He slows the kiss, tightening his hand at my hip, pulling me flush to his chest so our hearts pound in tandem. Music drifts up from downstairs, and when I place the song, crooned by Al Green, it seizes me by the soul.

Let's Stay Together.

"I thought the DJ was gone," I say against his lips, "but they're playing our song. Did you arrange that, by chance?"

"The owner put in a good word for me," he says, smiling and standing, extending his hand. "Dance?"

I nod, stepping close to him, slipping my arms up over his shoulders and laying my head on his chest. His hands wander past my waist and hips to squeeze my butt.

"When we get home," he says, "this ass is mine."

"This ass," I tell him, pulling the necklace with the wheel charm and my old wedding ring free of my dress, "is always yours, Mr. Wade."

Looking down at me, his eyes glow with love. "That's good to know, Mrs. Wade."

We don't speak for a few moments, but sway, letting the song douse us in memory. Two naive kids in a shitty apartment on a cold night, clinging to each other, thinking we knew what true love looked like. We had no idea how hard it could be to live out these lyrics, to stay together. Hearing this song used to remind me of my biggest failure, but now it is the anthem of my greatest triumph. Not that I lost this love, but that I believed in it so much, I ran back into the fire to save it. That when all hope was lost, I didn't stop looking until I found it again. Didn't stop looking until I found *myself* again. And this man, this moment—is my reward.

Let's stay together.

Words of deep love, acceptance, renewal. It's a pledge to stand as one when the world would divide us. When we would hurt each other. It's fidelity and longing refined over a lifetime. I'm sure the love we have is so powerful, it could endure for a dozen lifetimes, but it has been concentrated and then distilled into just this one. We found each other after being separated before. We could do it again and again until time ended, but in this life, I'll never let go of him.

"I have something for you," he whispers in my ear, his warm breath misting my earlobe and sending a shiver down my spine. "In my left coat pocket."

"Another pear?" I grin up at him.

"Look and see."

I slide my hand into the left pocket, my fingers brushing the silk lining, seeking. And then I feel it and freeze into a pillar of shock. He stares at me, all traces of laughter gone, replaced by something fiery and tender. Trembling, I pull the ring out and hold it up between us. It's a large square-cut diamond on a thick platinum band. I gasp, my breaths halting and starting.

"There's an inscription." He guides the tip of my finger inside the band. I trace the letters before flipping it to read the one word.

"Wheel."

"There's no beginning and no end." He takes the ring and holds it up between us. "It's our own eternity."

The tears roll unheeded down my cheeks, and as soon as he gently wipes them away, they're replaced by fresh ones. This moment is so enormous, so overwhelming, but it doesn't stand alone. It's not just the strength of our full circle, but it's all the times we were weak, and got back up. It's every hurt, every second we spent apart, only to reunite. Our union wasn't just made by the good. The pain and the grief and the sorrows forged us together as much as the joys.

"Will you marry me?" he breathes at my ear. "Again?"

Unable to speak, I bite my lip to hold back sobs and shouts of joy. He slips the ring onto my finger and it's a perfect fit.

A smile widens his beautifully sculpted mouth. "I want to spend the rest of my life with you. Have more children with you. Fight with you. Make up with you. Wake up beside you every day."

He rests his forehead against mine.

"I was meant for you and you were meant for me, and even when we got in our own way, even when we screwed up—because we *both* did, baby—even then my soul knew, my heart knew, it was wrong being away from you. I don't ever want to ache like that again. People don't often get second chances like this, Yas."

"There's a part of me that keeps thinking I don't deserve it," I confess.

"Did we deserve all the shit that happened to us? The things and the people we lost? I've learned that life isn't about taking what you deserve, it's about getting all you can while you can because it's short. Because it's fickle. Because it takes when we least expect it. Now everything I've lost makes me cherish the things I have, instead of always being afraid I'll lose them."

He kisses the tears on my cheeks.

"Most of all you."

When we lose things, we don't always get them back. Of Byrd, all I have left is a stack of recipes and memories I pray will never fade. Of Henry, a wall of wishes that will never come to fruition and a small scar decorating my skin in honor, reminding me he was, if only for the briefest lifetime, a part of me and so completely mine.

I press my hand over Josiah's heart, and it beats a fervent rhythm of reunion. I look into his eyes and lose myself in the acceptance, the trust I thought we'd never recover.

"Don't leave me hanging, Yas." He brushes his thumb across my lips. "You haven't actually answered the question. Will you marry me...again?"

There are a thousand things I could say to capture how I'm feeling, to tell him what his devotion means to me. That instead of escaping into the dark, I'll find him in it, and we'll guide each other to the light. I touch the necklace at my throat, testing the familiar shape of the wheel, the precious weight of my first wedding ring. I tossed this into a well of wishes, certain that what I really wanted, the one I truly wished for, I would never have again. There are a million words I could utter to assure him he never has to worry about me wavering, but with an uncontainable joy and a teary smile, I choose one.

"Yes."

DON'T MISS KENNEDY'S NEXT BOOK,
COMING IN EARLY 2024

READING GROUP GUIDE

DISCUSSION QUESTIONS

Please note that the following discussion questions contain some spoilers. We recommend not reading ahead if you want to be surprised.

1. In the prologue, we see Josiah and Yasmen young and in love. Later in the book, we get a very different view of their marriage soon after Byrd and Henry have died. And then we see several years post-divorce. Compare and contrast their relationship dynamics in each stage. Who were they then versus who they are now?

2. Details of the two catastrophic losses and Yasmen's subsequent depression unfold over the course of the first few chapters. What emotions did you feel as it became clearer what had happened and how Yasmen had responded?

3. What were your first impressions of Yasmen's two closest friends, Soledad and Hendrix? How did they help with Yasmen's recovery? How are the women alike, and in what ways are they different?

4. Yasmen comes home to find Vashti having dinner and playing games with the kids and Josiah. How did you feel about Yasmen's response?

5. How did reading Josiah's point of view affect your impression of him after the opening chapters of the book from Yasmen?

6. Therapy plays a huge role in the book, and there is a lot of discussion about grief and depression. In some circles, therapy is still stigmatized. How did therapy and perceptions about therapy impact the characters and story? Did it change your views in any way? What were some of the things the story asked you to consider about grief and depression?

7. Did you see any ways in which Yasmen and Deja's relationship was reflected through Yasmen and Carole's? How do mothers and daughters influence each other? And how about Aunt Byrd's role? In what ways do people live on through others?

8. *Before I Let Go* is a romance, but also leans into elements of women's fiction and empowerment. What were some of the elements that highlighted the unique challenges women sometimes face and the various choices the women in this story make? Was there one woman's journey you identified with most?

9. Food is crucial to the story. Discuss the ways—beyond the fact that Yasmen and Josiah own a restaurant—that food is significant.

10. Did you understand Yasmen and Josiah's rationale for keeping their "affair" a secret at first? Did you agree with their reasons?

11. Were Josiah's initial fear and skepticism when Yasmen asked him to come home justified? How did they make you feel?

12. There is some debate about what makes a romance novel and how it should end. If Yasmen and Josiah had decided *not* to remarry but took a page from Ken and Merry's book, would you consider it a happily ever after? Did you agree with their decision?

RECIPES

Aunt Byrd's Limoncello Pound Cake

Ingredients

For the cake

- Cooking spray or vegetable oil, for the pan
- 2 cups all-purpose flour
- 1 teaspoon baking powder
- ½ teaspoon baking soda
- 1 teaspoon salt
- 1½ cups unsalted softened butter
- 1¼ cups sugar
- 3 large eggs
- 1¼ cups sour cream
- ¼ cup limoncello
- Zest of 3 lemons

For the glaze

- 1 cup powdered sugar
- 2 tablespoons limoncello
- Lemon zest
- A pinch of "bless your heart"

Directions for the cake

Preheat the oven to 350°F.

Spray a Bundt pan lightly or coat with oil.

In a bowl, mix the flour, baking powder, baking soda, and salt.

In a separate bowl or stand mixer, beat the butter and sugar on medium speed until light and fluffy. Continue beating the butter while adding the eggs, one at a time.

Add one-third of the flour mixture and mix on low. Add one-half of the sour cream and beat. Repeat these steps, ending with the flour mixture. Add the limoncello and lemon zest. Mix until it's smooth.

Pour mixture into the prepared pan. Smooth the top. Bake for 30 minutes on the center rack. Rotate the cake and turn the temperature down to 325°F. Bake for 25 more minutes.

Let the cake cool in the pan for about 15 minutes, then turn the cake out onto a wire rack or cake plate. Let it continue to cool while you prepare the glaze.

Directions for the glaze

Stir the powdered sugar, limoncello, and lemon zest in a bowl until smooth.

Drizzle over the completely cooled cake.

Josiah's Sweet Potato Pie Pancakes

Ingredients

- 1¾ cup all-purpose flour
- 2 teaspoons baking powder
- ½ teaspoon baking soda
- 2 teaspoons brown sugar
- 1 teaspoon kosher salt
- 1 teaspoon cinnamon
- ¼ teaspoon ground nutmeg
- ¼ teaspoon ground ginger
- 2 cups milk
- 2 small sweet potatoes, roasted and pureed until smooth (about ¾ cup puree)
- 2 large eggs
- 1 teaspoon vanilla extract
- Butter, for the pan
- A full cup of swagger

Directions

In one bowl, whisk the flour, baking powder, baking soda, brown sugar, salt, cinnamon, nutmeg, and ginger together.

In a second bowl, whisk the milk and sweet potato puree together. Add the eggs and vanilla.

Combine the wet and dry ingredients and stir.

Melt the butter in a large nonstick skillet or griddle over medium-high heat. Once it foams a little, reduce the heat to medium-low and ladle about ½ cup of pancake batter into the skillet. Cook until you see bubbles form in the batter and the pancake is golden underneath, about 2–3 minutes. Flip and cook it another 2–3 minutes, until golden.

Serve with maple syrup, pecans, or whipped cream—your choice!

My Aunt Evelyn's Corn Pudding

Ingredients

- Cooking spray, grease, or butter, for the pan
- 3 eggs
- 1 tablespoon vanilla extract
- ⅓ cup milk
- ¼ stick butter, melted
- ½ teaspoon salt
- 2 tablespoons all-purpose flour
- ½ cup sugar
- 2 cans cream-style corn
- 1 cup whole corn (frozen, canned, or fresh—your preference)
- A heap of Southern hospitality!

Directions

Preheat the oven to 350°F. Prepare a 9 × 13 baking pan with cooking spray, grease, or butter.

In one bowl, beat the eggs. Add the vanilla extract, milk, and melted butter.

In separate bowl, stir together the salt, flour, and sugar. Then whisk them into the egg mixture.

Fold in both cans of cream-style corn.

If using canned corn, drain half of the water from the can, leaving the other half. Pour the remaining water and corn into the bowl with the other ingredients. If using fresh or frozen, just pour all the corn in.

Stir all the ingredients together and pour them into the prepared pan.

Cook for 45 minutes (the eggs should be set and the top should be brown).

Let the pan sit for 15 minutes and serve!

Soledad's Vinaigrette

Ingredients

- ¾ cup avocado or extra virgin olive oil
- ½ cup sherry vinegar
- Juice from half a lemon (or a whole one if you want more twang!)
- 1 tablespoon Dijon mustard
- ½ teaspoon pepper
- Lil' bit o' salt
- 1 tablespoon honey
- 1 hefty dollop of bad & boujee!

Directions

Whisk the ingredients together and pour this over your fave salad! It also makes a great marinade.

ACKNOWLEDGMENTS

This book was both a labor of love and a catharsis of sorts. It's the first book I ever wrote, drafted nearly 15 years ago, before I'd even published anything. Though the title, characters' names, and so many of the details changed, the kernel of hope that spurred the idea remained. This story became increasingly personal. While writing *Before I Let Go*, I, like Yasmen, was diagnosed with depression. I say that I wore the skin of this book. I don't know if that made it harder or easier to write, but I know tasting some of Yasmen's experience made this story richer and more real. It made me more empathetic and taught me to judge less and offer more grace. My hope is that someone out there struggling or stumbling reads it and feels hope, feels joy, and is encouraged to continue.

There are so many people without whom I could not have written it...*finished* it!

There were several women who assisted me in understanding still-birth, grief, and depression from the perspective of a mother and/ or as a therapist/counselor. Leticeia, Gloria, Ebonie, Valerie, Angela, Shelly—thank you for all of your assistance, for your compassion. In every interview, every conversation, each exchange, it was so apparent you wanted someone to see themselves in this story. You had counseled clients like Yasmen, or you had *been* Yasmen. Your insight shaped her healing and helped stitch this fictional family back together. Your help was priceless and you have my unending gratitude.

Joanna, thank you for being my alpha, for always reading first and not letting me get away with much of anything. My work would not be the same without you. Your support and friendship continue to be one of my greatest blessings on this journey.

Keisha of Honey Magnolia, thank you for reading and pulling no punches. For finding new passion for everything I do on and off the page. Your vision and expectation of excellence inspire and provoke me in the best way.

To Lauren, for always reading early with a magnifying glass and for holding nothing back—thank you.

Chele, Shelley, Kelsey—thank you for reading early and encouraging me. I'll never take it for granted.

To my editor, Leah—THANK YOU for being so patient with me. There may never have been a worst first draft. LOL! I was in a very tough place personally and you handled me with care. You didn't panic and helped me find the best in this story. I hope! I'm so glad we took this journey together and cannot wait for what's next!

Dylan, you are not only my best friend and loudest cheerleader, but during this book especially you were a safe place for me. I'm not sure what I did to deserve someone as kind, talented, generous, and encouraging as you for a best friend, but I'm never letting you go.

To my mom. When I was at one of my lowest, darkest places, unsure if I'd even be able to finish this book, you dropped everything, hopped on a plane, and came to me. What's spectacular is that you've always done it. You've always known how to be there for me, how to help. You are wise, intuitive, resilient, generous, and compassionate. I hope I'm an apple that hasn't fallen far from your tree.

To my son, Myles. Every book is yours. I thought I understood what motherhood would be, but you turned that inside out, kid. You taught me that I was truly capable of unconditional love and I wouldn't trade it for anything. I wouldn't trade *you.*

Finally to my husband, Samuel. *Before I Let Go* wouldn't exist if you hadn't said, "Whatever happened to that book with the divorced couple?" That's you, though. As invested in my hopes and dreams as you are in your own. Humble and secure and caring and passionate. You are great and rare, my love. Josiah asks if people know the exact moment they fall in love, and he says it's not one moment, but a million. Here's to a million moments over the last twenty-five years when I fell in love with you and to a million more. It's been tough sometimes, but I'd do it all again as long as I get to do it with you. <3

ABOUT THE AUTHOR

A RITA® Award winner and *USA Today* bestselling author, Kennedy Ryan writes for women from all walks of life, empowering them and placing them firmly at the center of each story and in charge of their own destinies. Her heroes respect, cherish, and lose their minds for the women who capture their hearts. Kennedy and her writings have been featured in *Chicken Soup for the Soul, USA Today, Entertainment Weekly, Glamour, Cosmopolitan, Time, O* magazine, and many others. She has a passion for raising autism awareness. The cofounder of LIFT 4 Autism, an annual charitable book auction, she has appeared on *Headline News*, the *Montel Williams Show*, NPR, and other media outlets as an advocate for ASD families. She is a wife to her lifetime lover and mother to an extraordinary son.

Find out more at:
  KennedyRyanWrites.com
  TikTok: @kennedyryanauthor
  Facebook.com/KennedyRyanAuthor
  Twitter: @KennedyRWrites
  Instagram: @KennedyRyan1